# Death Under the Stars

**C.A.** Larmer is a journalist, editor, teacher and author of four crime series, two stand-alone novels and the non-fiction book about pioneering surveyors in Papua New Guinea, *A Measure of Papua New Guinea* (Focus; 2008). Christina grew up in Port Moresby, PNG, was educated in Australia, and spent several years working in London, Los Angeles and New York. She now lives with her musician husband, two sons and a cheeky Blue Heeler on the east coast of Australia.

Sign up for news, views and free book prizes:
**calarmer.com**

## ALSO BY C.A. LARMER

The Murder Mystery Book Club series:
*The Murder Mystery Book Club* (Book 1)
*Danger on the SS Orient* (Book 2)
*When There Were 9* (Book 4)

The Ghostwriter Mystery series:
*Killer Twist* (Book 1)
*A Plot to Die For* (Book 2)
*Last Writes* (Book 3)
*Dying Words* (Book 4)
*Words Can Kill* (Book 5)
*A Note Before Dying* (Book 6)
*Without a Word* (Book 7)

The Posthumous Mystery series:
*Do Not Go Gentle*
*Do Not Go Alone*

The Sleuths of Last Resort:
*Blind Men Don't Dial Zero*

PLUS:
*After the Ferry: A Gripping Psychological Novel*

*An Island Lost*

# C.A. LARMER

# Death Under the Stars

## The Murder Mystery Book Club
### (Book 3)

LARMER MEDIA

Death Under the Stars © 2021 Larmer Media
Second edition 2021
Previously published as *Evil Under The Stars: The Agatha
Christie Book Club 3* (© 2017 Larmer Media)
**calarmer.com**

Published by Larmer Media
NSW 2482, Australia
calarmer.com
ISBN: 978-0-6452835-1-8

Cover design by Stuart Eadie & Nimo Pyle
Edited by The Editing Pen
& Elaine Rivers (with heartfelt thanks)

For my friends and fans, old and new,
nearby and afar, who read my books religiously
and quietly cheer me on from the sidelines,
without fuss, without reward.

You're the ones I'd share my blanket with
at a moonlight cinema.
*Thank you.*

# PROLOGUE

As she stared, gobsmacked, at the woman sprawled under the cashmere blanket, looking as if she were simply asleep, the irony was not lost on Alicia Finlay.

She glanced at the blank screen behind her and back again.

*Ah, Agatha,* she thought. *You have a lot to answer for.*

"Is she dead?" someone asked.

"As a doornail," someone replied, someone without tact.

"Let's move back, please, people. Let's give the woman some space," came a third voice—Anders, of course, the good doctor, taking charge.

*"What on earth happened?"*

That was the husband, wild-eyed, shocked. He'd been asking a version of the same question over and over for the past five minutes, ever since he'd pulled the blanket from his wife's sleeping body and found, instead, a lifeless corpse.

There was no way to answer, of course, at least not yet, but the thick purple smudge around her neck gave plenty away. Not that the crowd was privy to that. The young woman's body had been covered over again by the blanket, and so most of the group melted away—homes to return to! babysitters to be paid!—while the sound of a siren shredded the still night air.

Lynette leaned down to whisper in Alicia's ear. "Looks a little familiar, don't you think?"

She nodded. Eerily familiar, in fact.

The words of Hercule Poirot—uttered only minutes ago—circled Alicia's brain like a childhood nursery rhyme, only more sinister and foreboding:

*"The sky is blue, the sun is shining, but you forget everywhere there is evil under the sun."*

But this time it was not evil under the sun that she was witnessing. It was evil under a starlit sky. And instead of a secret murder on a secluded cove in Devon, this poor woman had met her fate in a park packed with people in a fashionable suburb of Sydney.

That made it so much worse, of course, not the suburb so much as the very public nature of the attack. How did no one see it coming? How did no one hear her cries? And how could the Murder Mystery Book Club have been lounging just metres away and missed the whole event?

"What on earth *happened*?" uttered the husband again, and then a new question, "Who would do such a thing?"

He looked directly at Alicia then, and she met his gaze, softened her features, and tried to offer him a comforting smile.

She had an answer for him, of sorts, but she swallowed it back down for now. It wasn't the time or the place to be clever, but there was one person who had to accept at least part of the blame, Alicia decided, tearing her eyes from the man to the corpse and then back to the screen now looming like a black blotch on the horizon.

If only it hadn't been *Evil Under the Sun* showing at the outdoor cinema that night.

If only it had been a more mundane movie, a less riveting plot, then surely more eyes might have strayed more often and more people might have noticed a cold-blooded killer before he got away.

*Oh yes*, thought Alicia, glancing back at the lifeless lump beneath the bright scarlet rug. *Dame Agatha has a lot to answer for.*

# CHAPTER 1

Dame Nellie Johnson came in for some ridicule when she built herself a grand house on the flats of outer Western Sydney in 1898. What on earth was a woman of such social standing doing living out *in the sticks*? Wouldn't the Dame be better suited to an elegant apartment in the beating heart of the city, where she could wine and dine her many admirers with ease?

Little did her detractors realise, Nellie was a trend setter, and very soon the city's heart would be beating a path to her door. In just a few years, Nellie's semirural mansion, with its lush, wide meadows and fresh running stream, was swamped with neighbours and then businesses and, eventually, thanks to a sweeping, state-of-the-art bridge, offices and, yes, even apartment blocks, although elegant they were not.

Today Balmain is considered an *inner* suburb of Sydney, and a trendy one at that, and just a small patch of that once-secluded greenery remains, now given back to the people as a public park. It was on this patch that the inaugural Cinema Under the Stars was to be held in just under a week's time.

Claire Hargreaves, as elegant as Dame Nellie and as fiercely independent, stared at the film flyer with her trademark delight before placing it neatly in the middle of her eighteenth-century Chinese gold-and-polychrome-lacquer-panel coffee table, adjusting the angle so that it sat parallel with her spotless copy of *Murder at the Vicarage*.

She couldn't wait to show the Murder Mystery Book Club. They'd be equally as enchanted; she just knew it! She glanced at the mantelpiece and frowned.

That is if they ever arrived.

"Sorry, possum, sorry!" came the breathless tones of Missy Corner just a few minutes later as she thrust her arms around Claire on her way through the doorway. "Couldn't get my act together *at all* today."

"Don't worry, Missy," Claire replied, disentangling herself. "No one else is here yet."

"Really? Goodness me. I beat them *all*? Stop the presses! That's got to be a first."

She readjusted her zebra-print cat's-eye spectacles and headed straight for the couch where she took up her favourite position, slam-bang in the middle of the three-seater, just where she liked it. The book club had become the young librarian's fortnightly group hug, and she was shameless about that.

"Can I get you anything?" the hostess asked just as the doorbell rang again.

Claire held a manicured fingernail up and said, "Hold that thought."

This time it was Perry Gordon at the front door, also issuing apologies, something about romance and how it could take a flying leap. Claire heartily agreed as she welcomed him in.

The Finlay sisters arrived next, Lynette with a handful of her famous freshly baked scones, Alicia with their shared copy of the Agatha Christie book. It looked like Claire's copy after a rough night on the town, with yellow Post-it Notes poking out on various pages, and—horror of horrors—bent corners and scribbled pencil marks.

Claire was just about to close the door when she spotted Anders Bright striding down the footpath towards her house. He had his arms wrapped around a book and was staring at the path in front of him, a grim expression on his face. She shrank back and swept around to look for

Alicia, who was now making her way towards the couch.

"Everything okay?" That was Lynette, one thickly pencilled blond eyebrow cocked high.

"I didn't think he was coming," Claire whispered. "I… I thought…?"

Lynette frowned, then followed her gaze out the door. Her frown melted away. "It's okay. Anders is still welcome."

"But won't it be a bit…?"

"Awkward?" Lynette said, finishing her sentence, and Claire nodded.

"Probably, but that's what happens when you sleep with a member of the band. You've still got to face them at gigs when you break up."

Claire looked at her, bemused, and Lynette smiled.

"It'll be fine. Alicia and Anders are both grown-ups. Or at least I hope they are."

She then sat down on the other side of the couch.

Claire took a deep breath and pasted a smile to her lips as Anders approached.

"Welcome, Anders! Welcome!" she said loudly, as though reinforcing the point, and he looked up with a start.

"Thank you," he replied tentatively, before entering the house.

When he reached the lounge room, he didn't quite meet Alicia's eyes, just offered everyone a general hello and took his usual seat—a lone armchair—and turned his attention to his book.

Lynette gave her sister an encouraging smile, but it was lost on Alicia, who was now hostage to her wild imagination. She had been preparing herself for this moment ever since the book club returned from a cruise to New Zealand, which along with a few corpses, saw the demise of her relationship with the fellow club member.

If truth be told, it had never really got off the ground. Anders could never quite get over his errant wife, and

Alicia couldn't quite find the energy to drag him there.

So they had decided—by mutual consent, she kept reminding herself—to go their separate ways. The fact that she had fallen for another man on the ship was a whole other matter and one that didn't bear thinking about today.

Perhaps it was because of this new beau that Alicia didn't feel she had the right to boot her ex from the book club. It was a *book* club after all, his club as much as hers, and it felt unfair to send him packing when he hadn't, strictly, done anything wrong. If anything, she was the guilty party.

Still, it didn't stop Alicia from imagining the day's progression with dread. She pictured Anders's sulk intensifying, she imagined him snapping at her every comment and then making a final, fiery ultimatum: "This simply won't work! Either Alicia leaves or I do. You can't have us both!"

Of course that wasn't going to happen. They would all be very civilised, except perhaps for Perry and Missy, who kept glancing from Alicia to Anders and back again, looks of delight on their faces, waiting, perhaps, for some fireworks.

Alicia was determined not to provide any.

"Right," said Claire, clasping her hands together and dragging everyone's eyes front and centre. "Welcome, everybody. I've got a lovely pot of Earl Grey to bring out and some sweet citrus cakes I whipped up this morning, and then we'll get started."

"I'll help," Alicia said, desperate to avoid the scrutiny, and Claire nodded, leading the way.

"Are you okay?" she asked as soon as they were out of earshot.

"I will be if everyone would just act normal."

"Of course, yes, of course."

She reboiled the kettle and, as it worked its magic, pulled a plate of lemon tarts and another of orange-flavoured cupcakes from the fridge.

"And our dishy detective?" she asked, peeling off the clinging plastic wrap.

"Hm?"

"Is he still in the picture?"

Alicia matched her smile. "Yes, but now may not be the best time to discuss my love life."

"I understand. Here, be a pet and take these out."

Claire handed her the plates and then reached for the steaming kettle.

Within ten minutes, the atmosphere in the room had settled, but it took another ten minutes before Anders managed to meet Alicia's eyes and a further ten before he was able to smile reassuringly at her.

She knew she had hurt him—clearly more than he had hurt her—but she hoped their mutual love of Agatha Christie would ease them through. And today, at least, it came close.

The book they were discussing—*Murder at the Vicarage*—was the penultimate book before they switched to a different author, and an obvious and belated choice. The first full-length novel to feature the beloved Jane Marple, the "nosy spinster" from St Mary Meade, was all Missy's idea and a brilliant one at that. She was shocked the club had focused so heavily on Hercule Poirot in the past and mentioned it again as she handed out some notes with neatly typed questions and discussion points.

"It's really very naughty of us," she said. "And a little sexist, if I'm being completely honest. I mean, especially for a book club filled with so many strong women!"

"Who are you calling a strong woman?" said Perry in jest, but Missy hadn't finished making her point.

"Miss Marple never did get quite the same acclaim as Monsieur Poirot, but I, for one, think she's better. She was an *amateur* sleuth, after all, and couldn't just strut in and take over. She had to eavesdrop and encourage gossip and pretend to be fetching a ball of wool while the clues were being sprinkled about. That would be so hard, don't you think?"

Claire agreed. "Oh yes. By comparison, Hercule Poirot had it easy."

"Now that you put it like that," added Alicia, "he's what you'd call a 'mediocre white male'."

"Steady on!" said Anders, and the women laughed.

"We're just teasing," Alicia said, "but Missy is right. Miss Marple did have to work smarter and harder than Poirot. He had his sidekick Captain Hastings to do his legwork and Inspector Japp firmly in his pocket. Miss Marple was just a little old lady living in a quiet village. She wasn't a celebrity detective, so she had to somehow ingratiate herself into an investigation—no easy feat."

"As we know," said Perry, referring to past mysteries this batch of amateur detectives had helped solve. "Still, I prefer Poirot. Miss Marple has none of the sophistication and brilliance of that little Belgian. Bit of a dithering old gossip, if you ask me."

Missy stared at him aghast. "But that was her *strength*! That was her ruse; it was how she managed to wheedle the truth out of people and work out *whodunit*. It was a ploy, you must know that!"

Lynette sighed impatiently. "What I know is that time is ticking away and we haven't even got to the book yet. Can we drop the feminist lecture please, Missy, and focus on the actual mystery? I think it was epic."

And so they returned to the plot, something they all had to agree was as good as any mystery starring the indomitable Hercule Poirot.

It was not until they were finishing the dregs of their second pot of tea and smudging the last cake crumbs onto licked fingers that Claire remembered to mention the upcoming event.

She rescued the flyer from beneath a china plate and presented it to the group with a caveat. "I know we've already read and dissected this one, some time ago, but I'd love it if we could all go along this Saturday night. It'd be such a laugh. Who's keen?"

Perry snatched the flyer from her hands and read it aloud.

## An evening under the stars...

the inaugural
### BALMAIN MOONLIGHT CINEMA

featuring Agatha Christie's
### *EVIL UNDER THE SUN*

Starring: Peter Ustinov & Maggie Smith

Cost: $15 adults / $5 children

Gates open 6pm / Screening from 8.15pm

at the DAME NELLIE JOHNSON PARK

**BYO cloche hats and blankets**

*All proceeds go towards the maintenance of the park.*
*Brought to you by the Balmain Ladies Auxiliary Club.*

"Ooooh I'm in," said Missy, and Perry rolled his eyes.

"Well there's a shock. I guess I could do it. Now that I have my weekends back."

Alicia glanced quizzically at Lynette, who explained, "He got dumped unceremoniously yesterday."

"Oh no, there was plenty of ceremony," Perry retorted. "There was a long, elaborate letter, left under a white carnation, no less, with a bottle of—wait for it—*Chardonnay*! Tacky? Anyone?"

Alicia thought a bottle of wine was a lovely break-up gift and wondered if she should organise one for Anders. She shrugged the thought away and said, "This film will cheer you up then." She looked at Claire. "I'm definitely in. I've never made a secret of the fact that it's one of my all-time favourites."

Claire smiled. "Mine too. And you, Lynette?"

"Sure. Can we bring partners?"

Claire really wished she hadn't asked that and snapped her eyes to Anders, who was busily checking his smartphone.

"You know cheating husbands don't like public events, right, Lyn?" This was Perry, who hadn't cottoned on to the *faux pas* and was having a dig at Lynette's usual predilection for older, richer, unavailable men.

Lynette grabbed a plush cushion and smacked him with it, which helped defuse the tension. For a moment at least.

"Maybe we should just restrict it to club members," Claire began, but Anders was shaking his head as he got to his feet.

"I'd like to bring someone. Sounds like a plan."

Now all eyes swept to Alicia, whose jaw had tightened considerably.

*So that's how he wants to play it, hey?*

"Good," she said. "Let's all bring someone along. That'd be great!"

The book club ended a little awkwardly that day.

# CHAPTER 2

The stars were not out yet, the sun still clinging on to the horizon, and thank goodness for that, thought Alicia, as she plucked her way carefully through the crowd and around the numerous brightly coloured rugs and cushions towards the right-hand side of the park where, she had it on good advice, she would locate the rest of her book club.

For now all she could see was a writhing mass of bodies, some standing, some seated, some billowing blankets, others opening picnic baskets, many texting, probably reaching out to equally lost friends.

In front of them all was an enormous white screen, blank at present, and beyond that a stunning view of the twinkling bay, bookended by the Sydney Harbour Bridge at one end and a smattering of apartment blocks at the other.

Alicia noted that some of the audience had dressed up for the occasion, and she was delighted to see lots of cloche hats, as requested on the flyer, as well as a few wider Chinese straw hats, in keeping with the movie's plot. There were dainty day dresses and beaded "flapper" frocks, and several men had gone out of their way to wear cream linen suits and bright silk cravats, old-fashioned pipes unlit in several mouths.

"Spotted them yet?" asked the man behind her, and Alicia looked around at Liam Jackson, who had been following closely, a small icebox esky in his hand.

She looked out into the crowd again. "It's really hard, isn't it?"

From her vantage point, it all just looked like a tangled mass of limbs and rugs and picnic paraphernalia, and it was hard to tell one individual group from another.

"Ah! There." She pointed. "Not too far from the back, on the right-hand side, near the big white tent. I can see Missy's bright pink hair."

"Thank goodness for Missy," Jackson said, and Alicia agreed, although she could just as easily have spotted Perry's trademark lurid coloured suits or Claire's eye-catching ensembles.

Jackson had met the gang, of course, but he didn't know them that well, and she wondered what he would make of this motley crew that had come to mean so much to her. That was part of the reason Alicia had invited him along—to get to know them all better. The other part was staring at her now, an inscrutable look on his face, a stunning brunette by his side.

Ignoring the aforementioned brunette, Alicia made her way across and then sang out, "Hi guys," as she approached.

The group all looked around with welcoming smiles and sang their hellos back. Anders got straight to the introductions.

"Alicia, this is Margarita. She's Spanish and a literary professor."

"Oh, hi, Margarita," Alicia managed, wondering what her nationality or education had to do with anything. "And this is Liam Jackson," she told the newcomer, wanting to add, "He's Australian and a kick-arse cop" but decided to take the high road tonight.

The Spanish woman smiled vaguely at them both, then held out a plastic wine cup for Anders to fill with the bottle he was holding out. He did so dutifully, and Alicia caught Perry's eyes. He was rolling them.

"Come and plonk down next to me, lovelies," Missy

said. "More room on this side."

Alicia did as requested, and Jackson followed, waiting with the esky while she spread their blanket over the remaining patch of grass.

"You brought cushions!" Alicia noted, and Missy giggled.

"Well, I do have a tubby butt. It can get very uncomfy sitting on the ground. Here, you should take one." Then she gasped. "Not that I'm saying you have a fat bottom! Oh my goodness, you didn't think that's what I was saying, did you?"

Alicia laughed. "It's okay, Missy, no offence was taken. But thanks, I don't need a cushion."

"She's got a lovely cushion of her own," Perry noted with a wink at Jackson. "He's not plump, but he'll do the job."

This caused Alicia to blush, and she slapped him with a *Watch it!* glare.

Jackson didn't seem to notice any of this and simply placed his esky on the blanket before dropping down to join it, leaning back on his elbows, his legs out in front.

"Not on duty tonight then, Detective Inspector?" Claire asked, and Jackson tapped his mobile phone, which was in his hip pocket.

"Hope not. Time will tell, I guess."

"Speaking of which," she said, "Lynette's going to miss the start if she doesn't hurry."

"Oh there's plenty of time, panic merchant," Perry said. "We haven't been barraged with ads yet."

As if on cue, the soft jazz music that had been streaming across the crowd came to a screeching halt, and the overhead screen flickered to life, inducing an eruption of cheers from the crowd. It began showing a series of advertisements, much of which got lost in the waning light. It did send the audience into a fluster, however, and many made a dash back to their blankets, others off to the portable toilets or the refreshment tents to stock up before the main entertainment started.

Within ten minutes, the sun had vanished, the last of the advertisements were showing, and the crowd had been lulled into a quiet murmur. Alicia glanced around, getting her bearings before everything went dark.

She guessed there were about a hundred people at the park, maybe more. It was hard to tell with the colourful quilt of blankets and cushions and the many bodies sprawled out. She noted that the closest white marquee, just a few rugs to their right, was dubbed the Booze Bar, and farther down there was a food tent, several Portaloos and a side exit.

There was still a sizeable queue at the Booze Bar, and she was glad they had brought their own alcohol, happily accepting the bottle of Sapporo Draft that Jackson was now handing over.

"I don't need it, Mum, cut it out," came the snippy tones of a teenage boy nearby, and Alicia watched as the woman directly in front of them tried to wrestle jumpers over the heads of an assortment of wriggling children, all white-haired and freckle-faced. Alicia counted five kids, aged anywhere between five and fifteen, the eldest now sighing dramatically and trying to distance himself on the brown rug where his family was perched.

It was no mean feat. They were squashed right in, and she was not surprised when the boy stretched his legs out on the bright red rug that was lying temptingly empty in front of them.

"Ezekiel!" hissed a stern-looking fellow with a trim beard and John Lennon glasses. The father, no doubt, and the teenager folded his legs back and hugged his knees tight, looking both uncomfortable and mortified.

Alicia felt a pang of sympathy for him and then wondered why any of the children were there. It wasn't exactly a family movie showing tonight. She was about to comment on it to Jackson when a burst of machine-gun-style laughter snapped her head up and to the right. On the other side of the red blanket, closest to the Booze Bar, two men in their early thirties were squatting on the bare grass, both heavily tattooed, with caps on head and tall bottles of beer in hand, their glowing cheeks and loud laughter suggesting this was not their first drop.

*I hope they're not too distracting*, she thought just as she locked eyes with some elderly ladies seated in low camp chairs between her blanket and the men. They were clearly thinking the same thing and gave her a conspiratorial frown, before turning back to help themselves to a magnificent cheese platter they had set out on the tartan rug in front of them.

*Some people really know how to picnic*, Alicia thought.

"I'm here! Don't despair!" came a familiar voice from one side, and the group all looked up to see Lynette hovering with a half-bottle of wine, a block of vintage cheese and a punnet of fresh strawberries.

"No, I didn't have time to cook up a feast. This is all I could muster."

"It's all you need, my darling," said Perry, tapping the sliver of rug between him and Alicia.

"Where's...?" Alicia had forgotten the name of her sister's latest beau but was saved by a loud sigh.

"Don't even mention that man to me. He's not coming."

"Trouble in paradise?"

"He's a fool."

"Afraid he'll run into his wife?"

That was Perry, of course, and she just glared at him before asking, "Who's got glasses? I need a drink."

"I have plastic cups," Missy said, but Claire tsked loudly.

"We can do better than that, my dear."

She produced a silver goblet from her handwoven willow picnic basket and handed it to Lynette, who promptly filled it up, then offered the bottle around.

For once, Alicia was disappointed Lynette had not

brought a man along. It meant the only partners were hers and Anders's, and it felt a little like Battle of the Beaus. At least they were separated by a few book club members, some plush cushions, two picnic baskets, and an icebox.

Still, it didn't blind Alicia from the fact that the Spanish woman was stunning—slim *and* voluptuous, which seemed cruelly contradictory. Alicia had always struggled with her weight, having to exercise regularly and watch what she ate. Right now Margarita was thrusting what looked like a large chunk of prosciutto into her mouth, and Anders was watching her like he'd never seen anything so sexy.

"She's probably a right bitch," whispered Perry, following Alicia's gaze.

"Behave," she whispered back, trying hard not to laugh.

Then she glanced at her own beau who, again, seemed oblivious to this exchange, his finger tapping away at his smartphone.

"What's going on?" she asked.

"Not sure yet. Incident nearby. I think they've got it under control."

She nodded, thinking nothing more of it just as the giant screen went dark and then lit up again with a flourish of orchestra music. The crowd gave out another cheer.

*Evil Under the Sun* was just starting.

# CHAPTER 3

**B**y the time a pasty-looking Hercule Poirot was making his way across the glassy Adriatic Sea to the boutique island resort, Alicia was taking another moment to glance around. In front of the squirming family, the red blanket remained unoccupied, and she wondered about that.

*Who would spread out a blanket and then not bother to show up?*

Perhaps they were stuck in the toilet queue, she decided.

"Sorry, oopsy, don't mind us!"

Make that the *bar* queue, Alicia corrected herself, as she watched a late-twentysomething couple giggling and swaying their way through the crowd. They were both wielding bottles of champagne and looked very drunk, the man helping the woman who was swaying on her feet and giggling with every step.

They were a good-looking pair, your classic hipsters, both in matching grey fedoras. The woman, petite with dirty-blond locks splaying out from beneath her hat, had a silk camisole on over a flowing floral skirt and a brown suede jacket slung across one arm. Her white, oversized eyeglasses were almost falling off, and the man beside her, a hovering six-foot-plus, stopped to push them back into place before smacking a kiss on her cheek and continuing their shuffle across.

He had the hunky look of a Hemsworth brother about him, wide shoulders, a trim, straw-coloured beard, and a checked shirt over dark blue jeans.

They seemed to catch everyone's attention, Poirot forgotten for now as they reached their blanket and fell down onto it—well, onto each other, in fact, with a snort of laughter that saw the nearby parents scowl and a neighbouring pregnant woman, who was nearly bowled over in the process, shift her blanket a little to their left.

"Sorry, babe," the man said to her, and she gave him a cold smile before saying something to the man beside her.

He smiled sympathetically and shook his head.

Within minutes, however, all eyes were back upon the screen, and even Alicia managed to forget the early distraction and settle in to enjoy the film.

And enjoy it she did.

It had been a good few years since she had watched the Hollywood version of her favourite book, and while she was none too pleased by the poetic licence they had taken with the plot—relocating to a fictional island in the absurdly named Kingdom of Tyrania and creating whole new identities for almost every character—she knew the central crime remained unchanged and enjoyed looking out for the many clues that were being sprinkled on the screen above her head.

"I've never seen this one," Jackson whispered in Alicia's ear.

"But you've read the book, right?"

"Nope."

She turned to look at him, eyes wide. She didn't know whether to be jealous—he got to enjoy the plot for the first time—or shocked.

"I didn't know there was anyone left on the planet who hadn't read this one," she whispered.

"Well, I've already guessed that the smarmy chick in the turban gets it, but I don't know anymore than— oh hang on a sec."

He reached for his phone, which had been vibrating in his pocket, and pulled it out.

After reading the screen, he sighed and said, "And it looks like that's not going to change, at least not tonight."

He downed the last of his beer, then leaned over and gave her a quick kiss. "Duty calls. Sorry."

Alicia tried to mask her disappointment. "You haven't even got to the murder yet."

"Got a murder of my own. This one's real life."

"That trumps this one then."

He nodded. "I'll call you tomorrow, find out *whodunit.*" He got to his feet, then leaned down again. "But I got my money on the husband. It's always the husband."

She raised her eyebrows knowingly. "Fifty bucks?"

"Okay, so it's *not* the husband…"

"Shhhh!" came an angry hiss from someone in front of them, and Alicia looked around to find the bespectacled father glaring at them.

"Sorry," she mouthed, then watched as Jackson quietly waved goodbye to the group and began plucking his way around the rugs and stretched legs and off to one side.

Alicia sighed. *What is it with her and unavailable men?*

"Everything okay?" Lynette whispered, and she nodded, then caught herself.

"Well, not for some poor soul. Sounds like a homicide."

"Yikes, poor Jackson."

Alicia glanced back at the screen, thinking how ironic it was. Here they were, paying good money to watch a murder play out for their own entertainment while Jackson had to be paid to deal with murder in real life.

~~~~~~~

Alicia didn't know if it was Jackson's homicide that had her on edge or the long, slow build-up to the murder on the screen above her head, but she felt a trickle of impending doom, and she couldn't put a finger on it.

There was still some time before the body of Arlena

19

Marshall would be found at the sandy cove, but she felt it intensify. It was silly, really. She knew the death was coming, could recite the scene off by heart, and yet her nerves were feeling a little frayed.

Not so others in the crowd, however.

The hipster couple, who were now lying down on their rug, two empty bottles beside them, had been kissing for some time but were now so amorous it was causing much irritation among the audience around them. Alicia's eyes were dragged from the screen again as she watched the family man scoot forward and growl something at the couple.

The younger man looked around with wide-eyed innocence, then snorted with laughter while the elderly ladies tsked loudly and the tattooed blokes chuckled. They had clearly been enjoying the off-screen entertainment.

The hipsters behaved themselves but only momentarily. Within minutes they were back to their old tricks, but this time they had slipped underneath their blanket, and while still smooching, it was not as obvious, and the cranky father returned to watching the movie. Alicia noticed that his teenage son still seemed interested in the blanket antics, however, and was sneaking surreptitious glances at them from time to time.

By the time intermission hit and the surrounding fairy lights twinkled back to life, the passionate duo had been forgotten again as the gripping storyline played out in front of them. The flighty leading lady had finally been discovered lying, lifeless, at Pixy's Cove. It was a captivating scene—a dark moment on such a bright and sun-drenched day—that there were audible groans when the plot was put on hold for a short interval.

"Snack anyone?" Missy called out cheerily, not at all perturbed by the interruption. "I noticed sushi, kebabs and what looks like the most delectable crepes."

"We'll come and grab something with you," Anders

announced before turning to help Margarita to her feet.

"Alicia?" Missy asked. "Anything?"

"I'll stretch my legs in a second, thanks," she replied, wanting to keep some distance between herself and her ex.

As the group plucked their way towards the well-lit snack bar, Lynette stood up and stretched her long, lean body like a cat, catching the eye of the tattooed men nearby. They said something to each other and then continued staring, sly smiles snaking onto their lips, but, as usual, Lynette was oblivious to the attention. Alicia, less so. She wanted to reach over and smack them about the head with their cruddy old caps.

"So, she's your classic nightmare," Lynette said, nodding her head in Margarita's direction.

"Sorry?"

"Miss Barcelona 2017."

"What about her?"

"She is painfully good-looking, don't you think?"

"Hadn't given it much thought," Alicia said, now batting her eyelashes up at her sister. "Why do I care?"

Lynette dropped her head to one side. "If it helps, I think she's a fraud."

"Excuse me?"

"Paid escort."

Alicia laughed. "Oh for goodness' sake. I'm the one who's supposed to have the overactive imagination."

Lynette reached down and pulled the lid off Jackson's esky. "Think about it for a minute. That woman is hot and pretty damn sexy. No way Anders would score her under any other circumstances."

"I'll try not to take that personally, thanks, Lynny." She shook her head. "Besides, Anders is a good-looking man."

"Sure, but he's not hot and sexy. And where did she come from suddenly? He was dating *you* about five minutes ago. She's appeared out of nowhere."

Alicia said, "I think your theory is insane, but, once

again, what do I care? We broke up by mutual consent, remember? I have a boyfriend, yes? And he's not too shabby either." She frowned. "What are you looking for?"

Lynette had been rummaging frantically. "Where's the champers?"

"We just brought beers."

"To a moonlight cinema? How dull! Shall we go and see what we can get at the bar?"

Alicia nodded. She could do with a stretch. Allowing her sister to help her up, she glanced around again and noticed that most of the crowd were now standing or moving about. The hot-blooded hipsters had disappeared, hopefully to sober up, as had the two elderly ladies and most of the young family, just two kids left, sleepily munching homemade Vegemite sandwiches. Alicia did spot the heavily pregnant woman, huddled under her blanket, one arm wrapped across her stomach, looking bleak, while the two men were now checking out a teenage girl in a denim skirt to their right.

Alicia cringed as she reached for her purse.

By the time they got to the bar, the queue had swollen, and they were in for a long wait. Alicia wasn't sure she even wanted to bother until raised voices caught her attention at the front.

"Let's just get some water, babe. I think we're done."

"You're soooo boring!" came a slurred reply.

The sisters peered through the crowd to find the amorous couple at the counter, the woman with her purse out, the man shaking his head.

"Hey hon, come on now. If we drink any more, the old farts around us will attack." He turned to the young waiter. "A couple of mineral waters, thanks."

"Noooo," the woman scoffed. "Bugger them all! I'm allowed a drink or five." She snorted with laughter at this and then swept upon the barman with a flirtatious, "Hello there! We'll have a giant bottle of your finest champagne!"

The barman flicked his thick black fringe from his face and gave her a stiff smile. "We only have sparkling wine, madam. And we do it by the glass."

"Spoilsport! Okay then, give us a glass of your finest *sparkling wine*."

"Ah, no, thank you," her partner interjected. "Just the mineral water, thanks."

"Oh piss off!" the woman replied, her tone less flirty and more irritated now. "When did you get so booooring?"

"Honey, shhh." The man glanced around as though he had only just twigged that the entire queue was watching, enthralled by the mid-movie entertainment. "Seriously, we're done. Remember what your sponsor says."

"Piss! Off!" she said more clearly this time, sweeping her long blond locks from her face and turning back to the bewildered barman. "Well, let's have it! What do you want me to do? Beg?"

The barman scowled openly now and glanced from the woman to the man and back again before reaching for a bottle of Australian sparkling wine and pouring it into a fresh plastic flute.

"Keep going, keep going, keep going!" she cried, causing the barman's scowl to deepen and the partner to reach a hand to hers.

"Kat...," he began, but she shook him off.

He smiled apologetically at the barman and lowered his voice. "Come on, babe, we were having fun, but enough's enough."

"Shut the hell up, Eliot!" she spat back at him, grappling through her purse for some money.

The man's patience had worn off, and his expression had turned sour. "Seriously, Kat, now you're just being a bore. If you buy that drink, I'm out of here."

She snorted at that. "You're not going anywhere, baby. I've got the car keys, remember? You'll be walking home. Ha!"

She located a fifty note and thrust it at the barman, who looked deeply unimpressed and then reached for some change.

Realising his partner was not about to acquiesce, the man sighed heavily and then turned away, backing through the queue and out.

"Good riddanth!" she slurred after him as she plucked her glass from the counter and snatched the change from the barman's hand, saying, "Victory!"

A few people laughed as she stumbled off in the direction of the snack bar, but Alicia did not find it amusing. The woman's partner was right. She'd had enough, and now she would be drinking alone.

It was silly of her, really, but at least it meant no more smooching loudly under the blanket—an upside for everyone else.

By the time the sisters had purchased some drinks of their own and returned, they noticed the handsome hipster had parked himself on the grass just on the other side of Claire, now a good distance from his wife.

Alicia met his eyes, and he gave her a slight smile, but it was full of sadness and something else, a kind of weary resignation, perhaps. She imagined the couple's reunion at the end of the night, pictured him plucking the empty champagne flute from his wife's hand and helping her uneasily to her feet. She expected all would be forgiven eventually and was in no doubt they had danced this waltz many times before.

*Relationships were extraordinary*, she thought now. It's a wonder anyone ever left the dance floor together.

As the lights lowered again and the crowd all settled back in to watch the second part of the film, Alicia noticed the drunken woman return unsteadily to her blanket, the glass of sparkling wine already drunk, a half-eaten satay stick in one hand. She ripped the last of the chicken off with her teeth, dropped the stick into the glass, then dumped it on the rug behind her, before collapsing beneath the blanket again.

*At least alcohol has a debilitating effect*, Alicia thought. She'll settle down now and stop being so annoying.

The eldest Finlay would come to regret that ungracious thought.

# CHAPTER 4

After the distracting first half, the second part of the evening was relatively uneventful, and the crowd was mostly mesmerised by the unfolding mystery they'd come to watch. People did get up from time to time though, and Alicia noticed that the Booze Bar to her right maintained a fairly healthy trade, but for the most part the crowd was captivated.

By the time Poirot had assembled the hotel guests in the decorative lobby to perform the "big reveal," there was not a stray eye or a wandering foot.

Alicia smiled to herself. She adored the final summation, the chance for Poirot to prove his brilliance and point the finger from one trembling suspect to the next before finally settling on the real culprit. Or *culprits* as the case may be.

*Evil Under the Sun* had a particularly wonderful twist at the end, and even though she already knew *whodunit*—as did most of the crowd, no doubt—it still brought a gasp from her lips. It was as captivating now as it had been the first time she'd watched it. She felt suddenly gloomy, wishing she could have shared it with Jackson.

When the credits finished rolling and the lights flickered back on, Alicia joined in as the audience applauded loudly and cheered the darkening screen.

"She's just brilliant, isn't she?" said Claire, and they all agreed.

"I love it when she turns the facts on their heads,"

added Missy. "Yet makes it all seem so annoyingly obvious."

"You know, the nasty daughter kills herself in the book version," Margarita said, and they all stared at her.

*Where had that come from?* Alicia thought.

"Actually, it's only a suicide *attempt*," Missy replied. "She does survive, but that's so typical of Ms Christie, don't you think? She was always so unpredictable."

"Heartless, I reckon," came a voice nearby, and they swung around to look at the bearded hipster who was still squatting near Claire. "I'm glad they cut that bit out in the film. Hate it when they hurt kids."

"You have kids?" Margarita asked, and he scoffed.

"With that woman?" He indicated towards where his wife was still snoozing under her blanket. "You think I'm a sucker for punishment?"

He laughed, then added more seriously, "I don't think you have to have kids to feel empathy for them."

"Not at all!" agreed Claire, and now he turned his eyes to her, smiling as he swept them across her stunning face.

"You're an interesting bunch. Are you work colleagues?"

Missy beamed. "No, we're the Murder Mystery Book Club!"

He stared at her blankly for a moment as if waiting for a punchline, and when one was not forthcoming, said, "Brilliant! I love that. I must tell Kat. Agatha's her favourite, which is the whole reason we're here." His smile slipped a little. "Pity she missed most of it." He forced his lips upwards again. "Can she sign up? For your club?"

"Oh, well... ahh..." Missy looked around desperately for Alicia, who had been watching the exchange quietly.

She felt her own stomach lurch. After the disastrous "miserable housewife" from the first book club, she was not sure they wanted to enlist another.

"We're a completely closed group, so no can do," Lynette said unapologetically, and Alicia offered the man a sympathetic shrug.

"Fair enough. I wouldn't want the young lush either."

"No, it's not personal—" Alicia began, but he was getting to his feet and dusting himself off.

"Don't worry about it. Enjoy the rest of your evening, guys."

He smoothed his hair back under his fedora, then stepped around their blankets and the blanket of the family who were now scrambling about gathering their things, to reach his own.

Half the crowd had already fled, but many, like the book club, had chosen to remain until the rush was over and were finishing off their food and drinks.

Alicia was considering whether she really needed to polish off the final beer from Jackson's esky as she watched the man approach his wife. She continued watching as he reached down and gave her a gentle nudge, then leaned in closer and shook her again, more firmly this time.

A shiver ran down Alicia's spine. Something was off.

The man pulled the blanket down a little and then recoiled, scrambling backwards as though he'd just seen a ghost.

"My God," he cried, his whole body shuddering.

Then, "No… baby… nooooo!"

# CHAPTER 5

**A** passing couple was the first to reach the husband's side, followed soon after by a barman and then the two elderly women who were seated just nearby.

"What's going on?" someone called out while the young barman cried, "We need a doctor! Is there a doctor in the house?"

Alicia's eyes swept to Anders, who was obliviously chatting with Margarita, deep in conversation, one hand expressing something languidly.

"Anders!" Alicia called out, and he looked up, a glint of expectation in his eyes.

She waved towards the red blanket. "Someone needs help!"

He followed her gaze and looked confused for a moment before it sunk in. He scrambled to his feet and strode quickly across.

The rest of the book club watched the scene unfold from their rugs, not keen to crowd the poor woman who, Alicia initially thought, must have passed out from all the alcohol. But Anders's behaviour soon put paid to that.

He spent a moment leaning over the woman, but instead of helping her up or, at the very least, putting her in the recovery position on her side, he swiftly pulled the blanket back over her body and then, more tellingly, her face.

Alicia knew exactly what that meant, but the husband clearly didn't or wasn't accepting it, because he barked something at Anders and went to pull the blanket back before Anders grabbed his arm and tugged him firmly away. He must have told him the terrible truth because the man cried out in anguish and then fell to the ground again, his head in the palms of his hands.

As he shook his head over and over, Anders took a step away and reached for his mobile phone.

"Must be calling paramedics," Lynette said, but Alicia knew better.

She knew there was no point.

The way he was holding the husband back, the way he glanced around furtively as he placed the call, she knew he was phoning the police.

As he did so, he caught Alicia's eyes and, using his free hand, waved to her.

"I think he needs help," she told her sister, and together they swiftly made their way across.

Anders was now moving the gathering crowd back, begging them for some space, while the husband continued sobbing beside his wife.

"What on earth happened?" the distraught man was asking. "What happened? What *happened*?"

"Not sure yet, mate," Anders said gently, pulling the Finlay sisters aside as they walked up. "Where's Jackson?"

"He left ages ago," Alicia said, surprised he hadn't noticed.

"Can you get him back?"

"I can try. Why? What's going on?"

Spontaneously he reached a hand to his throat. "Can't say exactly, but it looks suspicious." Then he lowered his hand and his tone. "There's contusion marks around her neck. I think she's been strangled... *murdered*."

Alicia gasped and reached for her iPhone.

Liam Jackson smiled when he noticed Alicia's number pop up on the screen of his smartphone and hesitated for just a moment, shaking his head. His first reaction was that she wanted to implore him to return to the park, then he had another thought—she was being her trademark nosy self and wanted the dirt on his current crime scene.

He looked across the desolate rooftop, towards the man who was sitting up against the concrete wall, his legs spread out in front of him, his sinewy arms to his sides, one with a leather strap around it. The man's chin was down, his oily hair covering his face, and if it wasn't for the tourniquet and a nearby syringe, you would think he was just a drunk, fast asleep in an old car park. There were various crime scene officers hovering nearby, one taking photographs with a large, external flash, another pulling on plastic gloves and chatting to a similarly dressed woman to his right. Various officers were spread throughout the roof, all with their heads down, searching the immediate environment, and he watched them as he took the call.

"Hey, Alicia, what's up?"

"We need you here," she replied.

"Can't live without me?"

"At least one person can't."

He tore his eyes from the scene and said, "What was that?"

"There's a deceased woman here. Anders says it looks suspicious. Can you come back?"

He waited a beat, expecting a punchline, and when it didn't come, he said, "Are you for real? You're not talking about that poncey lady in the movie are you?"

"Wish I was. Nope. We've got a live one or a dead one, I should say. A woman a few rugs in front of us has been found dead under her blanket; she'd been watching the movie. Anders thinks she's been"—she lowered her voice—"strangled."

He didn't hesitate this time. "Okay, hang on a second."

He glanced back around the rooftop, crooking a finger at a nearby police officer, who walked straight over. "Where did Bleekers go?" he asked.

"Checking for cameras on the ground level. There's none up here, and he's not happy."

Jackson nodded, returning to the call. "Alicia, tell me, has Anders called someone?"

"I assume so. Hang on."

He heard Alicia mumble something to the side before she said, "He dialled triple zero about a minute ago, says the police have been alerted."

"And it's definitely suspicious?"

"Contusion marks around the neck, he says."

Jackson looked around again. "Listen, we're almost done here. Looks like a textbook overdose. I'll just check in with my colleague and make my way back. Are you okay? How's everyone else?"

"We're all fine. Don't worry about us."

"Anyone acting suspiciously?"

Now it was her turn to look around. "Not that I can tell."

"Any idea who did it? Was she sitting with a partner or friends?"

"There's a partner, but he was nowhere nearby."

"Okay, listen carefully. Tell Anders help will arrive shortly. I noticed some officers on duty when we first got there. Always is at public events. I'm surprised they haven't noticed what's going on, but if he's reported the strangulation, then the area command will be there soon, followed by my people from the serious crime squad. Just tell him to hold tight until then, and don't let anybody touch anything."

That made sense.

"But do one thing for me, Alicia," he quickly added. "Look around, soak up the scene, look for anyone or anything you feel is suspicious. You've got a good nose for that stuff, so don't waste the opportunity. These are crucial minutes; you could see something important."

She felt a rush of pride. He wasn't urging her to butt out, he was imploring her to help.

*How refreshing.*

"What exactly am I looking for?" she asked.

He gave it some thought. "If it's strangulation, as Anders suspects, I'd be looking for stray men, people who don't look like they belong but who are lingering. Often criminals like to check out the scene, make sure the corpse doesn't suddenly spring back to life. And you don't think it was anyone in her party?"

"I don't know! It's only just happened."

"Okay, no worries. Just keep a sharp eye out. I wasn't joking earlier; it's often the husband."

"He couldn't have done it. He was right next to us the whole time."

"What was he doing next to you?"

"It's a long story."

"Well, just stay sharp, all right?"

"Will do," she said, her voice shaking a little.

"And Alicia?"

"Yes?"

"Watch your back."

As she hung up, Alicia felt that ominous trickle down her spine again. She returned to Anders, who was now kneeling beside the husband, patting him on the back.

The husband had his hat off and was rubbing a hand through his hair over and over, saying, "Who would do such a thing? Who?"

Alicia tapped Anders lightly on the arm, and he stood up, moving out of the man's earshot.

"Is he coming?"

"He's just finishing up another job, but he's on his way. Says the place will be crawling with police soon enough. Listen, Jackson wants us to take note of anything odd or suspicious, anything that might help the investigation."

"Like finger marks around her throat?"

His tone had a note of sarcasm, and she was about to comment when three uniformed officers came rushing up.

They had to be the aforementioned park security, she realised, as they were each wearing laminated tags around their necks, and she wondered what took them so long.

"What's going on here?" one man demanded as he approached.

Anders quickly filled him in, pointing out the dead woman and her weeping husband. And so for the next few minutes they did as Jackson said they would, taking charge of the scene as the wail of a police siren could be heard in the distance.

One officer checked the woman, confirming the obvious, while another pulled the husband away and sat with him on a nearby blanket.

The third turned his attention to the crowd, who were now closing in again, eager to see what all the fuss was about. This officer was like a giant bear with a portly stomach and the booming voice to match. He pulled up a large icebox and stood on top so that he hovered above their heads.

"Attention, everybody!" he called out. "Attention! We've got a bit of a situation on our hands here. A woman is deceased, and there appear to be suspicious circumstances. We're going to need *everybody* to remain in the vicinity until we get some names and statements."

Some of the crowd looked alarmed at the thought of this, others began to back away, as if hoping to make a sneaky exit. This real-life incident was all very entertaining, but everyone knew it wasn't a Hollywood flick. Nobody wanted to be caught there for hours in the cooling night, being interrogated by the police.

Sensing their reservations, the officer repeated the request, louder than before, adding, "It's *extremely* important, folks, that we get all your information! We need to know if anybody saw anything. If anybody knows the deceased or has any information to report—*anything at all*—can you present yourself to one of my men, please?"

The crowd mostly stared at him blankly, so he began

pointing at various blankets and rugs that were positioned near the deceased.

"In particular, we're going to need to speak with anyone who has been sitting in this immediate vicinity, that means anyone belonging to any of this property *must* remain on the premises, please. That includes the blue-checked rug there, the grey one beside it, the pink one on the left, and the black-checked rug behind that."

There were more audible groans, but he had not yet finished.

"Everybody else can start to vacate the premises but not—I repeat, *not*—before you have provided my officers with some identification and a current contact number, please."

Again more groans, but the crowd did as they were asked, some dropping back to their rugs with a sigh, others grappling for their things or reaching for their drivers' licences, including the book club members, who, unlike the rest of the crowd, were disappointed that they had *not* been singled out.

Jackson was right. They were a nosy bunch with a taste for trouble.

# CHAPTER 6

Claire began placing the empty goblets carefully back into her picnic basket. "Come on, gang, you heard the man. We need to skedaddle."

"Is that even a word?" Perry said, brushing off his trousers. Then, "Hold your horses, backup has arrived."

They looked around to find two more officers quickly approaching the scene, one talking into a two-way radio that was clipped to a holster on his shoulder, the other heading straight for the body. After a few minutes glancing around, they spoke with the bearlike officer who then hauled himself back atop his icebox and called out to the crowd again.

"Sorry, folks, just one more thing! If anyone has any information about any of the people who have already left, please let us know." He pointed again, this time to a patch of trampled grass just behind the deceased. "I believe there was a family sitting there. If anyone has any helpful information on them, please step forward. We need to speak to them urgently."

"They took off the second the credits were over!" someone yelled out, and the officers waved him over.

"Do you know their names, by any chance?" one of them asked.

The man, one who'd been sitting a few blankets back, shrugged. "Nope. Cranky bunch."

"I think they belong to a local church group or something," one of the elderly ladies called out, and the officer looked at her, then held a palm out.

"Just… stay there, please. I need a word." He turned back to the crowd. "Just one more question, folks." He pointed to the bright pink rug and matching backpack to the side of the deceased. "Whose property is this, please?"

The pregnant woman stepped out from the crowd. She looked nervous and was holding her bulging belly, her curly red fringe flopping into her eyes. "That's me."

He indicated a finger to draw her forward.

"Name, please?"

"Maz," she said, adding quickly, "I mean, Mary Olden."

"Are you with the deceased."

"No. I was just, you know, watching the movie."

"Wait there, please madam, I will need to question you further."

She frowned a little.

"I'm not…," she began and then sighed. "Yes, sir."

The officer was now approaching the elderly lady who had returned to her deck chair and was clearing away her platter.

"Madam, we spoke before, is that correct?"

"Yes, Officer. It's Florence Underwood."

"That's right. And what can you tell me about the missing family, Mrs Underwood? You mentioned something about a local church?"

She nodded. "I heard them when they were in line to use the amenities, during the intermission, you see. The woman was telling the children to…" She glanced around and then lowered her voice. "She said they'd pray for the souls of the devils in front of them tomorrow in church, then she suggested the kiddies say a quick prayer then and there. They all began chanting something. Caught a few eyes I can tell you that."

The officer looked a little confused, so she added, "She was referring to the couple, the dead woman and her husband."

"She called them devils? Why do you think she would say something like that?"

The lady glanced again at the husband who was still being questioned by one of the officers.

She nodded her head towards him. "They were being rather frisky, you see—lots of shenanigans going on under their blanket. I mean, it was scandalous, really. Very uncalled for. The young people these days, they just don't have any boundaries, do they?"

"And the family was not happy about this?"

"No, and I can't say I blame them! They had little ones, and it was getting a bit out of hand. I was about to step in myself and tell them to behave. I mean, this is a *public* park, Officer. Not exactly the right environment for that sort of nonsense."

"Oh they were just having a little wrestle under their blanket, Flo," said her friend. "It was innocent enough. Besides, that was just in the first half, remember?"

"And you are, madam?"

"Oh, I'm Veronica Westera, but everyone calls me Ronnie." She smiled politely. "That couple had settled right down by the end of the film."

Ronnie pronounced the word like *fill-im*, and Alicia, who had been listening in, couldn't help smiling. It reminded her of her own grandmother.

"That's only because he'd been given the boot," said Flo now, her lips drawn downwards. "The husband had moved over there, you see, next to those people."

The woman nodded a head towards Alicia's book club, who were slowly packing up their things, begrudgingly moving it along.

The officer looked confused. "He moved over there? During the film?"

"Yes, dear, next to that lovely group, the one with the young lady with the rather lurid shade of pink in her hair. It's a strange sort of colour for a young lady, don't you think?"

"Now, now, Flo," said her elderly friend.

"I'm just saying, Ronnie. Anyway, Officer, the husband, well, he upped sticks and went and wedged right in with them. I thought, dearie me, that's a bit rude! He had a perfectly good rug over here with his wife, taking up more than his fair share of lawn, I might add, and *they* were crowded in enough as it was. He went and perched very close to that lovely Eurasian lady."

"Oh, Flo!" Ronnie's eyes were bursting behind her spectacles. "Are we allowed to say 'Eurasian' today?"

"I don't see why not, Ronnie, but honestly dear, this man isn't the PC police." Her brow furrowed. "You're not *politically correct* are you?"

He smiled despite himself and said, "That'll be all for now, thank you. Just wait here, please."

He then strolled across to where Claire was now dusting off her blanket. Perry and Missy watched him approach, and their eyes lit up.

"Oh yes," Claire said when asked about the husband. "He did come and sit next to us, in the second half."

"And he remained there the entire time?"

"I believe so. Didn't he, guys?"

They all nodded, except newcomer Margarita.

"He may have moved, how would we know?" she said. "We were all watching the movie."

"He didn't move," Alicia said decisively, turning to Margarita and telling her, "*We* would have noticed."

Perry was nodding his head vigorously. "Absolutely. He didn't move an inch. I know that for a fact."

"And how can you be so certain, sir?" the officer asked.

Perry grinned. "He had such divine shoes, black velvet Creepers, if I'm not mistaken, and they were crossed over, almost touching Claire's Mary Janes." He nudged his eyebrows up and down. "Claire might have been blasé, but I think he was trying to play footsie with her."

"Oh for goodness' sake, Perry!" she said.

He looked unapologetic. "Just telling it like it is."

The officer nodded. "Okay, looks like we're going to need you lot to hang around as well, I'm afraid. We'll need to question you further."

"Oh if you *insist*," Perry replied, winking at the group, who dropped back onto their blankets, all with smiles except Margarita who was scowling.

"Should we tell him how we've helped solve a bunch of murders before?" whispered Missy, and Perry tsked.

"I think they've got this one under control, Missy. Let's just hang back and enjoy the show."

"You're a disgrace," Claire said, and he smiled, looking delighted by the comment.

"Thank you. Thank you very much."


Over the next hour, the growing band of police officers got busy, taking down names and numbers and working their way from blanket to blanket, questioning those who were closest to the crime scene. The witnesses had all been moved back, keeping the perimeter around the deceased clear, and Alicia watched as first the homicide detectives and then the forensics team arrived in dribs and drabs to do their jobs, one of which was to cordon off the red blanket with police tape.

The book club was yet to be questioned, and stifling a yawn, Alicia was beginning to wish they'd get on with it when she spotted Jackson closing in. She felt a sliver of relief.

"How is everyone?" he called out as he approached.

"Well, we're alive," quipped Perry.

"We're fine," Alicia said. "How are you? How was your other job?"

"Bit tragic, yeah. Another junkie lost to his vice. I had to make a pit stop to inform his folks, although they didn't look too shocked. Didn't even look like they cared, to be honest. Good riddance was the general vibe. Sadly. Not like that fellow."

He nudged his head to where the distraught husband

was now seated in one of the older lady's deck chairs, just to the side of the bar area. Someone had placed a cup of something hot in his hands, and there was a woollen blanket around his shoulders, but neither seemed to be providing much comfort. He was sobbing into his chest.

"The husband?" Jackson asked.

They all nodded as he continued glancing around.

"Ah, good, Singho's got this one. Give me a minute, yeah?"

He strode confidently across the grass and under the police tape, towards a woman in black trousers and a man's white dinner shirt. She welcomed him with a brisk handshake and then waved Anders over. The doctor had remained in the cordoned-off area and was now showing Jackson the body, pulling the blanket back carefully and pointing to something on the woman's neck and then lower down.

Jackson was nodding slowly, thoughtfully. Eventually he shook Anders's hand, said something to the female detective and strode back to the book club.

"Okay, I've spoken with the detective in charge and vouched for you all."

"Told her we're fine, upstanding citizens, did you?" Perry asked, and he scoffed.

"I wouldn't go that far. But you're all off the hook for now. You can shoot off any time you like, just be sure to report to homicide headquarters sometime tomorrow to give your full details and official statements. Alicia knows the address."

She nodded, having driven out to his Western Sydney office before dinner just the week before. She knew from the quick tour he had provided that it was a large and sprawling building, buzzing with almost one hundred detectives investigating everything from organised crime and Middle Eastern gangs to robbery, sex crimes and child abuse.

She never imagined she would be back there under

such tragic circumstances.

"Hang on," said Perry. "I know it's Sunday, but I've actually got to work tomorrow. We're prepping for a function this week. Can it wait?"

"No, it can't. You're going to need to make some time."

He handed each of them a card. "Detective Inspector Indira Singh is running the show."

"You're not in charge?" Alicia asked.

"I'm sure I'll be on the team, but Indira's the senior detective on this one. Give her office a call in the morning and organise an official interview. You might be able to see her out of hours, Perry, if she's available."

They took the cards with some relief. The night had dragged on, and the excitement of earlier had now worn thin. It was well after midnight, and each of them was keen to get out of the cool night air and into their warm beds.

As they packed up for the final time, Jackson pulled Alicia aside.

"I need to hang around for bit, but I'll get one of the officers to drive you home, okay?"

"We're fine," Alicia said. "I've got Lynny, remember. We'll get a cab."

"You sure?"

She nodded, so he grabbed her hand and squeezed it. "Maybe send me a text when you get there, hey? Just to be safe."

"You think the killer is still lurking around?"

"I have no idea what the killer's doing at this point, but you're officially a witness, which puts you in danger, so just be careful, okay?"

She nodded again, trying not to let his words wreak havoc with her imagination.

Despite her best efforts, by the time the friends had said their goodbyes and the Finlay sisters were ensconced in a taxi, heading home, Alicia was feeling rattled again.

Jackson's words kept circling through her brain.

He was right, of course. There *was* a killer on the loose, and who knew where he now was and what his motives were. One thing was certain, however. The man—and she had to assume it was a man, judging by the brutality of the murder—had not only killed a woman in the middle of a public park, but he had done it with dozens of potential witnesses wedged in nearby.

It was such a bizarre crime, she realised, looking out over the expansive Gladesville Bridge as the taxi rattled along.

*What kind of person does that?*

*What kind of person spots a lone female lying on a blanket and somehow wanders over, strangles her to death, and then simply vanishes into the night?*

It was the boldest crime she had ever come across, bolder even than the death they had watched hours earlier on the big screen. At least in Agatha Christie's story, the killer waited until the suspect was alone on a secluded beach before going in for the kill.

This assassin was as brazen as he was terrifying.

# CHAPTER 7

The brutal sound of coffee beans being smashed to smithereens woke Alicia from a deep sleep. She sat up with a start and, for just a moment, contemplated the ridiculous dream she'd been having, before realising it was no dream at all.

A woman really had been murdered in front of a crowd of people at a moonlight cinema, and she was one of the witnesses. Yet she hadn't seen a thing!

She pulled her quilt back and reached under her bed for her slippers. Finding only one, she groaned and called out, "Maaaax!"

The lustrous black Labrador was in the kitchen, of course, both eyes watching Lynette at the cooker, a stray slipper under one paw.

Alicia snatched it up and, noticing it was now soggy with dog drool, held it with two fingers and groaned again.

"What have I told you about munching my shoes?"

Max had the decency to look sheepish, but Lynette was having none of it.

"Leave poor Maxy alone. It's all my fault. I was late with breaky this morning. He'd been scratching at my door for ages, and when that didn't work, he tried waking you. I found him shoving your slipper in your face. You didn't notice?"

Alicia laughed. "No, I did not." She bent down and gave the dog a big scratch on the belly he was now producing. "Sorry, Max. I was dead to the world." Then she winced, remembering the deceased. "What a night," she added, disappointing Max by standing back up.

Lynette nodded. "What a night indeed."

She placed a fluffy cappuccino in front of her sister and reached towards the fridge.

"Who would've thought?" said Alicia. "You go to watch an innocent murder mystery and wind up in the middle of one."

"Are any murders innocent?"

"You know what I mean. We're going to get a bad name for ourselves."

"Not our fault," Lynette retorted. "So who do you think 'done it'? I've got my money on the hubby."

"You sound like Jackson. Didn't we establish he was too far away?"

"He could've done it earlier."

"Except he didn't. We saw them arguing at the bar, remember? She was very much alive then."

"And it was really her?"

"Yes, it was really her! This isn't Agatha Christie, Lynny. They argued, he sat next to us, she returned and flopped down on her blanket alone, and less than an hour later she was dead."

Lynette looked annoyed. "Yes, that does kind of upset that theory. Then who?"

Alicia thought about that. "It's hard to answer *who* until we know *why*. I mean, we don't know them at all. It could be some grievance unrelated to anyone there."

"Except the cops are right. It had to be someone in the *immediate vicinity*." She mimicked the officious tone of the police officer from the night before, then added, "Had to be someone with access, otherwise we would've noticed a stranger plop down, strangle a woman and then choof off again, right?"

"Not necessarily. We were all pretty transfixed by the film by then, but even so, people were coming and going all the time, skipping off to the loos, answering phones, grabbing mid-movie drinks and snacks. There were a lot of people there, a lot of movement. I, for one, wasn't strictly watching who was sitting where. What about the people around her? That father was a pretty angry man."

"But would he strangle a woman? In front of his kids?"

"Well, since you put it like that."

"Maybe those two guys sitting nearby could've been a part of it. They were a bit sleazy. Did you see how they watched them a lot? One of them seemed to be getting a thrill out of it."

Alicia nodded. "*And* they took off early, before things had wrapped up, remember? That's a bit suspect. There was also that pregnant lady, she was right there."

"Now you think a pregnant lady killed her?"

"I'm just saying, she had access." Alicia stopped. "Wasn't she with someone? A man? Where did he disappear to? I didn't notice him at the end either. Why would he bail and leave his pregnant partner all alone? That was weird."

"I don't recall who she was with, just that she looked miserable. I wondered why she was even there."

"I thought the same about the family. It was hardly a Disney flick."

Lynette pulled two large white plates from a cupboard below the bench and then shared the breakfast between them—a poached egg for each of them, a few slices of bacon and some mushrooms, dripping in garlic, and then a couple of cooked cherry tomatoes on top. Alicia grabbed some cutlery from a nearby drawer and was about to tuck in at the kitchen bench when her sister held a hand up.

"Not so fast!"

She produced a small saucepan and scooped a thick yellow sauce over the top.

"Hollandaise?" Alicia asked.

"Give me more credit for originality than that, please," Lynette said. "It's my special breakfast béarnaise, actually."

"Isn't that the same thing?"

She stared at her. "One has white wine vinegar, one has

lemon juice. My brilliance is wasted on you! Tuck in."

They ate in silence for a few minutes, Max now watching intently, waiting patiently for someone—*anyone*—to accidentally drop a bit of bacon into his mouth. Within minutes Alicia was doing just that, and Lynette was frowning.

She adored Max, wasn't averse to spoiling him herself, but she took it as a personal affront to her cooking whenever her creations were shared with the mutt.

"What are your plans today?" Lynette asked when their plates were virtually licked clean.

"Apart from presenting ourselves to that trim-looking detective, you mean?"

"Oh dear, you're not jealous are you?"

"Of Jackson and Detective Inspector Singh?"

"Singho, I think he called her, yes. I'm sure she's just a colleague."

"I *know* she is. I'm fine with it."

Lynette watched her closely as she sipped her coffee. "Don't let your mind go there, sis. You will drive yourself insane."

"It's not! I'm not. It's okay." She smiled. "Honestly, I can't seem to muster up a suspicious thought of any kind. Isn't that, well, *odd*? I should be jealous, right?"

"No, you shouldn't. That's the whole point. They're just work colleagues."

"Yes, but the old me would be riddled with neuroses, imagining them in some kind of stationery closet tryst." She blinked several times, staring at the kitchen wall.

"Nothing?" Lynette asked.

"Nothing," Alicia said.

It was a revelation.

Lynette waved her hands in the air. "She's cured! Hallelujah!"

Max barked, confused by the sudden commotion, and Alicia laughed.

"Don't worry. I'm sure my imagination will be back to

its old tricks before the day is over. Speaking of which, what are *your* plans?"

Lynette reached down and patted the dog, calming him down. "I'm taking this one to the beach. It's finally warming up, and he could do with a surf."

"And by 'he' you mean you, right?"

"Who else?"

Alicia's phone buzzed then, followed almost immediately by Lynette's. They had both received the same message—Claire and Missy were meeting with the detective at eleven that morning and suggested they come along.

"There goes my swim," Lynette grizzled as she located a 'thumbs up' emoji and pressed send.

# CHAPTER 8

Detective Inspector Indira Singh had a confident, no-nonsense look about her. Dressed in a slimming black suit with a starched cream top underneath, she had a tight black ponytail and a light dusting of make-up, two tiny gold earrings at her ears, a small gold cross around her neck. In her midforties, she commanded attention, her staff quieting down instantly and stepping back as she passed them down the long hallway, book club in tow, towards an interview room.

Claire thought she looked cool, calm, and collected, but Missy was suddenly a basket of nerves, bobbing her pink head around and giggling unnecessarily as she always did when she felt out of her depth. Alicia just watched the detective closely, keen to get to know her better. She had heard Jackson mention "Singho" before—had always assumed it was a man—and only recalled words of praise and respect.

She was determined to like her, too, even if it killed her.

Apart from Anders, the entire book club was present, Perry having found some time to slip away from his busy schedule. Newcomer Margarita was there too. She'd arrived on her own and looked even more stunning in the cold, hard light of day, her luscious black hair scooped into a top knot, and her tanned limbs glowing beneath a white summer dress. Her surly expression did not match her sunny style, however, and she seemed deeply annoyed by the whole business, asking the detective several times how long it would take.

"It'll take as long as it takes," was DI Singh's clipped response.

The group was soon directed towards several sofas in a small, warmly lit room that was less interrogation and more relaxation. There was a kitchenette at one end, as well as bright beanbags, a shelf of children's books and a box of plastic toys.

"This is the family room," Indira explained. "You're not here for a formal interview as such. You're friends of Detective Inspector Liam Jackson's I believe?"

Lynette glanced across to her sister, who was now wondering how much Jackson had revealed of their relationship and whether it even mattered.

"He's just clearing up another case at the moment, so he won't be joining us this morning. Is anyone after a cup of something?" She caught the eye of a tall, chinless man who was standing at attention in the doorway. "We have tea that tastes like dishwashing liquid or coffee with the consistency of mud. Anyone?"

They all grimaced and shook their heads no.

"Good choice. Let's get cracking then, shall we? So, about last night."

She nodded to the other detective who sat down at a high-back chair on one side of the room, then pulled out a notepad and pen.

After asking each of them to spell out their full names, birthdates and contact details, she launched in. "I spoke with Constable Thompson from last night, the first officer on the scene who questioned you guys briefly, and he tells me you are Mr Mumford's best friends."

"Mr Mumford?" Alicia said.

"Eliot Mumford. Husband of the deceased."

"Oh we don't know the man," Claire began, but Indira waved a hand.

"Forgive me. By 'best friends' I mean, you have provided the deceased woman's husband with a very neat alibi. Is that correct?"

The group all nodded, except Margarita. Indira caught that and turned her gaze upon her.

"You have some reservations, madam?"

"Yes, I cannot vouch for him. I was not watching that man the entire movie, so I have no idea if he moved or if he did not move. How can I know that?" She glanced irritably at the officer who'd been taking notes.

Indira said, "Make a note of that then, Pauly. This woman cannot vouch for Mr Mumford's whereabouts, but the rest of you?" She turned back to the group.

"Oh he didn't move, not one inch," said Perry, flashing Margarita a quick frown.

"Margarita wasn't actually sitting next to Eliot Mumford," Alicia explained. "She was probably sitting the farthest away."

"So, what? You think I am clueless?"

This was Margarita, and she sounded deeply offended.

Alicia held a palm out to her. "Not at all. I'm just saying, some of us were closer to Mr Mumford so…"

"So I know nothing?"

"No, I'm not saying that." Alicia sighed and gave up, slouching back in the sofa.

Indira watched the exchange with curiosity and then studied Alicia for a moment. "And you are again?"

"Alicia Finlay," she said, thinking, *Okay, so Jackson hasn't mentioned me then.*

"Right, well, thanks for clarifying that."

Indira then turned to reach for a plastic container below the table.

"Okay, now for the fun bit." She pulled out a large scrapbook. "So I have a little game for you all, a combination of Pin the Tail on the Donkey and a treasure hunt."

Missy giggled again, looking delighted, while the rest shared curious glances.

Indira began tearing blank pages from the book and handing them around. As she did so, the officer produced a box of coloured crayons and placed them in the middle of the table in front of the sofas.

"We've brought you to the kids' room for a reason," Indira explained. "They've got the best resources when it comes to this kind of thing." She rummaged through the container again and pulled out a carton of sticky red dots. "Terrific. Thought I'd find something like this."

Next to the dots she added some gold stars and some marker pens.

"So has everyone got a sheet? Good. Here's how it goes. I want you all to work independently and try to recreate the scene from last night, using the pencils and dots. Place a red dot where the deceased was lying, and try to work out from there. Sketch in exactly how the area looked to the best of your memory, with the screen at the north, so make that the top of the page, and the main entrance at the south, or the bottom."

"You want us to do a floor plan of the park?" Claire asked.

"Exactly. Scribble in where you were seated in conjunction with the victim, and then fill in any other blankets that you recall. You can draw them in as circles or use the stars or whatever."

"So you mean draw in where we were sitting as well as that big family, that kind of thing?" asked Missy, and Indira nodded. "But what if we don't remember it all correctly? It was dark, and there were so many people there, and well, what if we get it all wrong?"

Indira said firmly, "Just do it to the best of your recollection, that's all I ask. Don't embellish; don't guess. If you're not sure, just draw a question mark or leave the space blank. We only want the facts please, people, no creative interpretations. And don't—I repeat—*don't* check with anyone else. I want your individual impressions because the more of them that line up, the clearer the picture will be."

"Do you want the snack bars and Portaloos, that kind

of thing?" Lynette asked.

"If it helps to add perspective, sure." Indira glanced at the wall clock. "I need to run out for a bit, but I'll give you ten minutes. I don't think you'll need longer. And Pauly here will hang around in case you need him. Okay?"

Perry raised his eyebrows sceptically, but the rest of them looked happy enough to do as instructed, so they got busy scribbling. Several times Missy went to check on someone else's drawing, but each time the officer intervened.

"DI Singh has asked that you work independently, please."

"Sorry, sir!" she said, then whispered, "It's just like being back at school, hey, guys?"

"Humph," said Perry. "If I'd known we'd be tested, I'd have scribbled a floor plan down my arm last night."

Ten minutes and six rather clumsy sketches later, the detective in charge had returned and was gathering the pages together. She asked them all to wait as she quickly glanced over them, then smiled.

"Jacko's right. You *are* an observant lot. These, for the most part, are replicas of each other. No one cheated, right?"

Missy glanced guiltily at the officer while Alicia was still staring at Indira. Did she just call her boyfriend Jacko?

*So they have nicknames for each other, do they?* She was not quite sure what to make of that.

"No, they didn't cheat, ma'am," the officer replied.

"Good. Well, apart from one or two minor things, they basically tell the same story." The group gathered around to inspect the results, and Lynette scoffed when she saw Alicia's attempt.

"What is that? The celebrity green room?" She pointed at a stream of gold stars down one side.

"They're the Portaloos," Alicia replied.

"They're stars!"

"Yes, and if you were desperate to go, they were the star of the show," she retorted. "They were the best facilities I'd ever seen—spacious, clean, and plenty of them."

"Okay, guys, that's not really the point," said Indira, coming to Alicia's aid. "The general idea is intact."

She was right, almost to the person, they had the general positioning correct. With the screen at the top of each page and the main entrance at the bottom, it was clear that the Mumfords' red blanket was towards the back of the circular park, on the right-hand side near the bar. No one recalled who was seated directly in front of the Mumfords, but beside them, on the left, was the pregnant woman and a man, and on the other side, closest to the exit and the Booze Bar, were two men with beers and wandering eyes. Just behind the Mumfords sat the family of seven, and to the right of them, also closest to the bar, were the two elderly ladies, Flo and Ronnie. The book club had been spread out across four rugs, just behind the two women and the family, two blankets back.

Next to the club, everyone had sketched in Eliot Mumford, with words to the effect of "Hubby—2nd half."

Indira tapped one of the drawings where the words "2 slimeballs" had been scribbled.

"Do any of you have any information regarding the two gentlemen who were seated to the right of the deceased?"

"They weren't gentlemen, I can tell you that," said Claire.

"Which is why I want to follow them up."

"I know they left early," said Alicia, "like sometime before the lights came back on at the end. But I can't tell you much more than that."

Indira seemed disappointed but let it drop.

After clarifying a few other things, she then placed the sketches aside and asked each of them to recount what they could from that fateful night. And so, over the next hour, they repeated each other's stories, although there were several important differences.

It seems only Lynette and Alicia had overheard the Mumfords arguing by the bar, although the others had noticed the husband, Eliot, come straight from there and sit down on the grass beside Claire's blanket. Everyone had noticed the two men leering at the amorous couple earlier in the evening, and everyone, except Alicia, had spotted the heavily pregnant woman making a dash for the toilets during the first half, clutching her stomach. Only Missy, however, had deduced that the two elderly ladies seated near the bar area were part of the organising committee.

"At least I think they were," she explained. "They had those thingamajigs around their necks, same as the security guys. You know those Access All Areas passes you see at music festivals and that kind of thing? My sister, Henny, got one of those when she helped out at the Carols by Candlelight at the Domain last year. It meant she could go absolutely everywhere, even into the Green Room, and, oh my goodness, I can tell you, possums, that was soooo exciting for her! You wouldn't believe what stars she got selfies with—"

"Thank you, Ms Corner," Indira said, cutting her off abruptly and making her blush behind her spectacles. "We have spoken with the committee and have their statements."

"Speaking of green rooms, I wonder why those ladies didn't get a better position?" said Lynette, not noticing Indira's developing frown. "They could have been in the VIP section up the front. I saw a cordoned-off area there, with lovely plush beanbags and low deck chairs." She then turned to Alicia and said, "That's where I put my gold stars."

Alicia didn't take the bait. She could tell Indira was fast losing patience with their banter.

Indira said, "If we could just focus for a little bit longer, please, then I can let you get on with your Sunday. So, I want to get this straight, you all say you saw the deceased, Kat Mumford, return to her rug, *alone*, at about nine thirty-five last night, is that correct?"

"I don't remember the exact time," said Margarita.

"If that was just after the end of intermission, then yes we did," countered Perry.

"Can you recall if she was wearing glasses and a hat when you last saw her?"

Most of them nodded but less assuredly this time.

"Does anyone recall her carrying an iPhone, the latest model?"

This time no one moved a muscle.

"She had a jacket on," said Lynette. "Was probably in her pocket, why? Is it missing?"

Indira ignored that question and asked, "Did anyone notice her get up again in that second half?"

There were vague looks.

"She might have," said Missy. "Sorry, I can't remember."

"And none of you saw Mr Mumford, the deceased's husband—or anyone else for that matter—approach Mrs Mumford again after she returned to her rug post-intermission, is that correct? No one just sort of drop down next to her, lean in or anything?"

This time there were head shakes all round except for Margarita, who wanted to clarify, yet again, that she could not account for Mr Mumford's whereabouts at any time, nor did she want to.

"I can't say what I did not see," she stated.

Indira exhaled loudly. "Well, that's very inconvenient. Jacko assured me, if anyone was going to spot a killer lurking, it was going to be you lot. You've really let me down today."

They stared at her, a little taken aback, before she smiled.

"I'm just pulling your chain. You've been very helpful,

thank you." She stood up, shook her shoulders out. "Okay, so this is the bit where I tell you not to skip town, we might still need to question you further, yada, yada, yada. Oh and if you do think of anything, get in touch immediately, okay?"

They agreed to do just that, then gathered their things and followed the young detective, who showed them out.

~~~~~~~

"That DI Singh's an efficient operator," said Claire as they made their way to a nearby café for a deconstruct.

"I found her a bit frightening, actually," said Missy. "There was something about her tone, don't you think? Reminded me a little of an old English teacher I used to have. Mrs Tantlepiece. We used to call her Mrs Terrifying Beast, she was *so* intimidating!"

"DI Singh is a detective, Missy, and she does have a job to do," Alicia replied, selecting a table on the sidewalk and dropping down into a wooden chair. "I thought she was quite nice."

Perry said, "And why wouldn't she be? We are her most useful assets after all."

"Or so Mr Jackson tells everyone. He's our biggest fan, huh?" said Lynette, but Perry scoffed.

"I think it's a different Finlay sister we can thank for that."

"Not true," said Alicia, plucking a stray menu from a nearby table. "He was really impressed with our help on that cruise ship. It's genuine, Perry."

"Sure it is, honey." He winked at her. "But I ask you, *what* is that Spanish woman's problem? I think she's got it in for poor Eliot Mumford."

Margarita had not chosen to join them at the café, and it was just as well because Perry had a few things to get off his chest.

"And talk about Ms Contrary. She's obviously been

hanging out with our grumpy doctor too much. Did you see the way she glared! Could wipe out an entire army with one lift of those bushy eyebrows!"

"Put the claws away, Perry," said Claire. "Margarita's just being candid about what she saw. She's absolutely correct. She can't say the husband never moved if she wasn't watching him, now can she?"

"Nah, I'm with Perry on this one," jumped in Lynette. "That woman definitely didn't want to be the husband's alibi. Seemed almost *determined* to smash his alibi, in fact."

"Which is madness," said Perry. "As if the man could have slipped away from all of us, scooched across two blankets full of people and murdered his wife, then slipped back without anyone noticing. That's ridiculous! Besides, what motive could he possibly have? The way he and his wife were carrying on, they were clearly smitten."

"We did see them argue," Alicia said. "Which is why he moved next to Claire."

"A lovers' tiff, sure," said Perry. "But that's nothing. Goodness, my lovers would all be six foot under if every lovers' tiff ended in murder!"

He snatched the menu from Alicia and said, "So what are we having?"

A waitress appeared soon after, and they all ordered coffees except for Missy, who insisted she needed an iced chocolate and a blueberry muffin to get over the interrogation. By the time their orders had arrived, they were back to dissecting the case.

"So what do we all think?" Claire asked, reaching for her ristretto.

"You mean *whodunit?*" asked Lynette, and Claire nodded. "Goodness, that's a hard one."

"Could've been almost anyone," Perry agreed. "Except for the husband, of course. It definitely couldn't have been him. I don't care what that Spanish vixen thinks."

Alicia smiled. She had a feeling Perry's animosity towards Margarita had more to do with his friendship with her than the woman herself, and she appreciated the sentiment.

"I just can't believe a woman could have been lying there and no one spotted a thing," Claire was saying now.

"Like a corpse in a morgue," added Missy, taking a bite of her muffin.

They all glanced up from their cups, and she giggled, spluttering crumbs everywhere.

"Sorry, luvies, I'm just recalling that line from the movie last night. Don't you remember?"

They shook their heads. Nobody's memory was as good as Missy's; they had learned that a long time ago.

"He said something like, 'Look at them all lying in rows like corpses in a morgue. They're not men and women, there's nothing personal about them, they're just bodies, like butcher's meat.'"

"*Like steaks grilling in the sun,*" Alicia said, finishing the quote as Missy clapped, delightedly.

Alicia's eyes widened. Yes, she did remember that bit, and it sent a fresh wave of chills down her spine.

Kat Mumford had been lying half-comatose on a blanket in a park, as though spread out on a platter, as though meat on display. And some butcher had seen his opportunity and taken it. She wrapped her arms around herself and shivered again.

# CHAPTER 9

The restaurant ticked all Alicia's boxes. The room was dimly lit, with individual candles on each table, the ambient music was a soft twelve-string blues, and the prices were low enough to ensure you could indulge without breaking the bank.

"It's my old faithful," Jackson explained after he'd sent the waitress off with their wine order. "And not just because it's close to headquarters. The food's terrific." He indicated the menu. "Asian fusion, I think they call it."

"Asian Confusion, according to Lynette. She says few Aussie chefs can pull it off properly, herself excluded, of course."

"I thought she was waiting tables at Mario's Café in Paddington?"

"Wash your mouth out, Mr Jackson, that's a temporary glitch in Lynette's grand plan to become Master of the Culinary Universe. She's still waiting for her ship to come in."

"She doing anything about it?"

"Don't be ridiculous. It's just going to land in her gorgeous young lap! Actually that's not quite fair. She has been setting up some social media pages to show off her cooking, but it's just a start."

She shook her head. She had given up on lecturing her sister about old-fashioned cooking courses and—heaven forbid—commercial cookery apprenticeships long ago.

"Speaking of which, the starters look amazing."

He smiled. "I thought you'd like it."

They made time to order, then sat back and drank their wine, smiling at each other across the candlelight.

Alicia couldn't believe Jackson had time to meet for dinner, just a night after two bodies had been discovered, and told him as much. He shrugged.

"I told you when we met, I don't play by the rules. If I'm hungry, I'll stop and eat, and not just a sandwich at my desk, thanks very much. I'm not going to starve for this underpaid job. And if I like someone, well, I'm going to see her, dead bodies or no dead bodies."

"Such a romantic sentiment," Alicia quipped, and he laughed.

"Don't get too excited. I do have to run off after this. But I wanted to touch base and see how you guys are all coping after last night. I would've invited the others along, hell I would've shouted Anders dinner—he did a bloody good job under trying circumstances."

"He done good?"

"Better than good. He did everything right, really protected the integrity of the crime scene. I know he's a doctor, but I can't tell you how many medicos get that part wrong—moving bodies, letting loved ones paw all over them. I owe him big time, but I figured I'm not exactly his favourite person right now, so dinner with you and me mightn't go down so well."

Alicia was glad he'd come to that conclusion on his own. "So what's the goss? Did the doc get his diagnosis correct?"

"Yep, according to the preliminary forensics report, Kat Mumford died of asphyxiation by manual strangulation sometime between nine thirty-five p.m., when she was last seen returning to her rug to watch the second half, and ten thirty-five p.m. when her body was discovered. One or two witnesses said she *may* have got up at some stage in that second half, but we can't confirm that. Must have been a gripping plot by then. In any case, she was definitely murdered during the latter half."

Alicia thought about that. "Could the hubby have done it at the *end* of that second half? When he went to check on his wife?"

"Good question, but we don't believe so. We have enough witnesses who saw Eliot Mumford approach the body and then jump straight back—including you, yes? No one believes he lingered long enough to place his hands around her throat. Manual strangulation does take a little time and effort. I know she was a sparrow of a thing, and he's a big boy, but I honestly don't believe he could just throttle her in one second and no one would notice."

There was a small cough, and they both looked up to find a waitress hovering by the table with a plate of roast duck and rice paper rolls in her hand. She didn't look at all perturbed by their morbid conversation, just impatient to get the plate down and away.

"Thanks, Penny," he said, then to Alicia's raised eyebrows added, "She's used to this kind of talk. Singho and I have come here a few times to dissect cases."

Alicia smiled. She waited. Where was the pang of envy? Why was she not rattled by that comment?

He breezed on. "So, definitely killed sometime during that second half. And definitely by bare hands." He placed his own hands at his throat. "There was clear circular bruising around the neck and some obvious contusions where the fingers and two thumbs were pressed into the surface."

She grimaced. "Poor thing. Could it have been a woman by any chance?"

"Not unless she was very large and very strong. According to Frank Scelosi, that's the coroner, the bruising from the digits was wide, about two centimetres. The fact that no one heard her struggle indicates that whoever it was, he had control quickly and it was over in less than two minutes. But not two seconds, which is why we have to eliminate the husband from our enquiries."

She smiled. "It's not *always* the husband then."

He smirked back. "Pity that. There's a half-decent life insurance policy and a couple of properties in the will, but no, that would've been way too easy." His smirk turned sullen. "There was something else though, something pretty disturbing that points to a random stranger."

"What's more disturbing than strangulation?"

He lifted a shoulder. "Probably shouldn't be telling you this…"

"…but you will because you know I won't take it any further."

He looked at her sideways.

"Okay, I might mention it to the book club. But you know *we* won't take it any further."

"Make sure you don't, or it's my head on the chopping block. Indira's strictly 'by the book'."

He took a good gulp of his wine, and she wasn't sure if he was dragging it out to tease her, but she bit her tongue and waited.

"The thing is, there is some indication of sexual assault."

Alicia dropped her glass to the table and sat back with a mental thud. She hadn't been expecting that.

"How… on earth?" she managed after that horrendous thought had settled in.

Jackson reached out and took one of her hands.

"Sorry, that's not exactly pleasant dinner conversation."

She waved him off. "How?" she asked again.

"As I said, it's not confirmed yet. Scelosi's doing the full autopsy tomorrow, but her clothes had been disturbed. One of the straps from her camisole top was broken and"— now he was lowering his tone—"her skirt line was up near her waist. Everything else was still in place, but well, it makes us wonder."

"Makes me feel sick!" Alicia blinked madly. "She was right there in front of us! How did no one notice?"

He squeezed her hand tighter. "It might be nothing.

I probably shouldn't have told you."

She almost wished he hadn't. She was struggling to believe it.

"You said that the couple had been quite frisky, right?" he said, and she half nodded.

"But that was the first half, and she looked perfectly decent when we saw her at the bar during the break. At least she looked fine to me." She paused. "I think she might have been wearing her jacket then though. Maybe I didn't notice the broken strap."

"Yeah, her suede jacket was located near the body. She'd obviously taken it off at some stage in that second half. Can I ask, was she wearing her glasses when you last saw her?"

"DI Singh asked that too, and I'm pretty sure she was. Have they gone missing?"

He nodded. "And her iPhone. We've searched the whole park, can't find either. Both were very expensive. The phone was Apple's latest, with all the bells and whistles, and her glasses were some posh brand. Husband reckons both cost well over a grand."

Alicia whistled. "Wow, so maybe it was as simple as a robbery gone wrong?"

"Nothing simple about it when the victim ends up assaulted then dead."

Alicia shuddered as dark images began to swirl through her head. She pictured a sweaty thief reaching in for the valuables, then spotting a comatose drunken woman, seizing his chance. As all eyes were fixed on the screen, he slunk down beside her, placed a hand over her mouth and...

She gave herself a violent shake.

"I just don't believe it. We were all wedged in fairly tight. How could no one see some weirdo molest the poor woman?"

There was another cough, and this time Penny was back, a plate of coriander pork in one hand, a bowl of jasmine rice in the other. Again she seemed completely unconcerned by the dark conversation happening at their table and simply waited while they shifted their wine glasses so she could do a dump and run.

Jackson offered Alicia the serving spoon as he said, "We'll know more when we get the toxicology report back. Always takes a few days."

She glanced up from the rice. "You think she was drugged?" She felt almost relieved. "That might explain it."

"Yeah, it might. Bloody hell, I hope she was, might have made her last moments less horrifying."

Now he appeared to shudder. Jackson had seen plenty of horrors in his fifteen years on the force, but there was something very unsettling about this one.

They ate the next course in melancholy silence. Burglary was one thing, murder much, much worse. But *assault*? At a public park? Neither could quite get their heads around it.

"Anyway, as I say, it's not confirmed yet. Maybe she just tossed and turned while she was watching the movie."

"Who tosses and turns so much they break their strap? Besides, she looked asleep for most of that second half. I saw her return with an empty champagne flute and then settle in, so I just assumed she'd drifted off. She was certainly drunk enough. Or I thought she was drunk enough."

So many of Alicia's first impressions were now being obliterated.

"What happens now? What's the next step?"

He finished his mouthful. "It's early days. We've got a lot of loose ends to tie up."

"Like?"

"Like where's the missing phone and glasses? What about those two dodgy blokes? Where did they go?"

She nodded fervently. "You think they might have done it? Now *that* I can understand. They were watching the Mumfords pretty keenly that first half and leering at anything in a skirt during the break. Maybe they saw their chance when she returned to the blanket alone. They were certainly close enough."

She cringed at the new set of images that were flooding her brain.

"That's partly why I'm telling you all this, Alicia. We need to find those two men, and fast. But we have almost nothing to go off. Not like the family who were seated nearby. Glad we've been able to track them down. We're interviewing the man tomorrow."

"How did you manage to find them?"

"Bit of police work, bit of luck. Pauly spent all afternoon going through the bookings, and they were one of only a few groups who'd booked children's tickets. Thank goodness it wasn't *Finding Nemo* showing last night."

"But you can't locate the sleazoids?"

"Nope. We're still trawling the online bookings, but almost everyone booked double tickets, and most people paid cash at the entrance anyway, so chances are they did that."

"I'm sure they did. It didn't seem like the obvious film choice for those blokes. A bit like that family, the guys were ducks out of water. I don't recall them having any blankets or chairs with them. I bet they just saw the crowd and wandered in. Bet it wasn't premeditated at all. Unless, of course, they spotted Kat earlier and followed her in."

Her facial expression showed him what she thought of that, but he was shaking his head.

"I think your first instinct was correct. I think—if it was them, and we don't know that yet, of course—but if it *was* them, I think they'd had a few brews and just saw an opportunity and went for it. That's why I need you to think. Can you remember anything about those men? Anything you've forgotten to tell us? Anything at all?"

She sat back with a frown. Gave it some thought.

"They were what some would call 'white trash bogans,'

you know? Caps on their heads, lots of tatts—"

"Any tattoos stand out?"

She gave it some more thought. "Not really. Just lots and not just on the arms. They had them all over their legs, and I think at least one had them up his neck. I'm not the biggest fan of neck tattoos."

"Oh I don't know. You'd look pretty good with some barbed wire curled up around your chin." He chuckled. "So they were wearing caps? Any logos, emblems, that kind of thing? Maybe the name of an auto shop or something?"

She sat forward. "One was in a fluorescent shirt, you know, the kind that tradesmen wear."

"Oh that's helpful. We'll start questioning all twenty thousand tradies in the area." Now he was smirking. "Sorry, it's a start. Anything else? Anything at all?"

She shook her head slowly.

"Can you do me a big favour and ask the rest of the club? Maybe Missy or Perry or someone might remember something else, something specifically related to those two guys."

She promised she would, but there was something about his request that had her feeling a little tense. Was this dinner date really a chance to catch up, or was he scouting for more clues for his latest case?

She gave herself a shake, deciding it didn't really matter. He knew she loved mysteries and was simply asking for her help.

So why did she have to go and ruin a perfectly lovely evening with that mean-spirited thought?

# CHAPTER 10

"Were they even wearing caps? I can't remember that," said Missy as she settled into a seat at the dining room table between Claire and Perry.

Perry slapped her across the thigh. "Yes! My goodness, how can you forget? They wore those big, truckie caps, the kind you see in those road movies where the creepy trucker goes berserk."

Claire frowned. "Thanks for that, Perry. It's not like Alicia's news didn't just creep us all out enough."

It was early Monday morning, and the group had gathered again at the Finlay sisters' cosy terrace house on the shoddy side of the inner-city suburb of Woolloomooloo. Alicia had lured them over with promise of a free gourmet breakfast before work, but they would have come even if Cheerios were on the menu. They all loved a good mystery and were determined to help out, but when Alicia put Jackson's request to them, they didn't have anything useful to add.

"They were just these big, boofhead-looking blokes," said Missy, reaching for her cup of English Breakfast tea. "The kind I don't often see in the library."

"Or in the museum," said Perry.

"Or in my vintage clothing shop," Claire said, adding, "Thank goodness, might scare my lovely clients away."

"They weren't *that* bad," said Anders, who had also agreed to come but had been fairly quiet so far. He looked dashing in his tailored work suit, and Alicia remembered now why she had fallen for the guy so fast. "I just assumed they were a couple of mates having a few beers and watching a film. I think everyone's reading way too much into it."

And then she remembered why they'd broken up just as quickly.

"Well, they are the most likely contenders for assault," Perry snapped. "I can hardly see the old biddies or Mr Family Guy having a crack."

"But it could have been anybody; there were plenty of people coming and going nearby," he said, and not unreasonably. "We were close to the bar, remember? Plus we don't even know if she really was assaulted yet, do we?"

Alicia shook her head begrudgingly, saying, "Her clothes *were* dishevelled."

"Which is odd, agreed, but it's not really proof of anything. Jackson, of all people, should know that."

There it was again, that familiar, patronising tone that made Alicia want to slap him around the head with his shiny blue tie. She'd forgotten how much Anders relished playing devil's advocate and how much it annoyed her. She was suddenly very jubilant that they had split.

"The point remains," she said, trying to keep her tone light, "Jackson has to find them and question them in order to eliminate them from his enquiries, and that's what we need to focus on. He just wants to know if any of us saw anything that could help to identify those two men. That's the sum total of what he has asked."

She glanced from face to face. "So just give it some thought, that's all. He wonders whether any of us can recall any identifying marks. Like I said, maybe there was a business logo on one of their caps? Or the name of a football club on the back of a shirt?"

"One of them was wearing yellow fluoro!" Claire announced, and Alicia nodded.

"Yes, I already told him that. Anything else?"

They all sipped their drinks quietly.

"Oh! Oh! I've got it!"

That was Lynette who was busy whipping up a cooked breakfast in the neighbouring kitchen. They looked around with enquiring eyes, the delicious smell of smoked salmon causing their taste buds to water. She pushed the saucepan off the hotplate and turned to face them.

"They had bad taste!"

The group stared at her, confused.

"Last time I noticed them, they were munching down on Dagwood Dogs. Have you ever eaten a Dagwood Dog? It's like a battered sausage on a stick. Gross."

Alicia groaned. "If it wasn't for the fact that you're cooking us breakfast, I'd throw you out!"

She laughed. "Sorry, couldn't help myself. So come and get it, guys. You can grab a plate and help yourself."

Over the next half hour, they devoured the salmon-and-green-pepper omelette with relish, and gave Jackson's question some more thought, but nobody had anything remotely useful to offer.

By the time they had all rushed off to work, Alicia couldn't help feeling disappointed. She had secretly hoped she could provide the missing link.

"Stop beating yourself up," Lynette said, giving her arm a bump. "It's not actually your job to solve every mystery for Jackson, you know that, right?"

"Yeah, yeah." She helped Lynette stack the dishwasher. "You know what I'm like. I just feel so bad that that poor woman was lying there, being… Well, I just feel like I need to do something, to make amends."

"Again, not your fault, Alicia. You can't save everybody from everything."

"I know. I know!" She slammed the machine shut. "I need to get to work. You going in today?"

Lynette shook her head. "Rostered day off. I'm going to work on my site, load these images up."

She had photographed the hearty breakfast on her smartphone, as she often did, and was keen to show off the pictures on her Instagram page. Dubbed FinlayFeasts, it already had well over thirty-five thousand followers and counting, and Lynette was beginning to field advertising and sponsorship requests. She was no longer holding out for a spot on the *MasterChef* TV show but attempting to conquer the digital world instead.

"Do people really care what we had for breakfast?" Alicia asked, incredulous.

"They do now, darling! Besides, apparently I'm not being 'present' enough online, need to up the ante, post a lot more images, or at least that's what sponsors say. The nags. Six posts a day they say. Can you believe it? Six! And that's just on Instagram. I also have to post to Twitter, Snapchat, Facebook. Arggh!"

Alicia stopped in her tracks. A tiny bell was ringing softly at the back of her brain, but she couldn't quite work out why. It had something to do with the case, she was sure of it. She gave herself a little shake.

*Oh well, if it's important, it'll come to me eventually.*

"See you after work then," she said, bending down to pat Max, who had been salivating all morning. "You keep this one out of trouble, okay?"

Max wagged his tail like that was the very last thing on his mind.

# CHAPTER 11

Pastor Jacob Joves was not a happy man.

It was bad enough that his work at St Thomas's Church had been so rudely interrupted, but now the two upstart detectives were asking all kinds of impertinent questions, like why any decent parent would take children to an Agatha Christie movie.

Of course, it was a question that had circled his own brain over and over last Saturday night as they endured the ridiculous and quite trivial plot.

He blamed Agnes Gerrymander for that one.

*"Oh you'll love it,"* she had declared without any trace of sarcasm. *"It's got a lovely pastor in it, and it really poses the important questions, like good versus evil, dark versus light. Plus there's a very wicked child who comes to no good in the end, so it will be a good lesson for the kiddies, especially your Ezekiel. Don't you think, Lorna?"*

Her friend had nodded like a mad wench. *"Oh yes, it's a real battle of the demons. Right up your alley, I'd say."*

That had piqued Jacob's interest, and yet it had been a major disappointment, more a celebration of excess and promiscuity than a battle of good versus evil as far as he was concerned. *And* there wasn't a pastor in sight! He told all of this to the detectives as they sat frowning at him in the garden just outside the rectory.

"Of course it didn't help that that filthy Jezebel was up to her evil antics under the blanket right in front of us," Jacob added, his top lip curling up slightly.

"You are referring, I assume, to the deceased woman,

Kat Mumford?" said Jackson, keeping his tone indifferent.

"I don't know the girl's name, but yes, that one."

"Perhaps somebody tried to teach the *woman* a lesson?" suggested Indira who had little patience for men who called grown women 'girls', especially when that 'girl' was twenty-seven and married, as Kat had been.

Jacob glanced at her and back to Jackson, telling him, "If you believe in divine retribution, as I do, then that sinner certainly got what she deserved."

Jackson smiled at him coolly. "You think kissing your husband in public is punishable by death?"

He held his face up and to one side, looking down at Jackson through his spectacles with a sneer. "You're putting words in my mouth there, Detective. That is not what I said."

He glanced again at Indira, who had been taking notes. "I am just saying, she was not exactly a good person. A holy person."

"She was just a passionate young woman enjoying a night out with her husband, Reverend Joves," Indira said, trying to keep the venom from her tone. She tried a change of tack. "Your family was sitting closest to the deceased that night. Did you notice anything suspicious during that second half of the movie? Did you notice anyone approach the victim at any time?"

"No, I did not."

"Can I ask why you took off so quickly when the film ended?"

He frowned. "You answered your own question, Detective. The movie was over. I have young children who needed to retire." He smiled slightly, revealing a row of crowded teeth in his lower gum. "And did I not adequately explain how woeful that film was? How dreadfully disappointing?"

"So it wasn't the Mumfords you were escaping then?"

"Why on earth would I be doing that?"

She ignored this and said, "And you didn't happen to

pick up a spare set of glasses or a smartphone when you were packing up?"

He seemed taken aback by the question, maybe even a little shaken, his brow furrowing deeply and his eyes darting across her face for several seconds as though wondering what she was getting at.

Eventually he said, "Are you accusing my family of theft?"

"I'm not accusing your family of anything, Rev Joves, simply asking if you picked anything up by mistake. Your blanket was closest to the Mumfords. As you say, you do have children, it wouldn't be beyond the realm of possibilities that one of them accidentally—"

"My children are not in the habit of stealing other people's possessions, Detective." He interrupted her, his voice colder and more controlled this time.

Indira ignored this and asked about the two men in caps seated nearby. Joves did not recall any identifying features but did remember them watching the Mumfords, just as the book club had. Unlike them, however, he believed Kat deserved the odious attention.

The pastor's eyes sparkled again, and he stared off into the distance. "He has dug a pit and hollowed it out, And has fallen into the hole which he made. His mischief will return upon his own head, And his violence will descend upon his own pate." Then he glanced back at them and said, "Psalm 7, passage 15."

The two detectives shared a look.

Jacob continued. "Then the Lord rained on Sodom and Gomorrah brimstone and fire from the Lord out of heaven. Genesis 19."

Indira didn't know what to make of this, but Jackson was smiling.

"I just need to get this straight, Rev Joves. Are you saying the victim deserved to be leered at, burgled, murdered, or all of the above? I'm a bit confused."

The pastor tsked loudly. "Ahh, now you're taking the

words out of *our Lord's* mouth, not mine."

"But you do believe that, right?"

"It may sound unforgiving to you, Detective, but sometimes sinners must pay the price."

Indira frowned at that comment, but Jackson was as cool as a cucumber.

"Except maybe Mrs Mumford *wasn't* paying the price. Maybe her wanton behaviour was going unchallenged. Perhaps you wanted to teach the evil Jezebel a lesson yourself, show your children what retribution really looks like."

His eyes narrowed. "I leave the punishing to God," he said, then he smiled widely, his cluttered teeth reminding Jackson of a Great White. "But it looks like someone beat him to it, doesn't it?"

"Arrgh. I need a long, hot shower now," Indira said, shaking her limbs out as they made their way back to their car. "What a creep! I mean, I'm a big believer in karma, but that man is just plain twisted."

Jackson agreed. "Twisted enough to take things into his own hands, do you think?"

She thought about it as she unlocked the unmarked police car and settled into the driver's seat. "What are you saying? He was so disgusted with Kat Mumford's frisky behaviour that he kills her for it? Bit unlikely. Creepy's one thing, but I'm not sure he'd stoop to murder and certainly not in front of his kids."

"And yet he took them to see a murder mystery, and all to teach them a lesson. What do you think he meant by that? And who's Ezekiel, do you think?"

"One of his boys, I assume—poor thing." She revved the car. "I never saw the flick. Does something happen to some naughty children?"

"Don't know either, but I know someone who does."

He clicked in his seat belt and reached for his mobile phone.

"Oh, wow, yeah, that is creepy," Alicia said, soon after Jackson had reached her at work and made his enquiry.

A journalist by trade, Alicia had been deep in concentration, editing an online article about vegan Instagram stars, and was happy for the distraction. All the bright images of watermelon and quinoa salad were making her hungry—and not for watermelon and quinoa salad. She could go for a greasy hamburger and fries and suggested as much to Jackson.

"I wish," he said, glancing across to Indira, who was hissing under her breath at a slow driver in front. "Still got a bit to get through before we break for lunch."

"Fair enough. Okay, so there's a teenage girl called Linda in the book, right? She's also in the movie. She's the stepdaughter of the murdered woman, and they loathe each other. In the book, Linda turns to some voodoo to try to kill her stepmum and, believing she's succeeded, ends up attempting suicide. But none of that appears in the film version. That's probably why he was disgruntled. Creep."

"And Ezekiel?"

"I think that was the name of the oldest kid. A boy. He looked about fourteen or fifteen, bored, embarrassed. Your typical teenager."

After hanging up, Jackson repeated Alicia's words to Indira, adding, "So it sounds to me like he deliberately chose to take his children, one as young as five or six I might add, to a movie thinking they would get to watch a teenager try to kill herself. A lovely little life lesson for the kiddies."

"Oh what a nasty piece of work." Indira pulled the car up at the lights. "'Divine retribution' I believe were his exact words." She mock shivered. "I seriously feel sorry for those kids."

"Do you think he had it in him to lean in and extinguish a life?"

She shrugged. "He certainly had an air of the psychopath about him." She tapped the steering wheel. "Although fondling the victim first seems a stretch. As for the thefts…"

Jackson chewed on a thumbnail and watched the traffic flow. "I want to speak to his wife, see what she has to say."

"Good idea although I have a feeling she'll just back up the husband. From what the other witnesses say, she was the meek kind. Despite his gruff complaints, no one heard her utter a word. Except at the lines to the Portaloos, then she made all the kids pray. Talk about embarrassing! I'd curl up and die if my mother made me pray in public like that."

He laughed. "Yeah, bad enough just hanging out in public with your folks. Still…"

He wished they'd asked about the wife and wondered how they could get hold of her without him knowing. Jackson had a hunch she'd be more forthcoming without the pious pastor lurking nearby.

"What about the two women who were part of the organising committee, Florence Underwood and Veronica Someone-or-other?" Indira said. "It was Mrs Underwood who noticed the mother praying. Maybe she saw something else that could help us."

"Good idea. Know where we can find them?"

She nodded, then checked her iPhone. "But you'll have to face them alone. Jarrod's just texted. Kat Mumford's parents have arrived from Perth. They're distraught— as you would expect." She sighed. "I'd better get back. Face the music."

"Want me to join you?"

"Nah, I've got this one. Besides, I have a feeling the old ladies would prefer you all to themselves."

Jackson wasn't sure whether to be flattered by that comment or frightened.

# CHAPTER 12

The headquarters of the Balmain Ladies Auxiliary was located at the far western end of the small Balmain park, in a crumbling brick mews that had also been donated by Dame Nellie Johnson's family many years earlier.

The club had cleaned it out and freshened it up and now used it as their base to raise funds for park maintenance and other more worthy causes.

The place was bustling with life when Detective Jackson creaked open the large barn door, causing the lively banter to come to a grinding halt as every face swung in his direction, most eyes bespectacled, all with raised eyebrows above. They didn't see many people under the age of sixty at their weekly gathering, let alone men or cops.

Recognising him immediately, Florence Underwood waved to Jackson and ushered him across.

"Here's the handsome police detective I was telling you all about," she said to the curious onlookers.

"Welcome, handsome police detective," someone called out.

"Care for a cup of tea and a biscuit?" someone else offered.

"I'm good, thank you," he replied, pulling up a pew— a literal church pew, mind you—and sitting beside Florence. She had a ball of wool and some knitting needles in front of her.

"We're knitting beanies and scarves for the poor refugee children to keep them warm next winter," she said, and he felt a pang of sadness.

Here was one group of people offering comfort to children they had never met; it contrasted starkly with the behaviour of the so-called family man he had just left.

"We're still so shocked by the dreadful incident at the film night last Sat-dee," said a woman beside Flo, a skinny thing with a bright yellow cardigan.

"It was our very first moonlight cinema," said another woman, a larger lady to her right. "We've got another one planned in a fortnight. We're supposed to be showing *Grease*. What if the reprobate comes back and does it again?"

"That's why I'm here," Jackson said. "I'm hoping you can help me solve this thing."

"We'll do everything we can, Detective," said Florence. "Won't we, ladies?"

There was a fervent nodding of heads before most of the women returned to chatting about other things, their needles clickity clacking away, like a chirpy soundtrack around them.

Jackson turned to Florence. "How are you holding up, Mrs Underwood?"

"Flo, please. And I'm perfectly fine, young man, don't you worry about me. You don't get to my age without seeing one or two dead people, I can tell you that. I'm just glad those beautiful young children beside me had left before it all got too gruesome."

"That's exactly why I'm here, Flo. I'd like to see how they're doing, maybe chat to their mother. I know you had some information on her the other night. Is there anything else you can tell me? Anything at all?"

She looked down at her ball of wool and began to knit. Jackson wondered for a moment if she had not heard him, but it was soon clear she was giving it some thought.

"Her name evades me," she said eventually, "something odd, I know that. Well, they were both odd, really. *Him* more than her."

"You mean Reverend Jacob Joves?"

She looked up at him. "So you've tracked him down then?"

He nodded.

"But you want to chat to her separately, yes, smart move, that."

Jackson smiled. She was savvy, this one. He wondered if she wanted to join a book club. Flo continued knitting for another minute or so.

"Right, well they all had biblical names, I remember that. There was a Hannah and a Zemira and, oh, I can't remember the older child's name."

"Ezekiel?" he suggested, and she nodded.

"That's it. Ezekiel. He looked a bit glum that poor lad. Bit like my eldest grandson whenever he comes to stay. You just know they'd rather stab themselves in the eye than hang out with us oldies." She cackled at that. "But now, what was the wife's name; it was something strange…" She continued frantically knitting. "Something *sinister*…" She looked up with a start, causing her spectacles to slip down her nose. She pushed them back and smiled. "Azaria! That's right. I kept thinking of that poor child who was taken by that dingo up in the Northern Territory. You know the one, back in the 1980s?"

He nodded. "Azaria Chamberlain. So Mrs Joves's name was Azaria, you think?"

"I'm sure of it. And I can go one better for you if you like."

"I do like. What have you got?"

She cackled. "I believe the oldest lad goes to St Matt's, the Anglican school in Drummoyne. If you're clever, you might catch her picking him up from school one day."

Jackson smiled. Flo Underwood was really growing on him. "And how do you know that, Flo?"

"He had a backpack with him with the school emblazoned across it." She smiled smugly. "I know the place well, Detective. Several of my grandchildren have been through it. Not a bad school as far as schools go, quite strict, but not so strict that they take all the fun out of life." She frowned. "Unlike that father of his. He was certainly the fun police that one!"

She cackled again.

"You didn't happen to notice anything about the two men who were sitting to the right of the victim? Two men in caps who were drinking a lot of beer?"

"Oh yes, they were a rough sort, I know that. But they didn't give me a second glance, of course. I'm invisible to men now I'm afraid." Then she shrugged as though it didn't bother her a jot. "But let me think..." She went into one of her knitting frenzies again, and Jackson glanced around, catching the eye of another lady, this one very tall, with a helmet of stiff, dyed-brown hair.

"You should ask young Brandon!" the woman called out. "He was the one selling the drinks. He'll be able to help."

She had obviously been listening in, and now Flo was nodding.

"Oh you're right, Alice, thanks for that. Yes, Officer, Brandon Johnson's your man."

"He worked the bar that night?"

She was nodding. "Him and his team. He's been at a bit of a loose end since his mother passed."

"Poor Dana, bless her soul," someone else said, and there was a communal sigh.

"Gone far too young," agreed Flo. "Such a waste; such a tragedy. Now, I wonder where you might find Brandon at this hour." She glanced around again. "Alice? Alice! Sorry to disturb again, dear. Any idea where we'd find young Brandon today?"

"Top Shop I reckon, usually works there during the week."

"Oh of course, yes." Flo turned back to Jackson, who was just about to ask the question she was answering.

"Top Shop's the trendy coffee shop up on the corner of High Street and Beattie, I think it is. Five smackeroos for a cup of Joe! *Five*, can you believe it?"

"That's cheap for Sydney," Jackson said, and she gulped.

"It's daylight robbery is what it is, Detective. You should lock *them* up while you're at it." Then her lips drooped south. "I really don't understand the current fascination with those newfangled coffee machines. You can buy three-month's worth of instant coffee for the price of a cup-oo-chino, *and* it tastes just as good if you ask me. Anyway, dear, Brandon's your man. He would have been serving those lads their beers; he might know something."

The detective glanced at his watch, then thanked her for her time and threw out a group thank-you to the other women in the room. They waved and smiled back, and he could have sworn he heard a soft wolf whistle and a couple more cackles as the front door creaked behind him.

~~~~~~~

"Get anything from our ladies down at the mews?" Indira asked after he had returned to the station where she found him in the communal kitchen, staring forlornly at a tin of the aforementioned instant coffee.

"You mean apart from a cheeky wolf whistle?"

She scoffed. "You're not that hot, Jacko."

He let that slide as he relayed his conversation with Flo and her friends.

"I think this Brandon Johnson could be a good lead. Barmen see everything at those events, and if my memory serves, the bar was not too far from where Kat Mumford was lying."

"We spoke to all the bar staff that night and again over the weekend. Don't recall a Brandon."

"You should have. They tell me he ran the bar."

"Did he now? Hm, that's funny. I recall a Mayan and a

Wally, a Jacki and a Lin, but no Brandon. Know where we can find him?"

"I know just the place."

He dropped the tinned coffee back onto the bench and added, "And we can grab an overpriced *cup-oo-chino* while we're there."

Fifteen minutes later, the two detectives had found the café but not the barman. And they'd abandoned all thought of ordering a coffee. The queue for the takeaway coffee bar snaked through the café, out the door and onto the street.

"Brandon's usually here," a flustered-looking barista told them. "But he cancelled today. Swapped with Wally, I think."

"Wally Walters?" Indira asked, causing Jackson's eyebrows to rise.

The barista shrugged. He didn't have a clue what Wally's last name was—nobody used last names around this place—but it didn't matter. Indira had spotted Wally working a table on one side.

"He was also on bar duty at the cinema that Saturday," she told Jackson as they made their way across.

"Very cosy," Jackson said.

"Convenient too."

Once Wally had finished scribbling on his pad, Indira introduced herself, then allowed him to place the order in the kitchen before insisting he stop for a chat. The café manager, a man with a large bushranger beard and weary look about him, was not impressed, but their badges trumped the lunchtime rush, so he begrudgingly gave the waiter ten minutes off.

"But take it out the back," he said. "Don't need to scare the customers away."

*How many do you need?* thought Jackson as they battled their way through the crowded café, which was furnished with beat-up leather lounges, retro lamps, and dusty oil paintings. It was your classic hipster hang, and the clientele all appeared styled to suit—most in vintage clothing, baggy beanies, thick glasses and beards.

Jackson glanced around, sadly, knowing the victim would have felt right at home in this place. He hadn't known Kat Mumford, of course, didn't recall much about her from Saturday night, but all his victims brought a lump to his throat. Older colleagues had told him he would toughen up eventually—"get used to it"—but he found that he hadn't. If anything, he felt each death more keenly with each passing year.

He wondered if that made him a better person or a lesser cop, or both.

"I told you guys everything the other night," Wally was saying as he led them through the back door and out to a set of tables near the toilets. He sat down at one and reached for a packet of cigarettes he'd stashed in his apron pocket. As he lit up, Indira noticed his hand shaking a little, and she wondered why.

Was he scared of cops, as many people naturally are, or was it something else?

"We're actually here to see Brandon Johnson," she said. "You don't happen to know where he is, do you?"

That didn't seem to soothe his nerves any, and he began tapping the box on the table, his knee jerking up and down in his seat. "No, no. No, I haven't. Why would I?"

He wasn't meeting their eyes.

"Well he must have called you to take his shift," Jackson said, also picking up on the tension. "Did he tell you why he couldn't make it in today, where he was calling from, perhaps?"

Wally shook his head quickly.

"So what *did* he say?"

"Nothin'. Just could I do his shift? I need the cash, so I said yes. That was it."

"And you worked with him on Saturday night, at the

film in Balmain?" Indira asked.

He hesitated, dragged on his smoke again, then nodded.

"And Brandon was the one who ran the operation, yes?"

"The operation?"

"He was the one in charge of the Booze Bar that night?"

Another hesitation, then, "Sure. Yeah."

Indira sighed. "So here's the thing, Mr Walters. I don't recall interviewing any Brandon Johnson on Saturday night. Which means he wasn't there when my officers arrived. Any idea why?"

He shrugged. "Think he had to leave early."

"You think?"

Wally was having trouble meeting her eyes again. "Yeah, he, um, had something to get to. Asked if I could take over."

"Is that situation normal for him? Running out on a big job like that?" Wally shrugged. "It's just that usually the man in charge remains there until the end. So why the sudden exit?"

"Dunno, you'd have to ask him that."

"Oh we will," said Jackson. "You can be sure of that. He left the scene of a crime. That's a pretty serious thing." He leaned in closer. "So is aiding and abetting somebody who leaves the scene of a crime."

It wasn't strictly a hanging offence, but this nervous Nellie didn't need to know that. It had the desired effect, and now Wally had stopped twitching and was staring at them, gobsmacked.

"It had nothing to do with me, honest! He just had to run and asked me to finish up. So I did. Not my fault he fled."

"Why didn't you mention him to one of my officers?" Indira asked. "He could be a major witness to the murder of Kat Mumford. You're not covering up for him by any chance are you, Mr Walters?"

"No way!"

"All sounds a little shifty to me, hey, Jacko?" Her eyes were still firmly on the young barman.

Jackson was also eyeballing him. "Yep, very bloody shifty."

"Look, Brandon doesn't normally bail. I don't know what got into him. He's usually dead reliable. He just got a bit jumpy when that guy started wailing about his wife. Maybe he's got a phobia for blood, I don't know. He just said he had to run and asked me to take over, said not to mention him." He held a hand up. "He wasn't being dodgy or anything. He just thought it would confuse matters, said it'd be best if I said I was running the bar."

"He asked you to lie for him? You didn't find that just a little bit suspicious?" Indira said, and he shook his head again.

"Maybe he had a hot date or something, wanted to get out before the shit hit the fan."

"Except the shit had already hit the fan," Jackson was saying. "He was a key witness. It was his duty to stay."

"I didn't know that, did I? You should talk to him about that."

Indira smiled sweetly. "Which brings us full circle back to you. Any idea where we can find him?"

He went to shake his head, then must have thought better of it. He stubbed out his cigarette in the garden beside him. "Lives on Watsons Lane, few blocks away."

"Got a street number for us?"

"Nah." And then to their darkening expressions he quickly added, "Honest to God, I don't know what number it is, but you can't miss it. It's the boarded-up cottage just behind Woollies."

The boarded-up cottage was as deserted as it looked. If Brandon was there, he was not answering the doorbell, and after a few frustrating minutes, the two detectives gave up and returned to their car, feeling both disappointed and reenergised. The elusive barman had the smell of a serious suspect about him, right down to the sudden vanishing act.

"You thinking what I'm thinking?" said Indira, handing over the car keys to Jackson this time.

He nodded, letting himself into the driver's seat.

"Yeah, looks like we might not need to track down those cap-wearing pervs after all. This could be our guy. Why else has he suddenly vanished? And why'd he freak out when the officers arrived on the scene that night? You gotta join the dots. The bar he was working was pretty close to where all the action was happening. He was the one who was pouring the champagne that night. Our victim had an open glass of champagne."

"You think he slipped something in? Then had his merry way? Or tried to?"

"Maybe. He was certainly in a position to do all the above. We need that bloody toxicology report."

"I'm onto it." Indira reached for her phone and looked up the number for the lab.

"Pull rank and tell 'em to pull their finger out," Jackson said.

A few seconds later, Indira was in a heated conversation with someone in the pathology department. After a few feisty words, she placed a hand over the phone to block her voice, telling Jackson, "They tell me they *would* pull their fingers out and their toes as well, they say, except they're caught up doing your overdose."

"My what? Why?"

"Came in first."

"Yeah, but it's not urgent. That's an open-and-shut case. He was a habitual user, no suspicious circumstances."

"Still, it's protocol."

"Tell them to shove their protocol. Tell them the detective in charge has given them permission to put that one on the back burner and focus on this case."

As Indira returned to the call, Jackson couldn't help

wondering why his boring old overdose was taking up so much time.

"Okay, they're promising results by this time tomorrow."

"What? Why not first thing?"

"Apparently they have lives."

"Pity we can't say the same thing about Kat Mumford," was his gruff reply.

# CHAPTER 13

Alicia was slumped over her desk, struggling to focus on the digital layout on the screen in front. It had been a long day.

She kept coming back to the night of the crime and a throwaway line that was just on the tip of her tongue. It was something that Eliot Mumford had said to his wife, at the bar if she remembered right. Something important, she was sure of it. She just couldn't quite remember.

"Penny for your thoughts, sweet pea?"

That was Ginny, the office receptionist who was decked out in designer couture today, her black eyeliner uncharacteristically subtle, classy satin pumps on her feet. One of Arial Publishing's women's magazines was trialling her in their beauty department, and she was determined to make a good impression.

"I think they'll care more about your copy than your Manolo Blahniks," Alicia had told her when she'd first twirled in front of her desk earlier that day.

"Oh this stuff really counts! You don't know because you work on lame magazines that nobody under the age of sixty-five wants to read."

"Actually, get your facts straight, Ginny. Nobody of *any* age wants to read them, which is why I'm now writing digital content for all these inane websites. Apparently, everybody reads online these days."

Ginny was now leaning over Alicia's screen, inspecting her latest work. "Oooh vegan celebrities! I love veganism. Pity you can't eat meat though."

Alicia went to laugh, then realised Ginny was not joking. She turned back to the screen. "Well, it's just as well because there's no meat in the story."

She waited a beat for Ginny to appreciate her pun, and when that didn't happen, she continued. "It's just like everything else online, all just fluff. These days four hundred words counts as an article. When I first started writing, that was a photo caption."

Ginny snorted and began mimicking an old lady's voice. "Back in the good ole days..." *Now* she laughed. "You're so hilarious, Alicia, you'd think you were a hundred and five! Okay, so I have a very important message for you."

"Oh?"

"Yes, can you believe they've got me back on phone duty? As if I haven't got enough on my plate."

"Message please, Ginny."

"Right, well, that hunky policeman boyfriend of yours rang." She dropped her head to one side. "Does he kind of remind you of Matt Damon from *The Bourne Identity*?"

Alicia wasn't listening. She was grappling for the mobile phone in her handbag, wondering why he hadn't called, until she realised she had forgotten to charge it.

*Damn it.* She couldn't seem to get the hang of modern technology.

"He's kind of got that rough, good-looking action hero thing going on," Ginny was saying.

"Ginny! Focus."

"Oh, sorry, um, he's ditched you for the night."

"What? Really?"

"Yeah, bummer, hey? He says, and I quote"—she read from the message slip in her hand—"'Will make it up to you, I promise.' That's it."

Alicia slouched in her seat. She had been looking forward to catching up with Jackson tonight, not only to deliver the results from her breakfast meeting with the club but to find out how the case was progressing.

She winced then. Here she was suspecting him of ulterior motives when she had one of her own.

"I'm sure it's no biggie," Ginny said, a tiny frown crinkling her otherwise flawless forehead. "He's probably just heaps busy."

"I know. I know. Thanks, Ginny. How's the beauty gig going?"

Now Ginny deflated. "Hard work. They've made me run all over town, fetching clothes and cosmetics for shoots and stuff. My feet are *killing* me!"

Alicia didn't want to mention the fact that her designer heels wouldn't be helping.

"Just between you and me, I'm quite enjoying sitting down for a minute, answering the phones."

"Grass is always greener," Alicia said.

"True. At least they do have fabulous freebies. You should see the skin products that come in from all the advertisers and sponsors. And we get to help ourselves."

Alicia stared at her. "What did you say?"

"We get to help our—?"

"No, no! Sponsors! Oh my God, that's it!"

Ginny looked at her warily. She had seen Alicia go into one of these sudden mental meltdowns before and knew to bite her tongue this time.

"Sponsors. That's what he said. Now I remember."

"Remember what?"

"Kat the murder victim. She was an alcoholic!"

Ginny frowned, wondering why Alicia looked so happy about that.

Lynette had the same look of bewilderment on her face that Ginny was sporting earlier.

"You're going to have to explain it a bit better than that. I'm lost."

Alicia dumped her bag and sat down at the kitchen bench, where Lynette was still tapping away at her iPad, the rich aroma of an Irish stew coming from a slow cooker behind her. Alicia wondered if she'd even left the house today and shot a worried look at Max.

"So remember when we were in the bar queue, during intermission, and the hipsters were having their barney."

"Of course. They were arguing over champagne."

Alicia held up a finger. "Correction. They were arguing over her drinking."

"Isn't that the same thing?"

"Not really." She brushed a hand through her shaggy blond hair, trying to recall exactly. "He said something like, 'Come on, enough's enough. Remember what your sponsor says.'"

"I don't remember those precise words but, so?"

"So what did he mean by that? Was he referring to her AA sponsor?"

"*Alcoholics Anonymous*? Seriously? Isn't she a bit young for that?"

"Wasn't Drew Barrymore an alcoholic at like ten or something?"

Lynette contemplated this as she reached for a bottle of merlot on the kitchen bench.

"Dinner's ready, want a glass?"

There was not a trace of irony in that question, but Alicia felt a little hypocritical as she nodded her head, then jumped up to take care of it while Lynette scooped generous ladles of the stew into two bowls, added sprigs of fresh parsley, then headed for the dining table.

As they ate their meal, Lynette said, "You know I have sponsors and I'm not an alcoholic."

Alicia stared at her blankly, so Lynette explained.

"I now have two companies who want to sponsor my food blog. Eliot Mumford could have been referring to some paid advertiser or sponsor, you know, like a surf brand or a skincare range or something. She was fairly pretty. Could've been a model."

Then, changing the subject, she said, "No hot date with your detective tonight?"

Now Alicia just shook her head, looking glum, and they finished their meals in silence before dropping the bowls into the dishwasher and heading for the lounge.

Alicia yawned and reached down to pat Max's silky head.

"Did you walk him today?" she asked, and Lynette stared at her deadpan.

"No, I ignored him completely. Does he like to walk?"

"No need to be so sarcastic."

"He's had *two* walks. He's just cranky because I wouldn't give him the leftover lamb. I'm saving it for homemade kebabs." She reached for the television remote. "So how does this AA theory of yours progress the case?"

Alicia wasn't exactly sure. "I guess I just pass it on to Jackson, and he'll take it from there."

She watched as Lynette scrolled through various channels and gave it more thought.

"It could prove fruitful. Maybe Kat met a dodgy bloke through her AA meetings. Those gatherings must get quite intimate. They tell total strangers their life stories. Maybe someone there got a crush on her and wouldn't take no for an answer."

"Bit of a stretch," said Lynette, still flicking.

"Ah yes, but it's the stretchy bits I like, you know that." Alicia yawned again. "Looks like a dud night on the telly. Might grab a herbal tea and head to bed. You want?"

Lynette nodded, so Alicia made large cups of peppermint tea for them both, then carried hers up the stairs, Max at her heels. She waited as he curled his body into his plush pillow bed at the top of the landing, halfway between both sisters' bedrooms. They had agreed long ago that it was the only fair sleeping place for their cherished pooch, although they both knew he snuck into one or the other's bed occasionally, and left it at that.

As she settled onto her own pillow, her lamp lending a soft amber glow to her bedroom, Alicia couldn't get the creepy images of the two men out of her head, so she did what she always did when she needed cheering up. She reached for a crime novel, this time a classic P.D. James, opened the well-thumbed cover, and was soon lost in the complicated plot.

~~~~~~~

Liam Jackson was even less convinced of Alicia's AA theory than Lynette.

It was now early Tuesday morning, and he had shown up at Alicia's door, three fresh croissants and takeaway lattes in hand.

"Lucky me," she said. "Two tasty breakfasts in a row."

She put her sister's share aside, then led him and the bouncing dog out to the tiny back yard to catch up on the case without disturbing a sleeping Lynette.

Alicia loved that Jackson considered Lynette even though it was *Alicia* he had come to see. She loved that he always sought her sister out to say a quick hello, didn't ignore her as she was ignored by so many of Lynette's boyfriends.

Being the older, shorter, and far less gorgeous of the two sisters, she had gotten used to being eclipsed by Lynette, but Jackson always managed to be polite while making it crystal clear which sister he preferred in his orbit.

"Seems strange that the hubby never mentioned something as important as AA," Jackson said as he made room on the old wicker table for the coffees and then sat down in a wooden chair. "Maybe it just slipped his mind."

"You questioned him?"

"Not yet, doing that this morning." He handed her a flaky pastry. "But Singho spoke to him at length on Sunday and again yesterday when he brought Kat's folks in, and as far as I know, it was never mentioned."

"How is he?"

"Still a mess, still in shock, as you would be. Singho reckons his pain is genuine, but she's a lot less cynical than

94

I am. She's tough, Indira, but when it comes to victims of crime, she's a total pushover. In any case, Eliot couldn't provide any reason why his wife would be murdered. Said she was a model citizen, no enemies, loving family, the same old story."

"Well, somebody didn't love her. What did she do for a living again?"

"That's a whole other can of worms. She's what you call a YouTube star."

Alicia scowled. "Why is that even a *thing*? It's like fame is now a perfectly acceptable career choice." She was thinking of the vegan stars she'd just finished writing about and of Lynette too. "Like it doesn't matter why you're famous, just make sure you have truckloads of followers."

She placed that last word in finger quotes, and he laughed.

"Somebody woke up on the wrong side of the bed this morning."

"I think I woke up in the wrong bloody era!"

He agreed. "You would have suited Agatha Christie's day better. I can see you tapping away at your old typewriter, tweed suit on, pearls around your neck."

"Thanks," she said, adding, "I think."

He laughed again, reaching for his smartphone. "So, yeah, Kat Mumford had some kind of interior design blog—or *vlog* I think they call it now—huge following apparently. Gets paid ads through that."

"Sponsors?" she asked, and he nodded.

She pouted. *There goes her AA theory then.*

Jackson was busily tapping at the screen. "The problem with Kat Mumford's line of business is there's no actual office, no colleagues, and all her fans are anonymous strangers online. Ah, here she is."

He handed the phone across the metal table, and Alicia had a look at the vlog that was now showing on the minuscule screen. It starred a tiny blonde with flowing hair and a happy face. She was bubbling with excitement about some new "bespoke" chandeliers, steering the camera from her own perky smile to a high ceiling where a stiff-looking black contraption was hanging and back to her face again. Alicia had forgotten how pretty the woman was and how vibrant and full of life she had been.

"How epic is that!" Kat gushed, half out of the frame. "And just $3,999 from Bend & Vine! You can't go wrong, guys."

Alicia gulped. "Four thousand bucks? For a hunk of metal? I'd hunt her down too if I'd wasted that kind of money." She looked up. "Sorry, that was a bit insensitive, but honestly, what planet is that woman on?"

"Planet Gen Y."

"Okay, so let me get this straight. You think a follower might have become fixated with Kat and started stalking her? Maybe followed her to the park and grabbed the opportunity when the hubby moved elsewhere?"

"To be honest, no I don't. Or at least I bloody hope not, because it makes our job a nightmare. But it's a possibility we can't ignore. Like I said, she had hundreds of thousands of followers, most complete strangers. Could be any of them." He turned a little grouchy. "I don't think people appreciate the dangers of the internet. They don't realise how much they're putting themselves out there, like bait for psychos. If you watch to the end of that clip, you'll see Kat offers her email address, even a mobile phone number, should someone want to get in touch."

"But no home address?"

"No, true, but a clever psycho could probably do a little sleuthing. Scroll through her other clips, check out her profile on Facebook. The woman has a gazillion selfies, all over her house, her back yard."

Alicia glanced back at the screen and saw that Kat was now taking the viewer on a tour of a completely whitewashed kitchen with gleaming chrome appliances. "Her kitchen has all the latest gizmos. And four thousand dollars for a light isn't exactly loose change. How does she make her money? Surely YouTube ads don't pay that handsomely. What does hubby do?"

"He's a chippie."

"A carpenter? That suits." She remembered his broad shoulders and checked shirt.

"But you're wrong about YouTube. The biggest stars get paid ridiculously well. Eliot told Singho that his wife made close to half a million bucks last year in sponsorships and advertising deals alone."

Alicia's jaw dropped. "Wow, okay, I take it all back. I want my own Instagram following!" She shook her head. "So when Eliot referred to her sponsor at the bar that night…"

"He probably meant a genuine business sponsor. You wouldn't want to risk that kind of money for a drunken night out. You blemish your reputation, you blemish your brand." He nudged his eyebrows up. "You like that? I was doing a crash course on digital marketing last night."

"Very impressive."

Jackson dusted the croissant crumbs from his trousers and checked his watch. "I'd better get going. Just tell me, any luck with the clubbers? Anyone recall anything useful on those two blokes I asked about?"

"Sorry, no. They were uncharacteristically quiet on that."

He stood up. "Well, it was worth a try." He leaned across and gave her a long, lingering kiss that tasted of coffee beans and butter. "How about dinner tonight?"

"Love to. When can you get away?"

He shrugged. "I'll be in touch. I better fly. Indira wants to reinterview Eliot first thing. We're hoping he's moved out of shock and denial and into the angry stage."

She arched an eyebrow. "Why do you want him angry?"

"Because then he might start pointing the finger and give us a few decent suspects."

# CHAPTER 14

Three days had passed since his wife was murdered, and Eliot Mumford's shock was still palpable. He had not yet got to angry, or at least that's how it looked to the detectives when he answered the door.

After offering a stunned hello, he shuffled back through his hallway to the open-plan kitchen/living area, his shoulders slumped, his gait slow. He looked like he was half-drugged, like he had the world on those shoulders and at least a couple of other planets on top.

As they followed him through the house, Indira expected to be familiar with most of it. Like Jackson, she had studied Kat's blogs intensely. But as they entered the kitchen, she was surprised to find it wasn't quite as whitewashed as she remembered and not nearly as tidy. Old burger wrappers, coffee cups and dirty dishes were stacked high on a black-and-white marble benchtop, and there was an odious smell coming from an open garbage bin that was half-toppled over near the back door. Housework was obviously Kat's domain. Either that or he'd given up now he'd lost his soul mate.

*And who can blame him?* Indira thought as she glanced around.

For his part, Jackson couldn't help wondering what all the fancy sponsors would think.

"How are you holding up?" Indira asked, trying to keep the worried look from her eyes.

"Oh, I'm just numb. Confused. Sad. Numb," he said again.

She brushed a hand on his forearm and nodded. "Yep, it's a shitty, shitty time."

No point pretending otherwise.

Eliot looked around the kitchen blankly, like he'd forgotten why they were there, so Indira pointed at the kitchen stools and said, "Shall we take a seat?"

He nodded and sat down.

Jackson cleared his throat. "Sorry to do this to you mate, but we have some more questions. We've got a couple of suspects that we're having trouble tracking down."

Indira shot her colleague a frown. She had hoped to ease him in a bit first, but Eliot was now nodding keenly.

"Yeah, I guess you would. I've been thinking about it, the killer was…" He sighed, scratched his scruffy hair. "Well, they were very bloody lucky, weren't they?"

Now she swept her eyes to him. "How so?"

"A park full of strangers at night, nobody knows anybody, everybody's looking up at the screen. Endless people wandering around using toilets, fetching drinks. Everybody had a legitimate reason for being there. Nobody needs alibis; it's open slather."

"You've given it some thought," Indira said.

"It's *all* I can think about," he said stonily.

Eliot was right, of course. It wasn't like a private event where they could track down the participants or spot the odd one out. Public events were open to all, including psychopaths. Of course, that didn't mean that those same psychopaths didn't stand out, even in a crowd.

"I'm thinking about the two blokes who were seated to the right of your blanket, between you and the bar—they were bit out of place don't you think?" said Jackson.

"How so?"

"For starters, it seems a strange film choice for a couple of redneck tradesmen. I mean, *The Fast And The Furious*, sure."

"Jackie Chan?" Indira offered, and he nodded.

"The latest James Bond even, but an Agatha Christie flick? No offence, Agatha, but I was only there to cosy up to my girlfriend."

Eliot's eyebrows shot up. "You were there?"

"Just briefly. Had to take off. Missed all the action."

He hoped it didn't sound flippant, but Eliot didn't appear to take offence.

He just nodded and said, "Yeah, well, we were only there for a laugh as well; it wasn't supposed to end like that."

"Those two blokes I mentioned, any idea who they were? Whether they looked familiar?"

Eliot shrugged. "I'm not even sure who you're talking about, to be honest. Don't think I noticed them."

"They noticed you," Jackson said. "Or at least that's what the witnesses say. Reckon the two guys were enjoying your little blanket antics with Kat."

He dropped his head into his hands then. "Oh no way."

"So you can see why we want to track them down, right? Problem is they've vanished. So you have absolutely no idea who they were? Notice any identifying clothes or tattoos or—"

"I told you, man, I barely remember them!"

He had raised his voice considerably but calmed down again quickly, looking up at DI Singh with imploring eyes.

"Sorry. I… I'm just gutted. After you told me about my poor little kitten, about the assault… I… I just feel like I've been punched in the stomach."

Indira held a hand up. "That's also why we're here, Eliot."

She frowned again at Jackson, wishing he hadn't launched into his interrogation so quickly. She'd wanted to deliver this tiny sliver of good news first. Indira liked her fellow detective, but he was like the proverbial bull sometimes. He always rushed in, treating victims like suspects, never comprehending their pain or giving them the benefit of the doubt.

Smiling reassuringly at Eliot, she said, "The coroner handed down the official autopsy report this morning." Eliot's eyes widened. "As I explained yesterday, there's still some more tests to be done, but we wanted to let you know, first thing, there was no sign of sexual assault. None whatsoever."

Eliot closed his eyes and brought his fingers prayerlike to his lips, as though giving thanks, then snapped his eyes open again. "So why was her top torn?"

She stared at him blankly. She didn't want to tell him that someone had probably tried, was most likely interrupted during the process, but he must have come to that horrendous conclusion himself because he dropped his head back into his hands and moaned.

Jackson coughed. He knew his partner was the softly-softly kind, but he needed to get Eliot back on track, and fast. A killer had been walking free for three days now, and he was desperate for some progress.

"Listen, Mr Mumford. I need to ask you about the barman as well. Do you remember the guy working the Booze Bar that night? The one your wife bought her last glass of champagne from?"

Eliot looked up again, confused. "Yeah, I think so. Young bloke. Why? You think *he* did it?"

"Not saying that, not at all. He's just a person of interest at this stage, and we'd like to bring him in for questioning, but we're having a bit of trouble locating him at present. We need to identify him."

What he didn't tell him was that they were growing increasingly concerned. Despite putting an officer on Brandon Johnson's door last night, he never returned and there was no sign of him at home or work this morning.

Eliot looked lively suddenly, clearly buoyed by this new lead. "Um, okay, sure, let me think. Like I said, young dude, maybe nineteen, twenty max. Darkish hair, skinny, bit judgy."

"Judgy?"

"You know, judgmental, kind of scowled at us a lot. Well, at Kat really. She was pretty drunk. He kept looking at me as if to say reel your wife in. You think he did this?"

"Not saying that, no. But speaking of judgmental, do you remember the family of seven who were seated just behind you?"

He scoffed. "How could I forget? That dude had it in for us. Kept telling us to shut up. Said he had kids and we needed to be respectful or some shit. I told him maybe it was time to take the kids home to bed." He scratched the back of his head. "Actually, now I think about it, one of the kids was a bit of a weirdo."

Jackson's eyes narrowed. "How so?"

Eliot ran a hand through his beard. "Dunno. It was just a vibe I was getting. He was definitely checking us out."

Indira sat forward now. "You're sure of that?"

He nodded. "That's why we moved under the blanket. Kat felt a bit uncomfortable with him staring at us, but I thought he was harmless enough. I remember saying, 'Oh he's just a kid. In his dreams, kitten.'" He cringed at this, hunched over, dropping his head into his hands again. "Maybe I should have taken him more seriously!"

Indira reached out and squeezed his shoulder. "Eliot, it's very unlikely an adolescent boy did this thing. He may not have had the strength." She glanced at Jackson. They would have to check that with the coroner. "But I can assure you we will investigate that thoroughly."

"Thanks, Indira, I appreciate it."

She nodded and stood up. "And on that startling note, I think we'll leave you to it. You have my number if you think of anything else or you just need to talk."

She gave Jackson the nod and turned to go, but her partner stood his ground.

"Er, just one more thing," Jackson said. "I'm just wondering, Mr Mumford, was your wife a member of Alcoholics Anonymous?"

The younger man stared at him gobsmacked. "How did you—?" He stopped abruptly, his cheeks flushing bright red beneath his beard.

He clearly wasn't expecting that question and nor was Indira who turned back to stare, inquisitively at Jackson.

*Where had that come from?*

Even Jackson looked surprised now and silently saluted Alicia. He had simply chucked the question out there to stir the man up. Never in a million years had he expected the answer to be yes. His girlfriend really was in the wrong career.

"You were overheard mentioning your wife's sponsor at the bar that night," Jackson replied. "We put two and two together."

*Well, Alicia did, but he didn't need to know that.*

Eliot started shaking his head, his eyes back on Indira. "Sorry, but… but what has AA got to do with any of this?"

Indira raised her eyebrows at Jackson as if wondering the same thing.

He said, "It may be nothing, nothing at all. It's just that it's a whole other avenue of enquiry, and it's worth knowing about."

Eliot was now scratching his beard. "Seriously, man, don't bother. It's a dead end." Then he sighed and said, "Kat didn't need AA. She thought she did. I wasn't convinced."

"Yet she was drinking to excess that night. You were overheard arguing about her drinking."

The colour was rising in his cheeks again. "She'd had enough, that's all. We were both in a great mood, why ruin it by going over the edge?"

"And you thought another glass of champagne would send her over the edge?" Jackson asked, and Eliot looked at him warily. "Was she in the habit of overdrinking?"

"She just liked a drink from time to time! Who the hell doesn't?"

If he wasn't angry before, he certainly was now, vigorously scratching at his beard with both hands. After a few moments, he stopped and inhaled deeply, clearly trying to calm down.

"Look, it didn't happen often. Seriously, AA was a waste of time. Kat just went to one or two meetings, didn't have anything good to say about them. Pack of losers, she said. I don't even think she was going to go back."

"And yet she had a sponsor. Do you mind if we contact that person?"

He was shaking his head now. "I… I don't really even know them, yeah? It's all kind of anonymous."

"Do you have a name?"

"Oh, um, Tim? Tom? Something like that."

"Do you know which group she attended?"

"Huh?"

Jackson could feel his patience waning. "Where it was? Which community centre or local hall?"

He sighed, threw his hands in the air. "I think it was nearby, wherever the local one is. Honestly, you're wasting your time. She wasn't an alcoholic."

*Tell that to her sponsor*, Jackson thought before turning to his partner.

"Anything else?"

Indira ignored the question and addressed Eliot. "Thanks for your time. I know it's a very trying period." She gave him a sympathetic smile. "Don't forget you can call us if you need anything, anything at all."

Eliot nodded bleakly, and Indira led the way outside, feeling like a spare tyre and not liking it one bit.

It was only once they were back in the car that she rounded on him.

"What the hell was that?"

Jackson's eyebrows rose. "What?"

"Why didn't you mention AA to me?"

"Sorry, it was just a wild hunch. I didn't actually think

he'd say yes. Alicia mentioned it to me this morning."

"Alicia? Who the hell's… Hang on, *Alicia Finlay*? One of your book club friends?"

He nodded.

"What are you doing discussing—"

"She's my girlfriend," he added quickly, cutting her off.

Jackson wasn't sure why he hadn't mentioned the relationship earlier, but the way she was glaring at him now made him wish he had. He suddenly felt like a thirteen-year-old caught snogging behind the school canteen.

"Oh, your *girlfriend*? And how did she work it out?"

"She was the one who'd overheard the comment about a sponsor. Even she agreed it was most likely related to a website sponsor. I was just trying my luck."

"And your girlfriend didn't see fit to mention it to me? I know we're equal rank, but I outrank you on this case, right? You do understand the way this works? I'm the lead investigator. I spent two hours questioning Alicia and her mates on Sunday and not one word about it."

He turned his whole body to look at her. "Are you angry with Alicia for not telling you? Me for not mentioning it earlier? Or yourself for not figuring it out?"

*Or are you just angry that I have a girlfriend?* he thought.

Indira frowned and looked away.

"Look, this is a good lead," he told her. "There could be something in it. AA blows the case wide open. You know as well as I do the kinds of people who attend AA meetings. It's not all suburban mums and dads. There could be a sex offender in the mix, someone ordered to attend AA by the courts. There sometimes is. It's worth exploring." He nudged her with his elbow. "I know you're officially my boss on this case, but we're in it together, right?"

"Yes! You and me, together. Not you, me, your girlfriend, and her bloody book club." Indira took a few calming breaths. "Sorry. It just came out of left field, that's all. You know what I'm like. I like to be informed.

I'm supposed to be the lead detective on this."

*Not your bloody girlfriend*, she almost added but bit her tongue.

"And I'm sorry. I'll give you the heads up in the future. I know you're top dog. I'm not trying to take that away from you." She gave him a half smile. "And I know I'm only on this case because I was there that night. I know Gordon was your first pick."

"He wasn't my—"

"I know we're different beasts. I shoot from the hip. I run with my gut. I don't play by the rules."

"No? Really?"

Indira smiled properly this time. She had only worked with Jackson a handful of times before, but she knew his reputation, and she knew they worked very differently. But she liked the guy and she hoped they'd work together again. And he was right. She had asked for him on this case and not, as the other women in the office had suggested, to keep some eye candy about. Jackson had been at the scene of the crime earlier that night. He had a better idea of the layout and the mood of the evening than any other officer on the case. She needed him. Kat Mumford needed him. And so did Eliot.

"Just no more surprises, okay?"

"I'll try."

She started the car and pulled out.

After a few minutes' contemplation, she said, "Good work back there. That's the first time I've seen the husband look edgy. He really, *really* didn't want us to follow that lead, did he?"

Jackson smiled. "Silly bugger. Now *all* I want to do is track down that bloody sponsor."

"Then let's try to do it."

# CHAPTER 15

"**I'll** try to get there," Alicia promised Perry over the phone from work. "But I'm a bit behind with the latest website. And the advertiser wants changes." *For the fifteenth time*, she could have added, but kept that to herself.

She knew the palaeontologist's mind was preoccupied with Wednesday's big event at the museum where he worked, and he didn't need to hear her woes. He was organising a charity cocktail party, and it had him in quite a lather.

"How's it all coming along?"

"Ohhh, getting there. I've gone right out on a limb with this one, insisted the old fossils who run this place put the event on, and I'm just terrified it'll be a flop."

Perry was trying to get the community more engaged in the museum's work and was hoping that sipping cocktails and eating canapés among dinosaur bones and stone-age relics would not just entice thirsty journalists, it would result in some much-needed media coverage.

"I'll be there!" Alicia said, more firmly this time. "And I'll make sure all the other editors in the building know about it."

"Thank you. What about Lynny and Jackson?"

"I'll drag them by the hair if I have to. You can count on us. Now get back to it and stop worrying!"

He promised to do that and hung up.

Alicia waited a beat then dialled Jackson's number. Despite her assurances, she was not at all sure Jackson would be free to attend tomorrow night's event, and she was determined to lock him in.

Across town, Jackson was locked in an interrogation room, his phone on silent. He was currently leaning against the back wall, arms crossed, observing while DI Singh slapped a series of questions at a frustratingly unflustered Brandon Johnson.

Brandon had just been spotted, strolling casually into his lunchtime shift at the Top Shop Café, and was promptly escorted back out and across to police headquarters, much to the café manager's exasperation and the detectives' relief.

They had abandoned the AA angle for now and were staring at the young barman wondering what he had to hide.

Brandon was a handsome lad, just turned twenty-one, with thick black hair—probably dyed—and an earring dangling from one ear—probably pilfered from an unsuspecting girlfriend.

"We've been looking everywhere for you, Mr Johnson," Indira was saying. "Where have you been for the past few days? You're not avoiding us, are you?"

"Not at all," he said calmly, a little too calmly, before glancing at his lawyer, an elderly gentleman who looked better suited to a game of bowls than a police interrogation. The lawyer shrugged as if to say, *Whatever*.

Brandon looked almost as bored as his lawyer and leaned back in his seat. "Look, I've just been bunking at a mate's place, that's all. No biggie."

"And Saturday's film night?"

"What of it?"

"Why did you do a runner?"

Brandon glanced at his lawyer again, then back at Indira. "I didn't do a *runner*. Was just tired, that's all. Didn't want to get stuck there. Didn't realise that was a crime."

"You didn't realise that was a crime," Indira repeated, turning deliberately to share a very visible eye roll with

Jackson before turning back. "You left the scene of a crime, Mr Johnson. The officers on the ground specifically asked that all parties remain on the premises to provide contact details and witness statements before they departed."

"I didn't hear that bit. I just grabbed my shit and left. What's the big deal?"

"The big deal," boomed Jackson suddenly, causing both the lawyer and his client to jump, "is that a young woman was murdered last Saturday night right in front of your face."

It was a smug-looking face too, Jackson decided, a little too smug for his liking. He stepped forward, his eyes boring into the younger man's.

"This is the same woman who was lying not six metres from where you were serving drinks all night." He held up a hand. "The same woman you *did* serve a drink to just minutes before she was murdered."

He lifted a shoulder, trying to look nonchalant. "So that's sad and all, but sorry, I'm still a bit, like, confused." He made a show of glancing at his lawyer again. "What's it got to do with me again?"

Indira smiled. "Good question, Brandon. Do you mind if I call you Brandon?" He shrugged again. "Great. Let me ask you this, Brandon. Do you recall serving the victim her last glass of champagne?"

"I remember serving her *a* glass of sparkling wine, sure. She was hot. What of it?"

"Did you pour the sparkling wine from an open bottle?" Indira asked.

"No, I keep the cork in when I pour."

He chuckled at his joke, glancing at his lawyer, who did not chuckle along.

"You think this is funny, Brandon?" Jackson said.

Brandon held a hand to his mouth as if stifling a laugh. "Nah sorry, what were you saying about the bottle?"

Indira stared at him coldly. "Did anyone other than you

have access to that open bottle?"

The toxicology report had still not come through, and the detective was hedging her bets, but while Brandon looked at her, his smile now slipping, the lawyer appeared to have woken up.

He cleared his throat and said, "You don't need to answer that, son." Then he turned his watery eyes upon Indira. "I was under the impression you had not received a toxicology report yet, DI Singh."

"Not yet, no."

"So why this line of questioning?"

"Just filling in the blanks, Mr Morrie."

"Not on my watch you're not." He cleared his throat again, making an ugly guttural sound. "Is my client under arrest?"

"Not at this stage."

"Are you suggesting my client had something to do with the deceased's murder, Detective?"

"No, I'm—"

"Well, thank goodness for that." He gave her a silky smile. "As you well know, Mr Johnson is here under his own volition. He is being cooperative. But if you are going to start throwing accusations around, we might just take our leave."

He tapped Brandon on the hand and made as if to get up.

Indira held her own hand up. "I'm not accusing your client of anything, Mr Morrie. I'm just trying to get the facts."

"Then let's stick to those, shall we?" He relaxed back into his seat. "This young man lost his beloved mother less than twelve months ago, his grandmother just a few years before that. He's had a rough ride, and I think we all need to be a little bit more cognisant of that."

"Of course," Indira said, attempting a smile of her own. She sat back in her own chair. "Mr Johnson, is there anything you can remember about that evening? Anything else you'd like to tell us?" Then she added, "If you don't mind?" flashing the lawyer a stiff smile.

Brandon eyed her suspiciously. "Like what?"

"Like did you happen to see where the victim, Kat Mumford, was sitting during the film?"

"Sure, like you guys said, she wasn't that far from the bar."

"And did you happen to notice anybody approach the victim at any point in the evening but especially during the second half of the film?"

"Nope, but then I wouldn't have, would I? I was cleaning up at that stage. Wanted to get away quickly, like *I* said."

"So you never saw anyone of any description approach the victim at any stage?"

"Detective Inspector Singh—" Morrie warned, but Brandon was shaking his head.

"Seriously, guys, I was too busy at the bar. I didn't have time to watch every drunken chick in the place."

Indira sighed and pushed herself away from the table. She'd had enough. "Okay, we'll leave it there for now." She looked at Mr Morrie. "Please be aware that we *will* be getting the tox results in very soon and we may require your client for questioning again."

"Yes, yes, I'll make sure he doesn't do a Houdini on you, Detective."

"That'd make a nice change, thank you, Mr Morrie," she all but spat back.

"He's a smug little bugger isn't he?" said Jackson the minute Brandon and Morrie had left the room.

"You talking about the suspect or his crusty lawyer?" Indira replied, shaking her head. "It's the old ones you have to watch for. They look like they have one foot in the grave, but they can run rings around you."

She loosened her ponytail and crinked her neck. "So, the barman's a smart-ass and he's got good representation, but does that make him guilty?"

"I reckon he's hiding something."

"Why do you say that?"

He rubbed the stubble on his jaw. "Don't know. I just get a bad vibe from the guy."

"Vibes don't hold up in court, Jacko."

"Pity that."

~~~~~~~

"He's definitely hiding something," Jackson repeated to Alicia as they clinked oversized wine glasses then settled in on the chocolate leather sofa at his place.

"Like what?" she said before taking a sip.

The wine was delicious. A silky Margaret River Cabernet Sauvignon, and she let it slide around in her mouth before swallowing.

He had good taste, Jackson, but in a subtle way. His apartment, located close to his office, was a classy mix of creams and browns, a few pieces of modern art on the exposed brick walls and an old turntable with dozens of records nearby. It was a bachelor pad, sure, but it had style.

"Dunno," he replied. "Just found him so slippery. Bit too smug. Like he knew what he was doing. I mean, why bring a lawyer?"

"Because it's his legal right."

"Yeah, but who knows that at his age? We just asked him in for a casual chat, yet he shows up with his solicitor who, by the way, I'll bet any money is married to one of the old biddies at the Women's Auxiliary. They seem to have assumed the job of his guardian." He drank from his glass and mulled that over. "At least we finally got the tox results."

She raised her eyebrows.

"No opiates or other drugs that might have knocked her out. Nothing in her stomach except orange juice and alcohol."

"No roofies then?" she said, referring to Rohypnol, which they had encountered on a previous case.

"Nope, but she had consumed enough booze to keep a rugby team happy, so that explains why she didn't call out. She'd probably passed out by that stage."

"How much?"

"Let's put it this way, if she'd been breath tested afterwards, she would have been more than five times the legal limit."

Alicia whistled. "No wonder she was at AA."

"Except it clearly wasn't working."

"That's true. Kat sure did fall off the wagon that night. Did you contact her AA branch? Or whatever it's called."

Jackson nodded. "No-go zone. According to the husband, she was a member of a local group, had some sponsor called Tim or Tom or something. The only group near them is in neighbouring Rozelle, but when I called, they were having none of it. Told me they never disclose the full identity of members both to other members and to outsiders. Refused to even concede that a 'Kat' of any kind was a member of any branch. Said it was called Alcoholics *Anonymous* for a reason."

He scowled, showing her what he thought of that.

Alicia figured it was fair enough but asked, "Doesn't a murder enquiry trump that? Can't you get a warrant or something?"

"What for? They don't keep membership files or attendance records, they don't film the meetings, so what would be the point?"

"You could interview some of the other members, see if they remember her?"

"They're unlikely to tell us anything, and frankly, I'm not sure there's any substantive reason to keep going down that track. Kat Mumford wasn't killed on AA premises. There's no evidence linking AA to the crime. Indira thinks it's a red herring, and I'm inclined to agree with her. It was a great guess on your part, but I'm not sure it's got anything to do with anything…"

"…but?" She could tell he didn't quite believe that argument and waited.

He took another gulp of his drink and then wiped his lips. "But I still can't understand why Eliot Mumford got so anxious when I brought it up. It's the first time I've seen him break a sweat. I reckon he's hiding something, maybe protecting someone."

"Probably just protecting his wife's reputation."

"Bit late for that, don't you think? He took her to a public park where scores of people saw her sloshed and making a fool of herself. Cat's out of the bag on that one." He stopped and smiled at his pun, and Alicia smirked back. "In fact," he continued, "the AA angle almost redeems her in my eyes. At least she was seeking help for her problem, so why be so evasive about it?"

Alicia finished her wine and thought about that while he reached for the bottle and refilled her glass. As he did so, she thought about her own wine consumption and how alcohol was such a regular part of everyday life. At least it was for them. It had not dawned on either of them to pop the kettle on or have a soft drink when they rendezvoused late after work.

She wondered if everyone had the capacity to be an alcoholic if, indeed, she did. That gave her a sudden ingenious thought, and she was about to mention it when he spoke.

"Anyway, as I say, it's a moot point. Indira is off the whole AA bandwagon and says we have more important leads to chase."

"Such as?"

"Where do I start?" He held up his forefinger. "Brandon Johnson, the barman. Why did he run off so fast?" He held up a second finger. "Ditto the two cap-wearing pervs. And who the hell *are* they?" Then a third finger. "There's also that religious zealot who was sitting behind Kat. He was outraged by her behaviour, called her a 'Jezebel.' Did he act on his outrage? You gotta wonder. And fourth"—he held up a final finger—"what's the deal with his pervy teenage son?"

"The bored, embarrassed-looking one?"

He nodded. "Eliot reckons he was checking them out too."

"Yeah, I did see him look over, but then it was all happening in front of his rug, bit hard not to look, especially if you're a hormonal kid. Wow, you do have your work cut out for you. I'm shocked you even have time for a wine."

He smiled. "Enjoy it while it lasts."

"What about the people in front of the Mumford's rug? Any prospects there?"

He shook his head firmly. "Don't believe so. They were all quite elderly, all hung around and gave statements, no one has a record, all seem like upstanding citizens—your basic nightmare." He smiled. "We're still looking into their backgrounds, but we're not holding out hope."

"So what's the next step?"

"Singho wants to focus on the two pervs and the barman first. Reckons they're the best bet. Problem is we can't find the pervs and Brandon's lawyered up."

"What did the autopsy say?"

"No obvious DNA, no skin under the nails, nothing like that."

"Did they check the champagne glass for prints?"

"It was plastic actually and yep, three sets. One was Brandon Johnson's—" and to her raised eyebrows he quickly added, "as there would be because he poured the champagne into it."

Her eyebrows dropped. "Fair enough. And the second must be Kat Mumford's, right?"

"They're pretty smudged, but we assume so. It's the third set, a much clearer set, that has got us curious. Whose might those be? Of course they could be from a civilian early on the scene who inadvertently touched it

115

during the initial kerfuffle."

Alicia thought about that. "What about the husband? Or Anders maybe?"

"We've ruled them both out already, and the other officers on the scene are all in the clear."

"Anders gave you his fingerprints?"

"They were already on file."

"Really?"

"Sure. He consults the Drug Squad on a regular basis, didn't he tell you that?"

No he did not. She wondered what else he hadn't told her in their brief relationship.

# CHAPTER 16

**M**az Olden looked a little shaken as she opened her front door to the detectives, one hand clutching onto the doorframe, the other patting her pregnant belly, which was subtly concealed today beneath a silk dress that had been cut on the bias. She had swept her red curls up off her face with a black headband, and she looked younger than Indira remembered and a lot more vulnerable.

"Must be close now?" said Indira, herself a mother of two with only exhausted memories of her pregnancies. She had worked through until the birth for both her children— now thirteen and fifteen—and found stepping into a crime scene a lot less stressful than a delivery suite. She hoped the sheer horror of her own experience did not show on her face.

Clearly not because Maz just shrugged and said, "Still got six weeks."

"Oh sorry. I thought you were about to pop."

"I wish. Bring it on."

She waved them in, then shut the door and shuffled through to the living area where she fell down onto a cream sofa, adjusting her dress around the bump. It was a tiny apartment in the poorer end of the inner west, but she had prettied it up with bright cushions and fresh furnishings, and it looked cleaned within an inch of its life.

"This one's a kicker, driving me freakin' nuts!" Maz was saying, rubbing her ribs to indicate where most of the blows had landed.

Indira nodded sympathetically. "You've got others?"

There was something in the way Maz spoke that gave that impression, yet she couldn't see any evidence of other children about, no strewn toys, kids shoes, that kind of thing. Now that she thought about it, she couldn't even see a fresh bassinet or an IKEA flat-pack to indicate that Maz had been padding the nest.

The younger woman's eyes suddenly glistened. "No," she said quickly, "no others."

"Are you okay?"

Maz swiped at her face angrily as a tear trickled down. "I'm fine. Just... well, I lost one. A while back. That's all. Makes you wonder, don't it?"

Jackson looked around for a box of tissues, but the woman was reaching for a toilet roll at the edge of the sofa and breaking off a few squares. She blew her nose discreetly and then looked up at them apologetically.

"Sorry about that. Doc says I'm just hormonal."

Indira nodded knowingly, and then Jackson cleared his throat.

"Are you okay to answer some questions, Ms Olden? About the other night?"

She wiped her nose again. "Yep, let's get it over with, hey?" Then, "I did tell you lot everything a few times now. I don't know what else I can say."

Jackson said, "That's my fault, sorry. I wasn't in on the initial interviews, so I just want to hear it all myself. DI Singh is kindly humouring me."

Maz gave an acquiescent nod, so he forged on.

"From what I hear, you were the person sitting closest to the victim. Your rug was just to the left of Mrs Mumford's, is that correct?"

Maz's eyes darted back to Indira. "But... but I didn't do it. I swear I didn't!"

"No, no. Detective Jackson just wants to get a clear picture of where everyone was sitting, the lay of the land, so to speak," she replied, thinking, *Honestly, Jacko. Bulldozer, china shop!*

"Besides," Jackson added, "we're almost certain Ms Mumford was killed by a man. The strangulation marks are very clear. Large hands, brutal force."

Maz's eyes were like saucers, and Indira turned to Jackson, giving him an "Are you kidding me?" glare.

Jackson held a palm out again. "Sorry, I don't mean to upset you." He glanced at the bump under her dress. "I'm just trying to get things straight."

Maz nodded slowly. "Okay, sure, yeah, I was there. Well, only half the time. The other half I was in the loos throwing up."

"Bad morning sickness?" he asked, and now it was her turn to glare.

"Well, it wasn't all the water I was drinking, that's for sure." She shared a subtle eye roll with Indira before adding, "And it certainly wasn't from grog. I reckon I was about the only sober person in the park."

"The victim, she was very drunk, is that right?"

"Hell yeah. Him too, the husband, but not as bad."

"Did you notice the two have an argument during the intermission?" Indira asked, and Maz shook her head.

"And did you see Mrs Mumford return to her blanket alone in the second half?"

"Yeah, I told that other officer this. I was lying down, feeling pretty sick at that stage, and I remember her coming back on her own. I remember thinking, poor thing, she's been ditched, but then she kinda just scowled at me, like I'm white trash, you know? So I thought, good on him. I'd ditch her sorry arse too. Silly cow."

Then she blushed, realising how mean her words must have sounded and looked down at her hands which were now wrapped around her stomach.

"Did you see where the husband went?" Jackson asked. "No."

"Did you see the husband return to his blanket at any stage during that second half? Before the end, that is, before he found her?"

"No."

"Did you notice anybody else approach Ms Mumford? Anyone at all?"

"Nope."

"What about the two men who were seated on the other side of her blanket, the side closest to the bar?"

She thought about that. "Dunno. I mean, they could've, I suppose. I kinda wasn't watching by that stage."

"Yes, I hear it's a great film," said Indira, trying to keep things light, but Maz just shrugged.

"I wouldn't know. Wasn't feeling crash hot, so spent most of it moaning to myself."

"So why did you stay?" asked Jackson. "Why not go home with your partner?"

"Partner?" She almost giggled at the idea. "What partner?"

He couldn't help his involuntary glance at her bump, and she blushed suddenly.

"Oh! No, he's... We've..." Her blush deepened. "We're not together. I'm on my own."

"I'm so sorry," said Indira, also not able to wrench her eyes from the woman's pregnant belly and the new life that was forming in there.

Maz's eyes took on a defiant glow. "It's fine. We don't need him anyway." She rubbed her stomach gently. "We've got this under control, haven't we, bub?"

"Do you have a solid support network?" Indira asked.

Maz looked at her as if confused for a moment and then said, "Mum's coming in a few weeks, if that's what you mean, and I've got the girls from work."

"You're still working?"

"Just a few shifts at Bob's Backyards & BBQs, you know, the new place that's opened up in Birchgrove?"

"Oh yes!" said Indira. "I love that place. You guys have stunning outdoor furniture. I almost bought a wicker lounge set there just the other day."

"The four-piece setting? With the striped scatter

cushions?"

"That's the one."

Jackson coughed discreetly. This was all very lovely, but he wanted to get back to the case at hand. The women looked at him as though he were an annoying intrusion.

"Sorry," he said, "but something's not quite adding up. If you weren't there with your partner, Ms Olden, who was the man you were sitting with during the movie?"

Jackson was sure the book club had mentioned a pregnant woman and her companion.

Maz looked at him blankly for a moment, and then the penny dropped.

"Oh *him*." Her face softened. "He was on his own as well. Real sweetie. Helped me get up a few times, offered to fetch me water, that kind of thing." She smiled wistfully. "Pity I can't find a good man like that. Pity I always attract the scumbags."

"Pity you didn't get his number," Indira quipped, causing the younger woman to giggle, but Jackson didn't find any of that amusing.

He had assumed, foolishly as it turns out, that the pregnant woman had previously been questioned with her partner. Now, suddenly, they had *another* missing suspect?

"Did you catch that man's details, Indira? Did any of the first responders?"

She looked doubtful.

"I think he left early," said Maz. "Before the film finished. Don't reckon he was digging it much."

"What makes you say that?"

"Oh, he just seemed so distracted, yeah? Kept asking if I wanted anything at the snack bar, got up a few times for a smoke. I wasn't real surprised when he said he was taking off."

Indira looked more focused now and was pulling out a notepad.

"Can you give us a description of the man please, Ms Olden?"

She looked a bit startled. "Okay, yeah, I think. I mean it was kinda dark. But, um…" She gave it some thought. "He was big, greyish hair, peppery-black moustache."

"He was older?" Indira asked, and she nodded.

"Yeah, maybe mid to late sixties? Wearing blue, I think. Maybe like a blue shirt and jeans or something."

As Indira scribbled away, Jackson sat back, stunned.

*How on earth had they missed this guy?*

"Do you think this older bloke is really a person of interest?" Indira asked as they made their way back to the car, another interview completed leaving more questions than it answered. "As far as I can tell, he was seated on the *other* side of Maz Olden, so he would have had to scoot across her to get to the victim."

"Except Maz has already confirmed that she spent half the time heaving in the portable toilets, remember? He had so much access it wasn't funny. Just had to shift across her blanket subtly and wrap his hands around a sleeping Kat Mumford's neck."

She frowned. "I want to know who the hell he is. Maybe there's a connection."

"I want to know why he took off so fast and why the first attending officers didn't even make a note of him."

"Hey don't blame them. It was an impossible crime scene—people coming and going in all directions. And he left early, yeah?"

"Still, you think she might have mentioned him to someone."

"Except she wasn't *with* him, so it probably didn't even occur to her. Plus she wasn't exactly in top shape that night; she wouldn't have been thinking clearly."

Jackson groaned, running a hand across the back of his head.

"What I don't get is, if the film was so brilliant as Alicia says, why did so many people piss off before it finished? Think about it. You've paid the full ticket price, why not stay the final ten minutes or so? It was a mystery, for God's sake. Why wouldn't you hang around to find out *whodunit*? What's the hurry suddenly? It's not like it was a giant stadium packed with thirty-five thousand punters and you needed to beat the rush."

"Not exactly a ringing endorsement for the film, that's for sure." Now it was Indira's turn to groan. "Instead of ticking suspects off, we seem to be adding a new one every day. We still have to track down the guys in caps, we haven't even got to Mrs Joves and young Ezekiel, and now we have to start hunting for some mystery man with a dark moustache!"

She groaned again as she swung the car back towards the office.

"I'll drop you at HQ, then I want to have a word with those security guards from the film night. They were manning the exits, the only place smokers were allowed. If Maz's mystery man really did head that way for a ciggie, and not once but several times, they *must* have noticed him, might even have had a chat."

"Smart thinking. But forget HQ, drop me at the lab. I want to ask Scelosi about those handprints around Kat's neck. Could a man pushing seventy leave those marks?"

"While you're there, you might as well check if a fourteen-year-old lad could also pull it off."

They *both* groaned at the thought of that.

# CHAPTER 17

Lunch time had long passed, but Alicia had a hunch Jackson would not have found time to stop to eat today—despite his boasts to the contrary—so she grabbed two chicken salad sandwiches and then jumped in her old Torana and headed for his office.

Just a few minutes earlier, he'd texted to say he was back at his desk and would call her in the next half hour for a quick chat, so she assumed he would still be there and was rewarded with his smile when she was escorted in by an officer from the front desk.

"You're a sight for sore eyes," he said, jumping up to embrace her.

She held out the sandwiches. "One for you, one for your boss."

"I thought a juicy red apple was the usual bribe."

"Nah, that's just for my vegan stars." She indicated a chair. "Have you got a minute?"

He nodded and waved her into it.

"I know it's extremely late notice, and I cannot believe I keep forgetting to ask you this, but do you want to come to Perry's PR thingie tonight? We're all getting there around seven."

He glanced at the clock on the wall. That was four hours away, and he couldn't make any promises. He told her as much.

"I thought you were the renegade, the rule breaker, the one who didn't let work get in the way of your social life."

Jackson pulled the wrapping from one sandwich and

took a large bite, chewing as he spoke. "I'm also the man who gets really pissed off when a cold-blooded murderer still wanders the city freely." He swallowed hard.

"Fair enough. So it's not going too well, huh?"

"Nope."

He glanced at the door, then jumped up and closed it before sitting on the edge of his desk and filling her in on the latest developments.

He finished by asking, "What do you remember of the guy sitting near the pregnant woman? The one you thought was her partner."

"Not much to be honest. I vaguely recall a moustache now that you mention it, but not much else."

"And you never saw him approach the victim?"

"No, or I would have said something. But then I thought he was with Maz, so that's how observant I am."

"Hey, don't beat yourself up. It sounds like everyone got that impression, the way they were interacting."

"Yeah, but strangers *are* friendly at those kinds of events, aren't they? You get wedged in together so tight it'd almost be weird if you *didn't* speak to the people around you. We even got chatting to Eliot at the end, before he got up and found his wife." Her face clouded over. "So what did the coroner say? Could an older man or a teenage boy have strangled her?"

Jackson waved his hand in a so-so motion. "Depends on their size. Which is why I need to work late tonight. I need to find both suspects and cross them off this ever-growing list or, even better, lock one of the buggers up!"

Alicia got to her feet. "Then I'll leave you to it." She glanced at the sandwich. "Want me to drop that into Indira's office?"

"No!" he said quickly, a little too quickly for Alicia's liking. "I'll, um, I'll give it to her a bit later, but thanks."

She studied him for a moment. "Okay, cool." Then she leaned down to give him a quick kiss. "We will all miss you at Perry's soiree, but we'll survive. Unlike Ms Mumford.

Good luck, hey?"

Then she left him staring glumly at the sandwich on his desk.

Jackson wasn't thinking about Indira though or how a sandwich from Alicia would be received (not good was his initial guess), he was trying to decide how to track down a teenager without incurring the wrath of his kooky dad.

He glanced at the wall clock again. It was now close to three fifteen. School knock-off time.

He called out, "Pauly!" and grabbed his jacket.

~~~~~~~

Ezekiel Joves was a lanky boy with knobbly knees and pointy elbows. He had the standard short-back-and-sides hairstyle to match the stiff private school uniform, which looked a little too small and certainly overwashed, the light grey shirt fraying near the collar, his blue trousers more faded than most of the boys who were rushing past him and out of the school grounds.

The end-of-school bell had just chimed when Jackson first pulled his vehicle into the no-stopping zone, earning him a glare from a volunteer traffic warden who began to approach. Pauly, who was seated beside Jackson, quickly held out his police badge.

The warden's glare turned anxious, so Pauly waved her over.

"Everything okay?" the woman asked.

She had that jittery thing that many people get when encountering law enforcement.

"Just looking for one of your students," Jackson called across the car. "Ezekiel Joves, know him?"

She looked at him, doubtful. "Year?"

"Eight, I think," Jackson said, hoping she wouldn't enquire further, and she didn't.

She simply called out, "Ella! Ella Horton-James, come here, dear!"

A startled-looking girl of about fourteen or fifteen looked up from a gaggle of similarly aged girls, frowned and then skipped over.

"These gentlemen are looking for an Ezekiel Joves, dear. He's in your year, I believe. Know him?"

"Ezekiel?" The girl looked unsure for a moment, then said, "Oh, Zak! Yeah, I know Zak." She also didn't ask any questions, simply looked around, scanning the crowd.

After just a minute, she began to point. "There! Just coming through the gates now, the skinny one with the really white hair."

The three adults all stretched their necks to watch as Ezekiel loped away from the school gates and towards a rumbling school bus.

Jackson vaguely recalled the boy from the park on Saturday night but was glad he had a positive identification and thanked them both.

"You *will* need to move your vehicle, officers," the woman ventured now, her tone more assured. "There'll be another bus pulling up any second."

"Just doing that now, madam," Jackson replied, starting the vehicle and doing a slow U-turn, missing several scuttling children by centimetres, to settle into another no-stopping zone on the other side of the street.

"Can we question him without his parents' permission?" Pauly was asking, and Jackson shook his head.

"But we can check out his hands. That might be enough."

"Hands?"

He nodded, recalling the coroner's words from earlier that day.

*"It depends on the size of the lad,"* Scelosi had told him. *"If he's small for his age, like I was, he'd be lucky to break a twig. But if he's a big boy, like the bullies I used to face, well, then maybe."* Scelosi had smiled almost wistfully at that, then added, *"It's all in the hands. If they're man size and there's a fair*

*bit of teenage angst behind them, they could do the job."*

From this angle Jackson couldn't tell just how man-sized Ezekiel's hands were, nor could he assess how much anger was brewing behind his blank expression, but the way he was standing, hunched over, suggested he was ready for battle. The queue certainly resembled a war zone. There were kids pushing and shoving, some cutting in, some boys throwing punches, some girls throwing arms around each other, all yelping and squealing and moving about. And all the while Ezekiel stood quietly in line, hands in his pockets, not interacting with anyone, his eyes downcast.

Jackson wished the kid would give someone a high five or swing a punch at least so he could assess the hands, but he was clearly a loner. Either that or his mates didn't catch that particular bus.

"Come on," he told Pauly, switching the car off and stepping out. "We need to get closer."

They waited impatiently while a convoy of shiny SUVs purred past, most filled with moody-looking teenagers and merrily chatting mums, then sprinted across the street just in time to see Ezekiel board the bus.

"Damn it," Jackson said, motioning for Pauly to follow him back across the road to their car. "Now for Plan B."

It was a slow plan.

Not knowing exactly where the lad would end up—was he heading home? Basketball practice? An S&M parlour?—the detectives settled in and followed the school bus as it meandered its way from Drummoyne through the back streets of the inner west.

A good fifteen minutes and almost as many stops later, the bus reached a busy intersection and a skinny, white-haired boy jumped out.

"Bingo!" Jackson said, pulling his own car into the curb behind the bus just as a short, tubby girl in a very different school uniform slouched past the car and approached Ezekiel.

She was wearing a white blouse, an extremely short black-and-green-checked skirt, and a bashful smile on her face. They embraced for just a moment before she turned abruptly and skipped away.

"What was that about?" Jackson asked and then, "Damn it."

Ezekiel was striding back in the direction the bus had just driven.

Pauly turned to watch and said, "He's turning down that first street." He looked forward. "Chuck a left at this next corner and cross back."

Jackson manoeuvred the car back into the traffic, earning himself a blast from a nearby car horn and some vicious words from a passing cabbie.

By the time Jackson had circled back a block, Pauly was the one doing the cursing.

"We've lost him!" he said.

Jackson wasn't giving up so easily. He slowed the car down and ambled along the back street, his eyes searching the mixture of shop fronts and front yards.

"There!" Jackson announced, just as they were crossing over another intersection.

He braked swiftly and swung the car down the street. It was a familiar one, and now *he* felt like cursing.

"He's heading to his dad's church," Jackson said, pulling the car back to the curb.

"Something to confess, you think?" Pauly asked.

"Maybe, or maybe he's doing penance."

Pauly looked at him confused but said nothing as Jackson switched the car off again.

They watched from a respectable distance as Ezekiel loitered a few metres from the church gates, then glanced around, bent down and began removing his shoes.

"What's he doing now?" Jackson asked, watching as the boy pulled a black pair of shoes out of his school bag, then dropped the white ones he had been wearing into the bag and slipped the dark pair on.

"Looks like he's swapping his Nike trainers for school shoes," Pauly said.

Jackson frowned. "That doesn't make any sense. He's just left school. Shouldn't it be the other way around?"

They watched for a further minute as Zak zipped up his bag, straightened his tie and then strode the rest of the way to the church grounds, reaching the front gate and glancing around again before brushing his hair down and pushing the gate open.

No sooner had he stepped into the church grounds than his father appeared from one side. Was it good timing, or had he been watching out for his son?

Jacob had a long wooden stick in his hand and was waving it at the boy, barking something as he approached. Whatever he was saying, it was clearly a lecture, and he continued barking away for some time while the boy dropped his head and said nothing. Eventually the man thrust the stick at his son—a garden rake by the look of it—and then stepped back.

As Ezekiel began sweeping up the leaves from the front yard, his school bag still fixed to his back, Jacob continued to watch him, his hands on his hips, frown on his face. After what seemed an age, he finally turned and strode inside the church.

"That's our cue," Jackson said, stepping out of the car.

The first thing Jackson noticed as they approached the boy was the size of his hands. They were large. Not extra large, mind you, but relatively big for a boy in year eight.

Ezekiel stopped sweeping as they approached and stepped back, allowing them to pass, but they slowed down and Jackson held a hand out to shake.

Confused, Ezekiel dropped the rake and returned the shake.

*Yep*, Jackson thought. *He could pull it off.*

He said, "Hi there, Zak is it?"

The boy nodded tentatively.

"I'm Detective Inspector Liam Jackson, this is Sergeant Paul Moore."

"Dad's inside," the boy said quickly, and Jackson smiled.

"Yes, thanks we'll head inside in a minute. Helping your dad out are you?"

The boy nodded slowly.

"Hope you get paid some decent pocket money for that."

The boy wasn't nodding now.

"You here about that woman?" Ezekiel asked.

"We are indeed," Jackson replied. "You remember her then?"

He shrugged. "She was pretty." Then a sly grin crossed his lips. "Shit-faced but hot."

"Oh yeah? You liked the look of her did you?" Jackson asked, trying to keep his tone light, and the boy smiled brightly.

"Yeah, man, she was, like, smokin'! Not like the stuck-up scrags at my—"

The boy stopped suddenly and reached for the rake just as a booming voice called out, "Can I help you gentlemen?"

The detectives swung around to find Jacob standing at the entrance to the church, a book in both hands, his eyes narrowed.

"Ahh, it's you again is it, Detective…?"

Jackson glanced back at Ezekiel, who had his head down, furiously sweeping away. Jackson sighed to himself and then walked down the stone pathway towards the pastor.

"Yes, Detective Liam Jackson, and this is my colleague, Sergeant Paul Moore."

Jacob eyed them both suspiciously as they approached, then flashed a look at his son, who had almost disappeared around the side of the building now.

"More questions, yes?" They nodded. "Then you'd best

come inside, Detective."

"You've got a good lad there," Jackson said as he followed him to a pew at the back.

"And why do you say that?"

"Well, you don't often see kids helping out around the place do you?"

Jacob smiled his sharklike smile. "He is weak, and he is easily tempted, Detective. And now he must learn the consequences of that."

"I'm sorry? What do you mean by easily tempted?"

Jacob's eyes narrowed again. "What can I help you with, Detective?"

Jackson let it drop for now. He wasn't in the mood for more word games with the man and suspected, from their first conversation, that it wouldn't get him anywhere anyway.

He said, "We're actually here to see your wife, Rev Joves. We haven't had much luck getting hold of her."

That was a lie. They had not made any substantial attempt to track the woman down, but Jackson needed a reason for being there, and Jacob seemed to buy it.

"She's probably still on the school run," he said matter-of-factly. "Why? What's my wife got to do with any of this?"

"We'd just like a word, that's all."

"And what would that be about?"

Jackson held his stare for a moment and considered telling him that it was none of his damn business, but he knew he needed to keep this man on his side. He didn't want him rushing off to silence his wife.

Maybe Indira was right. Maybe he did go in too hard sometimes. He softened his tone.

"Just boring old procedure, sir, nothing more than that. Just crossing our *T*s."

He glanced up at the figure of Jesus on the cross and wondered if that was a blasphemous term in a religious place like this.

He smiled, nodding his head towards Pauly. "We've neglected to get statements from everyone who was seated near the victim that night. In fact"—he lowered his voice—"I'm in the dogbox with my boss."

Jacob's eyes narrowed. "The angry Indian girl you were with?"

What Indira's ethnicity or gender had to do with anything was beyond Jackson, but he kept his tone light as he said, "DI Singh can be a little, well, grumpy." He gave Pauly a conspiratorial wink. "She just wants us to get a statement from Mrs Joves, and then we're off the hook."

"And what do you expect to learn from my wife?"

"Probably nothing, sir. Really. We just need to see if she saw anything that maybe nobody else spotted."

"She saw nothing, I can assure you of that."

"That's all very well," Pauly spoke now, pulling out a notepad. "We just need to ask. Can you give us a contact phone number for her please, sir?"

Jacob looked for a moment like he was not buying the detectives' story, then simply glanced at his watch. "Now is not a good time. If my wife is home, she will be preparing the evening meal and seeing to the children's homework. It will have to wait until tomorrow."

"Not a problem," Jackson said, catching Pauly's eye. The younger officer looked ready to complain, but Jackson wanted to keep Reverend Joves on side.

He pulled a business card from his jacket pocket. "If you could just ask her to call me as soon as she gets a spare moment, that would be terrific."

Jacob read the card slowly, then turned it over and back again. "Certainly, Detective Inspector Jackson," he said eventually, his sharky smile returning. "See if we can't get you out of that dogbox, hey?"

# CHAPTER 18

**A** violin concerto tinkled gently across the marble foyer of the Sydney museum where Perry worked, barely audible beneath the loud chatter and laughter of the fast-growing throng, and Perry Gordon gave Alicia and Lynette a nervous smile.

"So far so good," he said, reaching in to air kiss them as they joined the rest of the book club who had gathered near the entrance. "No Jackson?" he added, his lips pouting.

"Sorry, he's a bit stressed with the case. But I can see a couple of my colleagues over there, looking very content." She waved as she caught the eye of three women from sister publications who were swigging on glasses of wine.

"Great crowd," Lynette said, also looking about, and Perry beamed.

"Did you catch the Lord Mayor? And at least three federal politicians have arrived!"

"I'm more impressed with the celebrities," said Claire. "Was that Cate Blanchett I saw gliding past?"

"Where?" squealed Missy as Perry waved a passing waiter over with a tray full of Prosecco punch.

They each helped themselves to a complementary glass.

"I'll have to flit like a butterfly in a second," Perry told them, refusing a glass, "but first I want the goss!"

"Goss?" Alicia replied, realising he was talking to her.

"Yes. How is the case going? What has luscious Liam discovered?"

"Not a lot at this stage, hence the reason he's so

stressed. I think it's stalled."

"Stalled? How?" asked Claire, and Alicia looked around to find everyone staring at her.

"Oh, just a lot of loose ends, lots of missing suspects."

"Like?" said Anders, oddly interested, and she took a step back.

"Guys, this is hardly the time and place. The focus should be on Perry and his fabulous museum tonight. We can talk about the case later."

"She's got a point there," said Perry. "Plus I really do have to spread myself about, so if you discuss the case in too much detail now I'll miss out."

"How about we meet at our place later?" Alicia suggested, glancing at Lynette.

"I've got a much better idea," he said. "Hang around and enjoy the event, then I'll take you into the bowels of the building. We can chat about it all properly then."

They agreed to do that and then left the host to tend to his other guests while they spent the next two hours enjoying fine champagne and canapés while ogling the extraordinary displays, which included Aboriginal artefacts, Theban mummies, and some rather imposing woolly mammoths. For some reason that got her thinking of Margarita, and she wondered why she wasn't hanging off Anders's arm tonight.

It was a pity Perry was so busy—he would have had the nerve to ask.

"Probably couldn't stretch the budget that far," whispered Lynette, reading her sister's mind as she stared at a 42,000-year-old calf. "Or maybe Margarita's on another escort job?"

Alicia slapped her lightly across the arm. "Stop it! That's a terrible thing to say."

Still, it made her laugh, and she was in the mood to laugh tonight. It had been a pretty harrowing few days, and she relished the chance to forget about blanket-creeping stranglers and enjoy the glittering, star-studded event.

Sadly, for Alicia's imagination at least, the respite was short-lived.

Before she knew it, the party was over and Perry was back, ushering them out of the expansive foyer and down the endless, wide corridors to the southern end of the museum, a conspiratorial smile on his lips.

"Let's slip into somewhere more comfortable," he said with a wink.

"That was a lot of fun, Perry," Alicia said as they walked. "Are you happy with how it all went?"

"Delighted and so were the people who mattered. The patrons were all thrilled, and the museum director even took me aside before he left and said, 'Brilliant job, Perry.' I didn't even know he knew my name! Okay, here we are."

They'd reached a set of elevators, and he pressed his ID badge against a button, causing the doors to glide open.

"Take the lift down to the lower basement, chuck a right and head to the office at the very end. That's my hovel. It's open. I'll see you there in ten."

By the time Perry got to his office, the friends were all settled in chairs around his desk and on the tiny faux leather sofa near the door, chatting happily. It was a plush office, plusher than they had been expecting. He'd griped so much about work they anticipated a dark broom closet.

"Let's get this party started!" Perry said from the doorway, holding a glistening bottle of Veuve Clicquot in each hand.

Lynette cheered and Alicia said, "Got glasses?"

"Cupboard to the left of the desk."

She jumped up to grab some while he switched on a table lamp and killed the overhead neon lights, then picked up a remote control from his desk. The room was instantly filled with the sounds of Ella Fitzgerald.

"Wow, you sure know how to make things cosy," said Claire.

"Honey, I do so much unpaid overtime, it's the only

thing that keeps me sane."

Then he popped a cork and poured them each a drop.

"Now, since it's late and a school night, I won't bother with any preamble. Alicia, you've got the floor!"

This time she didn't hesitate. As the group watched on, Alicia spent the next half hour talking them through the case or at least as much of it as she knew. She told them all about the missing barman and how he had eventually been tracked down and interviewed.

"And?" said Lynny, hoping the guy was in the clear. He was cute, if she recalled, but her sister was nudging an eyebrow high.

"He was acting a little too cool for school, and Jackson's spidey senses were on red alert. Reckons he could be hiding something. Unfortunately, there's no DNA evidence so they can't pin him to the body, and the toxicology report came back clean—well, apart from champagne of course—so their theory that she may have been drugged doesn't pan out."

"So how did someone manage to strangle her so quietly and in such a public place?" asked Claire.

"And how did they manage to tear her clothes without her crying out?" added Missy.

Alicia lifted her shoulders, telling them about her AA hunch and how it had reaped rewards.

"But even for an alcoholic, she had a staggering amount of alcohol in her system," said Alicia, before glancing at Anders. "Could alcohol render you so paralytic you wouldn't notice a stranger climb on top of you and strangle you?"

Anders shrugged. "She may have been aware what was going on, but the alcohol's effects on her motor skills meant she simply wasn't capable of resisting, I'm afraid. I mean, she may have *tried*, but if he was very strong and had his legs or torso restraining her arms, she would have found it almost impossible."

The women all squirmed at the thought.

"Who would be so stupid to do such a thing in such a public place with so many people around to notice?" asked Missy.

"Good point," said Lynette. "Aren't there enough lonely women wandering dark streets you can pick on privately?"

Missy giggled nervously, not sure if Lynette was having a go at her, but Alicia was shaking her head.

"Except we didn't notice, did we? We were all there, and we did not see a thing."

They chewed on that for a bit, sipping their champagne and feeling the mood drop considerably. It was a shocking thought. One they could not escape from.

"There are two more suspects," Alicia said, reenergising the group.

First she filled them in on Jackson's recent conversation with Maz, the pregnant woman, and her description of the mysterious moustached man sitting beside her.

"Can you guys remember much about him?" she asked, but no one had anything new to add to Maz's description.

"And then there's Ezekiel Joves."

Alicia hadn't spoken with Jackson since his chat with Jacob and his son, but she filled them in on Eliot's damning accusation against the teenage boy.

"No way that little boy did this thing!" said Claire.

"He's bigger than me, Claire," Perry retorted.

"I still don't believe it. They were such a lovely family."

Lynette and Alicia swapped a look but said nothing.

"Good Christians, too, by the sound of it," said Missy, reminding them of how the elderly ladies had spotted them praying by the toilets.

"Doesn't mean the son didn't do it," snapped Perry. "Criminals come in all shapes, sizes and religions, I'll have you know."

"I'd be hunting down those two sleazy men first," was

Claire's final word on the subject.

"You know I was thinking," said Lynette. "Could Kat Mumford have been drugged with Rohypnol? I remember last time, Anders, your saying that it goes through the system quickly and is hard to detect."

"We found Kat's body very quickly, postmortem, Lyn, so I don't think that's an issue here," he replied. "But it's a good question. Roofies aren't the only date rape drug available. People use all sorts of nasty tranquillisers now, like GHB—or liquid Ecstasy—and other benzodiazepines, scopolamine. I wonder if they checked for everything. I know the Chief Pathologist, and he's good, but toxic substances are not his forte. Perhaps I should take another look at the report."

"You think he'll let you?" asked Lynette, incredulous.

"I was the first to attend the body. I did confirm her death."

*Goodness me!* thought Alicia. *Anders just volunteered to help.*

She wondered if he even realised he'd just landed himself in the middle of the case, but his relaxed demeanour suggested otherwise. She nodded quickly lest he change his mind.

"So what can *we* do to help?" asked Missy. "I want in on the action too!"

"Ditto," said Perry.

"Er, it hasn't even been a week yet, people," said Claire. "A little too early for us to play Miss Marple isn't it?"

"Spoilsport," spat Perry.

"No, I think Claire's right," said Alicia, surprising herself along with Anders who was staring at her, amazed. She laughed. "Hey, I love a good mystery as much as the rest of you, but let's just give Jackson a chance to do his job."

Perry looked sceptical. "Defending our boyfriend's honour are we?"

Protecting his relationship with Indira was closer to the truth, Alicia thought. Jackson hadn't said as much, but remembering the chicken sandwich incident, she got the distinct impression she ought to keep her distance.

"Let's just be patient and let the detectives do their thing. But I promise to keep you all in the loop, okay?"

They begrudgingly agreed, Claire and Anders looking relieved while Missy tried hard to mask her disappointment. She knew what Alicia was saying and respected her for that, but as far as she was concerned, if the case continued to stall, she would step up and start investigating whether the cops liked it or not.

Miss Marple never shied away from poking her nose in where it wasn't welcome, and nor would she.

# CHAPTER 19

Liam Jackson was ready to snap. He'd been scanning security camera footage all day and, despite several promising leads, still couldn't identify the two "perverts" who'd somehow vanished, let alone the sixtysomething with grey hair and a peppery black moustache. He glanced at his phone, wishing Mrs Joves would call. He needed the distraction.

It was now Thursday afternoon, a good twenty-four hours since he'd asked Reverend Joves to pass on his number. He wondered what the woman was playing at.

*Why wouldn't she call him straight back?*

*What was the wife and mother hiding?*

"I thought Jarrod drew the short straw on that," Indira said, breaking into Jackson's thoughts as she stepped into the viewing room, a can of soft drink in hand.

He yawned. "Yeah, he did the hard yards, but I wanted to see the final cut. I'm a witness after all, but damned if I can spot any of the buggers. I mean, I can see a few blokes clearly smoking near the exits, but any of them could be the guy Maz was sitting next to. As for the capped blokes…" He rubbed his scruffy hair, scruffing it up further. "Just not sure which if any are ours. None look up at the cameras, not one. What are the chances of that?"

"Smart thinking or bad luck?"

He shrugged and stared at his phone again. "Maybe I should work the Joves angle. Pay Ezekiel's mum a visit? See why she hasn't paid us the courtesy of actually getting in touch."

Indira shook her head firmly, a smile lighting up her face.

"Leave that for now. I think we've got a break in the case."

"Really?"

"Oh yeah, baby." She offered him the drink, but he declined, so she placed the can down and leaned against the table. "Okay, so I had another chat with the security guys. One of them was working the front exit and swears he can't recall any older bloke with a dark moustache, smoking away. Doesn't mean there wasn't one. He just can't recall."

"Maybe our moustached guy didn't have a smoke. Maybe he just told Maz that, for whatever reason."

"Maybe," she conceded. "Or maybe he used a different exit. I've just learned that the man we need to talk to is Guy Peters. He was on the side exit, the one on the eastern side, and *that's* where most of the smokers congregated apparently, because it was close to the bar and it had a better view of the film from that angle and blah blah blah."

"Oh, so they could drink, puff and watch at the same time?'

"Yep, your classic multitaskers." She laughed. "Problem is Guy Peters has gone AWOL."

"You are freakin' kidding me?" *Not another missing person, surely?*

"Don't get in a flap. He's on actual leave. Took his family up the coast on Monday. I've had a quick word with him via mobile, and he's very apologetic, says Constable Thompson took his full statement and gave him permission to go."

"What else did he say? Did he remember the moustached bloke?"

"Maybe, maybe not. It was a bloody scratchy line, but he says he might be able to help. Has offered to return. Will be back by the close of day. I can question him properly then."

"Let's hope he's got something to contribute, otherwise you've just ruined his family holiday." Jackson blew a puff of air through his lips. "And the two mates, the ones in caps? What about them?"

"They are slightly more elusive, but we may have a break there too."

Jackson sat up straight. "Seriously? That's great news."

"I said 'may' so no need to high-five me yet." She took another sip from the can. "We still can't get a firm description from anyone. Those two guys are like ghosts who walk. It's extraordinary. Loads of people remember them loitering, perving, but no one can tell me anything other than 'two tattooed blokes in caps.' It's like the disguise you wear when you're not wearing a disguise."

"Did you speak to the barmen as well? Surely they can give you more?"

She held up one finger. "This is where it gets interesting. So Brandon's no use to us, all thanks to Morrie, but I did have another word with his buddy Wally Walters, and he reckons he never served them."

"Must have. Those blokes were knocking back beers like there was no tomorrow, apparently, and no one remembers them having an esky, so they must have bought them there."

"Or *brought* them in with them."

He sat up even straighter, his interest piqued.

"That's the good news," Indira said. "Luckily for us, Wally Walters knows his ale. I'm not sure he could pick the guys in a lineup, but he would definitely recognise the brew they were drinking. Says it wasn't his. Says he noticed two men in caps sitting on the grass, not far from the bar. Says he only noticed them because they were knocking back some crafted brew in a longneck bottle."

"And?"

"And they weren't serving any crafted brew in longneck bottles at the bar that night. So they *must* have brought them in. He only remembers it because he was wondering why Brandon hadn't insisted to the organisers that no one be allowed to BYO. Reckons the takings weren't as big as they should've been, and he's not getting the commission he was expecting, and whine, whine, groan, groan. Says Brandon couldn't run an ice-making business in the Antarctic."

"Ouch," Jackson said, and she laughed.

"Anyway, bitching aside, that might help you narrow things down. Any of your becapped blokes holding anything that might resemble bottles as they entered?"

He looked at her like she was mad. "You serious? Almost every single punter was carrying something in— picnic hampers, green bags, backpacks—the bottles could be in any of them. In any case, it doesn't matter. Like I said, none look at the camera, no identifying marks. Waste of time. Although I suppose I could check the cameras from nearby bottle shops, that might help."

"Before you do, Wally has an idea."

"Really? Wally's coming through with the goods today. Go on then, what else does he have to say?"

"He would swear on a stack of bibles they were drinking a dodgy home brew called Chuckies or Chuck Up or something like that. The label's got an illustration of a guy frothing at the mouth. He's seen it before, but for the life of him he can't remember where. "

"Sounds like classy stuff."

"I know, right. But it helps narrow it down. I mean, how many bottle shops sell something that enticing? I've never even heard of it."

"Me neither. Okay leave it with me. I'll check it out."

Another hour of trawling the phone books and contacting every bottle shop and hotel in the area, Jackson had two names: Chester's Chuck and the Jolly Codger. The former was the name of the brew, and the latter, the only hotel in the area that sold it. Located in the less glamorous end of Rozelle, it was a dank establishment that was just a few streets and a million miles from upmarket Balmain.

"You heading there now?" Indira asked when he dropped into her office later that day to pass on what he'd learned. "I'd come with you, but I'm waiting for Guy Peters to show." She frowned. "If I remember right, that place is a bit of a dive. Let me know if they give you any trouble. Maybe Pauly can tag along to help."

"Oh, I'll be fine," he replied, smiling smugly as he departed.

He wasn't about to tell Ms By-the-book, but he didn't need Pauly, he was taking his secret weapon along.

~~~~~~~~

Jackson's secret weapon tried to hide her disdain as she stepped out of the taxi and onto the cobbled road outside the Jolly Codger. Alicia had been warned to dress down, and she had done so, stripping out of her work gear into jeans and a flowing black top, but now she wanted to slash the knees of her jeans and add a bulletproof vest. The place before her looked like a bikie hang-out, and not just because there were several Harley Davidsons leaning out the front.

It was a world away from picture-postcard Balmain.

The front windows were all cringing behind thick security bars, and the paintwork was hanging on by its fingernails. As she peeked through a side door, she was slapped with a blast of death metal and the stench of fried onions and beer.

Smashing fingers through her chunky blond hair, hoping to mess it up a bit, she then blotted most of her pink lip gloss onto the back of her hand before pushing the door open and stepping inside.

Jackson was already waiting for her at the bar, nursing a schooner of ale and sharing a laugh with a middle-aged barmaid who was wearing a low-cut dress and a gummy smile. The smile slipped considerably as Alicia walked up.

"Hey, you made it!" Jackson said. "Beer?"

She nodded, adding, "Got anything bottled?"

She had a feeling the barmaid was the spit-in-your-glass type.

The older woman flicked her eyes towards the illuminated fridges behind her, and Alicia pointed to a standard brew. "Just a James Boag's Draught, thanks."

After the barmaid did the exchange, Jackson indicated a far table and led the way.

"Looks like you were making good ground there," Alicia said. "Maybe I shouldn't have come."

"Nah, she's no use to me. Too old." Then he heard himself and said, "Sorry, that came out wrong. I meant too old for our pervs. She can't recall serving them. But! She has a daughter who also works the bar Saturday nights, so I have a hunch they'd have zeroed in on the younger barmaid. At least that's the vibe I'm getting from you lot."

"Well, that's the vibe they were giving out. So how do we find the daughter?"

"Easy. She's on her way down." His eyes headed north. "They live above the bar."

"Very convenient. Until then?"

"Let's try to order something that doesn't give us salmonella."

After placing orders for beer-battered fish and chips at the bar, they returned to their table just as a young woman entered the room from a set of internal steps.

"The eagle has landed," Jackson said, checking out her peroxide-blond pigtail and overly made-up face. She was wearing something equally as skimpy as her mother and glanced around irritably before catching her mother's eye and then being nudged towards Jackson's table.

"Did you explain you're a cop?" Alicia whispered.

"Hence the scowl. Let me do all the talking, yes?"

"Gladly." She sat back.

The young woman strolled over, clearly in no hurry to

talk to a cop, even stopping to high-five a man at one of the tables before finally stepping across.

"Mum says you wanna see me," she said, her voice squeaky. "If this is about Tony, I don't even wanna hear it."

"Tony?"

Her eyes squinted. She folded her arms across her narrow chest. "What do you want?"

"Do you mind having a seat, Casey? I just have a few questions. Won't hold you too long, I promise."

She glanced around the room furtively, then did as instructed, pulling out the spare chair and dropping into it.

"So your mum told you I'm from the homicide squad?"

She shrugged, noncommittal.

"We're investigating the murder of a young woman at a park just near here, in Balmain, last Saturday night. Cinema Under the Stars. Know anything about that?"

She shrugged again. "Some old flick was showing. Something for old farts. That's all I know. But yeah, I heard some chick got attacked. What's it to do with me?"

"Nothing at all. I just want to ask about some patrons who came in here that night. We think they may be able to assist our enquiries."

"That's code for 'They're up shit creek,'" she said, and Alicia had to stop herself from smiling.

*Ah, so young and yet so cynical.*

Jackson produced a grainy picture from his jacket. It was an A4 printout, clearly taken from an aerial camera, of two suspects in caps, heads down, heading into the park with something in their hands. Bottles perhaps.

"Recognise these two?"

She stared at the photo. "You're kidding, right?"

He didn't respond, so she scoffed. "What's to recognise? Two blokes in caps. Pop a cap on anyone in here, and that's what they'd look like."

"Not just caps. They were covered in ink. One had a tattoo right up his neck."

She made a "Pfft!" sound and then turned to call out, "Hey, Bozza! Micky D! Jason!"

Several men turned from the pool table to look at them. They were all covered in tattoos, two with tatts up their neck, one with a giant eagle etched onto his shaved head.

Alicia stared at them and shook her head at Jackson. Those weren't the guys.

Casey scoffed and called out, "Sorry, false alarm!" She turned back to the detective. "You're gonna have to do better than that."

Jackson was not put off. "Take a closer look please, Casey. These two didn't just drink here. They ordered several bottles of that dodgy brew you guys sell—Chester's Chuck. Your mum tells me she never sold any that night."

"Yeah well she wouldn't—she hates the stuff. Says it tastes like turps, but the povos all love it."

"Povos?" Alicia asked, and Casey gave her a Duh! look.

"Yeah, povos, poor people. It gets 'em drunk fast."

"Sounds like their cup of tea then," Jackson said. "Problem is, if your mum didn't sell it to them it must have been you, right? You were the only other person working before eight that night."

"Could've bought it another time. We have a stack of casuals, you know."

She had a point, thought Alicia, but Jackson was not buying that either.

"Nope, I reckon they got it here that night, around seven, seven thirty. And it was just you and your mum at that time. I reckon they bought a couple of tall necks each and then headed off to the park. And I reckon you served them. Want to tell me why you're not cooperating?"

She sat forward with a start. "Am too! Just don't remember them, okay. You really think I remember every single loser that comes in this place?"

"This is important, Casey. These 'losers' might have strangled a woman. Might have tried to rape her first."

Casey's brow crinkled at that, but still she shrugged.

Jackson sighed and sat back, and Alicia wondered whether he was giving up. She sat forward, unable to help herself.

"You would remember those two," she said, and the younger woman snapped her eyes across, her brow crinkling further. Alicia continued, "They were oozing slime. Could undress you with one look."

She scoffed. "You really want me to start calling out more names? Sounds like every second bloke to me, including the middle-aged, married ones." She darted her eyes back to Jackson. "*Especially* the middle-aged, married ones."

Alicia shook her head. "Nope, these two were top-shelf slime. They would win the Oscar for Best Supporting Slimeball. They were extra creepy. I'm talking, don't get caught down an alleyway slime."

The young woman's scowl vanished, and it was clear Alicia's description had given her memory a kick-start. She scooped the picture up and looked at it properly this time.

"Yeah, okay, now you mention it, there were a couple of extra sleazy A-holes in here that night. Can't recall what they ordered, sorry, and don't recall caps, but yeah, I remember some A-class slime. Called me things like 'delicious' and 'tasty.'" She mock vomited. "I mean, I've been called plenty in my time, but tasty? Ew."

Jackson smiled, directing it to Alicia. "Sounds like our guys. What else can you tell us about them?"

"Nothing. Like I said, just slimy is all."

"Try and think, Casey. Like *I said*, it's really important. They could be dangerous."

She glanced at the picture again. "You think they did it? To that chick?"

"Maybe, maybe not. We have to find them."

"We have cameras, you know?"

"Yeah, your mum says they're broken."

"Typical," was her response.

"Did you hear their names? Maybe one of them called the other something? Did you notice any significant logos, that kind of thing?"

Again she shrugged. "Sorry, apart from the sleaze on steroids, they didn't really stand out. Like I said, could be anybody in this dump of a place."

"That's the thing," said Jackson. "They did stand out at the film night, and they did look out of place, which has got us wondering why they were even there. Wouldn't have been their style. Sounds like they would have been better suited to the dog track."

Alicia had a thought. "You said something before, called the movie 'a flick for old farts.'"

"So?"

"So how did you know about it?"

Casey went to shrug, and then it hit her. "Danielle! Oh I should've thought of her." She glanced around the bar again. "Bummer, she's not here. But Danni's your girl. She was in that night, talking about going. I said it sounded like a snore, she said something about her mum loving that shit, got her into it. That's right, and then those slimeballs said something."

"What?"

"I can't remember, but the thing is, they seemed to know her. I'm sure of it, because they weren't that sleazy with her. It's like they were old mates or something. You know you just get that vibe? Anyway, they were talking for ages. She might know more."

Jackson looked relieved. "Great stuff, Casey. Can you give us Danni's surname so I can try to locate her?"

"I can go you one better." She reached for her mobile phone. "I can tell you where she is right this second."

# CHAPTER 20

"Don't you just love modern technology?" Jackson was saying as they pulled up outside an all-night pharmacy in the downmarket suburb of Redfern.

Alicia was not convinced. "Big Brother more like. I can't believe people sign up to that app. It tells the whole world—and their stalker—where they are every minute of the day. Creeps me out."

"But it makes my job so much easier." He grinned as they got out, taking a moment to survey the scene. "Casey reckons she must work here, said she knew she worked somewhere in Redfern."

"Maybe she's buying some bleach to wash away the memory of those slimeballs."

Jackson chuckled as he led the way inside.

They found Danielle Ligaro stocking shelves at the side of the shop, a white uniform on and a box of multivitamins in front of her.

"Can I help you?" she asked as they wandered up.

"Hopefully." Jackson presented his badge.

The twentysomething barely bat an eyelid as he explained what he was after, and she didn't hesitate when he mentioned two sleazy guys in caps that she'd been spotted conversing with at the Jolly Codger the previous Saturday.

"Oh yeah, Scotty and Davo," she said, placing some vitamins on a shelf. "What about them?"

Jackson played it cool, but Alicia couldn't help beaming. They were inching closer to identifying two

151

potential killers! She loved being on the beat with Jackson, couldn't believe he was letting her tag along, and she was soaking it all up. Missy was right. Professional detectives had it so much easier than amateurs. Jackson could just flash his credentials, and people had to answer his questions whether they liked it or not. It was a much swifter process than the Miss Marple meddling caper she and the book club had been running for some time—not to mention a damn site more rewarding than writing for the internet.

Maybe Jackson was also right. Maybe she really was in the wrong profession.

"Any chance you know their surnames or where they live?" he was asking.

Danielle shook her head. "I only know them because they used to hang with my ex, over at the Horse and Spanner, near Central Station."

"Still go there, you think?"

"Dunno but my ex does, that's why I've started hanging at Casey's place."

"Anything else you can tell us about them?"

"I know they come across as flirty, but they're pretty harmless. Both got partners; one even has a kid and another one on the way."

*That never stopped anyone from committing a crime,* Jackson wanted to tell her but kept that to himself.

She continued, "Jeez, they're nicer than some of the blokes that hang out with my ex. Good riddance."

"Not a good sort?" Alicia asked.

"Good with his fists," was her reply.

After they left Danielle to her shelf stacking, Jackson called it a night.

"But aren't we going to head to the Horse and Wrench or whatever it was she said?"

He smiled as he shook his head. "I am, you're not."

And to her pouting lips he added, "I've overstepped

enough as it is. Indira won't be happy. But if those guys are our suspects, I'm not having you anywhere near them. Could get rough."

"I can do rough."

He just stared at her as if to say, *Yeah right.*

"Well, if it does get rough, you can't go in there alone."

He was already tapping a number into his phone. "I'm not." He held a hand to stall her as he said, "Yep, found 'em… Nope, pub at Central… Yep… Grab Pauly while I text you the address."

~~~~~~~

So much for letting her tag along, thought Alicia sulkily as she waved Jackson goodbye at her front door and let herself in.

It was now 9.20pm and Lynette was curled on the sofa watching a movie, Max in a matching curl on the rug below. The film looked familiar, but something was off.

"*Evil Under The Sun*, the David Suchet made-for-television version," she explained, putting the episode on pause as Alicia dropped her bag to the floor and slipped off her sneakers.

"I was just keen to see what differences there are from the one we saw the other night. It's not too far in. Want me to start from the top?"

"Nah, I'll catch up." She fell into an armchair. "It's not like I don't know the plot."

"Yes, but this one has lots of variations again."

She flung the DVD case towards Alicia, who caught it clumsily with both hands.

"The script writers all have to meddle, don't they? In this one, the Linda character is a slightly older boy called Lionel. Why make him a boy? I'm confused."

Alicia thought about it. Good point. "And where have they set this one? The last one was some ridiculous-sounding place."

"Oh this one's in Devon, which is partly why I wanted to see it. At least they kept to Christie's setting. I've been googling it. It's filmed at the Burgh Island Hotel, which was, apparently, the original place that first inspired the novel, so that's something. But everything else is so different. Watch."

She clicked the remote control, and the movie resumed, suddenly revealing the face of Poirot's loyal sidekick, Captain Hastings.

"Hey, what's he doing on the island?" Alicia declared, and Lynette laughed.

"I know! And guess who shows up later to investigate? Inspector Japp! He's not in the original story either."

Alicia frowned. She adored David Suchet as Poirot, but she wasn't sure she was up for more meddling with Christie's plot tonight. Sensing her reticence, Lynette pressed pause again.

"You okay?"

"Yeah, just tired."

"How'd it go with Jackson?"

She gave her sister the abridged version, causing Lynette to quickly lose interest in the movie.

"So Jackson might have Kat's killers behind bars tonight?"

"Maybe."

"So why the long face?"

Alicia didn't know. She had a vague feeling of regret and was trying to shake it off. She should be rejoicing. The whole thing could be done and dusted by morning. And yet she was feeling a little, well, melancholy.

She gave herself a mental shake.

Was she really so desperate for mystery and excitement in her life that she'd rather the killer was still out there for *her* to uncover? Was she really that pathetic?

She grabbed her shoes and stood up.

"I'm all right. Enjoy the rest of the film. I wonder if you'll work out who the culprit is."

They exchanged smirks as she made her way up to bed.

What Alicia didn't know as she slipped into her cotton pyjamas and then settled in with her book, was that the case was far from over. Like the movie Lynette was watching, it had just been placed on pause for a bit.

# CHAPTER 21

Liam Jackson looked through the one-way mirror with a growing sense of exasperation. It was now late Thursday night, and he was sure the man at the interrogation desk was lying through his yellow-tinged teeth, but he had no evidence and no cause to hold him any longer. At least that's what his lawyer would have said if he or his mate had demanded one, which, fortunately for the detectives, they hadn't.

Indira was not so convinced.

"I don't think they did it," she said, stifling a yawn.

She and Jackson had spent the past two hours going between the two interrogation rooms, first questioning Scott Jalezic and then his buddy David Crow. Both had healthy rap sheets, mostly involving burglary, stolen cars and police chases, although Scott had done time for king-hitting a mate into a coma at a pub a few years back.

*With friends like that,* thought Jackson, irritably.

Yet despite their seedy reputation, there was no record of any sexual harassment or assault or murder for that matter, and the detectives were now no closer to a confession.

"I mean, if being a slimeball was a crime, sure, it'd be open and shut. But just because these bozos 'like to watch,' so to speak, does not mean they acted on it, and there's no evidence they ever have."

"There's always a first time," Jackson said, turning from the mirror. "I'm just not buying it. They expect us to believe that, during the first half of the film, they couldn't keep their eyes off Kat Mumford, and suddenly when it matters, they didn't see a thing. How does that work?"

"Maybe they got hooked on the story. I heard it's a good one."

He stared at her deadpan.

She smiled. "I don't know, Jacko, but they did say things got quiet. She slipped under the blanket and fell asleep remember? So they lost interest. Look, they're very happy to admit they were perving on the couple earlier, which lends them a degree of credibility if you ask me. If they had denied watching the Mumfords and insisted they had watched the film diligently from the start, *then* I'd be doubting them."

Jackson considered this, and she had a point. The two perverts were almost boasting of the sideshow the Mumfords were putting on.

*"More fun than the boring crap up on the screen,"* one of them had said.

*"We weren't expecting porn that night,"* the other had sniggered, making Jackson want to thump him. *"But they cooled it in the second half. Pity that."*

*"That's because the husband moved away,"* Jackson had reminded each of them, and they both seemed genuinely surprised to hear this. Like they hadn't noticed.

*"So why'd you leave the park early?"* Indira had asked, and again they both seemed unfazed by the question.

*"Like I said, boring as batshit. Just all these stuck-up snobs poncing about,"* said Scott.

*"Didn't want to get stuck behind all the old geezers shuffling out,"* was Davo's reply.

*"And where did you go in such a hurry?"*

*"To the Horse and Spanner. Ask anyone."*

They didn't need to. Detective Jarrod had just confirmed the fact, having rushed through CCTV footage. They had been caught on camera, strolling through the front doors of the Horse and Spanner at exactly 10.29pm, looking perfectly relaxed.

"Doesn't mean they didn't do it before they left," said Jackson. "She was killed sometime between 9.35 and 10.35, remember?"

Indira wasn't buying it. "Their fingerprints don't match the one on the champagne flute. Neither of them is carrying a late-model iPhone, which might have provided motive. We've got nothing. No evidence, nada. I think we have to let them loose on the world again."

"Bloody hell, lock up your daughters then."

And so the two men were released without charge and the case had stalled all over again.

"Just 'cause we haven't got any evidence doesn't mean they didn't do it," Jackson said, sulkily, and Indira had to agree.

"But it does mean we can't hold them. And it also means we need to keep an open mind. I don't want to focus on those two and forget that plenty of other people had access and opportunity."

He couldn't disagree with that.

"So what'd our unhappy camper have to say?"

She looked at him, puzzled for a moment, and then said, "Oh, Guy Peters. He was a font of knowledge, that one."

It turns out the security officer did recall an older man with a moustache who loitered by the side gate a few times with the other smokers.

*"But he didn't seem real interested in the plot,"* Guy had told her earlier that evening. *"So we chewed the fat for a bit."*

*"What'd you talk about?"* she had asked.

*"This and that,"* Guy replied, rubbing his now sunburnt nose. *"Let me think."*

"He remembered a couple of very interesting things as it turns out," Indira told Jackson now. "Was under the impression the man was waiting for someone, might have got stood up. Reckons he checked his phone a lot and seemed increasingly agitated as the night progressed.

Said something about, 'That's the last time I trust women' or something like that."

Jackson sat up in his chair. "Say again?"

She laughed. "I know what you're thinking: Was he referring to the victim?"

"Well, was he? You've got to wonder. Was he angry with women in general or one woman in particular? And if it was one woman, maybe that woman was Kat Mumford. I mean, run with me here. I'm going to throw some wild theories about."

She winced but waved him on. She liked wild theories about as much as she liked wild hair, and the tight plait down her back demonstrated exactly what she thought of that.

"Okay, so what if this moustached man—let's call him 'Mo Man'—was Kat's lover or something? Maybe he was furious to find her kissing her husband at the park. Maybe he thought they were separated or something."

"That's a lot of 'maybes,'" Indira said. "Besides, wouldn't Kat have noticed him? He was about six feet away."

"She was blind drunk remember? And she arrived late, might not have seen him loitering behind the pregnant woman in the dark." He began madly clicking his fingers. "Oh no! I've got a better one! What if he was Kat's *sponsor*? From AA?"

He did a final click in front of her face, looking pretty proud of his hypothesis.

Indira was a lot less impressed. "Okay, so this 'sponsor' just happens to be at the film that night and just happens to be seated two blankets away. He notices Kat shit-faced and decides to strangle her? Why would he do that?"

"Maybe he was angry at her for falling off the wagon."

She laughed and looked at her watch. "Okay, I think we need to call it a night. Get some sleep, reboot our brains."

"What's wrong with that idea?"

"Jacko, you're saying Kat's sponsor killed her because he was angry that she wasn't looking after her health. Can you even hear how ridiculous that sounds?"

His shoulders slumped. She was right.

"Come on," she said, gathering her things. "Whoever Mo Man was bitching about, we do still need to find him, and it will help if we're fully rested."

As they switched off lights and made their way out, Indira said, "Eliot Mumford's right, you know. It *is* a problematic crime scene. A public park for goodness' sake! And at night! Loads of strangers, all with a right to be there, no one with any need to explain who they are or where they are from. So bloody frustrating! Agatha Christie had it so easy. She only ever had a handful of suspects, and they always had full names, addresses and a backstory to dig around in."

Jackson agreed. "So how do we find this bloke?"

"No idea," she said, stabbing at the elevator button.

Oh yes. They were firmly—infuriatingly—back at square one.

# CHAPTER 22

**A**zaria Joves was staring at the floral square, one hand on her hip. Something was not quite right, and it had nothing to do with the quilt she was making. She glanced at the card her husband had just placed on the table in front of her.

*What did the police want?*

*What had they discovered?*

*And why did Jacob tell her to be "very careful" when he slapped the card down?*

She placed the quilt on top of the card and tried to ignore it for the first ten minutes, but eventually, begrudgingly, she gave up. She plucked it from beneath the material, took a deep breath and called the number for Detective Inspector Liam Jackson.

A woman's voice answered, causing her to flinch. She glanced at the card again.

"Oh sorry, I... I was looking for, um, Detective Jackson," Azaria said.

"Oh sure, he's..." Alicia was about to say, "Just in the shower" but quickly said, "occupied, can I get him to—?"

The phone went dead.

Alicia dropped it onto her bed like it was ablaze. She couldn't believe she had just answered Jackson's mobile phone. Why had she done that?

*In this day and age, what kind of person answers someone else's mobile phone? Especially when that 'someone else' happens to be a police officer and a boyfriend!*

That was something desperate wives did in bad

Hollywood flicks, expecting the husky voice of a mistress on the other end.

*Why didn't she just let it go to voicemail?*

"Why didn't you just let it go to voicemail?" Jackson echoed her thought aloud, and she swung around to find him standing at her bedroom door with a towel wrapped around his hips, his hair dripping wet.

"Sorry!" she blurted, stepping away from the bed. "Just habit, I guess."

*It couldn't be her imagination guiding her actions again, could it? Was the honeymoon over on that?*

"Did they leave a message?" His tone was light; he didn't seem too annoyed. She apologised again as she shook her head.

"It was a woman. She hung up. She seemed a bit nervous."

He stared at her for a moment. "So do you. Are you all right?"

She nodded quickly, wrapping her arms around herself.

He scooped the phone from the bed and checked the number, his lips puckering up. He had no idea whose number that was.

"Excuse me a moment."

He pressed redial as he stepped out of the room. Two minutes later Jackson was back, reaching for the trousers he had dropped by her bed very early that morning.

"That was Azaria Joves, the mother who was sitting behind the victim at the film. I've been waiting for her call. She's finally agreed to meet me, at her place, in half an hour. I just texted Singho, and she's going to join me there. I'd better get my act together." He glanced around. "Where'd I dump my shirt?"

Alicia deflated a little. She had been hoping they could grab breakfast before he rushed off, but she tried not to show it as she helped him find the rest of his things.

This was the first time Jackson had appeared at her

door so late after a shift, and she had been thrilled by the visit, but now she couldn't help wondering whether she should be offended or irritated or both.

*Was that just a booty call? Was that all it was?*

"You sure you're all right?" he asked again.

She tried to smile. "Great, yes, never better."

*Snap out of it, Alicia,* she told herself.

"You all right?" came the question for the third time that morning, and Alicia looked up from her cup of tea to see her sister staring at her sleepily from the kitchen door.

She nodded unconvincingly.

Lynette yawned, scooped her long hair up and into a messy bun on the top of her head, and then shuffled over.

"What's going on?"

"Nothing."

Lynette stared at her sideways, so Alicia sighed and told her about Jackson's visit.

"So what's the big deal? He missed you, he dropped over, then he had to run off for work."

"I know. I know. It's not that."

"Then what is it?"

"It's the fact that my mind is now playing up on me again." She sniffed. "I thought I was cured. I thought Jackson was my saviour."

Lynette pulled her sister into a bear hug. They stayed like that for many minutes until Max came bounding over and jumped up, turning it into a group hug.

~~~~~~~

"Shall I prepare a pot of tea?" the woman asked as soon as Jackson and Indira were shown through the front door of the small cottage located in the block behind St Thomas's Church.

The house was tucked around behind the main building, hidden from view by a thick wall of banksias and a large ironbark.

"Tea would be lovely, thanks," said Indira, remembering the steaming cup she had to abandon when her colleague's text came through.

"Ditto," said Jackson, adding, "We both take it with plenty of sugar and milk."

As Azaria Joves got busy making a pot in the kitchen, the detectives busily inspected her living room where, among the fussy, ornate furniture, framed family photos wrestled for dominance with religious paraphernalia. There was a shiny cross on one wall and a framed picture of Mother Mary on another, as well as school photos, stiff holiday snaps, and images of the girls looking like miniature brides.

"First Holy Communion," Indira explained.

She reached for another photo just as Azaria reappeared with the tray of tea.

"Nice-looking lad," Indira said, and Azaria glanced at the photo and seemed to start a bit, the teacups clinking on the tray.

"Ye-ees?" she said.

Her rising inflection added to the sense of nervousness, so Indira held on to the photo and sat down with it, noticing that the woman eyed the picture as she did so.

Eventually when the tea had been poured and Azaria had taken a few deep breaths, Indira sat forward in her seat and looked at Jackson, giving him the nod.

This case was going nowhere fast, so today they would play by Jacko's rules, she had decided. Softly-softly could take a hike. Besides, she had a feeling this woman was accustomed to answering to authoritative men.

"We're here to talk about Ezekiel," Jackson said, launching straight in and causing the woman to blink rapidly.

"Ezekiel?" she squeaked, glancing back at the photo which was still in Indira's hands. It was of her eldest son in his full school uniform, a cheerless smile on his face.

"Wh-why? Is everything okay?"

Indira went to jump in then, to tell this anxious mother that her son was perfectly fine, but she bit her tongue and let Jackson continue.

"I don't know," he was saying. "You tell us."

"I beg your pardon?"

"Good boy is he?" Jackson asked, before taking a loud slurp of his tea.

"Ye-es?"

"Ever give you any trouble?"

She blinked rapidly again. "I don't think so? Er, not really."

"So why was your husband doling out the punishment two days ago?"

The words were like a fresh trigger on the woman's nerves, and she rattled her teacup onto the table and then placed her hands in her lap.

"Excuse me?" she managed again.

Again, the upward inflection indicated either serious nerves or something to hide. It was time for a sudden change of tack.

"Mrs Joves, we're investigating the death of Kat Mumford last Saturday night, and we're wondering whether you might have any information to assist us in our enquiries."

"I... er, I don't think so. I thought you spoke to Jacob, er, Reverend Joves?"

"Yes, and now we're speaking to you." He smiled. "Anything you'd like to tell us?"

She glanced at the photo in Indira's hands again. She had a terrified look in her eyes.

"It has nothing to do with my Ezekiel, surely?"

He said nothing this time, and she looked from him to the picture and back again.

"I mean, he can be a bit naughty at times, I know that. Sometimes he takes it a little too far, but the school has been very good about it, have been working very, very closely with us on that. They're helping us guide him in a much, er, *safer* direction."

"Safer for whom?" Jackson asked, but he didn't get his answer.

Azaria's cheeks suddenly paled, and she stared down at her lap, her lips wedged tight.

"Good morning, Detectives," came a deep voice behind them, and while Indira swung around expectantly, Jackson just closed his eyes.

*Damn it. They were so close!*

He opened them again and turned to face the doorway. "Good morning, Reverend Joves."

Jacob stepped across the room and stood behind his wife's chair. "I hope my wife has been cooperative regarding the incident on Saturday night."

They nodded, noticing that Azaria had not looked up.

"And I assume you have asked her all the questions relevant to *that night?*"

Jackson sighed. He stood up. This was pointless.

"That will be all for now, thank you, Mrs Joves."

Indira looked at Jackson, confused for a moment, then followed his lead and walked out.

"She was never going to tell us anything with him hovering over her," Jackson explained as they dissected the conversation back at their base. "In fact, I bet he was there all along, eavesdropping in the shadows."

"Creepy bastard," Indira replied. "Notice how she went quiet and submissive the moment he walked in?"

"Yep. Bit like the son." He rubbed at his head. "I think she was about to come clean on us. I think we might have got more out of her if he hadn't bloody walked in."

"Yes, but she was talking about something that happened at Zak's school, not the film night."

"Okay, so what happened at school? Could it reflect on this case? Maybe Zak was caught peeking up some girl's skirt? Maybe he has a pattern of abusive or aggressive behaviour towards women."

She shrugged. "Well, good luck getting the information out of either of them. I have a feeling creepy hubby is going to stick very close to his wife in the future. I think you're spot on. Whatever Zak—or Jacob for that matter—have been up to, that woman will never spill the beans. Not now."

He stopped scratching and dropped his head to one side. "No, but I wonder whether someone else might."

# CHAPTER 23

Jackson manoeuvred his vehicle through the tight entrance gates of St Matthew's College and then parked in the main quadrangle in front of a grand sandstone building, right beside the No Parking sign. As far as Jackson was concerned, there were few perks in being a copper, but illegal parking was one of them.

After a few wrong turns, he and Pauly found the school principal in a small garden behind the admin block, watering a prickly rose bush.

"Stress relief," he told the detectives after the introductions were made.

"Kid's a bit of nightmare, hey?" said Jackson.

"Not at all. It's the parents that get my blood pumping." He smiled apologetically. "Just had a meeting with a 'Mommy Dearest.' Suffice to say she was not buying the argument that Prince Boofhead could possibly have been smoking cigarettes down behind the gymnasium. Not *her* son! Never!"

And to their looks of surprise, he said, "What can I say? I'm six months shy of retirement, and it can't come fast enough. So what can I help you gentlemen with?"

"We're here about another Prince Boofhead, actually. An Ezekiel Joves."

Principal Taylor stopped watering and turned to face them. "He's not so much a boofhead as a broken spirit that one."

"Oh?"

"His parents are the polar opposite of the one I was

just referring to. Or at least his father is. Reverend Joves believes that all children are evil and must prove themselves innocent. Has insisted I keep a firm eye and an even firmer hand."

"Spare the rod, spoil the child?" Jackson suggested, and he nodded.

"Except the research has never borne that out, and Ezekiel Joves is the living proof of that. I shouldn't be saying this, but Jacob is a tough master and his son is a direct reaction to that. Rather than keep his child in line, his rigid discipline has made things much, much worse."

"Worse? How so?" Jackson asked, but Taylor had a question of his own.

"Can I ask what this is regarding?"

"He and his family were witnesses to a murder at a park in Balmain two weeks ago."

"Yes, I was informed."

"We're just chasing up leads."

"And Ezekiel Joves is one of those leads?"

Jackson said, "I hope not but, yeah, maybe. We know he was in trouble here recently, and we're wondering what that was about. Whether it might help shed light on the case."

Taylor thought about that for a moment, then placed the watering can aside and led them down the cobbled pathway, back towards admin.

"He was a good kid to start with," Taylor was saying. "A sweet twelve-year-old, like most of them are, but there's been a lot of angst at home, I gather." He swung open the front door and headed straight for the reception desk where a young woman smiled up at him.

"Can you get the Joves file for me please, Sonya. It's E. Joves. Year 8H."

She nodded and he led the way into his office, which was large and plushly decorated, in keeping with private school tradition—including two stiff, high-backed chairs in front of an antique office desk. The only oddity: an enormous fish tank bubbling away in the corner.

He headed straight for the tank and picked up a jar of fish food. "More stress relief," he explained just as Sonya appeared with a manila folder.

He thanked her and then abandoned the fish and sat behind his desk, offering them the chairs in front.

"Right, let's see…" He glanced through the folder and back up again. "I guess I should be demanding warrants, that kind of thing."

Jackson and Pauly looked at him sheepishly and waited.

"But you caught me in a good mood, Detectives. I'm on the side of the righteous today, and by that I don't mean the pastor. I am quite convinced you will find that young Mr Joves had nothing to do with your case, and by helping you today I am, in effect, helping my student." He paused and stared into the distance, frowning a little. "Or at least I hope I am."

He continued scanning the file. "That's right, yes. Well, if you were to chat with your colleagues at the local area command, you would be able to verify this information yourself anyway, so…" He dropped the file to the desk, leaned back in his chair and said, "Ezekiel Joves was caught trading iPhones last week."

"Trading iPhones?"

"It's a bit of racket that emerges every now and then, thanks mostly to the millennials' obsession with devices. He had a bag full of smartphones and was selling them to students for about a hundred a piece."

Jackson whistled, thinking *Bingo*!

He said, "How very industrious of him. And this is against school rules, I gather?"

"Absolutely it is. Students may not solicit any material for sale, whether it be a peanut butter sandwich for fifty cents or an iPhone for a hundred dollars."

"How many did he have?"

"Six, I believe. We know his father is a strict Luddite and keeps his son on a tiny 'stipend'—his word, not mine—so we can only assume he did not buy them with his own money. Where he got them from is anyone's guess."

"Ooh I think I have an idea where he got at least one of them," Jackson said, and the principal frowned.

"I was afraid of that." He closed the file. "He's not such a bad kid, Detective. He's just trying to keep up with the Joneses, or in our case, the Packers and the Murdochs."

"So those Nikes," said Pauly, finally cottoning on.

Jackson nodded, explaining to Taylor. "We saw him remove some expensive trainers before meeting his dad."

"The proceeds of crime no doubt. The poor lad is usually in second-hand clothing, a regular in our charity uniform shop. In any case, we made him pay back the money to the students, and we retrieved all the phones, so he's probably not the most popular person around here at the moment. But my guess is that's nothing compared to the wrath of his father."

"We saw him doing some work around the churchyard," Pauly said.

"If that's all he gets, then he got off lightly this time."

"Has Ezekiel been in trouble before?" The man nodded. "Ever had any issues with female students, aggressive behaviour, that kind of thing?"

Taylor seemed surprised by the question. "Not at all. He's usually very polite to the girls, almost scared of them I would suggest. As for aggressive behaviour? Only towards himself." He sighed. "We discovered him cutting himself in the boys' shower block about six months back. We've attempted to get him some counselling, but his father will have none of it." He shook his head sadly.

Jackson also felt some sympathy for the muddled-up kid, but he couldn't think about that now. He needed to focus. "And what happened to the phones, Mr Taylor? Where did they end up?"

"We dropped them down to your mob, at the local

police station. If they don't find the original owners, we have asked that they go to charity."

Jackson nodded, but it wasn't those particular phones he wanted. He needed the last phone Ezekiel was clutching, the one he now suspected Ezekiel had sold to a young girl fresh off the bus.

He got to his feet.

"Thanks for your candour, Mr Taylor, you've been most helpful."

Taylor stood and shook both their hands. "Like I said, Zak's not such a bad egg, not when you consider the nest he's come out of. I'm all for rules, Detective, and am a deeply religious man at that, but Reverend Joves is too Old Testament even for the likes of me."

They left the jaded principal to stare gloomily into his fish tank as they made their way out of the building and back to the car.

"Now what?" Pauly asked just as the final school bell began clanging.

"Now we see if we can't crack an egg."


It took all of two minutes for Ezekiel Joves to admit to stealing the smartphone from Kat Mumford and another two before handing over the name of his last buyer, a fifteen-year-old student from Meadows Public High School called Shayna Jones.

She was the girl they had spotted embracing Zak when he got off the bus a few days earlier. They were not actually hugging; they were making the exchange.

"But I wouldn't have taken the phone if I'd known that chick was dead," young Zak cried after they had bailed him up outside the school gate. "I thought she was just sleeping. Honest I had nothing to do with that."

"And the glasses?"

"Huh?"

"What did you do with the white Gucci glasses Mrs Mumford had on?"

"What? I didn't take any glasses. I promise."

Jackson stared at him.

"No way, man, honest. I mean, Ray-Ban I could shift, but Gucci? Too old for my buyers." He frowned. "And I only took the phone cause it was just lying there. Like she didn't want it, and she looked so rich, and I bet she's on some plan where they would've given her a free replacement one anyway and…"

Jackson stopped him there. He didn't want to hear Zak's justification, and he certainly didn't want any more of this backyard confession. He wanted this done properly. Reluctantly he put a call through to St Thomas's rectory and waited a further ten minutes before Jacob Joves arrived at the school, his face a black blanket of fury, most of which was directed at his son.

"What did you do?" he demanded.

"Shayna was desperate, Dad. She's never owned an iPhone before. She begged me!"

"Another Jezebel, is that it? Another girl leading a man astray?"

Jackson stepped in. "Let's take this down to the station, please, Rev Joves. We'd like to formally caution your son before we begin questioning, and we would like you to get some legal representation for the lad. If you cannot afford legal representation, a lawyer can be—"

"Yes, yes!" Jacob snapped. "I've already phoned my solicitor."

Jackson felt a flood of relief. *Good*, he thought. *The young fool's going to need one.*

As two uniformed officers escorted a very angry father and his jittery son down to the squad headquarters in Parramatta, Jackson and Pauly headed in the opposite direction. They needed to get hold of Kat Mumford's stolen phone and fast, and so, after a few phone calls, they made their way to the home of a young girl called Shayna, whose dreams of owning an iPhone were about to come crashing down.

# CHAPTER 24

"**Y**eah, we located the phone," Jackson told Alicia over the landline that night. "But it's not much use to the case. The only fingerprints on the device belong to Kat Mumford, Ezekiel Joves and Shayna Jones, which is what we expected to find."

"No mystery prints like on the champagne flute then?"

"No, but it's got me wondering about those glasses. Now more than ever I want to know where they ended up."

"Maybe one of the other kids pinched them? Or a passer-by, someone who just saw the opportunity and took it."

He sighed. "You could be right. I think I'm reading too much into it."

"Could be a red herring, like the pipe!" said Missy, two days later at Book Club.

She was hosting the Sunday meeting for the very first time and was so full of nerves Alicia, the first to arrive, tried to keep her distracted with news of the case.

"Pipe?" Alicia said now, watching as Missy dashed from one end of the living room to the next, plumping cushions, removing old newspapers, wiping down dusty tabletops.

"You know, like in *Evil Under the Sun*?"

Missy picked up an olive-green cardigan and stuffed it behind the sofa.

"Remember in the book, one of the killers plants

Kenneth Marshall's pipe at the bottom of the steps at Pixy Cove where Arlena's body was found, to implicate the husband?"

"Except the glasses aren't planted, Missy, they've been pinched."

"Yes, but maybe it's the same thing. Maybe it's either to implicate a thief or, as I say, just to get the cops looking in a different direction. Could be a deliberate ploy."

Alicia considered that as she watched Missy continue to fuss and plump and panic.

"Don't worry, honey, the place looks great."

Missy glanced up from a side cabinet where she was now stuffing a jigsaw puzzle onto a crowded shelf. "Really? Do you think so?" Then she glanced around and frowned. "If only it really was my place, then it wouldn't look so... *drab!*"

The club had never been held at Missy's home before, largely because, as she said, it wasn't strictly *her* home. It belonged to her parents, and it had taken some convincing to get them to decamp for the day. She'd received enough ribbing from Perry about the fact she still lived with her folks, and she was not about to have them loitering with their embarrassing questions and awkward smiles.

No, the plan was very simple. They were to go to her sister Henny's place and remain there until Missy gave the all clear. Of course, Missy had tried this plan before, but something always came up, usually her father's angina, forcing her to cancel. The other club members were always happy to step in on her behalf, but Missy knew it was time to step up.

The doorbell rang and she jumped.

"I'll get it," Alicia said, but Missy was already scrambling for the front door.

It was Anders, usually the first, and he asked, "How's it going, Missy?" as he walked inside.

"Really good! I've managed to remove most of my

parents' mess, and I think I've made enough space…"
She stopped. "Sorry, you didn't mean…" She giggled.
"Sorry, you just meant, like, generally, right?"

He smiled stiffly and was relieved when he spotted
Alicia already seated inside. He strode across and gave her
a hug. It was warm and unexpected, and she hugged him
warmly back. Maybe they were moving on at last.

A loud knock heralded the arrival of Lynette, who had
been working a morning shift, then Perry, followed quickly
by Claire. Everyone was eager to get to the book club
today, and this time it had less to do with Agatha Christie
and more to do with the real-life mystery that had landed
in their laps.

After Missy ushered them into the "good" lounge
room, the one her parents reserved for special guests, she
indicated a side table where a plate of chocolate-chip
cookies and a pot of tea had already been placed.

"Best I could manage," she said by way of apology.
"Not much of a chef, I'm afraid. Not like Mum and
Henny. Now they can put on a delectable spread!"

"It's fine," said Claire, helping herself to a cookie.

Lynette tried not to frown. She wished Missy had told
her. She would have baked something or pinched some
muffins from Mario's on her way out.

"Shall we get started?" Alicia suggested, knowing they
were on a tight schedule and had a lot to get through
today.

And so they spent the next hour dissecting another
Miss Marple favourite, and it wasn't until the tea had run
dry and the conversation began to peter out that Perry
reminded them all they had a second murder to discuss,
one starring a beautiful young woman and her shattered
husband.

"How is Eliot Mumford?" asked Claire, closing her
copy of *Sleeping Murder*. "Has Jackson had a chance to
interview him again?"

Alicia smudged her lips to one side. "I wouldn't know.

I haven't seen Jackson since Friday morning."

*Before he slunk out of my bedroom and never looked back.*

They were all watching her now, one or two looking worried, and she pushed her lips into a smile. "But I did *speak* to him today, so I have a general overview of how things are going."

"Oh that's a relief," Claire said, and she wasn't referring to the investigation. She was thinking this group had a dreadful track record when it came to relationships.

"So how is it progressing? The case I mean."

"Not great. Basically, they've questioned all the potential suspects who were seated in the area, all except that man sitting next to Maz Olden, the older guy with the black moustache."

"And?" asked Perry impatiently.

"And nothing. Jackson says they're all a bit too smug, but they just don't have enough evidence to pin it on anyone. It's been over a week since the woman was killed and still no conclusive answers."

"Tell them about Zak!" Missy said, having already heard the gossip.

And so Alicia filled them in on the iPhone theft, adding, "They don't know whether Ezekiel pinched it while Kat was sleeping or if she'd already been killed at that point."

"Urgh, gross," said Lynette. "His loopy dad will have him saying Hail Mary's until the cows come home."

"I know, poor kid."

"Poor kid?" said Anders. "He did steal someone's property, people. He's no innocent."

"He's like Linda from the book," retorted Missy, and as several of them rolled their eyes she said, "No, I just mean, he's probably not a really bad person, he's just reacting to his circumstances."

"I agree," said Alicia, "and so do the detectives, who expect he'll get treated fairly lightly. But that still leaves the missing spectacles."

"He must have taken them too, surely?" Perry said.

"Well, they did a full search of his home and school locker and so far, no glasses."

"Maybe they got lost in the chaos of that night?" said Claire.

"Or maybe the killer took them as a trophy!" said Missy. "Killers do do that, you know. That's how that creepy serial killer Ivan Milat got caught. You know, the one who buried those backpackers in the Belanglo State Forest? The cops found souvenirs he'd kept from his poor victims in his house."

"Thank you, Missy," said Claire. "Are we not all creeped out enough as it is?"

She shrank back. "Sorry."

"No, Missy's right," said Alicia. "That's what DI Singh believes. She thinks the killer took the glasses as a souvenir. There's no other explanation."

"And they're convinced the kid had nothing to do with her murder?"

She nodded. "They have to keep an open mind, and apparently his hands are sizeable enough, but Jackson's gut feeling says no. He doesn't even think the nasty father did it either. He now thinks that all the yard work Zak was forced to do at the church was penance for selling iPhones at school the week before. Jacob insists he knew nothing of his son's theft of Kat's glasses, and Jackson believes that too. Reckons Zak would have got more than a bit of raking work as punishment for that."

"Poor kid," Claire repeated.

"He's a *thief*," Anders reminded them. "I know his father's super strict, but can we not glorify the wayward kid please?"

Lynette rolled her eyes. "So what happens now? Where is it all at?"

Alicia shrugged. "I think Jackson's hit a brick wall and he's too ashamed to admit it."

She took a deep breath and pushed her shoulders back.

"I'm wondering whether we can't bash through that wall for him."

"What are you saying?" said Missy, her eyes lighting up.

"I'm saying, it might be time for the Murder Mystery Book Club to start meddling again."

She turned straight to Anders who, she guessed correctly, would be frowning and said, "Jackson has *never* had a problem with us helping in the past, as you will recall. He even asked us to keep an eye out for suspicious things on the night of the crime. Took me along to the Jolly Codger that night. So I really don't think he'd mind."

"But you haven't checked with him," said Anders, and it wasn't a question. He knew what Alicia was like.

"I *can't*. He'd be obliged to tell me to back off whether he wants to or not."

"It is still early days in this case, isn't it?" said Claire, who wasn't sure which camp to be in at this point. "The murder only happened a week ago."

"Doesn't mean we can't help," said Alicia.

Besides, she had an ulterior motive. The sooner the Mumford mystery was solved, the sooner she would get her boyfriend back.

"I agree with Alicia," said Missy. "We've been very well behaved until this point, but if the police are lost and can't see a way forward, perhaps we can help shed some light on a few things."

"But that's ridiculous," said Anders, quickly holding his palm out. "Sorry, I know I sound like a broken record, but they're the *police*. They have all the information, the leads. We have nothing."

Missy held her own palm out. "That's where you're wrong. We have our 'leetle grey cells' don't we, possums?" She tapped her head, and bravely ignoring Anders's exasperated expression, she added, "I bet you any money we can solve this thing before the police do."

He looked at her sceptically.

"Seriously!" She turned to Alicia. "Didn't you say that

the suspects are being tight-lipped? Lawyering up and refusing to speak to the authorities?"

"Which is their legal right," Anders said.

"Yes, but maybe they won't be quite so tight-lipped with a few friendly civilians who happen to ask a few casual questions."

Alicia smiled. "That's exactly what I was thinking, Missy. We spoke about this last time. It's Miss Marple's hidden strength—the ability to sneak impertinent questions to unsuspecting suspects. In fact, I have a plan up my sleeve."

She nudged her eyebrows up and down and added, "And it involves at least one of us becoming an alcoholic."

# CHAPTER 25

"You want to sign up to AA even though you're not an alcoholic?" said Claire, aghast.

"I have to do it!" Alicia replied. "Jackson and Indira tried to investigate that angle and got shown the door. Actually, they never got anywhere *near* the door. It's all anonymous and confidential, so the second their badges were out, they were out. If I go in undercover, well, I might have more luck."

Anders said, "Is that ethical?"

"I'm trying to help a murder victim, how can it be wrong? And besides, how would they know I wasn't really an alco'?"

"Because you're a 'straighty 180,'" laughed Lynette. "They'll smell your sobriety the second you sit down in the circle."

Alicia glared at her sister. "I drink, thank you."

"A few glasses of bubbly does not an alcoholic make," Lynette retorted, as though her sister's usual restraint was a bad thing, but Perry was holding a hand up to silence them.

"Alcoholics aren't just wild, party people, you know. Alcoholism is a disease, an addiction that afflicts all types, all ethnicities and socioeconomic backgrounds. You'd be *surprised* how many middle-aged housewives have got drinking problems, or respectable accountants for that matter."

Lynette raised an eyebrow at him. "Easy tiger. I was just joking…"

He wasn't finished. "In any case, that's completely beside the point. It's very, very easy to infiltrate AA, and the reason's in the name. Alcoholics *Anonymous*, people! They don't make you walk a straight line when you get in there, you know? They don't do background checks and ask for three referrals from local barmen. Anyone can just waltz in and take a seat. Hell, you can sit there for weeks and not say a single word if you want. It's all strangely, rather oddly, *relaxed*."

Now the eyebrows were all raised, and he rolled his eyes.

"Oh fine, I confess!" He took a deep breath and put his hand to his heart. "Hello. My name is Perry. And I am *not* an alcoholic, thank you very much! But my brother was." He sighed. "Still is, I suppose. I don't think they ever get cured." He shook his head. "Anyway, the point is, I attended a few sessions with him about ten years back, just for moral support."

Alicia smiled at him pointedly.

"What?" he said, and then, "Don't even think about it."

Her smile widened. "Come *on*, you'd be great! You're an old hand, you know how it works, and you're a self-confessed drama queen. Come with me. You'll help me fit right in."

He glared at her. "I refute your use of the word 'old,' but you got the rest right." He sighed dramatically. "Fine. I'll do it."

"That didn't take much convincing," she said, laughing.

"Hang on a minute," said Anders. "Can we just back up a bit here."

Alicia's laugh caught in her throat. *Oh dear, here we go…*

"I'm confused about what it is you hope to achieve by attending the AA meetings of a woman who is now deceased. What is the point?"

"I don't know, just poke around, ask a few questions, see if there isn't a stalker type who might have done this."

"And you think he'll just be sitting there, twiddling his

thumbs, looking guilty?"

Now she let a scowl rip. "We could recognise someone from the film night, someone the cops didn't spot. Plus!" She began waving her fingers around. "Don't forget Kat had a sponsor. Jackson says Eliot was pretty evasive about it, but did refer to a 'Tim or a Tom' or someone."

"So?"

"So the cops are wondering whether Kat's sponsor might be the elusive man with the moustache. At least that's what Jackson was thinking. We saw the guy with the moustache so we could clear that one up for him in two seconds flat. But even if it's not him, it'd still be useful to chat to her sponsor." She glanced at Perry. "Correct me if I'm wrong, but wouldn't Kat have told her sponsor all her little secrets? If there *was* someone dangerous in her life, or she had a jealous lover or something, wouldn't her sponsor be the ideal person to blab to about that? Maybe they have some information that really should go to the police."

"Oh you're doing this for the *police*, are you?" Anders said, and Alicia glowered.

"Actually, I'm doing it for Kat."

But Perry was unsure. "Sorry to burst your bubble, honey, but you probably won't get a sponsor to tell you any of that. They're supposed to keep all the dirty laundry to themselves."

"Can't hurt to try."

"How are you even going to find the right AA? There must be hundreds of groups across the city."

"Jackson reckons she attended one in Rozelle. Can only be one in that suburb, surely? We just have to look it up."

"I'll do it!" said Lynette, pulling out her smartphone.

As she tapped away at the screen, Anders continued to frown. "You don't think someone's going to spot you a mile off, asking questions about a deceased woman? You'll be booted out after the second question."

"Give us a little more credit than that, Anders," said Perry. "You keep forgetting that we've done exactly this kind of thing before."

"Okay, but then what?"

"Then we tell Jackson and he takes it from there," said Alicia. "I'm telling you, if we do find some important information, he'll be secretly glad I butted my big nose in."

"Well, you said it, not me," was Anders's final word on the subject.

"It's at the Rozelle Neighbourhood Centre," Lynette announced, swiping at her phone. "Says they meet at five thirty every Tuesday, Thursday and... Sunday. Oh, you could go this evening!" She stopped, deflated. "Damn, no you missed Sunday. That one was on this morning."

"Tuesday, five thirty it is then," said Alicia, nodding at Perry.

"So what about the rest of us?" asked Missy. "I want to go undercover too! I want to find some clues." She rubbed her hands together gleefully, like she was discussing a game of *Cluedo*. "Why don't we do like we did last time and all pick a suspect or a lead and follow it!"

Anders didn't get a chance to pour cold water on that idea as the rest of the group was nodding their heads enthusiastically now.

"You guys need to get a life," was all he could muster, smiling despite himself.

"I'm thinking," continued Missy, "that I should try to have another chat with those two lovely ladies from the organising committee. They were happy enough to chat with me that night, so..."

"Great idea," said Alicia. "Jackson found them in the old mews at the back of that park in Balmain, so try there first. In fact, if you go tomorrow, you'll probably find them knitting scarves for refugees."

"I'll come with you if you like," said Claire, her ears pricking up at the sound of industrious crafting.

Missy gave her two thumbs up.

"I could talk to that cute barman," Lynette offered, and Perry sniggered.

"Isn't he a little too young and lowly paid for your tastes?"

"I'm talking to him, not dating him, Perry!"

"No, he's perfect," said Alicia. "He's clamped up big time, thanks to his lawyer, but I'm pretty sure Jackson said he works weekdays at the Top Shop in Balmain. You should drop by. I bet he'd be more open to chatting to a pretty young blonde than a couple of surly detectives."

"Aw, thanks, sis," she said, slapping Perry with a smirk.

Anders said, "You really think he's going to tell Lynette everything over a cup of Joe? You're going to have to slosh a lot of brandy in that cup to get him talking I would suggest."

Lynette looked despondent suddenly. "True, and if it takes ages like it did that first case we solved, I'll have to take extra time off work, and my boss will kill me. I'm not sure I've got the time or the budget for this."

"Ah but I know a way you could get to know Brandon *and* get paid for it," said Alicia, and Lynette smiled back at her.

She liked the sound of that.

# CHAPTER 26

Lynette smiled to herself as she strolled towards the trendy Balmain eatery they called the Top Shop. It was Monday morning, just after the breakfast rush, a good time to chat with unsuspecting staff, and while she had been forced to beg Mario for another morning off, she was hoping it would be the last.

Alicia's plan was ingenious—a win-win for everyone.

Mario's Café was never open for dinner, so Alicia suggested Lynette get rostered onto Brandon's evening bar staff. They had heard there was another film showing at the park that Saturday night—as far as they knew, it hadn't been cancelled—and Alicia suspected it would be a good chance for her sister to get to know him better and be paid for the effort.

Lynette's smile slipped a little. She just hoped Brandon was on duty today, as Alicia guessed he would be, and that she would recognise him again. She had only seen him briefly at the moonlight cinema's Booze Bar, and that was now over a week ago, but as soon as she caught sight of a skinny bloke with a shock of black hair and tight black jeans, she felt her confidence return.

*Well, hello Brandon Johnson!*

After a few moments pretending to peruse the menu out the front, Lynette quickly deduced which tables he was working and then strolled nonchalantly towards an empty one in his section, dropping her handbag to the floor and settling into a seat.

"Can I get you a menu, or are you just after a coffee

today?" he asked, grabbing a pad and a pen from his apron.

Lynette promptly ordered an espresso, then waited until he returned before launching in.

"Cool place you've got here," she said as he placed the cup down. "D'you know if there are any jobs going at the moment?"

He stopped to look at her properly. Lynette was a good six or seven years older than him, but she was leggy and blond and he liked what he saw.

"Maybe." His eyes squinted. "You look very familiar. Been here before?"

She quickly nodded. "Yes! I come here all the time."

It hadn't occurred to Lynette that Brandon might remember *her* from the film night too, but for Alicia's plan to succeed, it was important he did not.

"Jobs come up fairly regularly," he was saying. "I can ask out the back for you if you like. You got experience?"

"Yeah, I work at Mario's in Paddington, but to tell you the truth, what I'm really after is some bar work at night, to supplement my income. Pity you guys haven't got a bar here."

He glanced around. "Yeah, I keep telling them they should put one in. They'd clean up." He looked back at her. "You good on the drinks?"

She nodded enthusiastically. The truth was she didn't have a whole lot of experience pouring cocktails but enough to know it wasn't exactly chemical engineering. As long as you had the right moves and a decent recipe, you could pull it off.

Luckily, he took the bait, glancing around again before leaning in closer.

"I know of some bar work if you're keen. I run a team, working local festivals, PR events, that kind of thing. Lot of it's evening work. You interested?"

She feigned surprise. "Wow, sure. Sounds perfect."

He smiled broadly. "Then how about we forget

Top Shop and I get you some bar work instead?"

"Even better. Got anything coming up soon?"

His eyes squinted again. "You're really keen. What's the rush?"

"Oh, just saving to go travelling."

Then she flashed her sexiest smile. It worked. He smiled back, rubbing a hand through his black hair before pulling a mobile phone from his apron.

"Give me your digits, and I'll give you a call if something crops up."

As she tapped her number into his contact list, Lynette knew her sister would have a fit. Alicia was so old-fashioned about handing over personal information. But Lynette knew how things worked with youth today. The easier she made it for Brandon, the greater the chance he'd be in touch.

She smiled again as she handed his phone back. "Just look up L for Lynette," she told him, just as a cranky-looking man with a Ned Kelly beard started closing in.

"L for 'Lovely Lady,'" he said with a sly grin before turning away.

~~~~~~~

While Lynette was flirting with the young barman, Missy and Claire were unloading a cardboard box and making their way into the Balmain Women's Auxiliary clubhouse back at the Dame Nellie Johnson Park. Like the younger Finlay, they also had an ingenious plan.

"I've had all this out the back for ages," Claire explained to Missy soon after she met her at the little shop she owned in the city. "Odd reels of cotton, jars of buttons, several quilting sets, *lots* of wool and fabric, that kind of stuff."

"Sounds like a treasure trove," said Missy. "And you don't want to keep it for yourself, possum? Use it for your own fabulous creations?"

Claire sighed. "That was the idea, but I've barely opened the box in years. Now it's just getting in the way. It's time to find it a better home, and who better than a group of ladies doing their bit for the needy?"

Missy couldn't agree more, and neither could the aforementioned ladies who all gathered around when Claire produced the box and began rummaging through, uttering cries of delight.

"Very decent of you," said one woman. "We struggle to get donations like this anymore and certainly not from young lasses like yourselves. Nobody has time for sewing and crafts these days."

"The truth is it all belonged to my grandmother," said Claire. "She'd be thrilled to see you ladies do something positive with it."

"Oh we'll certainly do that, dear," said another woman.

As they talked, Missy was scanning the room for the two women from the film night. She couldn't see them and was trying to mask her disappointment when she heard a sudden burst of laughter coming from near the back of the hall. She guessed there was a kitchen out there.

"Do you mind if I get a drink of water while I'm here?"

"Of course, dear," one woman said. "Just head out the back."

"Grab a scone while you're at it," someone else added. "Flo will see you right."

Claire caught Missy's eye and smiled. "I might grab one too, if that's all right?"

They waved the younger women away, keen to keep rifling through their treasure, so Claire and Missy clattered across the wooden floorboards towards the sound of laughter.

When they entered the kitchen, they spotted Florence Underwood first. She had a scone in one hand and a mug in the other and was regaling some women with a story so hilarious at least one of them looked like she was choking.

"Don't let us interrupt," Claire said when they looked around. "We were just going to grab a cup of tea."

"Oh, here, love," gulped one of the ladies, "have some of ours."

She pushed a chipped teapot across the old wooden table towards them.

The other was reaching down behind her to a cupboard full of mismatched crockery, while Flo was staring at them, her eyes narrowing.

"Haven't I seen you girls somewhere before?"

Missy stepped towards her. "Yes! Oh you've got such an amazing memory! You're right. We met at the film the other night. The night that poor lady…"

She let that dangle, and Flo's eyes widened.

"Of course, yes. I'd recognise that lovely shade of pink anywhere."

As she said it, the other women wedged their lips shut and looked away. "Lovely" was not an adjective they would have used.

Flo continued, "You were part of that sweet club, weren't you? Now, what was it? Don't tell me. I must exercise my brain cells, ward off the dementia."

She placed two bony fingers to her brow.

"Film appreciation club?" suggested one of her friends.

"No, no, that's not quite right. Ah! A book club, the Murder Mystery Book Club!"

Claire said, "You really do have a great memory."

She poured herself and Missy a cup and then indicated some spare chairs at the table. "Do you mind if we…?"

"Not at all, dear. Help yourselves. So what brings you here?"

"Oh we had some sewing supplies we wanted to donate," she said, reciting the line they had prepared. "We figured after the tragedy at film night you might need all the help you can get."

"Yes, yes, terrible business. And how have *you* all been since that dreadful night?"

Before they had a chance to answer, the other women were sharing a look and getting to their feet. "We'll leave you to it, ladies. Better get back to work."

After they had rinsed their cups and left the kitchen, Flo sighed.

"I think they're all a little tired of the brouhaha over that night. It's been very trying on us all. The press has been bothering us mercilessly, trying to get comments. *And* we've had a few customers demanding their money back. One woman's even threatening to sue, would you believe? For mental stress or some such nonsense!"

"That's terrible," Missy said.

"It's shameful is what it is. It was hardly our fault now was it? It's not like we *planned* it or could have predicted it. And it *was* a murder mystery they came to watch, not *Bambi*! Although... now I think about it, there was a death in that movie too, wasn't there." She sighed again. "Thank goodness we're showing *Grease* at the next film night. That shouldn't give anyone too many evil ideas."

"Except a few frisky teenagers perhaps," said Claire, remembering a few wild characters from the story, but Missy's eyes were now wide.

She had just one character in mind now—Sandy Olsson—and was getting an idea of her own. She quickly pushed the thought away and tuned back in.

"Well, if we get sued, we're done for," Flo was saying. "The coffers will be emptied and our good work will be kaput. Dreadful business! It's not like we ran the night to make a profit. It's all going back to the maintenance of the park and to the little kiddies in refugee camps. Shameful, I tell you!"

Claire reached a hand across to the older woman. "I'm so sorry. People can be thoughtless."

"And cruel," added Missy. "So it was this group, here, who organised the film night, was it?"

Flo nodded. "It was Alice Smith's idea, actually, and the rest of us chipped in here and there. We do our bit.

191

My friend Ronnie—you met her the other night too, I believe? Well Ronnie and I were on bar duty. Not actually selling beers, mind you. Nobody wants to buy booze from little old ladies!" She cackled suddenly. "We got ourselves some spring chickens who look the part—very handsome bunch. We just helped organise that part, that's all."

"So that's why you were seated so far back, near the bar?" said Missy.

"We wanted to keep an eye on proceedings, yes. I know Alice has a soft spot for young Brandon—he's the lad we hired to run the bar, see? But well…"

She shoved a piece of scone in her mouth and darted her eyes to the ceiling.

Claire and Missy shared a look, and then Missy said, "Bit dodgy is he?"

Flo finished eating, then said, "I wouldn't go that far, my dear. Lovely lad, really. It's just that, well, he has a few *issues*, that's all. And who wouldn't after everything that's happened to the poor lad."

"Happened? You mean at film night?"

"No, no, to his beloved mum." She pulled the teapot forward and inspected the contents. "She passed, you see, and so brutally, just a year or so back. He took it very badly, as you would. So Alice is… well, we *all* are really, keeping an eye out for the lad. His grandmother, Bette, used to be president of the Auxiliary many years ago, and we know she'd appreciate it."

"So what happened to his mother?" Claire asked, trying to keep her tone placid when all she could think was, *So Brandon's mum died brutally—that's a coincidence!*

She wondered now if the woman had also been strangled.

"Car crash, dear. Absolutely devastating. Really shook the poor lad up."

"Oh." Claire had to stop herself from adding, "Drats!"

"What happened?" asked Missy.

"Dreadful business. Poor Dana, she was simply crossing the street, minding her own beeswax, as you do, and the young woman came out of nowhere. Slammed into her on the pedestrian crossing. Cleaned her right up."

Claire's ears pricked up again. "A young woman, really? Who was she? Do they know? Did they catch her?"

"I don't know about any of that, dear, although they must have nabbed her because I heard she was drunk as a skunk. Terrible business, that. It really messed with young Brandon."

"Was Brandon also hit?"

"Oh no, he barely had a scratch, but it must have been hard, watching his mother... Well." She pursed her lips shut again. Then she tut-tutted. "Everybody struggles to deal with things *mentally* these days, don't you find? I suppose it *would* be very hard to see your beloved mum pass away right there in front of your eyes, knowing there's nothing you can do to help. It's no wonder he's struggled a bit since. That's why Alice gives him the work. I'm just not sure he's the right..."

She stopped midsentence again and pushed herself up from the table.

"That's enough of my gasbagging, boring you young ladies senseless."

"Oh, no, we don't mind," said Missy quickly, but Flo was already rinsing her cup at the sink.

"Just be sure to clean up when you're done if that's all right. We run a tight ship here; everybody pulls their weight."

Then she departed, leaving the two book club friends staring at each other jubilantly.

"Did we just uncover a motive for Kat Mumford's murder?" said Claire. "Do you think Kat might have had something to do with that car accident?"

Missy was bobbing her head like a bright pink yo-yo. "Yes! Oh my gosh, yes!" Then she lowered her voice as Claire held a finger to her lips. "Sorry, but wow! This could be it. Flo did say a young woman was driving. A young drunk. What if that was Kat?"

"Do you think Brandon recognised her on Saturday night and took his revenge?"

Missy didn't dare to nod now, almost couldn't speak. She grabbed Claire's cup and began cleaning up. Then she swung around to face her friend.

"We need to get Jackson to check the police report. Find out who the young drunk was that wiped out Brandon's mum. See if her name doesn't rhyme with rat!"

~~~~~~~

Alicia wondered how soon she could put Missy and Claire's excitable request to her detective boyfriend.

It was now eight thirty on Monday night. Lynette was out with some girlfriends, and she was currently entwined in Jackson's arms on her living room couch, watching the Ustinov version of *Evil Under the Sun*. They were having such a lovely evening, she was worried about ruining things. Would he be thrilled by their discovery or annoyed?

Jackson had appeared on her doorstep an hour earlier with some takeaway Chinese and the DVD, declaring, "Okay, let's see what all the fuss is about."

The truth was he wanted to get a better idea of the timeline.

"Witnesses keep referring to scenes in the movie rather than actual times of events that night," he told Alicia as he placed the disc in the set. "I'm trying to get my head around it."

He produced a stopwatch, a pad and a pen. Then, as he slipped off his shoes and settled on the sofa, she grabbed bowls and cutlery and placed them on the coffee table in front.

As Jackson pressed Play, he said, "Okay, so I recall the film officially started at eight fifteen because that's just as I got my first text about the overdose." He jotted something on his pad. "I know the Mumfords showed up a good ten, fifteen minutes after that, and I left ten minutes after that." He jotted something else down. "So be sure to tell me when the intermission hit. That's the time I want to lock in. I need to work out who saw what when."

And so they watched the film with an eye on the time, Alicia alerting Jackson to the exact scene when the film groaned to a halt, about an hour into the movie, just after the body of Arlena Marshall had been discovered and before Hercule Poirot pulled the shiny red hat up to reveal Arlena's dead, distorted face.

Jackson made a note of all that, but she was more interested in his view on the plot. She waited until it ended and then turned to him with enquiring eyes.

He shrugged, choosing his words carefully. He had a feeling a lot depended on this.

"Look, I enjoyed it, really I did, but..." She frowned. "Well, it was a *bit* outlandish, don't you think? I mean that kind of thing would never happen in real life now, would it? It's pretty over the top."

She blinked back at him. "But it's not real life. It's Agatha Christie." As though that explained everything.

He nodded quickly and fled to the kitchen with the dirty bowls.

Eventually, with the food cleared away and cups of green tea in front of them, Alicia decided to forget Jackson's derogatory comments and move on to Claire and Missy's discovery. Yet before she got a chance to open her mouth, he was pulling her into his arms.

"I'm sorry if it feels like I've been avoiding you," he said, "but it's been depressingly busy, and by that I mean lots of work, no results. We're getting nowhere fast."

"That's fine," she said, pretending it hadn't put her nose out of joint. "In fact, I may have some new information for you—might even help the case."

"Oh?"

A deep breath and then she told him what her friends had learned from the Ladies Auxiliary. "We know it's a long shot, but you've got to wonder—was Brandon's mother mowed down by a drunken Kat Mumford?"

Jackson stared at her. Hard. She gulped.

"What are you guys up to?"

She bat her eyelids innocently. There was something in his tone that forced her to lie.

"Nothing. They just wanted to help out, and by help I mean the film group, not you, *obviously*. They had some craft stuff they wanted to drop in. That's when they ran into Flo and got chatting."

"Ran into her did they?"

She sighed. "Okay, maybe they—*we*—did have an ulterior motive. But you said it yourself, you're getting nowhere and we wondered whether we might be able to, you know, find out more. And wouldn't it be amazing if that angle worked out?"

Jackson was frowning, but it wasn't really Missy and Claire he was cranky with. He recalled his conversation with Flo and Alice the week before, when he'd first spoken to the women from the Auxiliary. They had mentioned Brandon's mother and her premature death. He hadn't thought to enquire further.

*What an idiot he'd been!*

"They didn't mean any harm," Alicia was saying, misreading his frown.

"No, actually I'm grateful."

"You are?"

"Well, I'm not happy you poked your noses in. I can just imagine what Indira will say about that. But you might be onto something there. I can't believe I missed that."

He released Alicia and got to his feet. "I *knew* Brandon was hiding something. Maybe this is it."

"Where are you going?" she asked, watching as he pulled his shoes back on.

"I've got to get back to headquarters. I want to check

out the incident report for the crash that took out Brandon Johnson's mum."

Five minutes later, Alicia sat staring at the empty space on the sofa beside her, feeling a little morose. She was glad Jackson had a new lead, really she was, but she had not expected him to dump her quite so quickly to chase it up.

Still, there was a silver lining in all this.

It was pretty clear from Jackson's behaviour—his lack of genuine anger or annoyance—that he *did* need the book club's assistance and was happy enough to receive it. It also justified her ulterior motive: the sooner they helped solve this mystery, the sooner she'd get her boyfriend back.

Reaching for her smartphone, Alicia tapped in a message to Perry.

"Still up for AA? If so, let's meet outside the Centre tomoz at 5.20pm."

It didn't take long for Perry to tap her a reply.

"I'll drink to that!"

# CHAPTER 27

The driver's blood alcohol level had come back in at 0.11, making her just over twice the legal alcohol limit. No wonder she'd crashed her Subaru Liberty station wagon into Brandon's unsuspecting mother, Jackson thought as he scrolled down the screen, rereading the incident report.

Apart from a serious case of shock, the woman had sustained only minor injuries while Dana Johnson was killed instantly. She never knew what hit her.

It was now Tuesday morning, and Jackson was checking the information again, seeing if there was anything he'd missed from the previous night.

He felt a little foolish remembering how he'd rushed back to the office, almost elated, honestly believing that Claire and Missy were onto something. He fully expected to see Kat Mumford listed as the intoxicated driver who had caused Brandon's mother's death, or at the very least, Kat Mumford under another name.

But it was not to be.

The real culprit's name was Laura Jan McGinty, age forty-five, a store clerk from Wagga Wagga. Height: five five. Weight: nineteen stone.

He studied the woman's licence photo again. Whatever this driver's sins, whatever her secrets, being Kat Mumford was not one of them.

He thought about the film he'd watched last night and scoffed. Chucking a bit of tanning liquid on someone might have worked wonders for an Agatha Christie suspect, but nothing was going to turn the middle-aged, morbidly obese Laura McGinty into sparrow-sized twenty-seven-year-old Kat Mumford.

He groaned. That would have been way too easy.

"That would have been really bad policing," Indira added after she caught him staring at the screen soon after. "Don't you think someone would have joined the dots by now? We always do a thorough background check of all our victims at the start of every investigation, you know that."

"Yes, but I just wondered whether she'd changed her name since the crash. I just hoped…" He stopped. "It was worth checking."

She looked unconvinced. "You're chasing shadows now, Jacko. What's going on?"

"I'm angry," he snapped back. "We should have caught the bastard by now. He should be behind bars."

"It's been a little over a week, mate. Cut us all some slack." She lightened her tone and added, "Including yourself, hey?"

"It's been ten days. Ten whole days and nights. There's another film showing at the park this Saturday."

"So?"

"So aren't you even a little concerned?"

"You think our guy's going to strike again?"

"How do we know we're not dealing with a psychopath? A serial killer?" He swung around in his seat. "Has anyone checked whether there's been similar murders at film festivals before?"

Now she looked at him sideways. He really was shadow-boxing, but even she had to concede it wasn't the craziest idea she'd ever heard. She picked up the phone in front of him and stabbed a number in.

"Pauly? Got a sec?"

It took a good hour before Sergeant Paul Moore returned to Indira, a white notepad in hand, a defeated look on his face.

"You're not going to like it," he said, glancing at the notes he'd been making. "As far as I can tell, there's been nothing but misdemeanours and minor infringements. A bunch of people were caught with marijuana at a film festival in the Domain, and there's been some stolen handbags, that kind of thing at almost every event."

"No deaths?"

"One guy had a bad reaction to some dodgy MDMA at a jazz night in Bondi about two months back. Left him clinging to life in hospital, but he survived." He sounded disappointed. "But no homicides, no strangulations, no sexual assault—nothing even remotely resembling this case. Sorry."

Indira thanked him and turned to Jackson. "Happy now?"

Jackson nodded, but he wasn't feeling happy, not at all. He had a creeping feeling in his gut that just wouldn't dissipate.

"I'll go read through the witness reports again," he said, trying not to pout.

~~~~~~~

Alicia was trying very hard to look a little more "rock and roll" and a lot less "straight," Lynette's words echoing through her head as she smudged a bit of eyeliner around her eyes and pulled a dark T-shirt over her head.

"Honey, I keep telling you—alcoholism doesn't discriminate," Perry told her when she met him on the corner near the Rozelle Neighbourhood Centre where the AA meetings were being held. "Some of my poshest friends are pisspots."

Still, it didn't stop her from feeling out of place as she studied the dilapidated food van on one side of the street and the graffitied wall on the other, several scruffy smokers leaning up against it. She also spotted a homeless

200

man slouched nearby, swigging from a brown paper bag, and wondered if he ever found his way into meetings, then shook the sad thought away as she stepped inside.

This evening an Open Discussion Meeting was being held, and Perry assured her that didn't mean she had to *discuss* anything, and he reiterated this as they slipped into empty seats at the back of the old hall.

She had been expecting a circle of chairs, but here there were three rows, most seats already filled with people of various ages and ethnic backgrounds, some chatting as though old friends, others stiff-backed and looking more bored than bleak. Every single person offered them a heartening smile as they settled in.

The rich aroma of coffee enveloped the room, and Perry nodded towards a table on one side where he could see a half-empty plunger of coffee as well cups, milk and an urn.

"Refreshment?" he asked, and she shook her head.

"Let's wait until later. It's a good excuse to chat to people then."

He nodded, whispering, "Good plan."

At exactly five thirty, one of the men who had been chatting stood up and pulled his chair out, turning it back to face the group. He was in his midsixties, with thick, white-grey hair, flowing purple pants, and one dangling earring. Your classic "urban hippie" Alicia decided, with the warm eyes and nonjudgmental smile to match.

"Hey, everyone, great you could make it. Let's start with the Serenity Prayer, shall we?"

The rest of the group began reciting the words, their heads bowed, their eyes closed, and Alicia used the opportunity to check them out.

There were thirteen people here today, not including the chairperson, herself and Perry, and there were a wide variety of ages, from about twenty-five to seventy. There were more men than women, and some were dressed in business suits, others in T-shirts and jeans. Perry was right.

It was a mixed bunch.

When the prayer was over, the chairperson introduced himself as Trevor and then asked, "So, anyone new to AA?"

Everyone turned to look at Perry and Alicia, and she felt flummoxed for a moment, but Perry was already raising his hand.

"Please introduce yourself," said Trevor. "But no surnames, please."

"Sure. Well, hello everybody. I'm Perry," he said, "and I'm an alcoholic."

"Hello, Perry," they all chorused back.

Then they stared at Alicia, who batted her eyelids for a moment until Perry gave her a nudge.

"Oh, yes, um, I'm Alicia and I'm… well, I'm…"

"It's okay," said the Chair, gently. "You don't have to say it. Not if you're not ready."

"Hello, Alicia," the group called out in return, completely unfazed by her behaviour, reading it as nerves, no doubt, not guilt.

She smiled apologetically at Perry. Lynette was right. She was so straight she couldn't even pull off their first lie.

"First time to AA or just to AA in Rozelle?" Trevor asked, and Perry cleared his throat.

"Just to the Rozelle branch," he said, speaking for both of them.

"Then you know how it works. There's a list of names and numbers over at the refreshment table if you need to phone one of us. Feel free to do so any time. And just let me know at the end if you need a fresh copy of the Big Book."

He was referring to the AA bible, the one that contained the seminal twelve-step method, and Perry said, "Oh no, we're fine, thank you."

Trevor smiled. "Good-oh. So, before we start, is anyone celebrating an anniversary today?"

There was silence for a moment before an older man

with a receding hairline called out, "I'm on 355 days— almost there!"

The group clapped and Trevor smiled. "I look forward to celebrating with you in ten days, Timothy." He paused. "Now, before Jenny reads the preamble, I wanted to remind you all that we're discussing gratitude today, so be sure to have your thoughts on that ready to go. Okay, Jenny, take it away…"

As a middle-aged woman with dimples and a kindly smile stood up and began reciting something from a piece of paper, Alicia felt a cloak of warmth slowly slip around her shoulders, and it remained there for the duration of the evening.

She had never considered herself an alcoholic, nor had she felt the need to attend such meetings, but now that she was here, she could see the attraction of joining such a tribe. They seemed so sweet and supportive, and she wondered why Kat Mumford had dropped out of the program. Not one person had given her a judgmental look. They seemed kind and open to helping a complete stranger.

About thirty minutes and several emotionally charged discussions later, Trevor called a break to proceedings and suggested everyone "grab a cuppa."

"And drop some change in the tin by the urn if you can," he added. "Every bit helps."

*At last,* thought Perry, who wasn't feeling as enamoured as Alicia.

His brother, Theodore, still struggled with his addiction, and no sweet talks at a community centre seemed to be making a jot of difference. Last he'd heard, Theo had fallen off the wagon. Again. Perry wondered if his brother would ever see sixty; was certain he'd be on dialysis by then.

"Come on," Alicia whispered, "it's game time."

He shook the bleak thought away and followed her over to the table where a fresh pot of coffee was being prepared and the urn was bubbling away. They both selected a green tea bag from a glass jar beside it and made a cup, then gave each other a "good luck" smile.

While Perry followed some men outside, Alicia pocketed a copy of the attendees' names and numbers, then made her way to a group of women standing near the front, deep in conversation with Trevor. They were around Kat Mumford's age, and one looked similarly dressed, in a flowing paisley dress.

She and Perry had already prepared their backstory, and she mentally rehearsed it again as she slowly walked up. Trevor noticed her approach and said something quickly to the group before stepping away.

"The poor darling," the Kat lookalike was saying now, and the others were nodding along.

Alicia felt a prickle of excitement and wondered if they were discussing Kat's death, but as soon as they sensed her presence, they stopped talking and swung around with wide smiles.

She smiled back. "Mind if I join you guys?"

"No worries," said one woman, a tall brunette with wide, brown eyes.

"How are you doing?" asked the Kat lookalike, opening the circle to her. "Elsa wasn't it?"

"Alicia, actually. I'm okay. It's... well, it's been a tough month."

She cringed inside, feeling like a fraud. Anders's words echoed through her brain again. This *was* deeply unethical. There was no two ways about it.

"It'll get better," the third women said. She was very short with long, strawberry locks "Always does."

"Yeah, sure, right before it gets bad again!" said the copy-Kat, and she was smacked across the arm for that one. She laughed. "Sorry," she told Alicia. "I'm Zara, the *realist*."

"The cynic more like it!" said the first woman, who then introduced herself as Mia.

"And I'm Mia too," said the strawberry blonde, causing Alicia's eyebrows to rise.

"I know," said Zara. "How positively unoriginal of them! So, just moved to the area then?"

Alicia shook her head, taking this as her cue. "No, but my friend Perry and I aren't loving our local AA, so another friend suggested we come here. Said this group was really supportive."

"Oh? Who was that?" one of the Mias said, and the other Mia held a freckled hand up.

"Hey, guys, anonymity, remember?" She turned to Alicia. "You don't have to answer that."

"Oh no, it's fine." She *wanted* to answer that. "A woman called Kat." She waited but there was no visible reaction. She continued, "Kat loves this group." Alicia pretended to glance around. "Although I don't see her here tonight."

The three women were still staring at her blankly.

"Cat, like the animal?" one of them said, and Alicia nodded.

"Sounds a little familiar," said Zara, chewing on her bottom lip.

"I don't remember her," said the first Mia, the taller one. "Has she been in lately?"

"To be honest, I think she may have dropped out."

They all nodded knowingly.

"It happens," said Zara. She lowered her voice. "I notice we haven't just lost Mary this week. Brian hasn't been in lately either." She was addressing this to the others.

"Good riddance," spat tall Mia, earning a dark look from her shorter friend.

"Could just be having a bad week or a busy one," she suggested.

"Or maybe he's getting his fists patched up," said Zara, and she scored another quick swipe across the forearm for that one.

"Zara! Honestly, stop it! You'll have Trevor reading you the riot act again. You know how seriously he takes it all."

Zara giggled. "Sorry, but the truth hurts. Just ask his wife."

Before Alicia could enquire about that, tall Mia was saying, "I couldn't care less if Brian ever showed again, but I do hope Mary's doing okay. She's usually pretty regular."

"Yeah," said Zara. "I hope she hasn't fallen off the wagon and into a bottle of Dom Perignon."

This caused a little *ping!* to go off in Alicia's head.

"This Mary that you're talking about, she hasn't got long blond hair, has she?" She turned to Zara. "About your height?"

She wondered now if Kat had used a pseudonym—she wouldn't be the first to give a fake name at AA, surely? Alicia had even considered doing it herself. She also wondered if these women hadn't yet learned of Kat's fate.

Yet, annoyingly, all three were shaking their heads firmly.

"Nope, she's a lot taller, with dark, almost black hair," said the shorter Mia just as the chair began clapping his hands.

"Let's get on, folks! It's time!"

*Damn it*, Alicia thought. She still had so many questions to ask.

As she took her seat next to Perry, she noticed he wasn't exactly smiling either.

"How'd you go?"

He waved his hand to indicate so-so.

By the end of the second half, the group was gathering their things hastily and clearing out. Alicia had hoped the women would linger so she could question them again, but all three disappeared before she'd even picked up her handbag.

"Don't worry," Perry said. "There's always Thursday."

Trevor approached. "All good? Everything okay?" They nodded. "I didn't call on you today and I won't, if you don't want me to. But please feel free to raise your hands next time if you do want to say anything."

They nodded again.

Then Alicia said, "Actually I wanted to ask you about a friend of mine who promised to meet me here but hasn't made it."

He turned his eyes to her, his smile relaxed. "Oh yes?"

"Yes, we made a pact, a few weeks ago, to be here, but I didn't see her tonight. Her name's Kat."

Trevor's smile vanished. "Kat?"

"Yes, Kat Mumford."

He took a step backwards. "I never discuss other members. Never. And I don't expect my members to either." Trevor's warm tone had turned positively frosty.

"Of course, sorry. I guess I'm just worried. I hope she's okay."

He frowned at her, looking as though he was contemplating what to say, then he took another step back and said, "I've got to clean up."

He strode off to the other side of the hall and began stacking the chairs while Perry and Alicia shared a look, then grabbed their things and headed out.

"What was that about?" Perry asked as they hurried off.

"Don't know," said Alicia. "But how nervous did he look when I mentioned Kat?"

~~~~~~~

The inner-city wine bar was dimly lit, but being a Tuesday night, it did not take long for Alicia and Perry to spot their friends, who were gathered around a booth, clinking variously coloured drinks. They made their way across, first stopping at the bar to grab a glass of Pinot Grigio each, the irony not lost on either of them as they handed over the cash.

"What if someone from AA catches us here?" said Alicia, and Perry snorted.

"It'll just give us *more* credibility, honey, not less."

"So how'd you do?" asked Missy, swishing along the seat to make more space.

Alicia mimicked Perry's so-so motion with one hand, then proceeded to tell them what she had learned from the three women earlier that evening.

"So you didn't recognise anyone from film night, and only one of them vaguely remembers a woman called Kat?" said Claire.

Alicia nodded. "Not much help is it?"

"And this missing Mary. Could that be Kat Mumford?" asked Anders.

"That's what I wondered, but Mary didn't fit the description. I can tell you one thing though, that Trevor guy acted very odd, didn't he, Perry?"

Perry thought about it. "Maybe, or maybe he was just flabbergasted that you used Kat's surname, you naughty woman." He turned to the group. "I think our Chair takes the oath of confidentiality very seriously. Unlike someone else I met tonight."

He'd been waiting to reveal what he had learned although he wasn't sure it would be of any consequence. "So you know how I was chatting to those guys, out the front, Alicia? The ones having a cigarette in the break? Well, one of them was called Timothy, remember?"

"Oh yeah, the older guy, the one who was almost one year sober."

"Oh my God! Didn't Eliot say Tim was the name of Kat's sponsor?" Missy asked, and Perry's smile slipped a little.

"I got excited too, Missy, but this particular Tim says he only sponsors men."

"He's lying, obviously," said Lynette. "Protecting Kat's privacy."

"He *was* pretty convincing. Insists he never sponsors

women, always just blokes, although he reckons he's had such a bad experience of it he's never going to sponsor *anyone* again."

"Why?" asked Missy, sipping from a glass of what looked like sparkling mineral water.

"He told me the first guy he ever sponsored was an 'ungrateful hypocrite with a god complex' and the last guy was a 'violent hothead' who used to beat up his wife. Says a guy at AA tried to pull him into line a few times, but it didn't work. Maybe this hothead took a liking to Kat and wouldn't take no for an answer?"

"His name's not Brian is it? The hothead?" Alicia asked.

"Timothy didn't get a chance to say any more than that because Trevor came out for a smoke and everyone suddenly went quiet. Like I said, Trev's a killjoy." His eyes squinted. "Why do you ask?"

"Zara said something about Brian's fists, which sounded very suspicious."

"Sorry to sound like a killjoy as well, guys, but were you even at the *right* AA?" asked Claire. "If nobody remembers Kat, maybe she attends a totally different one?"

"Or maybe she lied to her husband about that and doesn't even go to AA," said Lynette. "Wouldn't be the first time."

"Or maybe her *husband* was lying and she didn't even have a drinking problem," said Anders, and they all looked at him inquisitively.

"I spoke to the coroner who did the autopsy," he explained, "just to ask about toxins, and he insists there's no sign of any drugs in her system. In fact, he was adamant that Ms Mumford was in excellent shape. I know she was young, but he found no signs of alcoholism in her liver either—usually there's some scarring or build-up of fatty tissues, that kind of thing. He was as surprised as I was to hear she was in AA."

"But didn't she have an awful lot of alcohol in her

system?" asked Claire.

"Sure, but that could be a one-off. There was no indication—physically at least—that that kind of binge-drinking was routine."

"So you don't believe she was an alcoholic?" said Alicia.

"I'm just telling you what the pathology says."

"So why did Eliot *say* she was an alcoholic? He must have known Jackson would investigate. Plus Trevor definitely seemed to know her. I could feel it! He recognised Kat's name when I mentioned it. I'm sure of it, Anders."

Claire said, "Let's just look at the facts for now. The victim, Kat Mumford, was most certainly drunk that night. Like, big-time drunk. That's indisputable. Maybe she was new to AA, had just started binge-drinking and wanted to nip it in the bud."

"That would explain her good physical condition," Anders conceded.

"What if she *said* she was going to AA but was really meeting up with a lover?" said Perry, heading off in a whole new direction.

They all stared at him, most of them sceptically.

"This is all so confusing!" said Missy, staring glumly into her water glass. "Is Kat in AA? Is she not? Is she at the Rozelle branch or somewhere else? And what does any of that have to do with a guy called Brian who beats up his poor wife?"

"Probably a dead end," said Lynette matter-of-factly, tapping at her smartphone. "However, I may have a new avenue to explore." She looked up at them all, eyes sparkling. "Guess who just texted me?"

"Your sugar daddy?" said Perry.

Lynette smirked. "Kind of. Brandon Johnson has just offered me work, Thursday night if I want it."

"That's lucky," added Missy.

"That was quick," said Claire.

"Is it even necessary anymore?" asked Alicia. "Jackson already looked into that. Kat Mumford had nothing to do with Brandon's mother's death."

"Doesn't change the fact that Brandon might have it in for drunken drivers," said Lynette. "Remember, Alicia, when Kat was fighting with her husband at the bar? How she said she had the car keys and he'd be stranded? She said something like, 'You can't leave me, I'm driving!'"

Alicia didn't remember those precise words, but it got her brain churning. "So you think Brandon heard that and thought, 'I've got to stop this drunken driver from destroying another family!'"

Lynette nudged her lips to one side. "Or maybe he just saw red and reacted. Spotted her on her own in the second half and seized the moment to avenge his mum's death on behalf of all drink-driving victims."

"Ridiculous," said Anders, bringing them both back to earth. "This is the man who runs bars, yes? Who serves *alcohol* for a living? You're saying he's on such an anti-alcohol crusade he would kill a drunk woman rather than have her drink and drive?"

They all looked dispirited, except Lynette.

"Only one way to find out for sure." She tapped her phone as she spoke. "I'm going to go along and bring up the subject of drinking and driving." She clicked Send and smiled mischievously. "See if our cute barman gets a little hot under the collar at that."

# CHAPTER 28

Jackson loosened his collar, staring at his screen just as his mobile rang. He spotted Alicia's number and smiled. It was now Wednesday morning, and he'd been meaning to call her back. He was just about to answer it when Pauly popped his head around the corner of his door.

"Got the coroner on line five for you, Jacko."

He nodded, sighed, then switched his mobile off and picked up the landline.

"Detective Jackson," came Scelosi's voice at the other end. "I've been waiting for your call."

"Sorry?"

"I've got the results for you."

"Results?"

Scelosi chuckled. "Been burning the wick at both ends, hey? Your overdose, Detective. I'm sorry it's taken so long, but Indira did say it wasn't a priority."

It took Jackson a moment to switch gears, and he did so as he switched the phone to his other ear. "Okay, I'm with you now, apologies, Frank. You're right. The Kat Mumford case is keeping us up nights. What did you find? Too much heroin, not enough sense?"

"Something like that. Your guy wasn't at the worst end of the scales, but there was some indication of habitual use of intravenous drugs, a few track marks on the forearms, a tiny bit of scarring. Took it too far this time though. Had such a large dose in his system his entire respiratory system shut down. He would have lost consciousness, then eventually fallen into a coma. Death not long after, it's all in my notes."

"Silly bugger. Any suspicious circumstances? Signs of coercion, that kind of thing?"

"Had some old bruising on his face, a broken tooth, but nothing too fresh. I'd say he was a fighter not a lover. Except when it came to the drugs. He clearly loved his opiates. There was one thing though."

"Oh?"

"Not that strange, really, when you think about it."

"Oh?" Jackson repeated.

"He had a fair bit of benzodiazepine in his system."

Jackson considered this. "Like Temazepam, the sleeping pill?"

"That's the one. That could have contributed to his death. Opiates and benzos don't mix."

"Yeah, well, didn't we just agree he loves his drugs? I'm surprised there wasn't a whole cocktail of crap buzzing about in that scrawny stomach of his."

"True. Still, you got to wonder: Why waste a shot of the top-shelf stuff if you're too sleepy to enjoy it."

"Except he didn't enjoy it, did he? He killed himself. Maybe he took some sleeping pills, and when they didn't work, he went for the heavy stuff."

"But you found him at a public car park, right? Who wants to fall asleep at a public car park?"

Jackson groaned. He didn't have the time or energy for this. "So do you know if it was an accident or suicide?"

Scelosi sighed now. "Do we ever really know? He certainly took more than his fair share of both drugs. Maybe with the sleeping pills in his system, he was groggier than usual, took more than he meant to of the heroin, might explain it. Sorry mate, you're the detective. You're going to have to work that one out for yourself. Anyway, it's all in the report, which is whizzing its way to your inbox as we speak." Then he chuckled. "If only the suicides would do the decent thing and leave a suicide note, hey? Put us all in the loop."

Jackson touched his mouse, bringing his computer screen to life. "Great, appreciate it, thanks, Frank."

"No worries." He went to hang up and then said, "Just one other thing, Jackson. What should I do with his effects?"

"Sorry, mate, you lost me again."

"His personal effects. We have a couple of cheap wrist bands, a fake Rolex and a wedding band."

"Wedding band? I don't believe he was married."

"My mistake, but the ring doesn't look cheap."

"Can you get it to his folks? I think their address is on the Next of Kin."

"Already tried. They told me in quite colourful language what I could do with that."

Jackson sighed again. He felt some sympathy for the unloved addict, but he was more interested in solving the murder of a young woman who may also have been an addict, but at least she was trying to clean up her act.

"Just send it across to me, thanks, Frank. I'll take care of it."

"No worries," Scelosi repeated, and this time he hung up.

~~~~~~~

Zara Cossington-Smythe gave Alicia a polite smile as she swept through the open doorway of the Tulip Café. If truth be told, she had been surprised to get the call from the AA newcomer, wasn't even sure who she was when she first picked up. But then Alicia had said something about AA and her friend Kat, and it all clicked into place.

"I've had some terrible news," Alicia told her over the phone twenty minutes earlier, "and I *really* feel like a drink."

"Don't do it!" Zara had responded, as Alicia suspected she would, and immediately arranged to meet her at the café just down from the Neighbourhood Centre.

"You're lucky you picked me," she had told Alicia. "I'm between jobs at the moment. There's no way the two Mias could spare you a second—they're both corporate types."

It was midday, midweek, and Jackson had ignored yet another of Alicia's phone calls. She knew he was busy—she understood that—but she was having great difficulty focusing on her own job and couldn't stop thinking about the case. She was determined to sort out the question of whether Kat Mumford really did attend AA and kept wondering whether they had lied to her about that.

Not that she would blame them if they had. After all, if someone strolled in tomorrow and started asking questions about a shaggy blonde called Alicia, wouldn't she want them to play dumb too? Whether it was standard procedure, protocol, or pure politeness, she had to concede she'd appreciate that kind of confidentiality if a stranger came asking.

The problem was, she didn't have the patience for protocol and politeness, and unwilling to wait for the next meeting to press them on it, Alicia decided to take matters into her own hands and look up Zara's details on the AA contact list. She had a hunch chatty Zara was her best shot.

Now reaching her table, the young woman glanced at the latte in front of Alicia and said, "Tell me that doesn't have a swig of something in it."

Alicia smiled. "Not yet. But I'm this close." She indicated an inch with her own fingers, and Zara frowned.

"Don't do anything silly for the next few minutes. I'm going to grab a juice."

A few minutes later Zara was seated beside Alicia, waxing lyrical about drinking and how everybody falls off the wagon every now and then, how it was "par for the course."

"You will move past this," she said, reaching for her pineapple juice. "So what's brought all this on then?"

Alicia grabbed a crumpled tissue from her handbag and feigned a sob. "The woman I was telling you guys about, the one who encouraged me to attend your AA?"

Zara sipped her drink, giving nothing away.

"I just found out why she wasn't there the other night."

"Because she gave you the wrong group?" Zara suggested.

Alicia blinked. "Oh, no, no, it's because she died. Last Saturday night."

"No!" Zara sounded genuinely surprised. She reached a hand across to Alicia. "I'm so *sorry*. That's terrible! No wonder you're reaching for the bottle. Overdose?"

"Sorry?"

"Did she, ah…?"

She indicated a slashing motion across her wrists, and Alicia gasped.

"No, no, she was murdered. Somebody killed her."

Zara's eyes widened considerably, and it was clear she wasn't expecting that. "Really? Another murder? This city is becoming unlivable!"

Alicia blinked a few times. That was not quite the response she was hoping for. She had been expecting Zara to fess up, to admit she knew Kat, had heard about the murder, and start spilling the beans. But here she was looking genuinely surprised.

Alicia squinted. "So you really never met Kat? She never came to the Rozelle group?"

"No, I told you that." Then it must have hit Zara, and she said, "Oh, you thought I was fibbing? Protecting your friend? God, I'm not Trevor! I couldn't care *less* if anyone knew I was attending AA. In fact, I use it to my advantage, darling." Her eyes twinkled. "Gets a lot of sympathy votes from the guys. Some are just glad they don't have to spend a fortune buying me expensive cocktails."

She laughed, then remembering what Alicia said, added, "I'm sorry about your friend, really I am. But I honestly never met her."

She took another sip of her juice, then had a fresh thought. "You know, I hate to speak ill of the dead and all, but maybe your friend was the one fibbing about AA. Lots of people do. We had an intervention for my bestie, Hannah, about oh a year or so back. She *promised* to attend meetings. Swore to get help. Never did of course. *Told* everyone she did, but I know otherwise. I've just let it go for now. You can't push people, honey. They have to push themselves. You can't save people from themselves."

She said it like it was a mantra, and Alicia nodded along.

"Reminds me of poor Mary," Zara continued.

"Mary and Brian, Mary?" she asked.

Zara frowned. "Oh, Mary and Brian aren't a couple. Goodness whatever gave you that idea?"

"Just the way you were talking the other night. You said they'd both dropped out..."

"Pure coincidence." She chuckled. "Mary would have a fit if she heard you say she was with Brian! No, Mary's all class. Brian, well, he's just a violent thug."

"Yeah, about that. How do you know he's violent?"

"He told us! Boasted about it, in fact, like it was some badge of honour. Said he was only at AA to get off some domestic violence charge, said he was told it would stand up better in court or something. But he seemed to hold it against his poor wife, like it was all *her* fault he was sitting there, listening to us lot." She shuddered. "I couldn't stand the odious little man." She smiled wistfully. "I mean, I know what Trevor was saying, 'You can't stop violence with violence,' but I was secretly glad when Eliot beat him to a pulp. Brian deserved everything he got."

Alicia dropped her coffee cup with a clunk. "What?"

"What?" Zara repeated, batting her eyelids.

"Did you just say Eliot?"

Zara reached a hand to her lips. "Oh God, there I go again. Don't mention that to Trevor, he'll have a coronary! I shouldn't be talking out of school, but, well you're one of us now, aren't you?"

"Eliot Mumford?" Alicia was still trying to catch up.

"Well, I don't know his *surname*. I mean, I might be liberal with first names, but *surnames*? I draw the line at that." Her eyes squinted. "You know him, huh?"

"He was married to the murder victim I was just talking about."

"Your friend? Wow, okay, so that was what Trevor was going on about last night. We knew there'd been a death in the family, but he didn't give us the deets." She thought about it. "Small world, huh? That must be why your friend's name sounded so familiar. Eliot used to call her his 'little kitten.' I never met her though, not properly you understand? None of us socialise outside of AA. That would be sacrilege!"

Alicia held up a hand. "Hang on, now I'm really confused. So Kat *was* a member of the Rozelle group, right?"

"No, I told you that."

"So how do you know Eliot?"

Zara looked as mixed up as Alicia felt. "Through AA! *He's* the member of our group. Didn't he tell you that?"

# CHAPTER 29

"No, he did not tell me that," came Jackson's grumpy reply when Alicia repeated this conversation over the phone to him an hour later.

She was back at work, attempting to catch up on some content for a parenting website this time, but could not get Zara's words out of her head, and after unsuccessfully calling several book club members (all busily catching up on work too, she imagined), she finally got a return call from her boyfriend.

He was not happy to hear about her clandestine trip to AA with Perry and told her as much.

"Look, you can stick me in the naughty corner later," she had said, cutting him off. "But what I've discovered may change your mind."

"Go on then. It better be good."

And it was. So much so, he wanted her to report to his office pronto.

"And bring that ratbag Perry. This needs to go straight to Singho. She's in charge." He paused. "And she'll be furious when she finds out what you've done."

"But we—"

"Look, I'll try to smooth it over before you get here. How soon can you come?"

Alicia groaned. "You're not exactly enticing me in."

"Your fault for sticking that nose where it don't belong." He softened his tone. "Come on, it's time to face the music. I promise she can bark, but she won't bite."

In fact, the first thing Detective Inspector Singh did when Alicia and Perry presented themselves at her office door less than an hour later was to snap both their heads off.

"I cannot *believe* you took it upon yourselves to interfere with a police investigation," she began, the previous Sunday's friendly tone now but a distant memory.

"We're sorry," Alicia began, but she cut her off.

"I doubt that. Jacko has already informed me of your interference in previous cases. I have a feeling this is standard procedure for you lot. Who the *hell* do you think you are? Do you have *any* idea how you may have compromised this investigation? If my perp ends up getting off on a technicality that you guys have brought about, I will throw the book at you both—and I'm not talking a bloody crime novel!"

Alicia recoiled, but Perry simply shrugged and stood his ground.

"You're right, DI Singh, it was terribly remiss of us," he said matter-of-factly, and she flashed her eyes at him. "Since it was all obtained illegally, we'll be sure to keep it to ourselves and head back to work." He glanced behind him to the door.

"Don't get smart with me, Mr Gordon," Indira snapped back, then took a deep, calming breath.

Alicia could tell her sense of outrage was wrestling with her natural curiosity, and she was eager to hear what they had discovered.

Indira exhaled loudly and waved them into the two chairs in front of her desk, saying, "You're not going anywhere. Sit down."

She then picked up her desk phone and stabbed some numbers in. A second later she said, "Get your butt in here. You might as well hear what your interfering buddies have got to say."

Then she hung up and turned back to Perry and Alicia, the latter withering further under Indira's furious gaze.

Over the next twenty minutes, the two friends filled Indira and Jackson in on everything they had learned at AA. They took them through their various conversations, and then Alicia relayed exactly what Zara had told her over coffee earlier that day.

"So this Zara woman says it was Eliot Mumford who had signed up to AA, not Kat?"

Alicia nodded. "She only knew his first name, but it has to be the same Eliot. She said he called his wife 'kitten,' so it has to be him."

Indira looked at Jackson. "So why'd he lie about that?"

Jackson shrugged. "Why indeed."

"I guess it is kind of embarrassing," said Perry, and Indira glanced back at him.

"What?"

"Well, it's hard enough admitting you have a drinking problem, must be even harder to admit you fell off the wagon the night your wife was killed. Maybe he feels bad about that. Maybe if he'd been sober, he could have protected her."

Indira cocked her head to one side. "Well thanks for that, Dr Gordon. Last I checked you were a palaeontologist not a psychiatrist."

Perry folded his arms with a huff. He'd had just about enough of this snippy detective. He and Alicia had just handed her an extraordinary lead, yet all she wanted to do was bite their heads off.

"You were happy enough to ask for our views last Sunday," he said, mostly under his breath.

She ignored that and said, "I still don't see what any of it has got to do with Kat Mumford's murder." Then she added quickly, "And I'm referring this question to *Detective Jackson* now. Thanks, Doc."

Perry huffed loudly again, and Jackson tried not to smile. He was used to Indira's temper, it rolled off him like water.

"Well, it proves Eliot Mumford's a liar for starters. Makes you wonder what else he's been lying about."

She nodded. Sighed. "We need to speak to him again."

"I also think we should get Alicia's new bestie in," Jackson said, adding, "Zara from AA. Let's show her some mug shots of Scotty and Davo. I'm wondering whether one of them might be Brian, under another name."

Indira held a finger up. "Remind me who Brian is again."

Perry spoke up. "He's the 'violent hothead' who was beating his wife up."

"And more importantly," added Alicia, a little meekly lest Indira jump down her throat too, "he's the one Eliot had a fight with."

Indira glanced at Jackson, and he smiled.

"Exactly. Maybe Brian is really Scotty or Davo? Maybe he didn't like being walloped by a trendy hipster and decided to take his revenge out on the trendy hipster's wife? Sounds like picking on women was more his style anyway. Maybe he followed them to the park or just spotted them there by coincidence and saw his chance to get even."

Finally Indira smiled. As far-fetched as it all was, she liked the sound of that.

Unfortunately for the homicide squad, Indira's smile did not last long. No sooner had Zara Cossington-Smythe been brought in, looking both outraged and delighted by the request to identify a suspect, she quickly informed them that "Bully Brian from AA looks nothing—I repeat, nothing!—like the two men from the film night."

Jackson had earlier swept Alicia and Perry from the office, telling them it might be best to put a brake on their "meddling."

"Indira's not like me," he said as he shepherded them towards the elevators. "She likes to play by the rules."

"You think?" Perry spat back at him.

"We'll behave," Alicia said more gently, not daring to mention that Lynette was booked to pour beers with Brandon the very next night. She wondered how easily Lynette could cancel that gig and whether she really wanted her to.

Once Zara arrived, Jackson showed her straight to Indira's office where she produced the mug shots of Scott Jalezic and David Crow.

"Who are they?" Zara enquired.

"We're hoping you can tell us that," Indira said. "Do you know or at least recognise either of these men?"

"Hardly," she said. "Should I?"

Indira's smile deflated, and Jackson sighed. He was really hoping his hunch would pay off and not just because it would mean case closed. It might also redeem Alicia in his partner's eyes.

Indira was saying, "So neither of these men goes to your AA? You can tell us, Zara. This is a murder enquiry."

"I *would* tell you, honestly. But I've never seen either of them in my life."

"So neither of them is this man Brian whom you say was beating up his wife?"

Zara blushed. "I am going to kill Alicia! She's going to get me in so much trouble with Trevor. I thought she was a *genuine* alcoholic. She's such a liar!"

"Just answer the question please, Ms Cossington-Smythe."

"No. Urgh. Brian's like a weedy thing, scrappy goatee. I mean he's got similar tatts, but he's super skinny. Was a muso, I think. I guess you'd find him handsome if you were into sinewy Iggy Pop types. Bit too punk rock for me. Can't say I'm exactly sorry he's dropped out."

A bell began clanging away in Jackson's head. He said, "You don't happen to know Brian's surname do you?"

She gave him a pointed look. "We don't use surnames. Does *no one* understand how AA works?"

"Okay, but this Brian guy. You say he dropped out of

AA? Since when?"

She thought about it. "I guess I last saw him, oh…" She tapped her long nails on the tabletop. "Let me think. He always comes nights. He wasn't there last night or the Thursday before that. But I think he was there the Tuesday before that."

"So he's been missing now for over ten days?"

"Well, I don't know if he's missing as such. He's dropped out. Most people do from time to time. It's standard procedure."

*Nah,* thought Jackson, *it's too much of a coincidence.* "And his name is Brian? Skinny, late thirties, you think?"

"Something like that."

Indira was watching Jackson closely, her eyebrows arched, but he ignored her and asked, "You told Alicia he had a wife. Did Brian wear a wedding band and a fake Rolex?"

She shrugged. "Never got that close to notice." Then she glanced at Indira. "Thank God."

Indira was still staring at Jackson. "What's going on, Jacko?"

He waved her off. "I'll tell you about it later."

She eyed him suspiciously, then turned back to Zara. She had a hunch of her own. "So the guy who runs the meetings, his name is Trevor? Correct?"

"Correct."

"Does he have grey hair? In his mid to late sixties?" Zara nodded. "Can you tell me, does he have a moustache?"

Now she shook her head.

"Did he *ever* have a moustache?"

"Not since I've known him, and I've been going for almost six months."

Indira said, "Fine, you can go, Zara. Thanks very much for your time."

Later, when Zara had left and it was just the two of

them chewing on Styrofoam coffee cups, Jackson smiled at Indira and said, "So my earlier theory that Mo Man could be Kat's sponsor doesn't sound so crazy to you now, huh? You think Mo Man might be this guy Trevor?"

She said, "He could've been wearing a fake moustache. That might be why Eliot never noticed him. Only one way to find out." She stood up.

"AA are big on keeping secrets," Jackson reminded her. "They'll just slam the door on you."

Indira smiled. "Ah but I know someone else who's pretty secretive, and he wouldn't dare slam the door on this gorgeous face."

# CHAPTER 30

Eliot Mumford was happy enough to open his door to DI Singh and barely bat an eyelid when she accused him of lying about AA. Perhaps he had been anticipating her questions, or perhaps it really was of "little consequence," which is what he insisted over and over as he poured both detectives a glass of water from the dispenser on the front of his enormous, two-door fridge.

He had cleaned the place up considerably since their last visit and looked like he'd finally showered and changed his clothes. He had a woollen beanie on his head, despite the warm weather, and his beard looked freshly trimmed.

Perhaps he was now in the acceptance stage, thought Jackson, eyeing him off.

"So why did you lie to us about AA, Eliot?" Indira was asking as he handed her a glass.

"Why do you think? I was embarrassed."

"Embarrassed?"

He pulled out a stool and sat down. "Yes, of course. Don't you think I haven't been beating myself up about this all week? I'm a drunk, Indira, an alcoholic. Happy now? And if I hadn't fallen off the wagon so spectacularly the other night, my beautiful little kitten might still be alive."

"Why all the secrecy?" said Jackson, whose BS monitor was buzzing loudly. There was something about this guy that was starting to grate.

"Like I said, I was embarrassed."

"You lied to us."

He shrugged. "A little white lie." He smiled sweetly at them both.

"A bloody big fat one I'd say," said Jackson, and Indira held a hand up.

She said gently but firmly, "Listen Eliot, we are trying very hard to bring your wife's killer to justice. We've been working around the clock. It really doesn't help her cause, or yours for that matter, to have people lie to us. I don't care how trivial or irrelevant or *embarrassing* you might think it is. You should have told us the truth on that."

Eliot looked suitably chastened. He dropped his head to the side and looked up at her through thick brown lashes. "I'm really sorry, honestly Indira. It was stupid of me. I get that. I just didn't think it had anything to do with Kat's death, so I didn't want to muddy the waters."

"Muddy the waters? It's practically a mudslide!" Jackson said. "We think someone from your AA may have some involvement in your wife's death."

He straightened up. "Really? Who would do such a thing?"

"Tell us about Brian."

"Brian?" Eliot blinked rapidly, his eyes darting between them. "From AA? What's that dirtbag got to do with this?"

"Is it correct that you got into a fight with him after an AA meeting one night?"

Eliot glanced between the detectives again, looking confused.

Indira said, "Just answer the question please, no lies this time."

"Sure, I slapped him around a bit. Lock me up if you want, but at least it was a fair fight. I wasn't half his size like his poor fiancée or wife or whatever she is."

"Did you see him beat her up?"

He hesitated. "Well, no. I've never met the woman, but he told us all about it in the sessions. Bragged about it in fact!"

"So how do you know she was half his size?" Jackson asked

"I don't. I'm just guessing. He was a bully. Look, I probably shouldn't have done it, but I just wanted him to get a taste of his own medicine, that's all."

"Do you know this man's surname?" said Jackson and, when he shook his head, added, "Any ideas?"

"No. Trevor makes sure of that."

"Did you see Brian at the film night in Balmain or anywhere in the vicinity that night?" Indira asked this time.

"No." He brushed his beard. "You can't really think Brian's responsible? Do you think he killed my little kitten because of what I did to him?"

He looked appalled by the thought.

"We're just checking all possibilities, Eliot. That's our job. You need to think clearly for me now, please. Did you *ever* see Brian anywhere near your home, your business, anywhere near Kat? Did she ever mention running into him, anything like that?"

"No, I promise, nothing like that. God, if I knew he was lurking about, he'd be the one throttled, not my beautiful wife."

"When did you last see Brian?" Jackson asked, and Eliot gave it some thought.

Like Zara, he recalled Brian attending AA about two Tuesdays back.

"And why haven't *you* gone back to AA?" Jackson asked.

"How do you know I haven't?"

"Just answer the question, Eliot." This was Indira and she, too, was losing her patience.

"For God's sake people. I just lost my *wife*. Last thing I need is to hear how Timmy's daddy used to expect straight As when he was in high school, and how poor Zara never made the ballet ensemble and isn't life hard. Boohoo. I just lost the love of my life!"

Indira nodded, giving him a sympathetic smile,

but Jackson wasn't feeling it.

"I would have thought they could help you through it," he said.

"You don't know shit," Eliot spat back.

Indira stood up. "Okay, that'll do it for now."

She gave Jackson a nod, and he eyeballed Eliot a moment longer, then stood up and followed her back through the house and towards the front door.

At the doorway, Indira turned back.

"You do need to process all this," she said. "Be sure to get some help before it's too late."

"You let him off a bit lightly," Jackson said as they strode back to their car.

"The man's right, Jacko. He's an alcoholic, and he just lost his wife. I don't think he needs us to beat him up when he's doing a pretty good job of that already."

"You're just defending him because he attacked that violent Brian," Jackson said and knew he'd gone too far.

She railed on him, her eyes fiery. "I do not condone vigilante justice, Jackson. You know that. Never have, never will. Eliot should have come to the police with his suspicions, not beaten that guy up. For all I know, that's what caused his wife's death. Brian might have taken out his anger on Kat."

"But we don't know that, do we?"

"No, we don't! Which is why I left the *victim's* husband alone and am heading back to the office to see if I can find some actual evidence. Okay?"

"Okay. I'm sorry. I just can't warm to the guy. There's something about him that gets up my nose."

"Well, it must be very bloody clogged by now because you've said that about every suspect in this case. You know that, right?"

He plunged his hands in his pockets but did not answer.

"Come on, let's get back to the headquarters, and I'll

get you some tissues, see if we can't blow a few suspects out of there."

He smiled at her then, glad to defuse the tension and said, "Fine. But first can you drop me at the lab?"

And to her curious glance he added, "I have to see a man about a dog."

~~~~~~~

Frank Scelosi was just peeling a set of blood-splattered gloves from his hands when Jackson walked in.

"Welcome to my humble abode," he said, waving the clean hand around the lab. "It's a rare day when we get one of you suits fronting up. I thought you preferred to read your autopsies online where the stench can't infiltrate."

"Actually I'm here for that package."

"Package?"

"Yes, you know the one belonging to my overdose. Brian Donahue."

He had a tingling feeling the Brian who'd recently had a hot shot of heroin on a lonely rooftop could be the same Brian who attended AA with Eliot Mumford. Zara's description sounded spot on. Of course Brian was a pretty common name around these parts, and even if it *was* the same Brian, he didn't know how that was going to progress the Mumford case. If anything, it wiped out a really decent suspect.

There's no way Brian Donahue could have killed Kat Mumford for revenge as Indira had suggested. He was already dead of a drug overdose a good two hours *before* Kat was strangled.

Still, Jackson didn't like coincidences, and he was determined to find out. He was wondering whether there was some kind of identifying object among Brian's possessions, something to prove his membership to AA.

He knew both Zara and Eliot could probably identify

him from his licence photo, but he was hoping to circumvent that.

"Sorry, mate. I handed Mr Donahue's things to a courier this morning," Scelosi was saying. "Probably being placed on your desk as we speak."

Jackson growled. "That'd be right."

"While I've got you," Scelosi said, washing his hands at the sink. "I've got something interesting to show you."

Jackson braced himself as Scelosi dried his hands then pulled on a fresh set of gloves and reached towards what looked like a chocolate milkshake.

~~~~~~~

The book club was gathered in Perry's living room, devouring gourmet pizza. All except Missy, who was there but insisted she'd already eaten, triggering looks of surprise from the others, and Anders, who gave no excuse and simply bailed for the night.

They had been meeting almost daily yet still had so much to discuss, starting with what Zara had told Alicia over coffee that day and ending with Zara's insistence that neither of the cap-wearing guys from film night was Bully Brian from AA.

"Or at least that's what she told Jackson," Alicia added.

"That doesn't mean Brian from AA *wasn't* at the film," said Perry. "We never met him; how would we know? He could have been sitting anywhere in that audience, keeping his head down so Eliot Mumford didn't spot him, then seizing the chance to kill Kat when Eliot moved away."

"Seems an overreaction to being beaten up," said Claire.

"Not at all. His ego was probably bruised the most, and he wanted to teach Eliot a lesson. Couldn't take the larger guy out so went for his usual prey, a small defenceless woman."

"You know, I was thinking," said Missy, and Perry looked horrified. She smirked at him and continued. "There's an awful lot of dodgy partners in this case. There's Brian the bully from AA, there's the pregnant woman's ex—didn't she say something to Jackson about being well shot of him?"

Alicia shrugged. "It sounded more like he was never really in the picture to start with."

"Okay, but then there's also that woman from the chemist. Remember, you were telling us about your night out with Jackson, the one where you went to the Jolly Codger?" She giggled. "You know that's so similar to the name of the hotel in *Evil Under the Sun*, right guys? That one was called the Jolly Roger. Did anyone pick that up? I mean, what are the chances, hey?"

Alicia said, "That's where the similarities end, Missy. I can assure you, if Poirot had stumbled into the Jolly Codger, he'd be lucky to get out alive."

She giggled again at that. "Anyway, you and Jackson went and interviewed that woman from the chemist, Demi someone or other?"

"Danni Ligaro?"

"Yes! And remember how Danni mentioned an abusive boyfriend?"

"Yeees," Alicia said slowly. "That's right, said she'd just dumped him, he was 'good with his fists.'" Her eyes widened. "What are you thinking?"

"Could the bully from AA, the one Eliot beat up, could he be the guy that Danni Ligaro was talking about?"

Alicia stared at her, trying hard to recall if Danni had mentioned her ex-boyfriend's name. She was sure she hadn't. "It's a major stretch," she said eventually.

"Yes, except that Danni went to the film night too, didn't she? She was the one who told Scotty and Davo about it. So we know she was at the crime scene at the time. Maybe she hasn't really broken up with her ex, or maybe he followed her there or was going to meet his two mates. Whatever. Maybe he spotted the Mumfords and saw his chance. When Eliot moved away, he slunk down next to Kat and... Well, you know the rest."

She finished with a bob of her curls while the rest of them looked at her with varying degrees of doubt.

Lynette said, "As far as stretches go, Missy, that's like Downward Dog on steroids."

"Still," Missy persisted, "you could always mention it to Jackson, Alicia, and get him to check."

Alicia recoiled at the thought. "I'm not sure Jackson's too thrilled with all our snooping, guys, so might be best not to mention that for now. Speaking of which..." Alicia turned to her sister. "Any chance you can cancel the bar gig with Brandon tomorrow night?"

Lynette looked outraged. "Why would I want to do that?"

"Jackson has asked us to step back, to stay out of it, so..."

"So too bad! I've already committed to the shift, and I'm not in the habit of bailing at the last minute. Plus it sounds to me like Jackson and Indira are flapping about like beached whales and can do with all the help they can get."

"Yes, but..."

"But Brandon's still a viable suspect." Lynette interrupted. "Yet you said it yourself, he's lawyered up and they haven't got a chance of getting him to talk." She recognised the anxiety flickering behind Alicia's eyes and softened her tone. "It'll be fine, sis. I'll go in very gently and just ask a couple of casual questions, see if I can't help them cross another suspect off the list. Besides"—she smiled—"I could do with the extra cash. There's a gorgeous pasta maker at Myers with my name written all over it."

# CHAPTER 31

The large wooden deck was bursting with revellers, some drinking in the extraordinary cliff view, most greedily quaffing wine and canapés, and Lynette was so swept off her feet she barely had time to blink, let alone query Brandon Johnson about his attitude to drunk drivers and whether he wanted to throttle any of them.

As she glanced across to Brandon now, watching him shovel ice into an empty carafe, she wondered if she was wasting her time.

Alicia had certainly tried to stop her from coming, fearful both for her sister's safety and her boyfriend's relationship with his boss. But it didn't feel right to cancel on Brandon at such late notice, especially as she had already been told that Wally Walters had bailed and he was one man short.

And so she had kept her shift, joining Brandon and two female bar staff, popping corks and serving wine and getting the crowd sufficiently drunk, which seemed to be the directive from the publicity women who were pushing some foul-smelling perfume from an Italian designer that probably smelled better with each glass of vino.

It was only when the event came to a grinding halt at exactly eleven, and the PR ladies swanned off, shooing the drunken stragglers in their wake, that Lynette found her chance to have a decent conversation.

Surveying the mess around her, she grimaced. Brandon was not the best employer she'd ever worked for. Not only had he left them short-staffed, he'd spent half the night on his mobile phone and the other half flirting with one of the publicists.

"Thanks for doing this," he said as he tipped the remains of a glass of wine into a potted plant. "You know I can't pay you any overtime, right?"

It explained why the other staff had taken off at the first opportunity, leaving her all alone with the suspect. While she felt safe enough, Lynette knew that Alicia would have a fit and just hoped it would all be worth it.

She was really going to earn that pasta maker tonight.

Taking the wine glass from him, she quickly rinsed it before slotting it into one of the boxes, then sealing the box up.

"That's fine," she told him, "happy to help." Then, keeping her tone casual, she added, "Did you see how much champers some of those women were throwing back? I hope they were all catching cabs home."

There was no reply, and she looked up from the box to find him back on his phone, texting something. Perhaps he hadn't heard her.

She tried again. "You know, it's amazing how many people drink and drive these days."

Brandon stopped tapping at his phone and stared at her a moment. His eyes narrowed slightly, and his jaw seemed to tense before he said, "Yeah, drink-drivers are scum."

"Yes! Total scum! I had a friend who got done for drink driving, and I have to say, I was not sympathetic. Not one bit."

He continued staring at her, his eyes now slits in his head. "What are you going on about, Lynette?"

She gave a quick shrug. "Nothing. I'm just saying…"

"Let's just finish up, okay? I'm beat."

She nodded, then reached for a dirty champagne flute and sighed. *What was she going to do now? She could hardly push him on it or ask about his mum. That would be way too obvious; it would give the game away.*

She sighed again. Maybe grumpy Anders was right all

along. Maybe this was all just a colossal waste of time. It was certainly an arrogant attempt on her part to solve what was clearly a complex crime.

How delusional they all were—Missy and Claire, Alicia and Perry—thinking they could outsmart the dumb detectives. They had all dashed off on their little interrogations, and yet what did they have to show for it? Nothing!

The truth was, people didn't miraculously confess to murder because a ditzy librarian or a shaggy-haired journalist, or yes, even a leggy young blonde asks the right questions.

*No wonder Anders has lost patience with us all*, she thought as she finished with the glasses and started folding tablecloths. *We think we're so clever, but really, we're just wasting everybody's time, including our own.*

Then she thought about that pasta maker and reached for a broom.

It took another hour of sweeping and scrubbing and packing and stacking, and they finally had the bar cleared away and the veranda sparkling clean.

"Thanks for staying back tonight," Brandon said as she helped load the last of the boxes into his van. "You can clear out now if you like."

He was parked in the steep driveway to the vacant Vaucluse mansion where the event had been held, but Lynette's car was about two blocks back, so she said her goodbyes, grabbed her oversized handbag, and began striding towards her Torana, using her iPhone light to help guide her way.

It was not until she was almost at her vehicle that she started scrambling through her bag for her denim jacket. The chill was setting in, but she couldn't find it among her things.

*Damn it.* She must have left it at the house. Groaning, Lynette swiftly turned back.

She was just coming around the bend in the road, about ten metres from the driveway, when she heard Brandon's voice. He was talking to someone. She wondered who it could be, certain that they had been the last two people on the premises. She looked up and saw that he was speaking into his mobile, his back to the street.

"Hey, that's not my fault," he said. Then, "I'll do things much smarter at the next film night, I promise."

Lynette stopped in her tracks.

*Hang on, what?*

"I'm telling you," he continued, "there won't be any cops, not this time."

She felt a flash of curiosity followed quickly by a prickle of alarm.

*Brandon must be discussing the night of the murder!*

Lynette froze for just a second before ducking behind a parked Mercedes, her pulse galloping like a racehorse.

"Just bring the cash," he was saying, "and I will make it happen."

Straining to hear him above her thumping heart, Lynette slowly poked her head back out. *Who was he talking to?*

"Yeah… Yes! Stop panicking. I told you already, I'll take care of it… She won't know what hit her, I can promise you that."

He laughed a little malevolently, then without warning, swung his head around and stared in Lynette's direction. She flung herself onto the tar between the Mercedes and a Maserati that was parked behind it.

*Had he seen her?*

*Was she about to be discovered?*

There was a long pause, and then she heard Brandon say, "Look, I'd better go. I'll see you on Saturday. Just give me the signal, and I'll do the rest."

There was another pause that seemed to extend forever before she heard the sound of a door slamming, feet crunching, and then a second door opening and shutting.

The car engine roared to life, and she waited a few more minutes while she heard the vehicle reverse out of the driveway, correct itself and then zoom past her, a terrifying sweep of headlights before it whooshed away.

Still crouched between the cars, Lynette let out a long, tremulous sigh. Her heart was thumping, her pulse was racing, and her mind was telling her that the Murder Mystery Book Club might not be such a waste of time after all.

~~~~~~~

"Oh my God, Lynny! Did he *see* you?" Alicia asked, alarmed when her sister recounted the incident back at their house soon after.

"Hope not," she replied a little too casually for Alicia's liking.

"I can't believe you were there with him in a dark, empty street. All alone! What if he'd found you cowering behind the car? What if he'd...?"

It didn't bear thinking about.

Alicia had stayed up waiting for her sister to get home, and it was almost one in the morning by the time Lynette pulled her Dr Martens boots off and accepted the herbal tea her sister was holding out.

"Stop stressing, Alicia. I'm *fine*, although I lost my best denim jacket thanks to bloody Brandon." She blew on the top of her cup. "So what do you think he meant by all that?"

The two sisters mulled over Brandon's words for many minutes, trying to come up with an innocent explanation for lines like, "there won't be any cops this time" and "just give me the signal and I'll do the rest."

"What does he mean 'she won't know what hit her?'" said Alicia, "and who the hell was he talking about?"

"You think he's a hit man?"

Lynette burst into giggles then, sounding just like

Missy. She was clearly full of nervous energy, adrenaline still bouncing about her system, and she tried to swallow back her laughter as she said, "He doesn't *look* like Al Pacino!"

Alicia scowled. "This is not funny, Lynette. Someone's life could be in danger here. We need to tell Jackson."

"No way! You said yourself he's losing his patience with us. He'll only bring Indira in, and she'll be even more furious than he is. Besides, it'll just ruin everything. They'll drag Brandon in for questioning, he'll deny everything, say I misheard him, and it'll completely blow my cover."

"Who cares? You're not working for him again, right?"

"I have to! I've signed up as part of his bar team for the next Cinema Under the Stars this Saturday."

Alicia stared at her, horrified. "You can't possibly do that! Not after what you just heard!"

"Now more than ever, Alicia. I have to go and see what he's up to. I might be able to catch him in the act."

"I don't want you to catch him in the act! I want to call Jackson and get *him* to catch him in the act."

"Brandon will spot Jackson a mile off, and it'll all be called off, whatever it is he's planning. This is the only option. He's already suspicious of the police. If he gets even a whiff of an undercover cop, it'll all be over and we'll be no closer to solving this thing."

"I thought you said it wasn't our job to solve Jackson's cases."

Lynette stared at her. "Since when do you listen to me? Come on, we're so close. Don't lose your nerve now."

Alicia thumped her cup down on the table. "I can't let you do it, Lynny. Forget it. It's just too dangerous."

"Now who sounds like Anders Bright? It's a public park, Alicia. I'll be fine!" Lynette softened her tone. "How about this: Why don't you and the rest of the book club come along? Pull up a blanket and keep an eye on things, make sure I'm safe."

Alicia thought about it, her frown relaxing slightly.

She wasn't sure they'd be much help, but it was better than sending Lynette in alone.

"And don't forget there's several security guards on duty, yeah?" Lynette continued. "I'll be perfectly safe, I promise. They'll protect me if Brandon gets out of line."

"Like they protected Kat Mumford?" Alicia said, feeling her stomach tighten again.

# CHAPTER 32

"We ever find those overpriced specs?" Indira asked, stretching out as she leaned her chair back.

It was Friday morning, almost two weeks since the murder, and still no arrest. Jackson looked up from his desk.

"Kat Mumford's?"

"No, Miss Marple's."

"Sorry," he said, "I've got my head in this other case."

"The overdose?"

"No, the shooter on the grassy knoll." He gave her a "gotcha" smile as he reached for the plastic bag sitting in the in tray on his desk. He looked through it again, turning the bag over, the contents clinking together as he did so.

"I think I need to get Zara back in here, see if my Brian is the same Brian who's gone missing from AA."

Indira looked alert now. "Yeah, about that. Tell me again why you think it's the same guy?"

"I know it's a long shot. I know Brian's a common name, but…"

He explained what the coroner had said to him about the old bruising on Brian Donahue's face and fists. "He was a scrapper, that's for sure. Those bruises could have come from Eliot Mumford. Plus the way Zara described AA Brian, it fits the description of my overdose to a T—he looks a bit like a skinny punk."

"Your Brian died earlier than Kat, didn't he? So he couldn't've done it."

"Yes, but if it is the same guy, well, what kind of a

wacky coincidence is that?"

"I appreciate your disdain for coincidences, Jacko, really I do. I'm not much of a fan of them myself, but can you please put your OD aside for a moment and try to focus on *this* case? We're getting desperate now."

A uniformed officer appeared at the door, a small thumb drive in hand. "Got the pix, ma'am."

"Good stuff," she said, waving her in. "Anyone spot you? Give you any trouble?"

"No, ma'am." She handed over the thumb drive. "No one suspected a thing."

"We'll make a detective out of you yet, Gertie. Thanks for that."

The officer beamed as she departed while Jackson stared at her, his eyes narrowing.

"What have you been up to?"

Indira ignored the question as she stuck the drive in her computer and waited. Within seconds a series of images began appearing on the screen. Some were a little grainy, some blurred, but most clearly showed a range of people all milling about outside a red brick building with graffiti tattooed across the sides. Some were smoking, some were talking, two just had their heads down and their hands shoved into their jackets.

"Last night's AA meeting," she told Jackson, whose ears suddenly pricked up.

He leaned over and started scanning the pictures, relieved to see that neither Alicia nor Perry appeared in the mix.

"You got Gertie to take these last night?"

She sniggered. "See, I can be as bent as the best of you. Any chance you can get that girlfriend of yours back in? I want to ask her some questions."

Jackson stared at her surprised for a moment, then placed the call.

An equally surprised Alicia made her way to squad

headquarters in record time. She could not believe that it was Indira asking for her help, not Jackson, and she hoped this marked a turning point in their frosty relationship. She felt emboldened and decided she would tell both detectives all about the conversation Lynette had overheard between Brandon and some co-conspirator on the streets of Vaucluse last night.

Yet no sooner had she stepped into Indira's office, the chill set in and Alicia quickly abandoned that idea. The DI barely smiled as she sat down, and her tone was clipped and officious. There was not even the slightest whiff of thawing ice in her demeanour.

"We appreciate your coming in, Ms Finlay," Indira said, "but I do expect that this conversation today remain confidential. And by confidential I mean you do not mention it to *anybody*. Okay? Not a soul. That includes your sister, your book club pals, your mother. Do I make myself clear?"

Alicia glanced at Jackson, who was leaning against a back cabinet, arms crossed, blank expression on his face.

She turned back to Indira. "What about my dog? Can I mention it to Max?"

Indira stared at Alicia, steely eyed, while Jackson tried to stifle a chuckle.

Alicia sighed. "I won't tell anyone."

She glanced back at Jackson, but he wasn't chuckling along. She didn't like Indira's terms one bit. Alicia told her sister everything. How was she going to keep this— whatever *this* was—from Lynette? Nor was she in the habit of keeping secrets from her "book club pals". Anders had done that in the past, and it was part of the reason they had split up. She loathed secrets between friends.

It wasn't just that though. Alicia didn't like the way Indira was speaking to her again today. *She* had called Alicia in to help, after all. She could try to be a little more polite about it.

But most of all, she didn't like the way Jackson was

standing there, smugly chuckling away, letting his colleague harangue her once again. She knew the DI was running this investigation, but she also knew that outside of this case, they were of equal rank.

*So why wasn't Jackson telling his colleague to pull her head in?*
She flashed him a frown.

Indira caught that and said, "If this is too difficult for you to manage, Ms Finlay, I'll get Jackson here to show you back out."

She turned her frown upon Indira. "It's fine."

The DI waited a beat and then twisted her computer monitor around to face Alicia. She tapped at the keyboard as the screen came back to life.

"I have some images here. I'd like you to take a look at them and let me know which of the gentlemen photographed goes by the name of Trevor."

Alicia glanced at Jackson, quizzically this time, then back at the monitor.

"Trevor from AA?" she said, and Indira nodded.

Alicia smudged her lips to the side, intrigued by the request now, and then leaned in closer to take a better look.

"There he is!" she said almost immediately.

Trevor was the first person pictured. A series of shots showed him striding towards the Neighbourhood Centre, glancing around, and then fiddling with the door— obviously unlocking it before a session. The next set of images revealed a variety of people walking past the building, some stopping and entering, others leaning against the wall to smoke a cigarette or converse. Trevor reappeared at one point with something in his hand, and there were several more images of him smoking and interacting with various AA members. Among the familiar faces, Alicia spotted Zara, Timothy and the tallest of the Mias.

Indira pointed to the clearest image of Trevor. "That's Trevor, yes? You're absolutely certain?"

"Yep, he's the one who chairs the meetings."

"Do you think that man, Trevor, could be the man you saw seated beside the pregnant woman on the night Kat Mumford died?" She held up a finger. "Just take a good look. Moustache or no moustache, could that be him?"

Alicia stared at the screen again. "I don't think it is, sorry, but I really didn't see him up close or even from the front. He was a couple of blankets in front of us, so I suppose it *could* be, but I'm not certain."

Indira made a note of something on a pad on her desk and then said, "Have another good look at the images on the screen for me please, Ms Finlay. Is there anyone else you recognise from the film night? Perhaps they weren't at the group meeting you and your friend decided to crash the other night." Her tone had turned icy again. "Just take a look and tell me, is anyone even vaguely familiar to you?"

Alicia let that comment slide and studied each picture individually. Eventually she shook her head, and Indira turned the monitor back.

"Right, well, thanks for that. We appreciate your help. Jackson will escort you out."

Alicia glanced at Jackson, who gave her a warm smile now and was opening the office door. They didn't say a word until he had walked her halfway down the corridor, then she rounded on him, her curiosity just nudging out her fury.

"She dragged me all the way in for that? Seriously? And do I *really* need to keep it from Lynette and the gang? What's the big deal?"

"I think Singho's concerned we'll have the civil rights nutjobs on our case for photographing a confidential AA group."

"Why does she want to know anyway?"

"It's just a hunch she's got, something she wants to clarify."

"Well, she can be a little nicer about it. What is that woman's *problem*?"

He placed a hand on her back. "We're at the business end of this investigation. She always gets a bit growly at this stage."

"A bit growly? She's bloody rude is what she is! *She* asked me in, remember? If it had been Perry, he would've told her where she could stick those pictures—and the camera!"

Jackson smiled. "Which is why you're here and not him."

They walked in silence until they got to the lifts. She stabbed at the button and turned her back on him.

"You okay?" he asked.

She turned to look at him. *Unbelievable!*

"What?" he asked, genuine confusion on his face.

She crossed her arms over her chest. "You could've stuck up for me in there, you know? Could have told her to play nicely!"

He went to put an arm around her, but she stepped back. Last night she had decided that Lynette was wrong, that she had to tell her boyfriend about Brandon's suspicious plans for the upcoming film night. Now she didn't want to tell him squat.

"I'm sorry, Alicia, but she is the lead investigator. I had to let her do her thing."

She stabbed the down button again a few times. *Where was the bloody lift?*

He put a hand on her arm, but she shook him off.

Jackson said, "Honestly, she's just like that sometimes." He paused as the lift went *ping*. "Alicia, please, you mustn't take it personally."

Her jaw dropped as she stepped inside the elevator. "She's rude to me, and I'm not to take it personally? Is she rude to *all* the witnesses in her cases. Is that how she *does her thing?* If so, it's little wonder you guys are getting absolutely nowhere with this case!"

Then she scowled at the floor as the doors slowly gobbled her up.

Feeling like he'd been beaten over the head with a hammer, Jackson was just making his way down the corridor when he heard the elevator sing out again. He swung around, relief on his face, thinking Alicia was back, but the other elevator door opened and a pregnant woman stepped out.

"Oh hi, Ms Olden," he said. "Come this way."

Maz Olden received a much warmer welcome than Alicia had enjoyed, and Indira even offered her a cup of tea as Jackson helped her into a seat.

She waved her off saying, "I spend too much time with my legs crossed as it is, but thanks."

Indira smiled kindly, and Jackson resumed his position behind her, wishing the DI could show his girlfriend the same courtesies and wondering where it had all gone wrong. He knew Indira was unhappy with the book club's interference, and he didn't blame her, but he also knew he was partially responsible for that, had given them the green light from the start. He just wished he'd smoothed that over better, wondered what he could have done differently.

"Thanks so much for coming in today, Ms Olden," Indira began.

"Maz, please. Ms Olden makes me sound so, well, *old*."

"Maz then." Indira clicked her screen back to life. "So we've asked you in today to see if you can recognise someone for us." She turned the screen around to reveal a magnified image of Trevor. All the other images from AA had been shut down, and Indira was pointing at Trevor's head.

"I'm wondering if this man looks familiar to you."

Maz heaved herself forward, leaning over her pregnant belly as she studied the picture. Her face scrunched up.

"Don't think so. Why?"

Indira frowned. *Damn it.* She smiled again. "Take a really good look, Maz. Imagine him with a dark moustache. Could that man possibly be the same man that was seated next to you at the film night?"

Maz looked a little alarmed now and stared back at the screen, studying it for a moment longer before shaking her short red curls. "Nope, sorry, I don't think that's him. That bloke was older, maybe thinner? Definitely had a moustache."

"Yes, but moustaches can be shaved off," Indira said. "Take one more look for me, please."

Maz sighed and looked again, then sat back and held on to her belly. "Wish I could help you, but no, that's not him."

Indira could barely conceal her disappointment as she opened the rest of the images from AA and pointed to the screen again. Like Alicia, Maz did not believe any of the faces looked familiar from the film night, and eventually Indira conceded defeat and shut the screen down. She thanked Maz for her time and then watched as she accepted the mug of tea that Officer Gertie was now handing her.

"So will your mum be in the actual delivery suite with you?" Indira asked, making conversation. "Please don't tell me you're doing it all alone."

Maz blew on her tea and shook her head. "Nah. Mum'll be in there. I'm one of four kids. She knows what she's doing."

"That's a relief. And will you be involving the father at any point? Or keeping him—"

"No way!" She blinked and then a sad smile enveloped her lips. "He doesn't even want to know about it, so…"

Then she patted her belly again, which was poking out from her skirt, looking flushed red and smooth as a bowling ball.

"We're going to be fine, aren't we, buddy? We're going to be *great*."

Then she smiled a little nervously before placing the cup back to her lips.

~~~~~~~

Liam Jackson held out a large takeaway latte and nudged his eyebrows in the air. "Truce?"

Alicia looked up from her desk with a start and quickly turned her smile downwards. "It's going to take more than cheap coffee, you know."

"I'll have you know this coffee cost five bucks! And you'll find, if you look a little closer, there's a little something extra on top."

Alicia narrowed her eyes and took the coffee he was holding out, noting the small love heart-shaped chocolate resting on the lid.

"Humph!" she said, unwrapping it and dropping it into her mouth.

He pulled a chair from a nearby desk and said, "May I?"

She shrugged as if she really didn't care and watched as he sat down.

"I'm sorry, Alicia. You're right. I should have told Indira to snap out of it. She's not normally that rude, or at least not to witnesses. I really don't know what her problem is at the moment. I mean, I know she's furious you guys got involved, but that's my fault, not yours."

"Exactly! *You* asked us to look out for suspicious stuff, remember? At the film night."

"I know. I just didn't think you'd *keep* looking out for stuff." He smiled. "I'll explain all that to Indira, but to be honest, I have a feeling there's more to it than that."

"Of course there is. She's jealous." Alicia knew all about the green-eyed monster.

"Of you?"

"Of you and me. She likes you, me not so much. It's obvious."

He shook his head firmly. "No way, nuh-uh. She's, like, ten years older than me, married to her career and her kids.

That's crazy."

"Doesn't change the fact. So how else are you going to make it up to me?"

He nudged his eyebrows up and down again. "What have you got in mind?" He stole a glance at her office door.

Alicia laughed. "Oh you're a long way from that, bucko!" She took a sip of the coffee. "But you can tell me what Brandon Johnson had to say."

"Brandon?"

"You just came from the Top Shop Café, am I right?"

"How did you—?"

She glanced at the latte. "Who else is going to charge five bucks for this crap?"

Actually, it was a wild guess, but it quickly paid off and Jackson proceeded to tell her about the brief chat he'd just had with the barman. Luckily, Brandon didn't mention a certain Lynette who had just joined his bar staff. In fact, according to Jackson, he was winding the bar work back.

"Says he had such a bad experience last film night, he's sticking to waiting tables at Top Shop."

"He's *not* running the bar at the Balmain Moonlight Cinema tomorrow night?" she asked.

He cocked his head to the side. "That's what he says. Why?"

She shrugged casually. There was no way she was going to tell him about Lynette's new gig now. "I just heard they were showing *Grease* this weekend. Figured the Ladies Auxiliary would hire him again, that's all."

"Oh I'm sure they'll have no trouble recruiting staff in this market." He smiled. "You wanna go? To *Grease,* I mean. It could be a laugh."

She shook her head quickly. "Oh, no. Urgh. Can't stand that flick."

She was lying of course, and he looked surprised.

"Wow, okay. I can't work you out at all. I really thought you'd be into that one. Want to do something else? I can probably get tomorrow night off. I'm owed a lot of overtime."

"No, I'm busy. Sorry."

"Busy?" He looked a little hurt.

"Yeah, I… I promised Lynny I'd, um, help her with her social media stuff this Saturday. Sorry."

Jackson's hangdog eyes were back. He was about to say something when his mobile beeped. He dragged it from his back pocket and read the message that had just come in. "Damn, okay, I gotta get back."

"Indira's probably snuck that GPS app onto your phone. She's probably tracked you down."

He smiled. "Are we okay?"

She shrugged. "Sure."

He looked at her for a few silent seconds, then said, "Maybe we could reserve Sunday then. Just you, me, nobody else? Not even Max."

She didn't laugh at that, just shrugged again.

Alicia knew she was being a bitch, but she was with Reverend Joves on this one. Retribution really did have its rewards.

"*Of course* he's running the bar on Saturday night," Lynette said over the phone to Alicia, ten minutes later. "I just got a text from him, like a second ago, confirming my hours. He wants me in Balmain at five on the dot. Why?"

"Hmm." Alicia tapped her pencil on the side of her desk, giving it some thought. "He told Jackson he wasn't doing the film nights anymore."

"He's lying, of course. Trying to get the cops off his tail."

"Yeah." Her stomach churned again. "I've got a bad feeling about this, Lynette."

"Well, that's a surprise. You didn't tell Jackson, did you?"

"No." But she wished she had.

"Good. This confirms that we're on the right track. The barman is definitely hiding something, and we need to find out what. Hang on, what?"

"What?"

"No! Wrong table, Carlos, number six! Six!" There was a muffled crackle before Lynette said, "Soz, gotta run. The place is going to hell in a handbasket. Oh shit, Mario's sending me dagger looks now."

"He should hook up with Indira."

"Sorry?"

"Never mind. Go, do your thing, we'll chat later."

As she placed the phone down, Alicia felt a small flicker of relief. At least she hadn't had a chance to tell her sister about her recent visit to Indira's office. It was one thing to lie to Jackson, but she was glad she had not had to lie to Lynette.

# CHAPTER 33

Claire did a quick twirl, her full, 1950s-style skirt swirling around her.

"Stunning," said Alicia. "I love it."

Claire was dressed up like one of the Pink Ladies from the movie *Grease*, complete with bubblegum pink jacket, high ponytail and requisite chewing gum.

She chewed noisily now as she placed her hands on her hips and said, "You, however, are a total spoilsport."

Alicia had a simple pair of black jeans and a striped shirt on. "Sorry, you know I'm not much of a clothes horse."

"Lynette already there?"

"Yep, unpacking plastic champagne flutes as we speak."

Claire frowned. "You think she's going to be okay?"

She had been reticent to attend the film event tonight, concerned for everyone's safety, but their enthusiasm had soon changed her mind, and so she had got into the spirit of the thing. Besides, Claire figured, the more of them there the safer it would be. Or so she hoped.

"Lyn tells me there are five other staff members on the team this time, and she has promised not to get stuck alone with Brandon for one second," Alicia told her. "So unless they're all in it together, I think she'll be fine." She glanced down the road. "Where's Missy? I thought she was coming with you."

Claire smiled mysteriously. "We're meeting her there."

"And why the cheeky grin?"

Claire began chewing nonchalantly again, then turned on her bobby socks and led the way to her blue VW Beetle.

The women reached Balmain with plenty of time to spare, parked the car and handed over their printed tickets, then began scanning the crowd for Missy. Alicia had a touch of déjà vu as she did so, coupled with a twinge of regret. She adored Claire, but she couldn't help wishing it was Jackson beside her instead and not just because he was stronger and had a police badge.

Meanwhile, Claire was looking out at the swelling crowd with a dash of relief. The film didn't start for half an hour, but it was clear they would have a full house, and she was glad of that. She remembered how worried the ladies at the Auxiliary had been and was happy the bad press had not damaged the event.

"I can't see her bright pink hair anywhere," Alicia said, staring at the section near the bar, the place they sat last time and the place they had agreed to meet.

"I see her!" said Claire, leading the way across.

It was only when they were close that Alicia let out a gasp.

"My goodness, you've gone platinum blond!"

Missy laughed uproariously at her reaction and gave her freshly dyed hair a little shake.

"You like?"

"I love it! Wow, what a change. I would not have recognised you."

Missy had also exchanged her zany zebra-print spectacles for a classic black pair, and she was wearing a slimming black top over a full red skirt and a black leather jacket over that.

"Sexy Betsy!" came a voice behind them, and they looked around to find Perry trudging up, a picnic basket in hand. "You've done a Sandy makeover."

Missy squealed. "I knew *you'd* get it! Flo gave me the idea when she first mentioned they were screening *Grease*.

I thought, if Sandy can make some changes, I can too. But I'm going further. I'm making over my entire life! I've applied for some rental apartments, and I'm moving out of home. It'll be costly, but it's time."

"So *that's* why you've been skipping all the expensive drinks and pizza?" Alicia said.

"Well, that and the desire to lose a little of this." She tapped her stomach and grinned.

Perry pulled a bottle of champagne from his basket.

"Let's drink to the new Missy," he announced, handing the bottle around, then he put one arm around Alicia and said, "Our baby is growing up."

Alicia laughed as they settled on a range of bright rugs, sipped their drinks, and looked around.

"Ooh there's Lynette," she said, catching sight of her sister, who was giving a subtle thumbs up from the bar area to their immediate right. She spotted Brandon just behind her, as well as several other bar staff, including a man who looked vaguely familiar. That must be Wally Walters, she decided.

"Listen, everyone," Alicia said, cutting through their chatter, "don't forget why we're here. We need to stay sharp and focused."

"Why *are* we here?" said Perry. "Sorry, luvie, but I'm really not sure what we can possibly see or do to help."

"Maybe nothing, but we're here to give Lyn some moral support and maybe some backup if it comes to that."

"You honestly think he's going to try something tonight?"

"I don't know, but Lynette swears he said something was going down tonight. There was going to be some signal—whatever that means. So we just keep our eyes peeled and our wits about us. Which means a little less of this," she held up her drink, "and a lot more of this." She placed two fingers to her eyes and then pointed them out to the crowd.

"Spoilsport," Perry said, giving her a wink.

"Hi, guys." This was Anders now, and he was on his own.

"No Margarita?" Perry asked, and he shook his head.

"She was just a friend, you know."

*Of course she was*, he thought, offering him some champagne, while Alicia gave him a warm smile.

The first half of the film was incident-free. Apart from a rowdy group of young women at the other end of the park, there were no major disruptions or overly amorous antics, although most punters probably wouldn't dare. Alicia noticed extra security tonight, not just on the exits but strolling through the crowd, and she wondered whether they were also putting a halt to any plans Brandon had—and whether that was actually a good thing.

As Sandy and Danny tried to reconcile true love and teen angst on the big screen, Alicia kept a subtle eye on the bar where Lynette appeared to be run off her feet. Alicia was surprised by the steady flow of customers, even after the film had started. This was certainly a younger crowd than the previous fortnight, although middle-aged women were still in abundance. They were the film's original fans, no doubt, and knew every word to every song, singing along at the top of their voices.

With intermission fast approaching, Alicia decided to touch base with her sister before the crowds built up. She whispered her plans to the book club and then slipped across.

"I'll have a glass of sparkling wine, thanks," Alicia said politely as she stepped to the front of the counter.

"Coming right up, madam," Lynette replied, giving her a subtle wink.

"Busy night?" Alicia kept her tone casual. They had agreed to stay incognito, but she was determined to get an update.

Lynette shrugged. "Not really, ma'am. Nothing much

going on here."

"Oh well, things may get more exciting for you in the second half," Alicia replied, handing over some cash.

After making her way back to the group, she went to sit down but was quickly intercepted by Claire.

"Wrong blanket, Alicia. This one's ours."

Alicia glanced around to find a thirty-something couple beside her, laughing, and she apologised to them as she resumed her place. At that moment, Alicia felt a little zap go off in her brain, but it vanished just as quickly and she gave it no more thought as she settled back in.

The second half of the evening was even less eventful than the first, and by the time the graduating class of Rydell High were driving off into the sunset looking bright and optimistic, the book club friends were glancing around looking anything but.

"No dead bodies?" said Missy. "No screams or cries?"

"Doesn't look like it," said Alicia. "And we should be thankful for that." She glanced at her watch. "Come on, we'll be late!"

They had previously arranged to rendezvous with Lynette just after the credits, behind the Portaloos near the snack bar. That way, if Lynette had anything to report, they'd have time to call Jackson and get him in before Brandon vanished into the night.

Yet Lynette looked even more disappointed than Missy.

"I didn't see any suspicious signals, and Brandon didn't leave the tent, not once!" she said. "Just poured beers, popped champagne corks and now he's over there with Wally and Jacki doing the clean-up." She hugged her jacket closer. "I have to be quick; he wants me back in five."

"Did you see him do *anything* suspicious?" asked Perry.

"Apart from work harder than I've ever seen him work before? No, nothing." She took a good swig of the water bottle she'd brought along. "He was really diligent tonight.

Took care of a few idiots who kept demanding stupid things like candy and champagne with ice."

"Champagne with ice?" echoed Perry, an eyebrow sky-high. "Well there's no accounting for taste!"

She laughed. "Did you see that hen's party? They were so out of it. But apart from them, it was all pretty dull."

"Do you think all the extra security might have curtailed his plans?" asked Alicia, and Lynette nodded.

"More's the pity," said Missy, who then slapped a hand to her mouth. "Sorry! That was a terrible thing to say."

"Don't beat yourself up," said Lynette. "I think we've all been expecting something to go down, as horrendous as that sounds. I'm so sorry I wasted all your time."

"No, no, not at all! You didn't waste our time," said Missy. "I would've come anyway." She turned to Claire. "I haven't seen Flo and Ronnie, but they'd be so happy with the turnout."

Claire agreed. "So what now?" she asked Lynette.

"Unless something dramatic happens in the next ten minutes, you guys might as well head off."

"You're coming with us, right?" asked Alicia.

Lynette shook her head no. "I promised I'd help them pack up. I've really got to get back."

"I'll wait around until you're done."

"Don't bother," Lynette said. "Honestly, I'm perfectly safe. There's a whole bunch of us over there, plus the security guards won't leave until the place is empty, so I'll be fine. You should grab a lift with Claire while you can, and I'll catch you back at home." Then she held a finger up. "And I'll make sure I'm never alone with Brandon—I promise this time!"

Alicia didn't look too happy with that arrangement, but she could see at least three bar staff still moving about in the white marquee, so she nudged away the dark images that were swirling through her head and gave her sister a warm hug.

"Be safe!"

As the book club packed up and eventually left the park, Alicia glancing back towards the bar, wondering whether to worry, Lynette remained behind to clean up. She dumped the empty bottles in the recycling bins at the back of the venue and helped lug boxes of unused champagne flutes and unopened alcohol into the back of Brandon's van.

After hoisting the final box into place, Lynette returned to the tent where Brandon, Wally and Jacki remained, now perched on a trestle table, sipping beers.

"Need a hand with the marquee?" she asked.

Brandon shook his head. "Nah, Wally and I will come back tomorrow and take care of it, but thanks. You were a great help tonight."

"No worries," she said, feeling remorseful again.

Lynette didn't know what the barman had been talking about on his phone the other night, but her doubts were creeping back in. Had he really been planning something sinister and been thwarted by the extra security? Or was there a perfectly innocent explanation for everything he said?

Maybe the Ladies Auxiliary were right, she decided. Maybe he was just a young man trying hard to get back on his feet. In any case, it was time for this amateur sleuth to retire to bed.

"You girls head home," Brandon was saying, "I'll make sure payment is transferred to your accounts tomorrow."

"Thanks," said Lynette, grabbing her things and then walking with Jacki out of the park, which was now abandoned except for a lone security guard on the front entrance.

"Need a cab, ladies?" the guard asked.

Jacki shook her head. "I'm just down the road." She waved to Lynette as she walked off.

Lynette pulled out her smartphone.

"I'll just book an Uber," she told the guard, stepping out onto the street so that her smartphone could pinpoint her exact location.

As she was tapping in her password, Lynette glanced up to find three of the hen's party staggering down the street. They had glassy eyes and were tearing into what looked like greasy hamburgers. She smiled at them and looked back at her phone just as one of the women tripped over and the others snorted with laughter.

"Oh my gawd, Jeanie, you are going to be sooooo wrecked at the church tomorrow! We really blew you away tonight!"

Then the other women giggled as they continued tumbling down the street.

Lynette stopped and looked up again. She blinked rapidly then clicked her phone off.

*My God.* She thought. *I've been such an idiot!*

Then she swivelled on her heels and made her way back inside the park.

# CHAPTER 34

Alicia stepped out of Claire's car at the corner of her block, then waved her off with an air kiss and a smile. It was only as she was grappling for her door key and walking towards her terrace house that she spotted the man lurking in the shadows just to the right of the letterbox.

She jumped back, her heart thumping beneath her shirt.

"It's okay," came a deep voice, a familiar one, and she exhaled as Jackson stepped into the streetlight.

"What the hell, Jackson," she said, "you scared me to death!"

"Sorry, I didn't mean to." Then, "Where have you been all night?"

He tried to keep the hurt from his voice, but it was difficult. She'd clearly been out having fun, not stuck at home working on Lynette's social media sites as she had previously claimed. As she had previously *insisted*, he thought sullenly, thrusting his hands into his jacket pockets.

Catching this, Alicia stepped towards Jackson and reached for his hand.

"We, ahh, we went to see a movie."

"Let me guess. *Grease?*"

Alicia's eyes widened.

"I'm a detective, Alicia. Not an idiot."

"Sorry," she said. "We were..." She hesitated. How did she tell him she had lied to him? That she was meddling again?

"You were doing some investigating of your own, weren't you?"

She couldn't meet his eyes. "Yeah... I guess."

"You guess?"

"Well, it didn't work out. I promise you, it was a complete waste of time."

"Why didn't you tell me?"

"Because I..." She stopped. She sighed. "I'm sorry, Jackson, it was silly, really. We had suspicions about Brandon—"

"Brandon Johnson?"

"Yes, but we got it all wrong."

"What suspicions?"

"Nothing. It was stupid. Look, I'm really sorry. We just thought you'd be angry, that you'd try to stop us."

"Like all the other times I've tried to stop you from helping in the past?"

She felt a fresh flood of guilt. He had a right to be angry. He might have been unsupportive in his office, but Jackson had never tried to block her from the investigation, not with any *real* conviction anyway, so why had she felt the need to keep this from him? At what point had she morphed into Anders, not trusting him, not keeping him in the loop?

"I'm really, really sorry, Jackson," she said again. "I just didn't want you to get into any more trouble with Indira, that's all. I was thinking..."

"What? What were you thinking?"

She smiled coyly. "Two words, Mr President. Plausible deniability."

He stared at her like she'd flipped. "Huh?"

"You know? Like in the movie *Independence Day*? The less you're told the easier it is for you to deny it."

He still looked confused, so she just shook her head and unlocked the front door.

"Come on. Let's see if I make more sense inside."

By the time the peppermint tea had grown cold in her cup, Alicia had brought Jackson up to speed on what the group was doing at the film night and what had transpired.

"Turns out Brandon was on his best behaviour, and absolutely nothing happened. It was all a complete waste of time."

"No dead body under a blanket?" he said. "Did you really expect another one?"

She scrunched her lips up, and he smiled. It warmed her heart.

"I don't know about *Independence Day*," he said, "but it's not *Midsomer Murders* either. There's not a dead body after every commercial break."

She smiled now, feeling her guilt ebb away. "I know. I'm a bloody idiot."

*Nah,* he thought. *I wondered the exact same thing.* He asked, "So where is Lynette now?"

"On her way home, I presume."

"You mean you left her there? With Brandon?"

Alicia felt a cold trickle down her spine. "Yes, why? I already told you, we got it all wrong. He wasn't up to anything."

"But you don't know that for sure, right? He is still a suspect in Kat Mumford's murder, Alicia. He might have been on his best behaviour tonight, but he's not off the hook for that one yet."

Now the trickle felt like a gush. "But... but she said Wally was still there and some other woman."

He frowned. "Tell me again what Lynette overheard Brandon say on the phone that night."

"Um... He said something about some woman he was going to take care of, how she wouldn't know what hit her—"

"And you're sure he wasn't talking about Lynette?"

The gush was now a tsunami smashing against her head. She could barely hear him from the ringing in her ears.

She grappled for her phone. "Maybe I should call her… just in case?"

He nodded quickly. "Do that."

As Alicia shakily stabbed the number in, she felt like she was drowning.

*What if Jackson was right? What if Brandon's victim was not some random moviegoer but a barmaid called Lynette who'd been poking her nose in where it wasn't welcome?*

She chewed mercilessly at her top lip and waited for her sister to pick up.

~~~~~~~

Lynette felt the phone vibrate in her pocket but ignored it. She was almost back at the bar tent now and had just seen Brandon handing a wad of cash to Wally, who was still perched on the trestle table and was smiling back at him.

"Hello, boys," she said boldly, stepping into the marquee.

Both men looked around with a start.

"I thought you took off," said Brandon, an edge to his voice now, and Lynette narrowed her eyes at him.

"And I thought you said we were all getting paid tomorrow."

She glanced at Wally, whose grin had been replaced by a bruising blush.

"Oh, Wal's just a bit skint, so, you know, I'm just helping him out."

She nodded, glancing around. Lynette noticed that the last of the security guards was packing up his things. He would be leaving the premises any minute. She didn't have much time.

"So how'd you do tonight?" she asked.

"Okay," he said slowly.

"Sell as much as you'd hoped?"

He stared at her. "No more than usual."

She nodded, wrapping her arms around herself. "And how much do you usually sell?"

"Sorry?"

"Candy? Champagne and ice? How much?"

Both men shared a glance then, before Brandon stood up from the table. She'd forgotten how tall he was, how he loomed over her. How strong he looked.

"What are you talking about?" he said.

"I'm talking about all that extra business you do on the side."

"*Lynette*," said Wally, his tone wary, but she held a hand up.

"You think I'm a moron, don't you?" Then she chuckled, but there was no joy in it. "I guess I have been. Talk about 'straighty 180'! Can't believe I didn't pick it up earlier."

Brandon's expression had darkened, and he took a step towards Lynette, but she was too busy piecing it all together to notice. She was glaring at Wally now.

"You must have had a real laugh when I tried to send that guy to the snack bar for 'candy.' You must have thought I was a moron when I didn't get the 'ice' request. Have a chuckle at me, did you?"

"Lynette," Wally tried again, but she was shaking her head at Brandon now.

"Here I was feeling *sorry* for you! Thinking how great it was that you'd sorted yourself out so well after your mum died. But selling drugs to customers on the sly?"

"Shh!" said Wally, glancing around, but Brandon was looming in front of Lynette now, an ugly scowl on his face.

She felt her heart skip a beat, and she stepped back, but he had her cornered. She glanced around furtively. They were now wedged into one side of the white tent. If the security guard was still around, there was no way he could see them. She wondered if he was within earshot.

"Take one step closer," she told Brandon,

"and I'll scream."

He stopped and held a palm up. "Just chill, okay? Just chill the hell out."

She watched him. "So this is your little business on the side, is it?" She glanced around. "Where did you stash the stuff?"

"It's not important, Lynette," Brandon said. "This doesn't involve you, just walk away."

Lynette's heart began racing trying to keep up with her head, which was now connecting dots at a rapid pace. "Did Kat Mumford catch you selling drugs? Did she threaten to tell? Is that it? Is that why you killed her?"

Now it was Brandon's turn to step back. "What the hell?"

"I know you had something to do with Kat's death."

"I had nothing to do with it!"

"Then why did you run off so quickly that night, why—" But she knew the answer even before he replied.

"Because I needed to get my stash out before the pigs started searching the place, why do you think?"

She turned to look at Wally, who had remained exactly where he was the entire time.

Wally nodded. "It's true. Brandon had nothing to do with that dead drunk chick. She didn't even buy any gear from him."

"But she did buy a champagne."

"So?" said Brandon.

"So you really didn't kill her to avenge your mother?"

He looked like she was insane, but she pressed on.

"You didn't kill her to try to stop her from drink-driving?"

Now Brandon was looking at Wally. "Did you give her some candy? She's lost the plot."

Wally shrugged no, but Lynette was not finished yet.

"So… so when you said, 'She won't know what hit her?' What did you mean by that?"

"Excuse me?"

Lynette forged on. "I overheard your phone call the other day. You said…" She stopped. The pieces moved around suddenly and were now clicking into a different place. She exhaled. "Oh, okay, you meant the bride, right?"

He seemed baffled for a moment and then nodded. "Yeah, Jeanie. Who else? The maid of honour phoned me. I'd sold her some…" He stopped, glanced around and dropped his voice. "Let's just say she got some party favours from me last time and wanted the same again tonight, but this time she wanted something special for her friend who's getting married. She wanted to surprise her with it."

"Some 'candy'?"

He nodded. "Yeah, some 'candy.' So I arranged it. That's it."

Lynette's shoulders dropped. She felt like a fool. As bad as it was, all she had done here was stumble on a sleazy drug trade. There was no conspiracy to murder, no case to answer with Kat Mumford.

Brandon had stepped right back now and was leaning against the table. "What are you going to do, Lynette?"

"You going to rat on us to the cops?" added Wally, his blush back.

She pulled her jacket tightly around her body and secured her bag onto her shoulder.

"None of my business," she said, watching as their faces flooded with relief.

Lynette stepped away from the men and out towards the tent exit again. "But I do know a lovely group of elderly ladies who might just think it's theirs."

Brandon held a hand out. "Please, Lynette, don't tell them."

She just shook her head and left them both staring at the wad of cash in Wally's hands like it had morphed into a tiger snake and was about to strike.

~~~~~~~

The herbal teapot was now abandoned as the trio helped themselves to a stiff drink, Alicia needing it more than her sister, who showed up at home just as Jackson was putting a call through to the Balmain Area Command.

As he called off the troops, Alicia rounded on Lynette.

"You gave me the scare of my life! Why didn't you answer my call?"

"Sorry, I was a bit distracted."

Tumblers of whisky in hand, they sat in the lounge room, Max asleep between them, as Lynette poured out the details of the night.

"You're just lucky they're amateur dealers," said Jackson. "I've seen plenty of people who accidentally stumbled onto the real deal, and let's just say most of them were lying horizontal on a slab."

Lynette shrugged nonchalantly, but Alicia shuddered. He was right. It could have gone so much worse. Yet it did throw a very different light on the Mumford case.

"I guess Brandon had nothing to do with Kat's murder then?" she said. "I mean, if he was willing to let you walk out after catching him."

"I don't know for sure, of course, but that's the vibe I got. He's obviously been selling drugs at those events on the side, and I think his only concern that first night was getting his drugs out of the park and away from the police, not avoiding a murder charge." She glanced at Jackson. "What are you going to do now? I did say I wouldn't take this to the police."

He slugged the drink back and blew out a breath of air. "But you did say you'd take it to the Women's Auxiliary, right?" She nodded. "Then I'm sure we'll hear about it pretty fast. As protective as they are, I can't imagine Flo tolerating that kind of nonsense."

"So much for the drink-driving crusade we thought he was on," said Alicia, staring into her glass.

Lynette glanced pitifully at Jackson. "So this leaves you back at square one, hey?"

"Not at all. We still have a few lines of enquiry."

"Such as?"

"Nuh-uh. I'm too exhausted to think about that now."

He stood up and held a hand out to Alicia, who was still nestled into the couch. "*Now* will you let me apologise properly?"

She let him pull her up, then she glanced back at Lynette.

"You going to be okay?"

"Always was," she replied, smiling.

As the couple headed upstairs, Lynette looked down at Max, who was sleepily thudding his tail near her feet. "That just leaves you and me, Maxy," she said softly before looking up and out through the window to the dark night beyond. "Not to mention a killer, who's still out there somewhere, free as a bird."

And then the smile slid off her lips.

# CHAPTER 35

Monday morning dawned bright, but Detective Inspector Indira Singh's mood did not match the cheerful blue sky outside.

"There's a killer out there, people, and we are no closer to finding him!" She stepped towards a large whiteboard at the front of the conference room. "And what have you lot been doing? As far as I can tell, having a wonderful weekend and delivering me no results!"

"Somebody woke up on the wrong side…," began Pauly in a hushed whisper to a colleague, before catching a venomous glare from his boss. He closed his mouth.

"I don't know about you, but I find it completely unacceptable," she continued, slapping a palm against a picture that had been magnetised into place. It was a headshot of a pretty blonde in thick white glasses.

"It's been over *two weeks* since Kat Mumford was brutally strangled in a public park, and what do we have? Bugger all!"

She pointed now to a large piece of paper that had been attached to the board. It was Missy's sketch of the crime scene, the one that best resembled the general layout.

"We have over a hundred people present during the murder, over a dozen witnesses—"

"Including one homicide detective," said a ponytailed woman at the back, and Jackson shot her a smirk.

"Hey, Gertie, watch your mouth! I'd left the scene long before the homicide."

"Let me finish!" Indira interrupted them, dragging both sets of eyes back to the board. "We have scores of suspects, at least ten of them viable, and yet we are not one inch closer to solving this thing. Why do you think that is, hey?"

All eyes had suddenly lost focus and were darting to the floor and to the ceiling, hoping their cranky boss would not pick them.

"What do you think we can do about it?" Indira persisted.

"We could get that book club back in," suggested Pauly, and Jackson winced, glancing back at Indira, waiting for the explosions.

Indira smudged her lips into an oversized smile. "The book club, you think? The Murder Mystery Book Club?"

Pauly went to nod, then sensing her vibe, stopped and played dumb.

Her smile was now almost a leer. "Great idea, Pauly." She turned to the room of detectives. "Let's give that man a medal!"

All eyes were now on Pauly, most brimming with pity, but Pauly was not sure whether to smile or shrink further into his seat.

Indira waved a hand around the room of six detectives and five support staff. "Who needs you lot when we've got the Murder Mystery Book Club? If only I'd thought of that earlier, Pauly! We should all just pack up and go home, leave it to the experts, hey?"

"No, I was just thinking—"

"No, you weren't thinking! This is not St Mary Mead, and Miss Marple is not about to come cycling in to save us! It is *our* job to reconcile this case, not a pack of amateurs. Do you understand?"

He nodded quickly and stared at his feet.

She sighed loudly. "Has anyone else got any bright ideas this lovely morning?"

You could have heard a pin drop.

Eventually someone said, "We could get those two perverts back in. They were dodgy."

Indira thought about that and stepped back to the board, pointing to the mug shots of Scotty and Davo. "And what would be the point of that, Jarrod? Do you have some fresh evidence I can chuck at them? Some extra questions we forgot to ask?"

He shook his head as his eyes followed Pauly's to the carpet.

Jackson cleared his throat and said, "I know this is a long shot..." Indira turned to glare at him. "...but I want to get Zara back in, the woman from AA. I want to see if she can ID Brian Donahue for me. See if her Brian is the same as my Brian, the guy who overdosed."

"I thought you were doing that last week."

"Er, no, you told me to give it up and focus on this case, remember?"

"That's right, because we'd already determined that Brian Donahue was dead long before Kat Mumford was strangled. So what would be the point of getting Zara in to ID him?"

"I know it sounds crazy, but it's just an itch I need to scratch."

She thought about that for a moment then said, "Can't you just ask Eliot Mumford? Isn't he the one who beat the man to a pulp?"

"Yeah, but if it's all the same to you, I'd rather check with an independent party." Then to her developing frown he added, "Just trust me on this."

She nodded. "Fine. I think you're barking up the wrong tree, but hell, at least you're barking at *something*." Then she turned to address the rest of the team. "See, people? *This* is what I'm talking about! Let's try to think outside the square today, hey? Let's try to think laterally! And let's try to catch this killer before his trail goes colder than my mood is going to be if we get through another week without solving this thing!"

~~~~~~~

Zara Cossington-Smythe couldn't think why the homicide detectives were dragging her back to their office, the novelty of being involved in a murder case now officially worn off. She smiled blandly as she was shown into a seat in front of DI Jackson and then watched as he placed an A4-sized print on the desk in front of her.

He didn't need to say a word. Almost immediately she gasped.

"Brian! What an ugly licence photo." She looked up at Jackson. "Why are you showing me a picture of Brian?"

Jackson had to swallow back his smile.

"You know this man, Brian Donahue?"

"I just know him as Brian, but yeah, sure, from AA. I already told you guys about Brian."

"*This* is the man who attended your AA, the same AA that Eliot Mumford attended?"

"Yes!"

"And this is the Brian that Eliot Mumford beat up after AA one night?"

She glanced at the photo and then back. "Um, well, that's what I heard. Why? Don't tell me Brian wants to press charges! What a lowlife. Now I wish I hadn't said anything. Eliot doesn't deserve to be arrested, he deserves a medal!"

Jackson took a deep breath. "Brian won't be pressing charges anytime soon, Ms Cossington-Smythe. Brian is dead."

She took a moment to digest that, then said, "Wow, okay. That's not too surprising, I suppose. So what happened? Bar fight?"

"He was found the same night as Kat Mumford. Heroin overdose."

Her eyes lit up. "I knew it! He should've been at NA!

I *told* Trevor he was in the wrong group and should sign up for Narcotics Anonymous. I could tell he was a junkie." She bristled with pride, then caught herself and dropped her smile. "Oh, well, may he rest in peace and all that, but I can't say I'm too sorry. He was not a nice person. So what does this have to do with your other death? Eliot's wife?"

*What indeed*, thought Jackson, taking the picture from the table and placing it back in its folder.

"You mentioned that Brian confessed openly during your meetings to beating up his wife, is that correct?"

"Well that's what he told us, yes."

"Do you recall his wife's name?"

As far as Jackson knew—as far as Jackson was *told*—Brian Donahue was not married. His parents were adamant about that, and there were no signs of a partner in the dingy bedsit he rented.

*"Who'd want him?"* the mother had said without sorrow or regret.

Zara was giving it some thought, shaking her head as she did so. "Sorry, I never actually met her; can't recall a name. I think he called her 'my girl,' like he owned her. He was a creep. I mean, it's sad for him, I suppose, but there's a very relieved woman out there somewhere I can assure you of that."

Indira Singh agreed wholeheartedly with Zara. She was now leaning on the edge of Jackson's desk, studying the printed picture of Brian Donahue closely.

"If there is such a thing as karma, this bloke got what was coming to him, and his wife is probably breathing a lot easier these days."

"Yes, except who is this elusive wife?" said Jackson, irritably. "Nobody's come forward to claim him, and I just spoke to his folks again. They're as surprised to hear about it as we are. Says if he really was married, he kept that one very quiet. We didn't see any signs of a woman's presence in his life either."

"No wedding photos at his house, or on his phone?"

"We couldn't find a phone. Figured it'd been nicked while he was out of it, unlike his Rolex which was so fake even a thief would've—" He stopped. Sat up straight. Then he began rifling through his in tray. "Where is it? Where did I put the bloody thing?"

"What?" said Indira.

"What is it?" said Pauly, who had also wandered in.

"The bag with his stuff."

Jackson yanked open a lower drawer and began sifting through the contents, then gave a yelp, dragging a plastic bag out and dropping it onto his desk.

"This is the stuff Scelosi sent back from the lab, the stuff the Donahues didn't want." He picked the bag up and studied it. "Scelosi said something about sending back Brian's wedding band. It just looked like an ordinary ring to me, I thought he'd just made an assumption, but maybe he was basing it on something more tangible than that."

He opened the ziplock bag and reached in to grab the ring. Indira leaned over the desk to watch, her eyes wide as Jackson turned the ring around and then peered inside the rim. He squinted.

"There's something engraved here. It's tiny. Hang on." He pulled his desk lamp closer and switched it on. Then he frowned and sat back with a start.

"What?" said Indira.

"What?" repeated Pauly.

Jackson looked a little shell-shocked. He scratched the back of his head. "I think it says 'Maz xo'."

He stared into Indira's saucer-shaped eyes. "What the hell is going on?"

# CHAPTER 36

$\mathbf{M}$az Olden looked confused, maybe even a little frightened, as the young sergeant showed her through to an interview room and left her sitting at the desk to sweat it out.

While she did so, Jackson, Indira and Pauly watched her through the one-way mirror.

"Mightn't be her, you know?" Indira was saying. "She can't be the only Maz in Sydney."

"It's her," Jackson replied. "She already told us she was glad her partner wasn't in the picture anymore."

"But she didn't say he'd died."

"Maybe she didn't know. Maybe she still doesn't."

"Maybe she killed him?" suggested Pauly.

"Oh wake up to yourself, Pauly," Indira shot back. "She was at the Balmain film night the same time he was taking his hot shot. Dozens of witnesses saw her."

"So why are we wasting time on this?"

Indira turned to Pauly. "We're letting Jacko scratch his itch."

Jackson frowned. "It's more than that. I told you before, I don't like coincidences, and this is a whopping great one. Think about it. What are the chances that the woman sitting closest to a murder victim is also the woman engaged to a man who ends up dead on the same night. *And* the woman whose dead husband attended the very same AA as the victim's husband?"

"Well, since you put it all so clearly like that," Indira quipped. "I know it smells fishy, but from a strictly logical viewpoint, these two deaths simply can't be related. If Brian Donahue is Maz's partner, he died by his own hands an hour or two before Kat died. So he can't have been involved in Kat's death. And Kat, Eliot, or even poor little Maz here can't have been involved in his death. All three were at the Balmain park."

"We need to check all the times again," said Jackson. "See exactly when everyone showed up at the park."

"You need your head checked is what is needed," was Pauly's assessment.

Jackson said, "Brian might have sought revenge on Eliot for beating him up. Maybe he organised a hit on Eliot's wife and then, I don't know, felt bad about it and tried to drown his sorrows with a hit of heroin that night and accidentally killed himself. Look, I know it's a bit wishy-washy, but it's a theory, right?"

Both Indira and Pauly looked at him like he was certifiable.

"Come on," said Indira, "let's see if we can't blow Jacko's ridiculous theory out of the water and get back to the Kat Mumford case."

The wave of relief that washed across Maz Olden's face seemed too genuine to be an act. Jackson and Indira watched the woman carefully as they produced the picture of Brian Donahue and placed it on the table in front of her. And both had to agree, she was either a very fine actor or genuinely relieved.

Her first reaction, like Zara, was to proclaim in a startled voice, "Brian!" Then glancing up at them innocently, she had added, "That's my fiancé. Ex-fiancé. What's going on?"

Jackson said, "I'm sorry to tell you this, Maz, but he died of a drug overdose two weeks ago."

And that's when her look of surprise morphed into a look of sheer, unadulterated relief. Maz dropped back in her seat, and her eyes welled with tears, then she buckled over her pregnant belly. "Thank God, thank God, thank God."

The two detectives watched her, trying to hide their surprise.

She looked up and said, "I'm sorry, it's just that he was so... cruel, so... violent. I... I know I should be sad he's dead. But... I... Oh, thank God!"

Then she grasped her stomach again and whispered, "We're safe now, bubba. He's gone."

Indira gave her a moment and then said, "You really had no idea your fiancé had died?"

She looked up, her eyes awash with tears. "No! I... Like I said, we weren't together anymore. I always thought he'd return. I knew he wouldn't ever let me go, but when he hadn't come back, I began to wonder." She sobbed again. "I began to hope..."

"Did you know he was attending AA meetings in Rozelle?" Jackson asked, and she nodded.

"NA in Surry Hills as well," she said, adding, "Fat lot of good that did."

"What is your relationship with Eliot Mumford?"

"What?" she said, sounding startled, and then, "You mean the man whose wife was killed the other night?" He nodded. "I... I don't have a relationship with him."

"So you had never met him or seen him before that film night?"

"No, never. Why? What's he got to do with Brian?"

Jackson left that question unanswered and asked, "So when did you first meet this man?" He indicated the photo. "Brian Donahue."

"About three years back. He was in a band back then. He was so cool, or I thought he was." She sniffed. "That was before he turned violent."

"When did he turn violent?" Indira asked.

"The minute I fell pregnant. The first time."

Maz gulped and her eyes filled with tears again.

"He bashed me so hard during my first pregnancy I lost the baby early. But he was *so* sorry, so apologetic." She gulped, then frowned. "I really thought he meant it. He was *so* sweet after that. He wrote me a love song, serenaded me outside my door…" She sniffed. "That's when he signed up for AA and NA, and I thought…" She sniffed again. Sighed. "Well, I was wrong."

"He turned violent again?"

"I should've left him, I know that. When I fell pregnant again, I tried to hide it, but he worked it out. He wanted me to get rid of it… of my beautiful boy." She rubbed her belly as the tears began to stream down her face. "He never wanted kids, said they ruined everything, but I wouldn't… I *couldn't!* I'd already lost one; I wasn't going to lose another. So Brian… He tried to get rid of him for me, like last time." She rubbed a hand across her nose and wiped at her face. "He punched me in the belly a few times. Threw me down a set of stairs."

"Why didn't you leave him?" asked Jackson.

"I did! Over and over. He kept finding me. It got worse each time."

"Why didn't you report him to the police?" asked Indira.

"I did that too! They just said he was struggling with the idea of fatherhood and told him to clean up his act. The fact that he was doing AA… well, they just let him off. They didn't care."

Indira shook her head angrily. "Who said that? Which area command?" Then she held a hand up. "Never mind, we'll get onto that later." She softened her tone. "I'm sorry Brian did that to you, Maz, and I'm sorry the police did not have your back, but we're trying to connect Brian to Kat Mumford's murder."

She glanced up at Indira, a look of alarm in her eyes.

"We don't believe he killed Ms Mumford directly, but I do have to ask, is there any way he might have known Kat? Did he ever mention Kat or Eliot for that matter?"

She wiped her nose with her sleeve. "No."

"Did he ever tell you that Eliot Mumford had beaten him up after AA one day?"

Maz almost smiled then, had to catch herself. "No, but... wow, good on him."

"You didn't notice Brian's bruises?" Jackson asked.

She glared back at him. "It's hard to see straight with two black eyes, you know."

He bowed his head by way of apology, then he had a thought and asked, "How come Brian's parents have never heard of you?"

"Parents?" She blinked, surprised. "I didn't know they were still alive. He said they died when he was like five. He went into foster care. I figured that was why he didn't want kids..."

"No, they live about two suburbs from his bedsit."

"What? Really?" She looked genuinely shocked by that and slumped back in her seat. "I... I never knew." Then she patted her stomach and said, "Fat lot of good they did us, hey, bubba?"

But this time, there wasn't just sorrow and relief in her eyes, there was a palpable sense of anger and betrayal.

~~~~~~~

The Orient Express restaurant was bursting at the seams, surprising for a Monday night, and Alicia was relieved when the waitress led them to a pokey table at the back, just near the swinging doors that led into the kitchen.

"Last table," the woman told her. "Sorry, all we can do."

Alicia assured her it was fine. She just needed somewhere to touch base with Jackson. They had gone part of the way to making up last night, but they needed some more quality time, some decent conversation, and a chance to rebuild the trust.

Jackson helped her into a seat and then sent the

waitress off to open the bottle of Sauvignon Blanc he had brought along.

"Are we really okay now?" he asked after the wine had been poured, and she reached over and took his hand.

"We're fine." Then she smiled. "I get why Indira is angry. I do understand. I know my book club can be a total pain in the neck and we overstep a lot." Then to his pointed look she added, "Okay, *all the time.*"

He laughed. "That's the understatement of the century. Still, I should have stuck up for you. I should have. I'm sorry. I'll do it in future, I promise."

Now she laughed. "Be careful, Jackson, that sounds like you've just given us the green light again!"

He groaned and then shook his head. "Somehow I get the feeling you'll do exactly what you want to do regardless of what I say."

She grinned and drank from her glass. That's what she loved about Liam Jackson, she decided. He wasn't trying to control her. He seemed resigned to the fact that Alicia Finlay and her friends were the world's nosiest book club, and love it or loathe it, it wasn't his job to change that. He also seemed to accept that she needed to stay informed, and no sooner had they ordered, he was filling her in on the latest developments in the Mumford case. It left her head reeling.

"Brian from AA is *your* overdose Brian. Well, that is quite the coincidence," she agreed. "So what do you think it means?"

He gulped his wine. "Beats me. According to Eliot Mumford, it means nothing."

"So you questioned him about it?"

"Of course, although this time instead of gently lobbing questions in his cosy kitchen, Indira finally hauled his butt into the station."

"And?"

"And it's another dead end. Eliot admits to beating up Brian Donahue but *insists* he never met Maz Olden outside

AA or at any other time and says it's a complete coincidence that she was sitting so close to his blanket that night. Reckons he never even saw the woman before that film night. Not even *on* that film night, in fact. He just vaguely recalls a pregnant woman on a blanket nearby. Recalls almost falling on top of her and getting a filthy look, but that's it."

Alicia blinked. Something he said made her synapses zap again, but this time an image was forming in her head. She let it go for now and asked, "Do you believe him?"

"No, he's a liar. He's lied to us several times now, but what evidence do I have? Maz wasn't a member of AA, her fiancé was, so it's highly probable that they didn't meet. Zara never met her, so why would Eliot?"

He chewed on the lip of his glass.

"What?" Alicia asked, knowing he wasn't finished with this topic.

He placed the glass back on the table. "I just *know* he's lying. I've sensed it almost from the start, but I don't know about what, and I don't know how to find out."

"What about Maz Olden?" Alicia asked. "Could she be lying?"

"Absolutely she could." He stopped to enjoy the first course that was being placed on the table then, and after a few mouthfuls said, "I have a mad theory if you're interested."

"Yes, I love mad theories. Shoot!"

He smiled and wiped his mouth with his serviette. "Okay, so what if Maz really loved Brian?"

"Brian the bully who threw her down a set of stairs?"

"Wouldn't be the first domestic violence victim to forgive and forget. We tracked down the officers who investigated the domestic incident she mentioned, and they say it was *Maz* who refused to press charges, not them."

"What? Why?"

"Some domestic violence victims do that for their own safety, understandably terrified of the repercussions.

But I'm wondering whether we've got it all wrong. What if her tears of relief are all an act? You have to remember, this is the guy she is about to have a child with, the one she was engaged to, the one she gave a ring to with a kiss and a hug on it. You don't give someone an engraved ring if you despise them, do you? What if she loved Brian Donahue, faults and all, and was furious with Eliot for scaring him off or turning him suicidal or whatever. In any case, she discovers he's dead—maybe he sent her a text saying goodbye, I'm not sure. I have to look into all that— but what if she is so furious she somehow tracks down Eliot and Kat to the Balmain park, slips down next to their blanket, and takes her revenge."

"Small, itty bitty problem with your theory," said Alicia.

"I know. Her hands are tiny; they don't fit the contusion marks around Kat's neck. But then she wasn't on her own, was she? She was with a man who—shock horror—vanished into the night."

"The mystery man with the mo!"

"Exactly. Who is this bloke? Maybe he's a mate of Brian's. Maybe he did the deed for her and then slipped away."

She sat back in her seat. "Wow, that's quite a theory."

"I know, right?"

"So how do you prove it?"

He scowled. "That's the tough part."

"The first thing you've got to prove is that Maz knew Eliot and Kat, otherwise how could she identify them at the park?"

"Kat was all over YouTube, remember?"

"Yes, but Eliot wasn't, and nobody ever recalls him mentioning Kat by name. How would Maz even know that Kat was his wife? Unless they met outside AA, of course! They must have crossed paths at the beginning or end of a session."

"Eliot insists he never met Maz. Maz insists she never met Eliot."

"Maybe Maz is lying. Maybe Brian pointed out Eliot and Kat one evening after a meeting, and she took it from there."

"But how do I prove that? How do I prove that Maz knew Eliot and Kat or could spot either of them in a busy park?" He groaned. "To be honest, I'm not even sure I should be trying to prove this. Singho thinks I'm wasting precious time and wants me to focus on other suspects, but I can't seem to let this one go."

"I know a way we can find out."

"We?" He held up an open palm. "Babe, this is the part where I remind you to stay out of it."

She just stared at him, waiting for him to come to his senses.

Jackson sat back and shook his head at her again. "Alicia, you *cannot* hassle Zara again! She's been interrogated enough."

Alicia smiled wider. "Oh it's not Zara I'm thinking of this time. And I won't be doing the interrogating, I can promise you that."

# CHAPTER 37

Perry straightened his silk tie and smoothed his goatee into place, then strode swiftly across the rain-splattered street towards the older man with the receding hairline. Timothy Iles glanced up and away then back again, this time with a frown.

"What the hell do you want?" he growled.

"Just five minutes of your time, that's all I ask," Perry said.

Timothy kept walking. "I've got an AA meeting to attend." Then he stopped and swept around. "And don't you dare try to follow me in."

"Please," Perry persisted. "I'm begging you, for Kat's sake, just give me five minutes and I'll explain everything."

Timothy's gait slowed just slightly, so Perry added, "I'm trying to find who killed Kat. This is extremely important. There's a brutal killer out there. We need to stop him."

The man picked up his pace again and kept walking towards the Rozelle Neighbourhood Centre, so Perry sighed sadly and was just turning away when he noticed Timothy continue past the Centre and down another block. He was heading towards the Tulip Café, the same café where Alicia had previously questioned Zara.

Perry smiled with relief as he followed him down the road and then inside.

"Can I get you guys anything?" a waitress asked breezily after they had chosen a table near the back. "We have a range of coffee, tea, a bar menu if you'd like to see one."

"I'll just have a latte, thanks," Perry said, and Timothy scoffed.

"Don't bother with the charade. I know you're a fraud. You might as well order a beer; it'd be more honest."

The waitress's smile slipped a little as she looked from Timothy back to Perry, who said, "I'll still have that coffee, thank you."

The waitress looked at Tim, her smile strained.

"Nothing thanks. I'm not staying."

"Oh, er, okay then." She glanced nervously between the men before dashing away.

Timothy stared at Perry. Hard.

"Zara told us everything, so you can drop the bullshit, mate. She told us to steer clear of you and Alicia. Is that even her real name? Are you really Perry?"

"Yes, we did use real names, and we're both very sorry that we lied to you all. But we did it for a good cause. We are trying to find out who killed Kat Mumford. Eliot's wife."

"Why not just ask us? Why all the subterfuge?"

"Good question, maybe we should have. I apologise profusely. Did Zara also tell you about Brian?"

"Couldn't have happened to a nicer bloke."

Perry nodded. "That seems to be the general consensus." He waited a beat. "Look, I appreciate your talking to me."

"I'm only here because I feel sorry for that poor woman. Kat. That's all." He folded his arms. "You've got five minutes, and then I'm history."

"Good. Thank you. That's all I need." Perry took a breath. "Can I ask, did you ever meet Brian's fiancée, a woman called Maz Olden?"

He looked confused by the change of tack but then shook his head. "Next question?"

"Do you know if Eliot Mumford or his wife knew Maz?"

"Again, no clue. Why don't you just ask your mate?"

"Mate?"

"Eliot."

Perry accepted the latte he was being handed and said, "Oh we don't know Eliot. Or Kat for that matter."

Timothy looked incredulous. "Then what the hell has all this been about?"

He held up a placatory palm. "We were sitting close by, the night Kat was murdered. It unfolded right in front of our eyes. Can you imagine how upsetting that would be? We've struggled to just look the other way, pretend like it didn't happen. Alicia's boyfriend is a detective, and they don't seem to have a clue. We're just trying to help. That's all."

Timothy rubbed his head. "Eliot sure doesn't deserve you guys. Pity it wasn't him who got strangled at the movie instead of his wife."

"You don't like him much, do you?"

He shrugged. "Like I told you, he's an ungrateful hypocrite with a god complex."

Perry sat up straight. "Hang on, that was Eliot you were referring to? You were *Eliot's* sponsor?"

"For a few months. Until I learned he'd beaten Brian up. I know Brian was a loser, but he was a *skinny* loser. Eliot is the size of Thor. Hardly an even contest. You ask me, Eliot was as bad as Brian. Came in, boasting about it at AA, acting like some kind of saviour, riding in on his white horse and protecting the little pregnant fiancée. All the women at AA oohed and ahhed, like he really was some Nordic god."

"So why'd you call him a hypocrite?"

"He might not beat up his wife, but he's as bad as Brian, if you ask me. Called Kat his little kitten but treated her like a dog."

Perry's ears pricked up. "How so?"

"Look, I never met Kat, right? But he showed me her stuff online once, soon after I caught him drinking at a pub just down from here. She looked beautiful to me.

She clearly worked hard. And she obviously adored him. If I had a woman like that waiting for me at home, I'd never look into a bottle of gin again. But there he was getting smashed, bitching and moaning about her, how she used to be such a party animal and how she'd turned into a bore."

"She was a party animal the night she got killed," Perry pointed out.

"I know, and that surprised the hell out of me. I kept thinking, but she's not the big drinker, he is. She's the reason he's at AA. Pity it wasn't him that—"

Perry's shocked expression finally must have registered because Timothy stopped talking for a moment and looked worried.

"Didn't Eliot tell your cop friend all this?"

"Tell him what?"

"He was only at AA on Kat's behest. All he had to do was attend meetings and try to give up the grog. That's all she ever asked from him. But he found that *unreasonable*. Every time we spoke, every bloody cigarette break, he bitched and moaned about how *demanding* Kat was, how it wasn't *fair*. Why couldn't he have his cake and eat it too? He was a churlish child."

Perry was stunned. "Did Eliot ever say what would happen if he dropped out of AA? If he didn't stay off the alcohol?"

"Sure. He said the 'silly bitch' would leave him, and he didn't want that."

"Why not?"

He rubbed his fingers together, indicating cash.

"But he's got a job; he's a carpenter isn't he?"

"Only when she drags him into one of her projects. Otherwise, no, Eliot's a man of leisure, haven't you worked that out yet? Spends most of his time at his mates' bars and cafés, supping lattes and stroking his stupid beard."

Timothy was watching Perry's expression closely.

"Why does this excite you? I mean, no one wants to pin Kat's murder on Eliot more than me, mate, but he couldn't've done it. I heard he wasn't even close by when it happened. He doesn't have what the cops call 'opportunity.'"

"That's true," said Perry.

*But he has motive in spades.*

"Anyway." Timothy was getting to his feet. "I've said enough. Have broken every single commandment in the AA bible."

"Sorry," Perry said, "but just one more thing, please. Just before, you said Brian's fiancée was pregnant. How did you know that? Did Brian mention it in the sessions?"

Timothy thought about that. "Probably." Then he stopped. "No, that's right. Eliot told me that's how he justified beating Brian up. Said he was doing it to protect Brian's unborn son."

"Unborn son?"

"That's what he said."

"But how did Eliot know Maz was pregnant—and with a boy—if he never met her?"

"Good question. I guess you'll have to ask him that."

Perry tried to hide his excitement. Not only had he just discovered a good motive for murder, it sounded like Eliot had lied to the police about knowing Maz Olden.

To Perry that was more intriguing than anything else. *Why would Eliot feel the need to lie about that?*

As the older man turned to leave, Perry said, "Thank you so much, Timothy. I don't know what to say."

Timothy didn't turn around as he called back, "The truth next time would be a good place to start."

~~~~~~~

Detective Indira Singh was saying something along the same lines to Perry and Alicia as the two friends sat stoically in front of her desk again, this time with Jackson standing behind them, one hand on the back of each of their chairs.

"I don't even know where to start with you two—interrogating witnesses, hindering my investigation…" She let that drop, took a breath, plastered a smile to her face. "But! Jacko here has *insisted* I be a bit more polite, so I'm going to try very hard to bite my tongue this time."

She inhaled deeply through her nose. Then exhaled through her lips. "You two are just lucky your guesses have panned out." She looked up just as Pauly walked in. "What did you find?"

"Apartment in Rose Bay," he said. "Purchased four months ago through a different agent. Lease is under her maiden name."

"That explains it. Thanks, Pauly."

As he walked out again, she smiled. It was a rare sight for Alicia, and she couldn't help smiling along.

"So it looks like Timothy Iles was right, and Kat *was* planning to leave her husband," Indira explained. "We already suspected she wasn't a happy camper—Kat's mum indicated there were problems in the marriage, but we couldn't find any actual evidence of that. For the past fortnight, Jarrod's been interrogating their friends, work colleagues, inner circle, but by all other accounts they were madly in love. It was almost nauseating, to be honest."

"It was obviously an act," said Perry. "Eliot's sponsor will attest to that."

"Except it's one man's word against everyone else. At least now we have proof that Kat was moving out. It's not quite divorce papers, but it's close." She turned to Jackson, who was pulling up a seat beside Alicia. "I kept wondering why the Mumford's house looked different to the one I'd seen online, and now I get it. I bet the all-white kitchen she posted on Instagram belongs to the new apartment, not the one they were living in. That has a black-and-white benchtop, yes?"

"Maybe Eliot saw those clips, too, and worked it out

for himself," said Jackson. "That's extra motive to act."

"It sure is. Better to kill his wife and get everything now than have her skip off to a new life and get written out of the will. We're checking Eliot's business too, seeing what kind of financial situation he was in. If it's dire, it'll strengthen his motive, but it still doesn't solve the question of opportunity." She looked back at Alicia and Perry. "You said yourselves, there was no way he could have done it. He stayed beside you lot the entire second half."

"Could he have hired someone?" suggested Perry. "Contract killing?"

"Except nobody noticed this killer for hire come out of nowhere, bend down and do the deed," said Indira.

"Which brings us back to Mo Man," said Jackson. "He had access, he had opportunity."

"Hang on," said Indira. "I thought you said Mo Man was working with Maz, not Eliot."

He shrugged. "I don't know what to think anymore."

Alicia cleared her throat and said, "Maybe they're in on it together? Have you thought of that?"

All eyes were now upon her, at least one set glinting irritably, so she quickly added, "Maybe Eliot and Maz planned the whole thing."

Indira frowned. "Why? *How?*"

She swished her lips to one side. "I don't know *exactly*, but maybe it happened just as Timothy said—Eliot saw Maz getting slammed about after AA one night and hatched a plan. What if he got in touch with her and agreed to take out her partner if she took out his?"

"I saw a fabulous film like that once!" said Perry.

Jackson was already clicking his fingers. "Yes, um, a Hitchcock one. What's it called...?"

"*Strangers on a Train* and it won't work," snapped Indira. "Sure, Eliot might have somehow given Brian the hot shot, then raced to the film with a very drunken Kat—they did get there late; we could probably make those times work. But there is no way that tiny, pregnant Maz could have strangled Kat. Not physically possible, remember?"

"Which brings us back to Mo Man," said Jackson.

Indira growled. "I haven't got time to track down the elusive bloody man with the moustache!"

"Maybe you don't have to," said Alicia, sitting forward more confidently this time. "It *could* just be the two of them. I've been thinking about this since *Grease* the other night, when I didn't recognise Missy in the crowd even though she usually stands out like a sore thumb. And then when I sat down on the rug that wasn't actually mine, that's when it began to dawn on me how easy it is to get your rugs mixed up…"

Now all three of them were staring at her with irritated expressions.

"Sorry," Alicia said, laughing despite herself. "I'm just trying to get it clear in my head."

She took a deep breath.

"I think I know how Eliot and Maz pulled it off right under all our noses." Her eyes lit up as she glanced at Indira. "I know you're not a fan of wild theories, but I've got a theory that might not be as wild as it sounds." Now her eyes darted back to Perry and Jackson. "But first we're going to need to pack our picnic blankets and head off to another moonlit cinema."

# CHAPTER 38

Centennial Park is a sprawling urban green space, not far from the centre of Sydney and as different from the cosy little park in Balmain as a sci-fi thriller is to *Evil Under the Sun*. But as far as Alicia was concerned, they would both do the job nicely.

Centennial Park's monthly Moonlight Cinema was screening the film *Gravity* the very next night, and she was keen to get the club back together to test out her theory and put her plan into place, and this time DI Singh would be the guest of honour.

On paper it sounded implausible, ridiculous in fact, but she remembered the words of Hercule Poirot, and it gave her courage as she watched Indira plucking her way through the crowd now, towards her blanket in the waning sunset.

It was Poirot who talked about "suntanned bodies lying like meat upon a slab" and how, to the casual observer, there was little difference between one body and another lying out in the sun. Well, it was not just on a beach where bodies looked similar but lying on rugs wedged in together at an outdoor cinema, under a blanket of darkness.

That wasn't the only thing Alicia was borrowing from the great Agatha Christie tonight. She suspected the answer to the puzzle lay in the plot line of *Evil Under the Sun* as well and wondered whether any of the players even realised that when they put their macabre piece of theatre into play.

Perry, who like the rest of the book club was privy to

Alicia's plan, was less circumspect. "I think Eliot's been dreaming of this for a while, but when he heard about the movie choice, it got his creative juices flowing."

"For the sake of grand theatre, I'd like to think so," said Alicia, "but I doubt it."

She didn't think real life was ever quite as clever as an Agatha Christie novel.

"Well you sure shoved yourselves in the middle of it all," said Indira as she stepped across an open picnic basket and onto Alicia's rug.

"All the better to prove my theory," she swatted back.

Alicia had decided that the best way to handle the prickly DI was to give as good as she got and, failing that, to let the woman's comments wash over, not to take it all so personally. Jackson insisted Indira was a good person at heart, and so she would give his partner the benefit of the doubt and see how that worked out.

Perry was not so easily swayed and could barely restrain his frown as he watched her dump her bag and then drop down on Jackson's other side.

The book club had all gathered tonight except for Anders, who had been dropping out of group get-togethers of late, and Alicia tried not to think about that now. For all their history, for all his combativeness, she enjoyed having him around. Somebody needed to play devil's advocate. It couldn't always be Claire, who was now slumped on her own blanket, rubbing her temple.

"I know we're here to help, Alicia, but I've got such a headache. I feel a migraine coming on."

"I've got some paracetamol if you need any," Indira offered.

"Thanks. I think I'll be okay," she replied, shaking her head at the beers that Jackson was handing around.

Indira took one while Missy held out a Tupperware container full of rice snacks topped with avocado and cheese. Her diet was clearly still on track, and she looked the better for it, her energy still high, her smile still in place.

A sudden burst of applause caught everyone's attention, and they looked up to find the movie was just starting on the big screen at the front of the roped-off section of the park.

"Now what?" asked Indira.

"Just settle in," Jackson said. "And enjoy the show."

She frowned at that idea but did as requested, pulling a pillow from her backpack and resting her elbows back against it, her legs out in front.

Jackson scooched closer to Alicia, who had also brought cushions this time, while the rest of the gang spread out on the myriad rugs and blankets that the Finlay sisters had prepared earlier. There were also several coolers, a picnic basket and three backpacks.

Alicia pulled a fresh red blanket out of one backpack and flung it over Jackson and herself, then they put their beers aside and settled under the blanket to cuddle. Within minutes they were kissing amorously, which didn't seem to bother anyone, except Indira.

"Jeez, you two, get a room," she hissed.

They tried not to laugh as they continued wrestling under the blanket for another five minutes or so. Eventually, as the film progressed, things settled down and Alicia was now huddled quietly, Jackson beside her, the others spread out in a range of positions, and Indira was feeling more relaxed.

She hadn't picked Jackson as the "public display of affection" type and was glad they had snapped out of it. She couldn't help feeling sorry for Claire though. The poor woman had dashed off to the toilets at one point, looking ready to throw up.

Other than those two interruptions, Indira soon got caught up in the Sandra Bullock blockbuster and was as surprised as everyone else when intermission hit soon after and the lights flickered back on.

"Anyone going to the snack bar?" Missy called out, and Perry nodded his head.

"Sure, I'll come."

They helped each other up, and then he held a hand out to Indira.

"Come on, stretch your legs. It'll do you some good."

Indira shrugged. "Sure. I could do with something more substantial than rice cakes." She glanced towards the red blanket. "Where'd Jacko and Alicia go?"

"Oh they're already in the queue," Perry said. "They were famished."

"Impatient buggers. Okay, what about you, Claire?" Indira glanced over to where Claire looked half-asleep under her pink blanket.

"I'll see if she needs anything," said Lynette, waving them on.

As the trio closed in on the snack bar, they noticed a long queue. Indira suggested they cut the line and join Alicia and Jackson, who were just visible at the front, but Perry was having none of it.

"Just because you're a cop doesn't mean you don't have to wait your turn like the rest of us plebs, you know."

"Fine," she snapped back, adding, "You don't like me much, do you, Perry?"

He turned to her, his lips wide. "I could say the same about you!"

"Well, if you did it wouldn't be true. You seem like a nice enough person. When you're not interfering with my investigation, that is."

He looked even more outraged. "Interfering, sure, but I'll have you know I've never been called 'nice' in my life—not even by my exes! I'm *fabulous*, darling, and a lot of fun. But *nice*? I don't think so."

Then he gave her a sly smile as he turned back to face the front.

Indira smiled too. It was as good a truce as either was prepared to make. She glanced back towards the counter where she noticed Alicia and Jackson were handing over some cash in exchange for a cup of hot chips.

"What are you going to get?" Missy asked, and Indira glanced back at her.

"The chips look good," she replied as the queue slowly snaked forward.

By the time Indira, Missy and Perry returned to their rugs, the second half of the film was just getting underway and Indira only had a moment to glance around before darkness descended again.

She noticed that Claire had made a good recovery and was helping herself to a snack while Alicia was lying down under her blanket, an empty bucket of chips behind her head.

Jackson was sitting upright next to Missy on a small deckchair she had brought along and was a fair distance from his girlfriend now.

"Everything okay?" she whispered across to him.

He glanced at her, then to Alicia and back. "Lying down's doing my back in." He stretched a little to emphasise the point.

Forty minutes later, the credits were rolling, the crowd was applauding, and Indira was wondering what the point of the evening was. She had enjoyed the movie, despite herself, but that was not the reason she had come. There was still so much work to do on the case, and she was starting to feel restless again.

She glanced across to Alicia, who was still snuggled under her blanket.

"Not a sci-fi fan?" she said to Jackson, who was laughing at some joke with Missy.

He looked up at her. "Sorry?"

"Your girlfriend's fallen asleep. I thought she had some grand plan for the night. I didn't realise it involved her catching up on her $z$'s."

Jackson frowned. "Hm, that's odd."

He stood up and stepped across several blankets to reach Alicia's rug.

He bent down and gave her a gentle shake.

He frowned, then gave her another shake, a firmer one this time.

Then he fell back on his thighs, looking stricken.

"Oh my God," he said, gasping. "Oh my God, Alicia, nooooo!"

Indira swept around to stare at him, her lips wide, her face as ghostly as the screen above her head.

# CHAPTER 39

Indira's colour had returned, along with her trademark glare, but she didn't know who to direct it at first—Jackson for pulling her leg or Alicia for pretending to play dead.

They were all sitting up now, every one of them nursing a beer, including Claire whose "migraine" had miraculously vanished.

"I'm sorry, Indira, really I am," said Alicia. "But I needed to see if my theory worked. And it did."

Indira glowered. "I don't think you've proven anything. So you lay there pretending to be dead. As a detective, I'd still point the finger firmly at the people closest to you in that second half. Nobody else came within a metre of you. I would have noticed."

"Except I'd been lying there, pretending to be dead since *before* intermission," Alicia said, causing Indira's jaw to drop.

She took a moment to digest that. "But... but I saw you at the snack bar, didn't I?"

She glanced at Perry and Missy, who giggled.

"No, Indira," Missy said. "That wasn't Alicia. That was Jackson and Claire."

Indira looked over at Claire, who was reaching into a backback and pulling out a short, shaggy blond wig. She gave the detective a sympathetic smile.

"I pretended to be sick and went off to the loos where I changed into the wig."

"But I looked at Alicia's blanket," Indira persisted.

"She wasn't there."

"That's because I had 'strangled' her earlier," said Jackson, using finger quotes, "while we were having our passionate little wrestle. Then when Claire left, I carefully nudged Alicia's 'lifeless body' closer to Claire's pink blanket so it looked like Claire had returned and was now snoozing underneath."

"Then," Claire said, "Jackson came to join me at the front of the snack bar where, from the back, it looked like he was standing with Alicia. We're a similar height and size, and dressed in similar colours, with the wig on, most people couldn't tell the difference."

"But I *saw*…"

"You saw what your brain expected you to see—Alicia and Jackson," explained Perry, "but really it was Claire and Jackson. You only saw them from the back, remember? I wouldn't let you get too close."

Indira's lips formed a perfect O. "That's right. You told me not to cut in. Cheeky man!" She shook her head. "Okay, so when I got back to the blankets…"

"You saw what looked like Alicia asleep, Claire awake and Jackson far, far away," said Perry. "A replica of another film night a few weeks back."

They all nodded along except for Indira, who was still struggling to get a clear picture in her head.

Jackson smiled at Indira's perplexed expression, opened a fresh bottle of beer for her and said, "Shall we start from the top?"

Indira took the bottle, sighed dramatically and said, "Go on then, wise guys."

And so, as the rest of the crowd gradually finished their picnics and headed off into the night, the Murder Mystery Book Club talked Detective Inspector Singh through Alicia's "insane" theory, one they had just proven was not quite as mad as they had originally thought.

Alicia wished the main players could be there to

witness the "grand denouement," just as they were in every Poirot novel, but of course, this wasn't a work of fiction. The revelation would be made to them with their rights read, crafty lawyers present and far less chance of a dramatic admission of guilt.

She took a sip of her beer and began.

"It all played out just as we performed it tonight," she said. "We don't know the exact details—"

"Of course!" Indira interrupted.

She smiled. "But here's what we think happened…"

# CHAPTER 40

It had been a glorious, sundrenched day, and the crowds had flocked to the small park in Balmain early to clinch the best patch of grass in front of the large white screen at the northern end of the park.

*Evil Under the Sun* would be showing that night, and they could not wait.

One of the early comers was a pregnant woman called Maz Olden. Maz could wait. Indeed she did wait, for over an hour, witnesses would later tell detectives, just leaning against a cement balustrade near the park entrance, watching the crowd, biding her time.

Whether she was waiting for a man with a peppery moustache she had lured there under false pretences or simply plucked him out of the crowd that evening, no one knew, not yet, but as soon as he spread his rug on the ground to the right of the screen, not far from the bar and, more strategically, close to the Portaloos, Maz finally made her way across, dropping down to claim the bare grass beside him.

Perhaps it wasn't the moustached man she was targeting but the large family who were seated just behind, knowing they would be distracted as all families are, and moving and wriggling a lot. Whatever the case, Maz spread her hot pink blanket out and, when no one was paying too much attention, pulled out another blanket, a red cashmere one, and spread that out on the edge of her own.

Latecomers, like the book club, would then wrongly assume that the Mumfords had placed the blanket there and gone away and come back.

And so the crowds continued to spill in, and dozens of colourful rugs became a bright quilt that spread across the entire lawn, a jumble of picnic baskets, backpacks, and bodies everywhere. So many bodies, in fact, that it was almost impossible to tell where one group ended and another began.

And that was what Maz and Eliot were counting on.

Earlier that evening Eliot had somehow managed to get his wife drunk, so drunk she was almost incoherent and barely able to walk. How he managed to do that would be a matter for the detectives, but Alicia had a hunch that Kat had drunk willingly with her husband for the final time. Perhaps she was drinking orange juice laced with vodka? Or perhaps he had convinced her to have a final hurrah before they broke up? In any case, by the time Kat arrived at the park and was dragged across the lawn to the empty red blanket, she was moving from giggly drunk to barely cognisant. She would have been legless if it wasn't for the firm hands of her sober husband helping her onto the rug.

And so they flopped down noisily, making their presence known, ensuring there were plenty of witnesses as they kissed and cuddled and carried on, Kat so intoxicated she probably had no idea what she was doing or even where she was.

Then, during that first half of the movie as all eyes were gripped by the murder of Arlena Marshall on the big screen, Eliot Mumford was gripping the neck of his wife, silently squeezing the life out of her, and nobody noticed.

Kat did not cry out or fight him off because she was so drunk by that stage that she barely knew what was happening. And nobody noticed a thing because they were a passionate couple, right? As several witnesses said: *"They were just having a little wrestle under their blanket. It was innocent enough."*

In fact, if the poor, intoxicated woman was still

cognisant, she was probably wrestling for her life.

No sooner had Kat gasped her last breath then the next part of the plan sped into motion. Maz, who had pretended to be an annoyed audience member to the left of the Mumfords, faked morning sickness, rushing off to use the facilities and making sure she caught the eye of several concerned witnesses as she did so. She needed to get away before intermission. She had a new role to play. Concealed under her pregnant stomach—a stomach that wasn't really as big as it looked—was a long blond wig and Kat's grey fedora, Gucci glasses and suede jacket. They had been pinched from the deceased woman earlier that evening, easy enough to do when the victim was drunk and her husband helping you out.

As Maz quickly changed clothes, Eliot carefully and slowly shuffled himself and his now deceased wife across from their red blanket to the hot pink one, moving inch by inch, so slowly that nobody noticed. As Alicia had proven tonight and during the screening of *Grease*, blankets blend into each other when laid out on the grass. It's easy to mistake them in the dark or shift between them with little fuss.

Then with his dead wife hidden beneath the edge of Maz's rug, Eliot slipped away to the bar just before the lights came back on. It was the most gripping part of the movie—the part where Arlena Marshall's body is discovered—and he was banking on the fact that nobody would notice that he was alone. Or if they did, they would later assume that Kat joined him at the bar soon after.

Meanwhile, Maz had morphed from a sickly, curly haired pregnant woman into a drunken blonde with her trademark white glasses and fedora, a flowing skirt, and a large suede jacket to hide her pregnant bulge.

And so she slipped out of the Portaloos and over to the Booze Bar to join Eliot near the counter. And there she played the role of her life—faking a fight with her "husband" in front of a queue of strangers, including

Alicia and Lynette, who had no idea it wasn't really Kat because, well, they hadn't really seen Kat properly, had they? She had been huddled under Eliot's arm when she first arrived.

And so the fight scene played out perfectly with one intention and one intention only—to provide Eliot Mumford with an airtight alibi. With the curious queue watching on, he stormed off to sit alone, a safe distance from his "wife," while his "wife" continued to make her presence known, staggering first to the snack bar, then when the lights were low enough, back to the red blanket to settle in all alone—and very much alive.

*Kat had to be alive at the start of the second half! Scores of witnesses had seen her, right?*

While Eliot perched beside the book club, fake Kat pretended to fall asleep below her blanket. Yet all the while, the real Kat was already dead and now lying with one arm over her stomach, under Maz's pink rug, looking like a sick pregnant woman, not a corpse.

At some point in that second half, only one witness could confirm, fake "Kat" slipped away to the Portaloos, returning five minutes later, *sans* her disguise, as the real Maz. Then all Maz had to do was plonk down on the *other* side of Kat's lifeless body.

With so many eyes on the screen above, so many bodies sprawled on blankets, and so many people reaching over each other to fetch drinks, cuddle up and move about, it would not have been too hard for Maz to then slip Kat's belongings back or to nudge her slowly but subtly to her original position under the red blanket.

And yet she made one niggling error.

While she had returned Kat's fedora, Maz had forgotten to give back the glasses. They probably got caught up in her own blanket or in the backpack she'd brought along. Alicia guessed that the police would find a pricey pair of Guccis somewhere among Maz's belongings. They cost a small fortune, and she wasn't exactly flush, so there was every chance she hadn't disposed of them.

Of course if that didn't pan out, there was always the champagne flute. Alicia would wager a bet that the unknown fingerprints would turn out to be Maz Olden's. After all, it was really Maz who had bought that sparkling wine, not poor Kat.

Meantime, with all that subtle shifting and shoving— by Eliot in the first half and Maz in the second—it's no wonder Kat's camisole strap was torn and her skirt was out of place. They had probably not even factored that in, but it worked in their favour, adding an element of menace that pointed away from the loving husband and towards a nefarious stranger.

That was just good luck for Eliot.

By the time the film was over and Eliot was making his presence known, chatting to the book club about the plot, Maz had morphed back into a heavily pregnant woman, sitting up on her pink blanket, looking sickly and glum.

After saying his goodbyes to the club, Eliot then returned to wake up his wife, pretending to discover her dead body and reeling back to begin Act 3: A Man in Shock.

"He played that part brilliantly," said Indira now, shaking her head as she polished off her beer. "If what you say is true, both Eliot and Maz are the most accomplished actors I've ever come across."

"I think desperation will make you do anything," said Alicia. "And Maz was desperate. She clearly believed that Brian was going to kill her and her baby, so she acted to save her life and the life of her unborn child."

"Fat lot of good that's going to do either one of them when she's locked up in prison," said Claire. "I can't believe she agreed to do it."

"Eliot can be pretty persuasive," said Jackson, "batting his big brown eyelashes and stroking his handsome jaw." He tried not to direct that comment at his colleague, who had seemed a little too quick to believe the victim's handsome husband. "He obviously convinced Maz that they had to work together to save themselves. In any case, I'm sure Maz felt she had little choice. Maybe she really couldn't escape Brian and thought it was the only way to save her baby. Or perhaps she was just seeking retribution." He shook his head. "Perhaps Reverend Joves got it half right. Except Maz was the real Jezebel here, not Kat."

At that stage the plan was less Agatha Christie and more Alfred Hitchcock, Alicia noted.

Indira nodded. "Yes, *Strangers On a Train,* we were saying that yesterday."

"Except it wasn't so much that they killed each other's partners as helped each other out," explained Jackson. "We still have to get our heads around that. Personally, I suspect Maz arranged to meet Brian at the deserted rooftop of that old shopping mall the afternoon of the film night. I don't know how she lured him there, but I suspect she had a peace offering for him, a chocolate milkshake that had been laced with sleeping pills—Scelosi found both among the contents in Brian's stomach when he did the autopsy. Maybe Maz told him she'd get rid of the baby or something, I don't know. In any case, she must have left him when he got drowsy then dashed off to Balmain. Perhaps she had already loaded up his syringe with a double dose of heroin, so when he woke up, groggy, he would give himself the fatal dose while she was giving herself an alibi at the film night."

"Or maybe she left him there and Eliot snuck in and administered the fatal dose while Brian was sleeping?" suggested Alicia. "Remember, Eliot and Kat got to the park later than everybody else."

"He was cutting it close," said Indira.

"That's true," said Perry. "If he did do it, he would have been rushed. Remember, he had to get back to his wife, somehow ply her with alcohol and then turn up to the park just late enough to ensure a grand and noisy entrance."

"Yeah, I've got my money on Maz doing it," said Lynette, but Jackson was shaking his head at himself.

"If only I'd given that man the courtesy of investigating his death properly. If I'd looked into his background better I would have learned there was a brutalised fiancée with a motive for murder. There's probably CCTV footage of Maz at the mall, buying that chocolate drink. Scelosi insists it's a chocolate Frappuccino from Starbucks—that can't be hard to check."

"Hang on," said Lynette. "The coroner can pinpoint the brand of drink?"

He smiled. "Yeah, it took him a bit longer, but he was able to work it out from the concentration of ingredients. Something to do with the mocha-flavoured sauce, apparently." He laughed. "I think Scelosi was just looking for an excuse to test milkshakes all day. In any case, he was very bloody proud of himself."

Jackson looked at Indira. "Eliot and Maz must have thought they were very clever, luring Brian to that old rooftop where there are no cameras, but I bet they didn't figure on Frank. I'm sure Starbucks would have working CCTV. Can't be too hard to check the footage and see if Maz purchased a Frappuccino on the day in question. I just can't believe I didn't join the dots faster."

"Oh don't beat yourself up," said Indira. "You joined them in the end."

"Still," Jackson said. "Still." And he left it at that.

Indira was standing up now to stretch her legs out. She said, "This is all very clever, guys, but we have one slight hitch."

"Evidence," said Jackson.

"Evidence," she repeated.

"I'll get that footage from the shopping mall. Maybe we'll get extra lucky and see Eliot entering the mall. It's a start."

"And that's all it is. We've got a lot of work ahead of us to prove the rest."

She glanced around. They were virtually the last group left at the park, just a few stragglers still lolling about.

"Come on, the security guards need to get their beauty sleep, and so do we. That's a lot of 'maybes' and 'what ifs' to substantiate tomorrow."

Then she flung her hands to her hips and said, "And I'm talking about the homicide squad now, people, not the Murder Mystery Book Club!"

They laughed and gathered their things, then headed for the exit. By the time they reached their cars, the group was exhausted and the thought of finding evidence was beyond most of them, but Indira was brimming with ideas.

She suspected that Alicia was right and would seek a search warrant for Maz Olden's apartment first thing in the morning. She was determined to find those Gucci glasses and hoped Maz had been greedy enough to hold on to them. She had assumed young Ezekiel had stolen them, and that was a lucky break for Maz. Another red herring, in fact.

Glasses or no glasses, it still left Eliot in the clear, but she had an inkling that a young woman with a baby onboard would quickly roll over if offered the right incentive.

"What are you smiling at?" Jackson asked as he leaned in her car window.

"Oh just plotting the next move," she said, then nodded her head towards the book club friends who were giving each other goodbye hugs. "You've got a nice bunch of mates there, you know, and a smart bunch at that."

"Really? You want to say that a little louder so they can hear it from the horse's mouth?"

"Who are you calling a horse?" She winked. "Nah, wouldn't want them to get too cocky and start applying for jobs. Cripes! Tell them thank you, but we'll take it from here. They can go back to their fiction and leave the facts to us."

"I think I'll just leave it at 'thank you,'" Jackson said, and she laughed as she drove off.

# EPILOGUE

The letter had been beautifully handwritten on thick blue paper, and Alicia read it aloud to the book club as they sat on recycled furniture in Missy's new lounge room.

She had found a place to rent just up the road from the Finlays, and while it was on the small and shabby side, she had done her best to brighten things up with cheerful furnishings that had been begged, borrowed and stolen. Yet the mood in the room was now subdued.

By the time Alicia had finished reading, several of the group were teary and most were lost for words.

Eventually Perry said, "Well, it's his loss, not ours."

Alicia shook her head firmly. "I, for one, will miss him."

Perry sniffed. "Yeah, I guess I will too. At the very least he was lovely eye candy."

"Anders was so much more than that!" Claire retorted. "He was switch-blade bright and slapped us with cold water whenever we needed a dose, which is often I might add."

"Sometimes that water was scalding hot," Missy said, then smiled despite herself.

Anders had always been a little impatient with her, but she understood why and would miss him as much as the others.

It had taken the good doctor over an hour to construct his resignation letter to the Murder Mystery Book Club, and he was not lying when he said he would miss them and wished them the best. But the truth was he hated being the voice of caution. He hated always trying to apply the handbrake.

"You're a very clever, underappreciated bunch," he wrote, "and you don't need someone like me to hold you back anymore. I just can't help myself. I'm clearly too cautious for this club. I've tried to fit in, but it's been, frankly, *terrifying*. Maybe it's because I'm a doctor or because I'm an official police consultant, maybe I'm naturally conservative or have a reputation to uphold, but I feel the time has come to move on. I was hoping Margarita could take my place. She studies literature, and I thought you'd all get along, but I learned pretty quickly after that first get-together, that she's even more cautious than I am, so I apologise for that. I do wish you all the very best, and I hope we can stay in touch."

"I *knew* she was a plant!" said Lynette, and Alicia scoffed.

"You thought she was a paid escort!"

The others looked at her, astounded, and she shrugged one tanned shoulder high.

"I just knew he'd brought her along under false pretences that's all."

"He was trying to audition his replacement," said Claire. "Which was very decent of him if you think about it, and the question still remains: Who *will* replace Anders? Our numbers are getting low, folks."

"That's right!" said Missy, putting an evil tone to her voice: "and then there were five!"

They all laughed and agreed it was time to recruit a few more members to plump up the club.

"How are we going to find the right people?" asked Lynette, but Perry was shaking his head wildly.

"Hold your horses!" he cried. "Before we get into that, I'm still waiting to hear how the case is progressing." He turned to Alicia, his eyes wide. "So did Eliot Mumford do the right thing and confess everything?"

"What do you think?" She laughed. "Sadly, this ain't no

Agatha Christie novel, folks. He's got himself a top barrister, of course, and is settling in for a fight."

"What about Maz?"

"Oh, she's been an easier nut to crack. It's just as Indira suspected—she's desperate to talk in exchange for a plea deal. Maz says it was *all* Eliot's idea, every last bit of it apparently—even the lethal dose of heroin. She says Eliot gave her that to pass on to Brian. The problem was, Maz couldn't be sure he'd even take it that night, and after she hadn't heard from the police, she was terrified he was still out there somewhere, alive. It's no wonder she looked so relieved when Jackson and Indira informed her of Brian's death. Jackson thought she was acting, but she was *genuinely* relieved to hear he'd died.

"She also didn't know about his parents and says if she knew they were still alive, she would have gone and pleaded with them to pull their son into line. Insists she would not have taken Eliot up on his plan to kill Brian."

"What a load of nonsense," said Claire. "She could easily have gone to the police at any time."

"She did, several times, but was too terrified to press charges. Even if he was convicted, she knew Brian would be back out one day and angrier than ever. She thought he might take it out on her boy."

"So how did Eliot convince her?" asked Perry. "He must have been very persuasive."

"He timed it beautifully, by the sounds of it. Approached her soon after Brian had thrown her down a stairwell and landed her in the Emergency Department, apparently. The baby survived, but she was now so desperate she was prepared to do anything."

"Humph!" said Claire. "So she robs another innocent life to save the lives of herself and her unborn child? I'm sorry. I'm still not buying it."

"You don't know what you might do when pushed to the point of desperation, Claire," said Perry before he turned back to Alicia. "So did it all happen as you said, at the film night I mean?"

She nodded. "More or less."

"They were bloody lucky then. It strikes me as very risky. How could Eliot be sure that none of us would spot his little switcheroo? How could he be sure that you and Lynette would not realise that Kat was Maz and vice versa? I mean, if you had started fighting with Jackson at the bar, Claire, Indira would have known immediately that it wasn't Alicia. She would have heard her voice, seen her profile. Sorry, but it takes more than a wig and glasses to impersonate somebody."

"This ain't no Agatha Christie novel," echoed Claire.

Alicia smiled. "You have to remember, guys, they had it easier than we did. None of us had ever *seen* Kat Mumford before, and if we had, it was probably only on a YouTube clip on a tiny device, or at least that was what he was banking on. Remember, too, when they first arrived at the park, the film had already started and it was very dark. He had planned for that. So even though that was really Kat at the start, she was huddled under Eliot's shoulder so none of us got a really good look at her when she was alive. All we really saw was long blond hair, white glasses and a hat."

"But what if someone in the bar queue knew her?" Perry persisted. "It could've happened; it's a smaller world than you think."

"I'm not saying he wasn't lucky," Alicia said. "His stars were certainly in alignment that night."

"All except for the bit where he came and plopped down next to us, of course," said Missy. "He wasn't counting on the Murder Mystery Book Club now was he?"

"Well, we're very good at theories," countered Claire, "but what *evidence* have they got against Eliot? Won't he just point the finger back at Maz and say it really was his wife at the bar with him at intermission, and Maz is just making the whole thing up? It is all rather outlandish when you think about it."

Alicia smiled. "They do have evidence, actually. They have proof that the woman Eliot was pretending to argue with at the Booze Bar could *not* have been his wife, and he must have known that. Which means he's part of the charade."

"The fingerprints on the champagne flute?" prodded Lynette.

"Actually, no. Turns out the third set of prints are from the wholesaler who sold the flutes to Brandon about three days before the film night. They believe the smudged set belong to Maz—she must have tried to wipe them off— but they're just not clear enough to pin on her. Doesn't matter though. They have something much better, something I never thought of."

She smiled wickedly and made them wait a beat before saying, "The chicken satay!"

The book club stared at Alicia blankly, and she laughed.

"Remember, after their fake fight at the Booze Bar, fake 'Kat' went and bought a satay stick at the snack bar? I saw her eat it and then drop it into the champagne flute before she laid down."

"You can't get fingerprints off a skinny little satay stick, surely?" said Claire.

"No," said Alicia, "but you *should* find traces of chicken satay in the dead woman's stomach." Her smile widened as the fact dawned on each of them. "The coroner found none. All she had in her stomach was orange juice and alcohol. Indira's kicking herself for not picking that up earlier. It means the woman Eliot was pretending to argue with at the bar, the woman who then walked off and bought a chicken satay, could not have been his wife. So he was lying. Even better, there's saliva on the stick, and they're testing for DNA now."

"Hook, line and sinker!" said Perry, delighted.

Lynette's mouth widened. "Eliot must be *furious* with Maz for eating that chicken!"

Alicia agreed. "I'm sure he is, and I'm sure that wasn't

part of the plan, but Maz was pregnant, so who could blame her for getting the munchies."

"Can I just clarify," said Missy. "Maz *is* really pregnant, right? Tell me they checked that!"

"Yes, just not suffering from morning sickness and not nearly as pregnant as she looked that night. Remember most of us recalled a 'heavily pregnant' woman, yet by the time Indira and Jackson interviewed her at her home a few days later, Indira was surprised to find she still had a good six weeks of her pregnancy left. She wasn't nearly as pregnant as the witnesses had claimed. That's because she no longer had a wig and jacket squished against her stomach."

"Why did she even hang around at the film night?" Claire asked. "Why not run off with Mo Man, and who *is* Mo Man anyway?"

Alicia shrugged. "They haven't found him yet. Indira thinks he's a random stranger who had nothing to do with any of it. Jackson thinks they lured him to the film through a dating website so Maz would have someone to pretend to be sitting with. They're still investigating that. As for *why* she hung around? My guess is, she didn't know if her violent fiancé had taken his hot shot yet and probably wanted to stay away from home as long as possible to give him a chance. She was probably terrified she'd get back and find him sitting there, fists clenched."

They all shuddered a little at that. They felt some sympathy for Maz Olden, but it didn't begin to excuse what she had done. It didn't come close to compensating for Kat Mumford's life.

"Okay," said Alicia, forcing a smile onto her lips and reaching for her handbag. "Enough of all this horror. We have more positive things to think about!"

She smiled more convincingly as she produced a notepad and pen.

"Claire's right—it's time to inject some fresh life into this book club. I think we should put another ad in the local classifieds, like I did last time, calling for new members. What do you all think?"

They nodded enthusiastically and began yelling out their priorities.

"They should be smart *and* suspicious!" said Missy.

"Fabulous and good fun!" added Perry.

"Exotic and handsome wouldn't hurt," added Claire, causing them all to stare at her aghast. "What? Why should Alicia have all the fun?"

"I'll just take anyone who can cook," said Lynette. "I'm a bit over feeding you lot."

They chuckled as Alicia scribbled down their ideas and began constructing a fresh advertisement for the Murder Mystery Book Club, Mark 2.

Just as they'd run out of steam, Alicia looked up and beamed, then took up the pen and wrote the final prerequisite:

*"Must adore crime fiction, have a passion for puzzles, and never be averse to solving a real-life mystery should one fall into your lap."*

Then Perry scoffed and said, "But what are the chances of *that*?"

~~ *the end* ~~

# ALSO BY C.A. LARMER

## After the Ferry: A Psychological Novel

IT'S THE 1990s, pre-mobile phones, and a young traveller must make a terrifying choice: Will she jump ship with a seductive stranger? Or stay cocooned on the Greek ferry with friends and miss what could be the love of her life?
One choice leads to true love.
One choice leads to murder.
*But which is which?*

"Larmer's plot is a clever one...The characters are finely honed and credible, and Amelia's contrasting lives and personalities are brilliantly rendered and made plausible."
*Jack Magnus, Readers Favorite*

## Killer Twist (Ghostwriter Mystery 1)

KILLER TWIST is the first stand-alone mystery in the popular 'amateur women sleuths' series featuring feisty ghostwriter Roxy Parker.

"A fun read with a well defined protagonist, interesting secondary characters and an easy style. Lots of local flavour which catches the imagination."
*Parents' Little Black Book @ Amazon*

"Roxy Parker is a compelling character and I couldn't help but adore her. She's 30, hip, very inquisitive, and fiercely independent. A great cozy. I enjoyed it immensely and will be ordering the second in the series."
*Rhonda @Amazon*

**calarmer.com**

Made in the USA
Monee, IL
02 June 2022